BROOKLYN PLAGUE

Dov Silverman

It was business at usual for Mac at Ridgewood Veterans' Hospital in Brooklyn. Times can be hard, and the struggle is real.

It was about to get a lot harder in the very real threat of a virus that would sweep through the city, taking the lives of both rich and poor as it went.

BROOKLYN PLAGUE

CHAPTER ONE:
A DAY'S WORK

RIDGEWOOD VETERANS' HOSPITAL, BROOKLYN, NY

"She's in cardiac arrest!" Nurse MacKenzie shouted.

A male nurse leaped onto the wheeled stretcher and performed CPR. The young woman did not respond. The gurney rolled into the emergency room where another male nurse, older and larger than everyone else present, expertly inserted a needle into the patient's left arm and announced: "Vein open!"

A short round female nurse noted: "Blood pressure low. No pulse. Oxygen level zero."

"JJ, keep pumping," MacKenzie ordered the man performing CPR. "Doctor to Bay Number One!"

The nearest doctor ran in through the entrance. "Mac, what have we got?"

"DOA. Multiple lacerations, a broken nose and left arm. Probable broken ribs on the left side. Jill, paddles!" she snapped.

The short round nurse dropped the blood-pressure bulb as the gurney entered cubicle #1 and dragged the electronic paddle table to the doctor's side. He rubbed the paddles together as Jill helped JJ from the gurney. Mac tore off the patient's blouse and pulled up her bra.

"Stand back!" the doctor ordered, and applied the paddles.

The young body arched and shuddered. All eyes went to the oscilliscope.

"Flat line," the doctor announced. "Up the voltage. Stand back!"

Again the body bucked. The oscilloscope blinked, sending a line of peaked yellow blips across the screen, accompanied by a bell sounding the heart's rhythm.

"Yes!" MacKenzie shouted. "We beat the devil. Implement Procedure One."

Big Bill Schmrsal held up the woman's pink wallet. "*Nien* allergies."

"What the hell is he talking about?"the doctor asked. "Nine allergies?"

"He means none," Mac answered. "Yiddish."

"You've got some crew," the doctor said as he parted the young woman's hair, revealing a nasty scalp wound. "Mac, I want a full body scan. JJ, you step out of this cubicle and close the curtain behind you."

The doctor examined the patient's eyes and asked: "Car crash?"

"No, that bastard over there." Jill pointed a pudgy forefinger to an unshaven young man watching from the entrance. He wore rumpled jeans and a leather vest and his bare tattooed arms cradled a motorcycle helmet.

"It's her third visit this year," Mac scowled. "I recognized them."

"Call the police," the doctor growled.

"They're worse than useless," Jill answered. "Cut his balls off."

"I'll do it," Big Bill offered.

"You stay out of trouble," Jill ordered. She turned on the doctor. "Why did you send JJ out?"

"It's the last time he'll work in this ER."

"Please, Doctor," Mac sighed, "Let me do it."

"I'd rather you did."

Jill placed an oxygen mask on the patient. Big Bill adjusted a drip infusion while Mac used a damp cloth to wipe blood from the young woman's face. Jill then handed the doctor a clipboard. He looked at and signed it, saying: "Get her to x-ray."

"Bill, you take her," said Jill. "I've got to make hot chocolate." And she walked out.

"Hot chocolate, in the middle of summer?" the doctor wondered.

"It's for him." Mac nodded toward the young man watching his woman being wheeled out of the ER.

"Just a minute ago she wanted to cut his balls off."

"She'll melt a package of Ex-Lax into the chocolate," Mac smiled.

"And then you'll ask the question, 'Vhere vere you vhen the shit hit the fan?'"

"I didn't hear anything," the doctor said, and left.

"Her eyes are open," Bill noted.

"You interview her," Mac replied. "Watch her vital signs. I'm going to speak with JJ."

"Will they fire him?" Bill asked.

Mac shrugged. "He does his job."

Mac found JJ at the ER entrance. "Can you help me?" he asked.

"Only you can help yourself, JJ. You've got to dry out. You're a veteran, and have rights to enter the rehabilitation unit. I'll have you admitted, but you have to swear on your sweet Irish heart that you'll follow the program to the very end. Then and only then will I decide on reinstatement."

"I've been thinking..." JJ hedged.

"It's about time. When you climbed onto the gurney your breath almost knocked us over. Had you given the girl mouth-to-mouth she would have gotten alcohol poisoning."

"The doctor didn't have to make such a big scene about it."

"Yes he did. Had she died, an investigation could have terminated all of us—because you were drunk on duty."

"...I'd like to take a week before going to dry out."

"You want a last binge?"

"...Well, yeah."

"No. You follow me right now to the Drug Dependency Ward or you get the hell out of here."

"Awww, Mac..."

"Now, JJ."

The head nurse held the door open, and JJ slowly followed her upstairs.

"Martha," said Mac, "This is JJ Dougherty. He can sweet-talk the angels out of their wings. He's one of my best ER people—and an alcoholic."

"I want to hear him say it."

"Say what?" JJ asked.

Martha dug her fists into her hips and cocked her head, staring at him.

"Okay. I'm...an alcoholic."

"Well, JJ," Martha asked, "Have you ever dried out before?"

"Never needed it."

"Bullshit! You think I got these gray hairs believing rummies and drug addicts?"

"I'm not an addict!"

"Doing drugs?"

"No, godammit!"

"Assume the position."

"Don't you trust me?"

"No. Up against the wall and spread the legs."

He did, and Martha patted him down from his hair to his shoes. She lifted his right trouser leg and pulled out a half-pint bottle of whiskey tucked into his sock.

"Turn around," she said, holding out the bottle. "Take it, and I'll never allow you on my ward. Turn away from it and walk through those doors, and I'll help you beat this disease."

JJ's right hand started toward the bottle. He caught Mac's eye and his hand dropped, tears welling in his eyes. Mac kissed him on the cheek. He turned away and walked into the ward.

"It won't be easy," Martha said, watching him go.

"I'll visit," Mac promised.

"Oh, congratulations are due."

"You mean on my Ph.D?"

"You're the first woman in America to qualify as a Clinical Nurse Practitioner in the Emergency Room. You can even write prescriptions."

"I'd like to write a few cyanide pills for a wife-beater."

"I have a couple on my ward."

"What can we do?"

"Kill the bastards before they can do more harm," said Martha. "Beating women—power over women—is as addictive as drugs or liquor. The courts slap their wrists because they were Under the Influence. One of them wasn't even drunk, but his lawyer told him to drink a bottle of booze before the cops picked him up."

"He got away with it?"

"The courts are lenient with veterans. It's worse in the civilian hospitals."

"You know, with my Ph.D. I got a counselor's assignment to four civilian hospitals in the area."

"Be prepared for more action. ER in the city should qualify you for hazardous duty pay. Women young and old come traipsing in and cut with guns, knives, and boyfriends who kicked the shit out of them."

"The women bring in the weapons?"

"No, the boyfriends have them. It stops the women from talking to the police."

"Martha, you used to be the Kings County supervisor of First Responders. Would you make the rounds with me some Friday night, show me the ropes?"

"Stoney, you're likely to hang yourself with the ropes I show you. That's why I resigned and took this job." Martha pointed to the sign: DRUG DE-PENDENCY UNIT. "I'm my own best patient."

"How's it working for you?"

"One day at a time. A year, two months and ten days sober."

"How do you spend your free time?"

"Free time is dangerous for an alcoholic. I eat with the patients, and sometimes watch TV with them."

"Where do you sleep?"

"Here and at home."

"Come folk-dancing with me tonight."

"I can't."

"Bullshit. I'll meet you at the ER entrance."

"I'm no dancer."

"Great! You'll fit right in."

The hospital loudspeaker announced: "Five-eighteen, call your station. Five-eighteen, call your station."

Martha plucked the phone from its wall-stand and handed it to Mac.

"MacKenzie speaking."

"You should answer 'Doctor MacKenzie'," Jill's voice chided.

"What's happening?"

"Rabbi Goldman is back. He's bleeding out."

"Put in two simultaneous under pressure. I'm on

my way."

She got up and headed for the elevator, saying: "Martha, six PM. Doctor's orders."

CHAPTER TWO:
THE PATIENTS

"Nu, Moishe," Mac asked, *"Vous maks du?"*

The pale-faced bearded man managed a weak smile. "My favorite nurse." He removed his fedora and adjusted the yarmulke on his balding head. "You going to save my life again?"

"Jill is capable of that."

"I don't understand a word of Yiddish," said Jill.

"It's close to German," Big Bill put in.

"That's another language I don't know."

Mac scrutinized the chart and ordered, "Call Doctor O'Brian on the double."

O'Brian came quickly. Mac questioned the Rabbi, then briefed the doctor. "Rabbi Goldman has been our hemophiliac patient for years."

"I thought Orthodox Jews didn't get hemophilia."

"He's Conservative. And he was given AIDS-contaminated blood."

"From this hospital?"

"Unfortunately, yes."

"Is he a veteran?"

"Vietnam, a chaplain with the paratroopers. He's

bleeding internally. Blood in the urine and feces. AIDS complications."

"Bill," said the doctor, "Take blood. I'll write the tests. Tell the lab it's a priority. Rabbi, I'm going to force two more bags of blood. I'll return as soon as the lab reports come down."

Then there was a disturbance in Cubicle 2. Mac parted the curtains and saw a boy being undressed by one of the nurses who was gently removing his trousers and underpants. His penis, scrotum and the lower part of his belly were colored angry red, and he was whimpering. Two young girls were trying to calm him. One said: "My brother took a pot of boiling water and spilled it on himself."

"Where are your parents?" Mac asked.

"We've got no dad, and our mama works."

Mac turned to the nurse. "Two OPT of Algin, and apply anti-burn cream. The doctor will stop by. After he's seen them, send them home. No charge."

Jill poked her head in and said: "The cops are questioning the wife-beater in the crapper. His wife is out of X-ray. You want to talk to her?" There was the slightest inflection in her voice. She and Mac exchanged glances.

"I'm going now," said Mac.

She entered the ward and went to the foot of the bed nearest to the nurses' station. The young woman had a full head-bandage and a patch over her right eye. Her nose was swollen and bent at a right angle. Her left arm and ankle were in casts. Pillows were arranged at her left side so she wouldn't roll onto her broken ribs. Mac heard sobbing, and looked up from her patient's chart.

"Don't cry, darling," Mac said. She filled a plastic cup full of water and held it to the woman's bruised lips. "Drink slowly."

"Am I going to die?" the woman whispered.

"Not this time, Rosie dear—but he did try to kill you."

"I can't see around this big nose. Do you know me?"

"It's Mac. You've been my patient twice before."

"Oh, good. I was hoping I'd get you again."

"That's pathetic. No one deserves such beatings. Lie back and try to rest."

"I'm afraid to close my eyes. He might come up here."

"I doubt it. The police are questioning him—in the toilet."

"...Is that normal?"

"Your husband is having... violent eruptions of the lower intestinal tract."

Just then Jill entered and came up to the bedside. "He's being de-shitified," she said, and took Rosie's hand. "I came to see how you're doing."

"The pain-killers are wearing off."

"I'll get something for you," Mac promised.

"You've got to press charges this time," Jill insisted.

"He'll kill me for sure!"

"I'm ready to kill *him*."

"Nurses don't do that."

"I'd be helping you by killing him. The last time, I set O'Rooney and Burke from the 83rd precinct on him. Did that help?"

"He was two weeks in the hospital and six months sober. Then he started drinking again and blaming me for everything."

"That's the problem," said Mac. She rolled up the pajama sleeve and injected Rosie. "Lie back. Close your eyes and enjoy a good sleep. We'll talk later."

Rosie closed her eyes and began breathing gently.

"Someone's got to do something." Jill pointed at the girl. "She's a former Army sergeant, with two tours in Afghanistan, yet she puts up with this. She's got to be protected."

"Will you come folk-dancing tonight?" Mac asked.

"Yeah. With Bill."

"Can he dance?"

"Floats like a butterfly. Oh, and the replacement for JJ is waiting to be interviewed."

"You do it. You're now the senior ER nurse."

"Upgrade in pay?"

"Of course. We're making America great again."

The applicant stood six feet tall, weighed 190 pounds, had blond hair, clear blue eyes, and broad powerful shoulders. His starched nurse's uniform was ironed with military creases, which bent crisply as he handed Jill his resume. She took it, noting: "Floyd Sorenson. Combat veteran?"

"Yes, Ma'am."

"Call me Jill. I'm not old enough to be a ma'am."

"Yes, Ma—uh, Jill."

"You served four years as a corpsman with the

Marines. Two tours of duty in Afghanistan, and two tours in Lebanon?"

"I'm restricted from speaking about Lebanon."

"You've been decorated twice, plus a Purple Heart and letters of recommendation. You made senior rank in less time than anyone I know."

"I enlisted in the Navy and became a combat corpsman. I loved the work." His voice was a tone lower than most men's, and he stood close when he spoke. His teeth were white and even in an easy smile.

"Why did you leave the Corps?"

"Uh, I got in trouble."

"For a military medic that usually involves drugs."

"No, Ma'am!—uh, Jill. I'm a vegan. I'm very careful about what I put in my body, or administer to others."

"Then what was the problem?"

"...Women. I like women, and they like me." Jill looked him up and down, said nothing, but shook her head and stared at him. He squirmed briefly, then amended: "I... got involved with some officers' wives."

"'Wives', plural?"

"Uh, yes."

Jill waved at him to stop talking and asked: "Why did you leave the San Francisco VA hospital after only six months?"

"...Grab-ass and women."

"Explain."

"Well, San Franciso is the Gay capitol of America. I don't care for that lifestyle, but hey, live and let live. The trouble was, some of them were sexually aggressive. On the ward and in the corridors, they were always grabbing my ass."

Jill considered that she wouldn't mind grabbing a bit of Sorenson's ass. "What about the women problem?"

"There weren't enough interested in men. I've made a study of women. I keep a notebook."

"I'd like to see that book!"

"I'm going to write a novel, really."

"Oh? What's the title?"

"'Getting Laid'."

Jill sat back and laughed. "You certainly are crazy enough to be on his staff. Now let's see what you know about nursing. In Cubicle 1, put up two more pints of blood under pressure for the rabbi. In Cubicle 2, if the child is calm give him some anti-burn cream, two OPT Algin before sleep, and send him home. Don't charge."

"How come we treat children?"

"Because we're goodhearted. Only Mac and I can be goodhearted."

"Free of charge?"

"We're a VA hospital, and have no system to charge non-veterans. It's a poor neighborhood. Now in Cubicle 3 there's an older vet complaining of constipation. He hasn't been able to pass feces in a week."

"May I borrow a stethoscope?"

"Take mine."

"How's the new recruit?" Mac asked.

"A gem," Jill smiled.

"That's a mischievous grin, what's wrong with him?"

"Nothing."

"Can't be. He's twenty-five, decorated for bravery under fire, rapidly promoted, has recommendations from everyone he's worked for, but he left Frisco after only six months. What's the problem?"

"Nothing's wrong, and that's the problem. You're going to have the entire female staff, patients and visitors lining up in the ER. He's that attractive."

"Really?"

"Hubba, hubba, hubba! I'd put my shoes under his bed in a New York minute. He looks like a Norse god."

"You said female patients?"

"I should have said all women."

"How about him and Rosie?"

Jill paused, rolled her eyes and smiled. "It might give her a reason to live."

"Tell Floyd to enthuse her, but no sex. She needs to be inspired to fight back."

"If he came near my bed, I wouldn't fight; I'd pull him in."

"Doesn't Big Bill give you enough loving?"

"Wait 'til you see this guy."

"He's your problem; you're responsible for the ER staff."

"Bless you."

"But can he do he job?"

"He knows his way around. Rather than send the

constipated guy in #3 to the operating room, he dug the feces out by hand, with a forceps."

"Great. And speaking of shit, how's the wife-beater doing?"

"De-shitified. The cops had to carry him out."

"Will they press charges?"

"Depends on Rosie, and she never did before."

"You think this new male nurse could inspire her?"

"He inspires me."

"Even a fire-hydrant inspires you. Send him to Rosie."

Mac retired to her office, and was an hour into paperwork when she was summoned by the ward nurse to Rosie's bedside. Rosie was hiding under the covers.

"What's wrong, darling?" Mac asked. "Why are you crying?"

"An angel came, and I look such a mess," Rosie sobbed.

"That eye-patch gives you a dashing appearance, like Superwoman. What did this angel look like?"

"Beautiful. He was all in white, with blue eyes and blond hair."

"A male angel?"

"Do you get female angels?"

"I never had an angel visit. I've brought a brush for you; let me do your hair."

"What about my nose? I can barely see around it with my good eye."

"The swelling will go down, and ice will help.

There's a woman plastic surgeon who I recommend. You can have any shape of nose you'd like."

"I had one like Barbara Streisand."

"She's beautiful."

"You really think so?"

"She used to live here in Ridgewood."

"Will the angel come back?"

"I'll see to it. Now you go to sleep. Your eyes are dilated; the morphine is still working."

"...Is it safe?"

Mac fluffed Rosie's pillow and kissed her on the forehead. "Sleep," she said.

An announcement sounded on the loudspeaker: "Five-eighteen, please call the administration office."

The Administrator invited Mac to lunch in the board-room, and led her to a seat on his right at the head of a large oval table. To his left sat two elderly, sophisticated-looking men. After them were Brooklyn's Borough President, next to him Monsignor Adolph Kline of Saint Barbara's Church, then Parker Wessels of the Salvation Army and then Congressman Elijah Waters, Chairman of the New York NAACP. The remaining three men and a woman were administrators of four Brooklyn hospitals that Mac was to evaluate and advise. She had no idea why she was invited.

The VA administrator spoke first. "I've requested your attendance to honor Nurse Elizabeth MacKenzie on being the first woman in our great nation to be awarded a doctorate in Emergency

Room Procedures. We have two guests here from the White House Veterans' Administration." He nodded to the two men on his left. They smiled, and cameramen took photos, while a TV team from the *Daily News* and the *Brooklyn Eagle* filmed. Speakers praised Mac for her twenty years of service and her new degree.

The last to speak was one of the gentlemen from Washington. "Doctor MacKenzie, we appreciate your attendance at such short notice. The President of the United States sends his personal congratulations on your achievements and your dedication. In fact, President Trump is the reason for this meeting. He recalled a stipulation in the 2008 budget, allowing fifty million dollars to be directed to an innercity budget for research on improving hospital emergency procedures."

"*Research*"? Mac thought, almost literally pricking up her ears.

"It requires a Ph.D in that specialty," the gentleman from Washington went on.

Oho! Mac understood.

"Doctor MacKenzie, you're the first person to satisfy that requirement." He paused for the applause. "That's the good part."

"Give us the bad part," Congressman Waters said.

"We have only to the end of the year before the appropriation runs out."

"Isn't that enough?" the Borough President asked.

The gentleman from Washington looked at Mac. "Only Doctor MacKenzie can answer that," he said.

"She will have to set up a program and show present constructive use of the funds. Then it must be certified by Congress, authorized by the Senate, and signed by the President."

Mac saw it all, and thought as fast as she ever had in her life. Basically, she had to write a grant proposal outlining how she would do a study on improving local emergency room services.

"I'll guarantee the Black caucuses," the Borough President stated.

"I'll guarantee the Democrats in both houses," Congressman Waters added.

"And the President will vouch for the Republicans," the man from Washington finished. He looked down at Mac. "Can you draw up a plan in that time to utilize all that money?"

Mac kept her expression solemn. Allowing a week for Waters and friends to kick it through Washington, she had a week to write her grant proposal. She could do it in a day or less. "I have conditions," she said.

"Such as?"

"First, my staff comes mostly from this hospital. When we appear at other hospitals, I choose those whom I wish to liaison with."

The other hospital administrators buzzed in a brief discussion, and quickly agreed.

"Second, I control the finances."

The smiling faces turned grim. "That's more than the yearly operating budget for this entire hospital," the administrator worried. "Mac, have you ever handled that much money?"

"You know the answer," Mac snapped. "I also know that, without proper control, money can be *inappropriately* directed—inadvertently, of course."

The whole group around the table broke into heated discussion.

Congressman Waters leaned close to Mac and whispered: "I'm glad you used the word 'inadvertently'."

Mac only smiled back at him.

The VA administrator demanded order, and got it. "For us to be awarded the money," he reminded them, "We must decide here and now just who will disburse the funds."

The second man from Washington was obviously military, and had done this sort of thing before. "I suggest," he said, "A financial committee, consisting of Dr. MacKenzie, one of you five hospital adminis-trators, and two from the remaining participants. Three of the four must sign every allocation of funds, and Dr. MacKenzie's signature must be man-datory."

"That amounts to veto power," one of the other hospital administrators grumbled.

"But she'll be doing most of the work," the VA administrator countered, "She'll be taking all the responsibility, and she's the sole reason we're being considered for this grant."

There was heated discussion, voices were raised, eventually a vote was taken and the recommendation was approved. The VA administrator helped Mac to her feet to receive applause and congratulations and subtle jockeying for favor.

The military man from Washington quietly said: "You have a golden opportunity to serve your community. Don't be afraid to use that veto power. Everyone here wants a piece of that 50-million-dollar budget; it's more money than was spent to build the Brooklyn Bridge."

Congressman Waters pressed his gray-whiskered Black face close to Mac and almost whispered: "I got this limp because back then the ER didn't take niggers. You have a great opportunity to serve the people of Brooklyn. I'm just a phone call away, and I sit on the government's Budget Committee. It's a key to many doors." He handed her a gold-embossed business card. "This is my personal cell-phone number."

After the guests departed the VA administrator pointed to the cluster of business cards in Mac's hands and smiled. "Those will prove important. Have your secretary write a personal note of appreciation to each of them."

"Secretary? What secretary?"

"You've got one now, plus an office down the hall from mine."

Mac collapsed into a chair.

"Welcome to the big leagues," he chuckled. "You have nine and a half business days to attain Congressional approval from both houses, plus the President's signature."

"Well, I'd like to personally thank President Trump. How do I address it?"

"To Mr. President, the White House, Washington, DC."

"Gee, thanks."

The loudspeaker came to life: "Five-eighteen, code one. Please call your station."

"Back to real life," said Mac.

She used the office phone. "Jill, what's wrong?"

"We're losing Rabbi Goldman; he threw up more blood than we pumped into him. I moved him to Saint Peter's, cubicle #10 so we can clean up."

"What did O'Brian say?"

"That the rabbi is on his way out."

"Did you notify the family?"

"They're on their way in."

"Don't tell them we call it Saint Peter's. His family alone is a crowd. The last time he was dying, half the Penguins in Borough Park and Williamsburg filled the streets."

"What are Penguins?"

"Religious Jews with black suits and white shirts. Arrange a private room on the ground floor near a side door."

"Will do."

"Come to dinner with me and Bill," Jill insisted. "We're celebrating Mac's promotion at the Gay Greek's."

"That name would be appropriate in San Francisco," Floyd replied. "I didn't expect to find it in Brooklyn."

"They named it in the 1930s, when 'gay' meant 'happy'. Ridgewood is an old German neighborhood.

There was a street called Brewers' Row: *fifteen* breweries, one after the other. Bill's family owned a couple. They settled here in the 1800s."

"What about you?"

"Nine generations Brooklyn, on my mother's side. My children are the tenth. Webb Street is named for John Webb, a great-grandfather and ship-builder. His great-great-grandfather came in 1775 to fight the Americans, and ended up joining them."

"I never thought of Brooklyn in terms of history."

"The biggest battle of the Revolution took place not far from here. General Howe had thirty-two thousand trained men, including the British battle-fleet, and he lost to George Washington, who had only ten thousand, mostly local militia and farmers."

"I never heard of it."

"That's because the Americans technically lost the battle, being driven off the field, but ultimately won the war. History is written by the winners. Further down Central Avenue is the *Brooklyn Eagle*. America's first poet, Walt Whitman, was a reporter during the Civil War—for the *Eagle*.

"We seem to be the first ones here," Floyd noted. "It gives me a chance to ask some questions. You put Big Bill in charge of handling the dying rabbi and his family. Is Bill German?"

"He and the rabbi are old friends. Bill speaks He-brew, Yiddish, English and German."

"He's Jewish?"

"No, but he learned their language on an Israeli kibbutz."

"How did he get there?"

"In his Munich high school he joined a group—of descendants of the Nazis—trying to make amends for the Holocaust. They work to establish Israel as a homeland for the Jewish people. Bill volunteered two years' work on a kibbutz. He helped with the wounded during terrorist attacks and wars, and he decided to become a medic. He joined the American army to become a citizen and a medic. He served in Afghanistan and Iraq, then used his GI Bill to study nursing."

"We could have crossed paths overseas."

"Unlikely: Bill's older than you."

"Are you and he married?"

"No, we just live together. I have three children: all married, and a grandchild on the way. My husband passed two years ago. Heart attack."

"I'm sorry for your loss."

"Well, yes, he was a beer-swilling, hardworking, fun-to-be-with guy—until he got whiskied up. Then he'd kick the shit out of me or anyone else."

"An alcoholic?"

"A full-blooded Cherokee Indian. Beer can be handled, but hard liquor makes them crazy."

"And what's the story with MacKenzie?"

"The brightest student to graduate from Stonybrook University Medical School. She earned her nurse's cap at age nineteen, and was snapped up by the Stonybrook veteran's hospital. She married a Marine captain. He was killed in Afghanistan. She transferred here because we tend to get the younger veterans. You know about her Ph.D?"

"That's why I requested Ridgewood VA. Cutting-edge new things will be happening here."

"They may already have started. Mac was invited to an important meeting this afternoon—"

"Oh, here they are now!"

Big Bill was reaching over the heads of Martha and Mac to open the chrome and glass door to the diner. The three came in and took seats at Floyd's and Jill's table, and Mac whispered to Jill: "Do you realize this table is surrounded by young women?"

"It's him." Jill nodded toward Floyd, who seemed oblivious to the attention. "He's a chick-magnet. What happened at the meeting?"

"Let's order first," said Mac.

The owner brought them menus and introduced himself as Georgee Prodromakeos Short. He was thin, muscular, in his fifties, and sported a chef's white hat, white jacket and trousers, and a handlebar mustache that curled at the tips. He placed a menu with a flourish in front of each guest, rubbed his hands together and asked: "May I bring a glass of wine, on the house, for my favorite Emergency Room people?"

Jill pointed to Floyd and explained: "He's a vegan."

"No problem," said Georgee. "I have vegan wine, from Greece."

"Do you know if it's strained properly?" Floyd hedged.

"I"ll send in my daughter," Georgee smiled. "It's her wine. She's vegan. Myself, I eat meat—lots of meat."

"Me too," said Bill. "I'll have a t-bone steak, fried onions and potatoes."

The wine arrived, served by a tall, lithe young woman wearing a short black dress, sheer black stockings, a dainty white apron around her narrow waist and a white lace blouse climbing both sides of a well-defined cleavage. Her features exemplified the Greek history of beauty and dedication to the human form. Her eyes were sparkling obsidian, matching her silky-smooth long black hair that was crowned with a rhinestone tiara. Her face was an aquiline outline of beauty and her skin was a rich, burnished cinnamon. Upon her entrance, an audible sigh swept among the male diners. Floyd's crystal eyes met her radiant smile, and neither of them blinked.

"Do you know if the wine is filtered?" Floyd asked.

Her long dark eyelashes fluttered. "This is ethical wine. My cousin lives near the acropolis, and he presses it especially for me. He filters it through carbon, bentonite clay and limestone."

"Thank you so much for sharing." Floyd stood and stepped closer to her. "Would you care to join us?"

She held her ground and replied: "I'm working. The wine is my present on your first visit." She smiled, and left.

"You're a fast worker," Martha grinned at Floyd.

"Heaven knows, I try," Floyd grinned back.

"I never saw Georgee's daughter before," Bill noted. "She's a knockout."

Jilll slapped his large shoulder. "That's why Prod never lets her out when you're here."

"I never heard of 'ethical wine' before," Mac mused.

"Can we hear what the big meeting was about?" Martha asked.

"Okay," Mac sighed. "I'm to be in charge of a government-funded project to improve ER services in Brooklyn. It's a pilot program to reduce inner-city casualties. The four civilian hospitals and this VA hospital will be our focus. We'll evaluate and improve Bushwick, Bedford-Stuyvesant, Red Hook, Flatbush, and our Ridgewood ERs."

"What's the budget?" Martha asked.

"Fifty million dollars, for two years," said Mac.

There was an instant's silence all around the table. Then Jill gasped: "Wow! They're putting their money where their mouth is!"

"Who decides how we spend it?" Martha asked.

"We do," said Mac. "Actually, I do—but I hope everybody at this table will help. Our team will serve each of the five hospitals for a month at a time, twice a year."

"They'll bitch like crazy when we use their ambulances and facilities," Jill gloomed.

"As my first allocation, I ordered a brand-new ambulance from International Trucks. As for the ER facilities, whatever's lacking I'll attempt to buy."

"How much will the ambulance cost?" Bill asked.

"Fully equipped, half a million dollars."

The resulting silence at the table caused Mac to add: "It's state of the art. Requires a four-man medical crew, driver and helper. The ambulance capacity is two stretcher patients and one seated."

"I would very much like to be included on your staff," Floyd murmured.

"You are, my boy!" Mac said. "I have a special task for you."

Floyd beamed. His white teeth reflected the diner's lights.

Mac asked: "Do you know how to folk-dance?"

Floyd blinked a few times before he answered. "I grew up in Oregon. My great-grandfather called dances on the Oregon Trail."

"Your family was on a wagon train?" Bill asked. "Did they fight any Indians?"

"By 1870 the Indians were no longer hostile. The train did have a few scrapes with White renegades."

"Bring on dinner," said Mac. "This celebration is on me, for my new staff of the ER Evaluation Committee."

CHAPTER 3:
JOINING THE DANCE

Folk-dancing was held in the basement of Public School 75. When the ER crowd arrived people were already doing stretching exercises while others changed into dancing shoes. Women wore jeans or gay-colored cotton long skirts. Most men wore jeans, with suspenders, over short-sleeved white shirts. Some sported straw farm hats, while others wore cowboy hats. They separated into groups of four couples each as more people entered and hurried to form their squares.

"This is my first folk-dance," Martha said.

"I'll help you," Floyd promised. "This looks like it's shaping up into square-dances, so listen to the instructions from the caller. In the old days, most people didn't know each other's dances, so someone stood up in front and shouted instructions like 'honor your partner' or 'honor your neighbor', where you turn and bow to each. Or things like 'grab your partner and swing her 'round. Not too fast, don't knock her down'. The last sentence is filler words to make the rhyme; don't pay attention to them."

"Ladeeeees and gentlemen," a tall thin man in a white Stetson hat spoke into a microphone.. "This evening we have the pleasure of the Ridgewood Trio providing our music: Mark Goldberg on fiddle, Whitey Hendricks on banjo, and Hairless Hogan the Elder on accordion. My name is Danny Block, and I'll do the calling and cueing for as long as my voice holds out."

The crowd applauded. Danny Block went on: "For you beginners, I'll start with simple moves and slow instructions. As the evening wears on I'll give you more intricate patterns. You can try, or watch and learn. At the conclusion, Elder Hogan will announce the best couple, and they'll lead the Grand March to finalize the evening."

He then nodded to Elder Hogan, who stamped his foot three times and swung into the introductory instrumental riff. The other musicians join in on the verse and Danny Block began to sing.

"All God's children got a place in the choir.
Some sing low, and some sing higher.
Some of them dance on the telephone wire,
And some just clap their hands—
—Or paws, or anything they've got.

"Boys and girls, form up your squares.
If you're a-sittin' then leave your chairs.
Boys to the right and gals to the left,
If you don't have a partner, don't fret.
We'll sort things out, you can bet."

The Caller partnered a man next to Mac and an elderly couple at the head of their square. He then started Calling the instructions—"Honor your partners, honor your corners" —while the Trio played on.

"Allemande left with your partner square.
Bring her home, and you know where.
All join hands and circle right,
And we'll all get home tonight—
—Get back home, pretty late tonight."

"With your partner, dance down the middle.
Keep in time to the sound of the fiddle.
Dosey-doe with your partners all,
Come back home and stand tall—
Come home and that ain't all.

"All four ladies now make a chain.
Go 'round the square and come home again.
Hey-diddle-diddle, the cat and the fiddle,
And the cow jumped over the moon.
Hogan laughed to see such sport,
And we'll all dance 'til noon."

Danny kept up his patter of filler words while he directed the dancers up, down, and around the floor until the song ended. Then he announced a "ballad" to give the older folks a breather. Hogan the Elder stepped back and the banjo-man moved forward. He plucked five notes, and Martha watched Floyd's face light up. He cried out "Rye Whiskey", and sang along with the Caller in perfect harmony.

"Way up on Cliff Mountain I wandered alone.
I'm drunk as the devil, and a long way from
home.
I'll eat when I'm hungry and drink when I'm dry,
And if whiskey don't kill me, I surely won't die.
"Rye whiskey, rye whiskey, rye whiskey I cry.
If you give me rye whiskey, I surely won't die."

The audience applauded the duet, and the Caller announced the next square. Martha took both of Floyd's hands and told him: "That song is the national anthem of my ward."

"What section is that?"

"Alcohol and Drug Rehabilitation. 'Dee-tox'."

Mac's emergency cell-phone rang, and she went aside to answer it. She wasn't gone long.

"What was that about?" Jill asked when she came back.

"Dosey-doe with your partner," Mac muttered, massaging her forehead. "Let's form up the square."

And the dance went on.

During one of the breaks the Danny Block cleared his throat and called out: "Does anyone know what a Diddly Bow is?"

"Some kind of musical instrument?" some man asked.

"Can you describe it?" There was silence. "Anyone want to guess?"

"My dad has one at home," Floyd called out.

"Ah. And where's that?"

"Portland, Oregon."

"Aha. Tell the folks what it looks like."

"Well, it's a single string of baling-wire, stretched between two nails hammered into a board. My dad had a whiskey bottle forced under the string to magnify the sound."

"Give that man a cigar! Yes, folks, that's exactly what a diddly-bow is. Now, gentlemen, honor your partners. Honor your corners. It's time for the Grand March and to end our evening's festivities. Ladies, join hands and circle right. Men, circle left. Will the lady and gentleman with the matching straw hats and red shirts step out and lead the Grand March?"

Outside the school, Mac addressed the ER group.

"I'd planned on finishing the evening with hot pretzels and cold beer at the Hofbrau House, but Rabbi Goldman died. I need you all to arrive at seven in the morning. Big Bill will liaison with the family for removal of the body. Now he'll tell us what to expect."

"It'll appear like chaos," Bill explained, "But it isn't. The *kevroat kadisha* is knowledgeable and experienced. Let them handle the crowd."

"Who are they?" Floyd asked.

"The volunteer Jewish Burial Society. They'll carry the body to the synagogue and everybody will follow with them. So will we. When you return to the ER, each of you pick up a haversack and two bottles of water. Most of your cases will be people overcome with emotion. If the person is unconscious, lift both legs by the heels; that's usually sufficient to bring them back. Very important: women treat women and men treat men, unless it's a dire emergency. Don't drive to work; there won't be any parking spaces. Use public transportation. It's a three-block walk from the hospital to the Ridgewood Talmud-Torah Synagogue. Expect some of the elders and pregnant women to need water. Arrival at the building to the left of the synagogue proper means our work is done. There the *kevroat kadisha* will take over and wash the body in preparation for burial. Any questions?"

"Will we have any support?" Jill asked.

"Two ambulances will follow the crowd," said Mac. "Beyond that, you can call on the police for assistance. See you all in the morning. Floyd, please walk with Martha and me; I have a special job for you."

The others chuckled and scattered to their cars.

"And I have a couple recommendations for you," Martha said. "Two excellent drivers, big men and ex-military medics. They work at the New York City VA, and they live here in Ridgewood."

"Why do you need big men?" Floyd asked.

"Crowd control," Mac answered. "What are their names?"

"Alphonso Constable and Percy Cook. They both speak Spanish, and Alphonso does Italian."

"I'll put them on a sixty-day trial," Mac promised.

"So what am I to do?" Floyd asked.

"You're to be my fox in the hen-house."

"What does that entail?"

"I'll place you in all of the four hospitals, in advance of our month-long visits. You'll write a private report on each staff before we arrive, then another after we leave."

"Oho. You want a spy."

"You want a job? Exciting things will be happening."

"...I never thought of myself spying on my colleagues."

"It's the quickest way I can think of to improve our medical service to the community. Are you with us or not?"

"As the caller said, 'All God's children got a place in the choir'..."

"After the funeral tomorrow, go to Bushwick's ER. It's nine blocks from here. They'll be expecting you."

"Okay. Look, can you tell me why the whole ER staff thinks this weekly folk-dance is such a big deal?"

"Besides letting off emotional pressure, and healthy exercise, you mean? Sure. This is a safe place to do our plotting, scheming, and politicking. We might be overheard at the hospital."

"I see. Goodnight, then," Floyd, chuckled, and he walked away to his motorcycle.

"Why did you pick him?" Martha asked.

"Why do you think?"

"Because he's God's gift to women. They'll open their hearts, and legs, to him."

"He's new. They don't know him."

"Oh, they will."

CHAPTER 4:
VIOLENCE

Mac entered the hospital parking lot at 6 AM and came in by the side entrance. The guard there smiled and saluted, and directed her to the administrative offices. The news had gotten around that quickly. Another guard showed her to the door next to the chief administrator's office, where her name had been freshly applied, along with the letters "Ph.D." She smiled, remembering. For five years she had held down a full-time nurse's job at night and a full credit-load of studies by day. Now she worked the day-shift, had those significant letters after her name, and an office of her own. She was quietly proud, and intimidated by the responsibility thrust on her so soon. She took a deep breath, pulled out her key-ring with the new key that the administrator had given her just those yesterday, unlocked the door and walked in.

Inside was a small vestibule almost filled by a huge filing cabinet, a secretary's chair and desk, bearing a computer, a printer-scanner, a fax machine, a sturdy office phone, and a name-plate saying only: "Ms. E. Basch". Mac recalled that the administrator had promised her a secretary along with the office, and clearly a secretary of enough status that she didn't have to start her shift until 8 AM, if not later. Whistling the theme song of "Nine to Five", Mac went to the door at the end of the vestibule and opened it, revealing her office proper.

It was larger than the vestibule but furnished much the same, with the addition of a battle-worn filing cabinet, a rear door and a single window looking out on the hospital's parking lot. Mac set her coat on top of the file cabinet, dropped her purse on the desk, sat down almost gingerly in the chair, and found it remarkably comfortable.

"Time for work, then," she murmured, as she fired up the computer. She pulled a blank-cased CD out of her purse, stuck it in the computer, and began typing her grant-proposal.

By the time she'd finished, the secretary's voice could be heard through the door to the vestibule, chatting with machine-gun speed on what had to be the phone. Mac took the CD out of the computer, set it carefully in its case, and carried it out to the vestibule to meet the mysterious Ms. Basch.

At the secretary's desk sat a horsey-looking middle-aged woman just hanging up the phone while pulling papers out of the fax machine with the other hand. She looked up to see Mac enter, smiled widely, and gushed: "Oh, Doctor Mackenzie, it's so nice to be working with you! I've heard such good things about you—one moment—here's a note from the Chief Admin and a letter from Congressman Waters—" The phone rang, and she picked up the handset without missing a beat. "Doctor MacKenzie's office, please hold.—And more notes from Financials, Purchasing, and International Trucks—" All was delivered at rapid-fire pace.

MacKenzie mused that if Ms. Basch resembled any horse, it would have to be Secretariat. "Ms. Basch," she wedged a word in edgewise as she held out the CD, "Here's the grant proposal that the Chief asked for. I think he'll want to see it right away."

"Oh, certainly!" Ms. Basch beamed. Her teeth were horse-like too. She took the CD with the hand that wasn't holding the phone, flipped the case open, pulled out the disc and inserted it into her computer in a single smooth motion. "Hello? Yes, Mr. Esterhazy, I'll relay the message." She muffled the phone against her flat bosom and asked Mac: "Do you want to talk to Admin at Bushwick?"

"Not now," Mac admitted, with a conspiratorial grin. "I'm going to the ER. Please rush that proposal to the Chief."

"Will do," promised Ms. Basch, as she turned back to the phone.

Mac made good her escape, reminding herself to send a note of thanks to the Chief for the gift of the hyperactive secretary. Her new office's paperwork, at least, would be in capable hands.

In the ER there were two patients under observation, the room was spotless, and all the apparatus was in place. Mac walked to the back of the room and down a corridor to the back of the building. In the last room she heard Bill Schmersal's voice speaking Yiddish, sounding as if he were consoling someone.

She walked in and saw that it was the rabbi's wife. Mac had expected a person devastated by grief, but instead the Rebbtzin Goldman beamed with joy. She was in her sixties, no more than five feet tall, wearing a gray wig and plain print dress and thick woolen stockings, and had a pair of the bluest, merriest eyes, which appeared to be squeezing out joy instead of tears. Mac leaned down and kissed the woman on both cheeks, murmuring: "I'm sorry for your loss."

"Don't be sorry for me," said the rebbetzin, smiling. "It is the community which has lost one of the world's greatest Biblical scholars. My husband looked forward to learning about life after death. He envisioned a great study-hall where all the Biblical geniuses taught."

Mac had been instructed by Bill that it was the place of a visitor to listen, encouraging the mourner to speak, but she could think of nothing to say to that, so she only nodded. She saw that behind the widow sat two bearded men beside the sheet-covered body on the bed. No doubt they had kept the night vigil, praying beside the body through the dark hours. They would accompany the body to the synagogue and then the grave, praying all the way. Mac chose not to think of how that custom must have originated. She excused herself and took Bill aside.

"Have you been here all night?" she asked.

"Yes. They needed someone to translate."

"But they speak English well enough."

"True, but the rabbi was a friend and I wanted to be here. We sometimes played chess..."

"Was he good at it?"

"Yes, but I usually won. He'd go off on some Biblical story, I'd encourage him, and he'd lose concentration. I think he guessed what I was doing, but he enjoyed it too much to call me out on it. ...Look, I need to speak to you."

"About what?"

"Not here."

"Then in my office after the funeral. It's right next door to the Chief's. Watch out for Secretariat."

Mac looked down from her office window and saw the parking lot full of black-suited bearded men. Beyond that, gray-clad women filled the streets. Mourners arrived on buses from upstate New York, New Jersey, and as far as Connecticut. An ambulance with lights blinking sounded its siren as it came slowly toward the ER. The crowd parted before it, like the Red Sea before Moses. Floyd followed it on his motorcycle. Martha sat behind him in her starched whites, in a red helmet with a black visor. A few paces behind them walked Jill, a lonely speck of white in a sea of black coats, hats and beards.

Mac's phone rang. "This is Alphonso Constable," said a voice from the speaker. "You asked that I and Percy Cook contact you."

"This is a job interview over the phone," said Mac. "If successful, you'll be given a six-month trial period. So describe yourself, and what you do, and how you do it."

"First, I'd like to hear what the job is and where it is,"

"Fair enough. You'll work out of Ridgewood VA hospital, but we'll be outsourced to the four closest private hospitals on a rotating basis."

"Why rotating?"

"We'll be evaluating and training them to improve ER and EMS services in Brooklyn, and hopefully we'll create a paradigm for the whole United States."

"You know, both Percy and I live in Ridgewood?"

"I also heard you were Army combat medics."

"We served together with the Rangers in Afghanistan, and we saw the elephant all right."

"My husband met the elephant over there, and didn't make it home."

"Sorry for your loss."

"Thank you for your service. I'll fax both of you a questionnaire. Don't discuss it. I want your answers to be given in a meeting tomorrow afternoon in my office."

"What kind of ambulance will we be driving?"

"The newest International, with the latest equipment."

"Wow! Right now we're driving a 1999 bucket of bolts, and have to steal to keep it stocked."

"Will Percy Cook agree to my requirements?'

"Yes, ma'am," said a different voice. "I've been listening in."

"Good. Tomorrow, in my office."

A vast mournful sigh swept Ridgewood as the body of Rabbi Yeshaya Goldman, wrapped in a white shroud, was carried out on a stretcher and placed on a gurney. There was pushing and shoving as the mourners tried to touch the gurney or the shrouded body, but an elder reprimanded the crowd and they became more orderly. A group of rabbis, followed by the crowd saying prayers and reciting psalms, followed the gurney away from the hospital and into the street. Most people had brought their own water bottles, and the ER staff had little to do. They returned to meet in Dr. MacKenzie's office.

Mac distributed copies of a fax she had sent to New York's VA hospital, and said: "Do not discuss these questions or your answers. If there are subjects you believe should be added, do so, but be brief. Your response should be no more than one 8 by 11 page for all the questions. Turn them in to Ms. Basch tomorrow morning. We'll meet in the afternoon. Bill and Martha, stay behind."

When the others had gone she asked: "Bill, you wanted to speak to me? Martha's my deputy. Speak freely."

Bill wiped sweat from his brow. "I think I'm in trouble."

"What did you do?" Mac asked.

"I killed Rosie's husband."

"W-what?!"

"Great!" Martha snapped. "That bastard deserved to die."

"Bill," Mac pointed to a folding chair recently placed in front of her desk. "Sit."

"I'll stand."

"Then I'll sit. Tell me everything. Do the police know?"

"Yes. I called them. They said not to worry, the husband was a piece of shit and they should have killed him first."

"Who were the cops?" Martha asked.

Bill handed her a card.

"Detectives O'Rooney and Burke, from the 83rd precinct," said Martha. "Good men. They knew the husband. How did it happen?"

"After the dance, Jill went to buy pig knuckles and sauerbraten. I went to the synagogue to get food for the men saying prayers over the rabbi's body. They only eat kosher. I delivered it and decided to look in on Rosie. The husband was there, threatening to kill her if she told the police about him beating her. All she asked him for was a bed-pan. He threatened to knock out her other eye. I pulled him away from the bed, and lifted the sheets to insert the pan under Rosie's *tush*—"

"What's a 'tush'?" Martha asked.

"Yiddish for backside. Her bare right leg and hip were exposed. The husband called me a pervert. We argued. Without warning, he snatched the pan out from under her and threw it in my face."

"Full of urine?" Martha guessed.

"Got it all over me and my uniform. I don't remember throwing the punch, but he came off the ground and the back of his head hit the bed's guardrail. He was dead."

"Rosie saw all this?" Mac asked.

"No. She passed out from pain when the husband pulled away the bed-pan. The charge nurse saw it all."

"She's your witness?"

"Yes. She gave a statement."

"Martha, you call the detectives. I'll talk with the charge nurse. Bill, you sit down."

"I could go to the electric chair!"

"No, you're only going to my chair." She pointed. "Take a seat."

Martha completed her call and announced: "It looks alright. The detectives will pick up Bill in an hour and drive him to the King's County courthouse. Bill, you'll be arraigned for trial before Judge Golding. He's a supporter of the Me-Too movement, and is hard on womanizers and child-beaters. The charge nurse is your witness. The detective said the sheets were wet, confirming that the husband pulled the pan away before the woman had finished urinating. And there's Bill's soaked uniform."

"Where is it?" Mac asked.

"I stripped it off after the cops left," said Bill, "Stuffed it in a laundry bag and gave it to the charge nurse, then washed off and changed into clean scrubs. The nurse kept the bag."

"Smart girl," said Mac. "How do they expect the judge to rule?"

"At best, dismiss the charges. At worst, involuntary manslaughter and Bill released on his own recognizance. The detectives recommend leniency for Bill, and the charge nurse will support them. She and Bill will wear their uniforms to the hearing."

"Will there be a trial?" Bill asked, unconvinced.

"A hearing, anyway," Martha said. "It's a legal formality. Not to worry. Get back to work."

After Bill left, Mac commented: "I've thought of killing some of these abusers."

"You aren't the only one. You're going to see more maltreatment cases in the public hospitals."

"...Did you ever consider it?"

"Killing? No!" Martha snapped. "Uh, I have to go finish handing off my department and answer your questionnaire."

"Wait," said Mac, pointing. "Look out the window. That's the kind of ambulance I'll order."

Martha looked out at the big International in the parking lot. "It's a beauty," she admitted, resting a hand on Mac's shoulder. "Yes, I've thought about killing some of these sick sons of bitches."

She turned away and started to leave the office, then stopped, and shut the door. She returned to the desk, leaned close and whispered: "I've done it."

"What?"

"I've done it. I killed a patient." The two women locked eyes. "It was the girls. The mother couldn't stand girls. She was perfectly caring for two sons, but she killed her first daughter. We reported it to the police. They charged her, but she had money enough to hire the best lawyers and they got her off on a technicality. The woman got pregnant soon afterwards, and birthed another girl. We'd get the little tyke beaten and bruised. We filed reports, but nothing happened. She even got a judge to sign a restraining order against me, the police, and Social

Services."

"What about her husband?"

"Less than useless." Martha collapsed into the chair, and tears streamed down her cheeks. "The little darling. Her name was Gwen. She had red hair, a freckled face and a pug nose... Her mother set her out at the bus stop forty minutes early. It was freezing cold. The mother had a pot of water, and she poured it over the child's head and down the back of her snow-suit. She went back to the house for another pot-full of water, and did it again. By the time the school bus came, Gwen couldn't move. The bus driver carried the girl into the bus and drove her to our hospital. By the time we got her, Gwen was dead."

"Surely they prosecuted!"

"Three witnesses saw the woman dousing the child. She even admitted what she'd done, but because she hadn't been Mirandized properly her confession was out. Her lawyer had arranged to have her tried before a sympathetic judge who had just lost a daughter."

"You mean she got off?"

"Until she came into my emergency room. A shot of air into her IV line. I did it."

"How were you able to live with that?"

Martha patted her eyes dry. "Quite well, thank you."

"If you were offered the opportunity, would you do it again?"

"Absolutely. And when I meet my maker, that's the first thing I'll tell him."

The two women sat in silence for a long time.

CHAPTER 5:
SETTING SPIES

BUSHWICK HOSPITAL

Floyd rolled his motorcycle into the Bushwick ER parking lot, its chrome sparkling in the sun. He tucked his helmet under his arm and entered the ER.

"You must be the temp fill-in this week." The woman who spoke to him was, according to her name-plate, Charge Nurse Mayzie Ivory. She pointed to his helmet. "If you/ve got a motorcycle to go with that, you'd better park it inside."

"Why?"

"We're on the border of Bedford-Stuyvesant. They'll steal the teeth out of your head so you can't eat your dinner. Then they'll steal your dinner."

"In broad daylight?"

"Get the bike. Put it next to mine in the laundry-room."

"You ride?"

"A 1999 Harley Softtail."

"Wow! I've got a 1979 Electra Ultra-Glide."

The two of them spent the next several minutes

talking about bikes.

"Enough," Mayzie said. "Get it safe in here. Vets' hospital ER people don't fit into the chaotic life of inner-city first responders."

"Why is that?"

"Comparing a vets' hospital to an inner-city ER is like drinking from a water fountain and drinking from a fire-hose." Mayzie pointed at a gurney being rolled into Cubicle 8 by an ambulance crew. "Take this clipboard and work that patient. I'll be nearby if you have any questions."

Mac telephoned Mayzie. "How did the new man work out today?"

"Hmmm. *Menza-menza.*"

"Why only so-so? He's a biker; I thought you two would get along."

"I'm old-school: nursing is for females. No, no doubt a male nurse's strength can be an asset. Floyd's also patient initiative. He enjoys nursing. I can see that..."

"Then what's wrong?"

"He's beautiful. Female nurses and patients were finding excuses to be near him. I gave him an assistant and she went all gaga, knock-kneed with her mouth hanging open, until I kicked her in the ass."

Mac sighed. "I had a similar problem."

"I might order chastity-belts for my staff."

"Put him on the ambulance. He was a combat medic, and he's used to treating high-impact injuries."

"That's an idea. Tomorrow is Friday, and Party

Time in the neighborhood. I'll put him on the grave-yard shift in the ER, then on Sunday evening with the first responders. If he survives, I'll keep him for the week."

"Let me know. Now I've got an interview and a staff meeting. Talk to you Monday."

Alphonso Diaz was six feet tall and wound as tight as any man MacKenzie had ever seen. The veins in his bare forearms stood out like miniature railroad tracks until they disappeared in the short sleeves of his pressed uniform shirt. He weighed in at one-hundred-seventy pounds, and had dark, piercing, Latin eyes.

The uniformed man next to him weighed a hun-dred pounds more and stood six inches taller. His bright chocolate skin reflected the office lights from his shaven skull. He had a square jaw, and met Mac's gaze without challenge or anxiety. She was surprised that the larger man spoke for both of them. He was articulate, and his baritone voice was steady and rich. "We both live close to this hospital," he said. "We're married and have two children, a boy and a girl, each."

"Will you pledge them in marriage?" Mac joked.

"That'll be their choice. But I have a question: if this doesn't work out for us, will we be able to return to our positions in New York?"

"I can't promise, but you'll be able to use your seniority to work anywhere you wish in the VA sys-tem. Is there any reason you think this position might not work out?"

"We understand this is an experimental program."

"Correct. And I have a question for you: your experience is with VA procedures. Four of the hospitals we'll service and evaluate are public hospitals. Those neighborhoods are rough."

"In New York we serviced Harlem," Alphonso spoke up. "You know we were trained combat medics. Although it wasn't our job Percy and I often stopped bleeding. In opioid cases we often neutralized the patients or their families when they got out of hand, and on occasion set up and inserted drips."

"I'd prefer you leave infusions to the nurses."

"What's so experimental about our group?" Percy asked.

"Did you fill out the faxed questionnaire?"

Both men nodded.

"Then come to the conference room. We're about to review them."

She led the way to where Bill, Jill, and Martha were waiting.

Mac introduced everyone, seated them around the oval table and took out their papers. Percy and Alphonso handed theirs over to her.

"Our Emergency Department," Mac began, "Is responsible for the provision of medical and surgical care to patients arriving at the hospital. Our ambulance service, or EMS, is accountable to arrive in the shortest time possible to the scene of an emergency, and to provide assistance. Your objective today is to suggest ways of improving both the ER and EMS services in all five hospitals. Martha will direct the discussion. Jill will take notes while I review your questionnaires. Go to it."

At Bushwick hospital on Friday night, Floyd pushed his bike into the laundry-room behind Mayzie's. He walked down the corridor, opened the doors to the ER—and fell back as the noise bowled him over. Orientals, Blacks, Hispanics, Haitians with dreadlocks, men, women and children wearing face-coverings and Muslim clothes, they filled the room and spilled out into the corridor, all in a state of animated agitation. To be heard you had to shout, and everyone did.

Floyd grabbed a passing nurse and asked: "Where can I help?"

She slapped a plastic infusion-bag into his hand. "Third gurney from the entrance in the hallway. Slow drip."

"How can you work like this?!"

"Hah. Just wait 'til 3 AM, when the bars close. Then the devil comes by in his motorboat."

At 8 AM the ER was finally quiet. It was full of patients sleeping—in chairs, on gurneys, in the cubicles, and on the floor. Most awaited transportation to other hospitals.

Mayzie supervised the morning staff turnover. She stopped Floyd and grabbed him by the front of his bloody uniform and asked: "Do you still want to work in the ER?"

"Yes."

"You have blood all over your jacket, puke on your trousers, and a bump on your forehead."

"A drunk hit me with a bed-pan."

"It's the weapon of choice, unless they bring their own. See you tomorrow night, and we'll do this again."

Saturday, at midnight, Floyd helped relieve the night crew. His pressed whites with military creases had five strips of 2-inch wide tape stuck on each leg and a short apron with several pockets. "What the hell is the butcher's apron for?" Mayzie demanded.

"Pressure bandages, a stapler for sutures, antiseptics, and your cell-phone number in case I go out of my mind."

"That's why they call me Crazy Mayzie; I've been in the ER too long. What's with the tape on the trouser legs?"

"To apply pressure bandages quickly. It's more efficient than a tourniquet to stop bleeding, and less dangerous."

"Ah. Good for direct pressure, but if there's arterial spurting use a tourniquet anyway, between the heart and the wound. If necessary, use a second one. I suggest you add a marker-pen to your apron. We write the time of tourniquet application on the patient's forehead and the tourniquet strap. You don't have the legal right to remove the strap; only an ER doctor can do that. Sunday you'll take the evening shift on ambulance #1."

"Is there a reason I'm not staying in the ER?"

"Your supervisor MacKenzie recommended it."

Thursday, Floyd showed up in MacKenzie's office.

"Why did you put me on the ambulance?" he asked bluntly.

"You drew too many females in the ER."

Floyd snorted. "On the ambulance, my first call was a spousal dispute. The husband kicked the hell out of his wife, and she hit him with an electric iron. They were covered in blood. I jumped in to help the cops."

"A mistake. That's their job, not yours."

"The husband was punching the wife in the face. When I pulled him off, she tried to hit me with the iron. I took it away, and she threw a pan of lye-water in my face. I would have gone blind, bur the female nurse cut open her saline infusion-bag and cleaned my eyes. I came back to the hospital as a patient."

"Did you go out the next night?"

"I answered the next call. A premature birth. A cop brought the child out; he's done it three times before. He calls his mother, and she instructs him. Everything was fine."

"Did you answer my questionnaire?"

Floyd handed her the printout. "After two nights in the ER and three on the ambulance, I'd change my priorities."

"How?"

"I filled in the answers before I worked Bushwick. Mayzie needs a bigger ER."

"More personnel?"

"More beds. Her staff is well trained, but they have to fight their way through the ER, the corridors, and even out to the loading ramps. It's impossible to wheel a gurney inside. The hospital has only a ninety-bed capacity. Half the patients needing hospitalization are farmed out to other hospitals; that occupies ambulances which should be answering emergencies. The patients have to wait until morning for rides to other hospitals. Some are on the floor, others in waiting-room chairs, and the corridors are full."

"To build a new ER would take a month of Sundays. Meanwhile, we couldn't close it dcwn."

"In Iraq and Afghanistan we serviced civilians from tents, and were well organized."

"There you had the guns. Here the civilians have them."

"The nurse who took care of my eyes was terrific, but while it was happening I kept wishing for a doctor."

"Bill and two ambulance drivers made the same suggestion."

"Why isn't there a doctor on every ambulance?"

"The AMA forbids doctors as first responders. Too many were injured."

"How?"

"Gunshots, knife wounds, Molotov cocktails. We have doctors on radio stand-by to instruct ambulance personnel, like that policeman's mother."

"That's not as good as a qualified MD on the scene."

"You're right, but the doctors are not wrong."

"Another thing. Why are there three policemen in every patrol car?"

"Two go out of the car to the scene. The third

locks himself in the car and calls the precinct, keeping the line open."

"Why?"

"In case of an ambush."

"They make a habit of ambushing cops around here?"

Just then a nurse came in and announced: "Ocullasses is back."

"Introduce him to Floyd. I have to fax this proposal to Washington."

"My pleasure." Her smile almost split the nurse's face.

"Floyd," Mac warned, "No matter how the patient tries to jolly you, he has serious issues and could become suicidal. Keep him busy until the psychiatrist arrives." She picked up the phone.

The nurse led Floyd out of the office, saying: "A thirty-five year old male, married, with three children. Considered a mathematical genius, but finds it difficult to interact with people. He tells jokes to avoid personal issues."

"What am I supposed to do?"

"Keep him talking until the psychiatrist arrives. Cubicle 3. Good luck."

A thin man wearing a winter jacket, rumpled woolen shirt, jeans and flip-flops without socks was sitting on a gurney, staring at the floor. Floyd automatically picked up the clipboard on the end of the gurney, looked at the chart, and asked: "Mr... Ocullasses? What's the problem?"

"Any fool can see I'm depressed," the man grumbled. "Where's Nurse MacKenzie?"

"She's been promoted."

"Ah. About time they put a competent person in a position of authority. The world is going to hell in a hand basket."

"Hmmm," said Floyd, sitting down beside him. "If you had the power to change things, what's the first thing you would do?"

"I'd pass a law forbidding gas stations from cleaning parts in the open."

"Really? What good would that do?"

"It's the whole point. That's why I'm depressed. A block away is a gas station, and they put some parts in a pan of gasoline and left it lying on the ground. You know it's hot out there. A scraggy old dog came up and drank the gas. The animal stiffened, bolted round and round the gas pumps, then fell on his back with his four legs stiff in the air."

"Dead?" Floyd guessed.

"No, he ran out of gas!" The patient slapped his knees. Floyd groaned in appreciation.

A doctor parted the curtains and came in. This was clearly the psychiatrist. "I see you've kept Mr. Ocullasses entertained," he said.

"According to his chart," Floyd puzzled, "That's not his name."

"Allow him to explain."

"It's the terminology of my affliction," the man said. "Ocullasses is a combination of two words: 'ocular' from the ancient Greek, meaning eye, and 'ass' from the American idiom. When the nerve of the eye is connected to the nerve of the ass, you see everything as shit."

Floyd groaned again.

"Hey, keep it down over there," a nurse from the next cubicle complained.

CHAPTER 6:
BEDFORD-STUYVESANT
COMMUNITY HOSPITAL

FRIDAY EVENING, 79TH POLICE PRECINCT

As instructed, Floyd wheeled his bike into the rear parking lot of the Tompkins Avenue police station. There the guard directed him to park, chain up his bike, and board the hospital bus. He took a seat in the rear where he could see the people and listen to their conversation.

The two starched points of a nurse's cap appeared coming up the entrance steps. The cap sat on curly black locks on a head with a broad Black face. Through pearly white teeth she bellowed: "Are my kittens ready to play?" Everyone appeared to ignore the greeting.

As the woman came up the steps she appeared to grow in size until she filled the aisle. She was easily as large as Big Bill. She waddled down the aisle, greeting each person by name, and they responded. She looked up, and her gleaming black eyes locked onto Floyd.

"Heaven help us," she bellowed, "There's a White man on the bus!"

"Guilty as charged," said Floyd, smiling, smiling.

"At least he knows where to sit," someone quipped.

"You must be Floyd. Call me Momma. Everyone does."

She sat down next to Floyd, and the bulk of her body shoved him sideways against the window. "Heard you alright with Crazy Mayzie," she said. "My ER is more organized. We used to be even more orderly until the Black Muslims moved out."

"Why did they leave?"

"Nobody knows. Farrakhan just ordered 'em out, and three hundred families just left. Half went to Georgia, and the rest to upstate New York. They used to volunteer in the ER and the hospital. Black Muslim guards kept the gang-bangers away. When they left, it hurt. They worked hard, and were clean and community-conscious."

"Are the gangs that big of a problem?"

"There are a hundred and thirty-five gangs in Brooklyn alone. Most are affiliated with the Bloods, Crips, or Crowns, and the Black Lives Mafia is probing into all of them. They live off drugs, prostitution, illegal cigarettes and liquor, and they'll fight hard to protect their sales-turf."

"In Bushwick and Ridgewood, the hospitals are neutral ground."

"The Muslims kept it that way in Bed-Stuy, but we're returning to Shame, Blame, and Glory. If a gang-banger is shamed, he blames someone and redeems his honor in a gang-fight."

"Don't you have assigned police?"

"The hospital has private guards—without weapons. The gangs are better armed. When push comes to shove, the guards hide. Stay close to me until people get used to your White face. If you have to, grab a CO2 fire-extinguisher and let the punks have it in the face. Sunday you go out on the ambulance." Mama reached into her enormous handbag and pulled out two magazines. "Tape these under your belt and over your kidneys."

"What for?"

"Protection against knife-wounds."

In her office Mac told Floyd: "We're meeting in the Gay Greek's this evening. It's mandatory."

"Will we go folk-dancing afterward?"

"That's up to you."

"Can I bring a partner?"

"The Greek's daughter?"

"I've been eating there every chance I get."

"She only works there weekends and Wednesdays."

"I thought she worked full-time."

"She studies at the New School for her MA as a hospital dietician."

"She's nice."

"She's beautiful," said Mac. "I'm trying to convince her to apply for a position at our hospital. Sloan-Kettering approached her already."

"Wow! Beautiful and smart."

"How did you feel at Bed-Stuy?"

"Like a fish out of water. Mine was the only White face in the neighborhood. Mama suggested I wear my helmet and get a pair of heavy gloves. I was useless in the ambulance. The drivers and I had to lock ourselves in the vehicle to keep it from being stolen or broken into for drugs. They got a cop to stand guard."

"Yet there are streets that are safe. Bergen Street is one of them."

"I saw. It was like finding an oasis in the desert. The street was clean, and we could leave the ambulance and walk around. I was told that streets like that are dominated by churches and their families. They screen people who want to move in."

"Possibly they could replace the Black Muslims in keeping order at Bed-Stuy. What did you think of their ER?"

"It's well-organized. Overcrowded on the weekend, but they have a three-hundred and fifty bed hospital to back them up. I think drugs are being sold, stolen, or traded through the ER."

"Is the medical staff involved?"

"I don't know. It's the type of characters who hang around the ER: they remind me of the problem at the San Francisco VA."

"Good observation. See you later at the Greek's."

As soon as Floyd was out the door, Mac picked up the phone. "Martha? I just heard from Golden Boy. I'd like you to inform your detective friends that drugs may be leaking from the Bed-Stuy ER."

"I'll call them."

"See you tonight for dinner and dance."

The diner buzzed with a capacity crowd. Waiters and waitresses—all relatives of the Prodromakeos family—moved swiftly, serving, cleaning, and setting up new tables. Georgee met Mac, Martha, Jill and Bill as they came in. "Your table is reserved in the back," he said. "It's quieter, and more private."

"Anyone else here?" Mac asked.

"Two rough-looking guys who say they're drivers. Floyd is in the kitchen helping Kula. He and she will serve."

"How come?"

"Kula decided you should all have a vegan dinner."

"Uhm, I'm sure it will be delicious. I'll keep an eye on Floyd."

"And I'll watch my daughter."

Kula came to the table, bearing menus printed on the office computer. "Welcome to the Gay Greek's," she announced to the ER staff. "Tonight I'm your chef and my father is your host. I thought to introduce you to veganism." She handed out the menus to the four, who smiled politely. "Our purpose is to prevent the exploitation of animals and promote a cleaner and healthier environment. I hope you enjoy dinner." She and Floyd hurried off to the kitchen while the ER staff studied their menus.

Ridgewood ER Vegan Menu

Tuscan Tomato Soup With Garlic Bread

Nachos With Veggies & Vegan Cheese Sauce
Stir-Fried Sugar Peas & Carrot Noodles
Black Bean & Avocado Burrito
Creamy Butternut Squash With Linguine & Sage
Vegetable Paella & Humus Quadrilles
Strawberry Sherbet & Prodromakeos Family
Wine

"...Just a little short on complex protein, and a shameless exploitation of plants," Martha muttered. "Did you know, there's a large and growing body of evidence showing that the higher plants have awareness? They fight wars, protect their young, and communicate with each other via chemicals in water, through the ground by their roots, and through the air by their leaves. The smell of new-mown hay is really grass-plants screaming in pain. Veganism doesn't guarantee moral superiority."

"You hush," Mac whispered back. "Let the kids have their fun. It'll taste great."

"Anything that comes out of this place tastes great," Martha conceded. "Bring it on."

At the end of the meal MacKenzie tapped her wine-glass, nodded appreciatively to Georgee, and announced: "We thank you for hosting us as members of your family. To your daughter, our compliments were extended by silence. When mouths are full and talk is little, it's praise to the chef for her excellent vittles."

She raised her glass again, and everybody joined in the salute to Kula.

Mac tapped her glass again and continued: "I'm certain we'll all have second thoughts about veganism and questions for Kula about that lifestyle, but this is a business meeting, so I'll just dive in. Congress has passed the allocation for our ER project, and President Trump has signed it."

There were multiple cheers. "You mean we've got the fifty million dollars?" Jill asked.

"Yes, minus half a million for the newest and most modern ambulance from International Truck Company. It'll be on view Friday morning in time for a ceremony. All the political bigwigs and news outlets will be there. Jill, as ninth-generation Brooklynite, you'll guide the Borough President. Alphonso and Percy, as residents of Ridgewood, you accompany Congressman Waters. Floyd, you'll escort the Undersecretary of the Treasury; she arrives at 10 AM at Kennedy Airport, and represents the President."

"What, will she ride behind me on my bike?" Floyd asked.

"Leave the bike at the ER. The Secret Service will pick you up there at nine."

"Bill, you attend the VA representatives from Washington. Martha and I will be with Mayor DeBlasio and his entourage. Please, be as accommodating as possible to your charges and the media."

"Showoffsky-fest," Bill snickered, quietly.

"Who will usher the other hospital administrators?" Jill asked.

"Our Chief will take them in hand. Congratulations are in order to Bill Schmersal; he was acquitted of all charges in Brooklyn District Court."

Everybody applauded and reached out to shake the big man's hand or at least pat him on the back. "He should get a medal," said Martha. "Rosie will be another two weeks in traction, and at least month in the hospital."

"We need to move on if we're going to make the square-dance," said Mac. "All of you are required to meet tomorrow morning in the hospital parking lot at 8 AM. The new ambulance will arrive with a team from International Trucking, who'll instruct you on its use and maintenance."

"How long will that take?" Jill asked.

"As long as necessary. There's a lot of new equipment, especially for the drivers: an updated computer program with Skype conferencing, bullet-proof windows you can see out of but not in through, and tires that won't deflate when slashed, stabbed, or shot."

"Sounds like a tank," Percy noted.

"Certain places in Brooklyn, you'll wish it was a tank," said Jill.

CHAPTER 7:
AND THE BAND PLAYED ON

LUNA PARK

The ER team entered the basement at PS 75 to a standing ovation. Danny Block announced: "Tomorrow Ridgewood Hospital will host legislators from Washington, and New York's five boroughs will present Ridgewood's Emergency Room staff with the world's most modern ambulance. Let's have a round of applause for Dr. MacKenzie and her staff!"

"Word gets around fast," Bill chuckled.

The evening was even more fun than the last time, and it ended with the Grand March led by Floyd and Kula. As they left the school Martha pointed to the helmet in Kula's hands and asked: "Where are you guys heading?"

"Coney Island," said Kula.

"To watch the submarine races?"

"Luna Park."

Floyd practically glowed. "Since I was a kid I dreamed of Luna Park: the roller-coaster, the Thunderbolt, the Cyclone, the Slingshot—Did you know the Slingshot propels you at ninety miles an hour?—and then there's skydiving over the Atlantic Ocean..."

"Enjoy!" Martha laughed.

Kula mounted the Harley behind Floyd, and they drove off up Central Avenue. He parked on Stilwell Avenue in Coney Island, chained the cycle to a lamppost, went to the entrance and presented the tickets he'd ordered online. He and Kula tried to hold hands while walking through the barrels at the entrance. They collapsed in a giggling tangle and had to be helped out into the park by grinning attendants who'd seen that before. The sounds of organs playing to the Merry-Go-Round, and the calliope with the Aerial Swings filled the park.

"You pick which ride we go on first," said Floyd.

"No, you choose; it's your dream."

"The Cyclone, then. It's the oldest and most famous ride in the world. It was built in 1927. Our tickets entitle us to any ride we choose, as many times as we want."

They rode the Cyclone twice. Then Kula chose Wild River, and they flew down the water-chute to the pool below. The Aerial Swings and the Thunderbolt followed.

At the Mechanical Race Horses there was a group ahead of them: four tough-looking Black men escorting a beautiful middle-aged Black woman dressed in a short, sequined, silk dress with matching shoes.

"She's stunning," Kula noted.

"If she takes a deep breath," said Floyd, "She's going to burst out of that dress. I'd like to see that."

Kula playfully slapped his arm.

He bought a bag of caramel-coated popcorn and a larger bag of salt-water taffy, and they shared. Kula declined to go with him on the Slingshot, and when he returned Floyd admitted she'd been right. His stomach couldn't take any more food.

Kula held her skirt down as the left the park, where an attendant slyly hit a button that blew air up her legs.

Then they both noticed something strange. The area in front of the Luna Park entrance was emptying quickly. There were no children at this time of night, but people were running away.

Several White men in suit jackets entered the empty square, reaching into their pockets. They were walking toward Floyd and Kula, but they were focused on the group of Black men escorting the beautiful woman.

The Black group came laughing their way out of the exit, behind Floyd and Kula. The woman guffawed, trying to hold her dress down as the park attendant pressed the air button.

One of her four escorts saw the group moving toward them, and whipped out a pistol.

Floyd's combat instincts cut in. He shoved Kula sideways and to the ground, and covered her with his body.

The White men fired, some right through their pockets.

The first Black man fell with his weapon in hand. The other three ducked back into the park. The Black woman, her attention drawn away from the air jet, raised her head. One of the White men raised a sawed-off shotgun and fired into her face. She dropped, and the park attendant fled. The White men holstered their weapons, turned and quickly walked away.

There were ten seconds of silence.

"Are you alright?" Floyd panted. "You sure you're okay?"

"Yes, yes, yes," Kula answered, "But you're crushing me."

Okay, I've got to help those two." He sprinted to the man and checked for vital signs. "Dead," he pronounced.

Behind him, Kula pawed out her phone and began poking numbers.

Floyd hurried to the woman. Her jaw and left side of her face were shot away, and she was choking on her own blood. Teeth and pieces of jawbone were lodged in her throat. He tried to pry them out with his fingers.

"Mothafucka, what you doin'?" The three remaining Black men were pointing guns at him.

"She can't breathe!"

"You gonna die!"

"I didn't do this; ask my girlfriend there. I'm a medic. Do you want this woman to live?"

"Yeah!"

"Then get a sharp knife and a ballpoint pen."

He heard the mechanical snap of metal on metal, and found himself looking at switchblade knife. He grabbed it. One of the men rummaged through the woman's purse and produced a ballpoint pen. The woman's body convulsed as her windpipe filled with blood and bone.

"Clean handkerchiefs!!" Floyd shouted "And take the pen apart. Give me the bottom part, without the ink or spring. Two of you hold her shoulders, and one hold her legs." He straddled her body, shoved her head back and placed the knife point at her throat.

"You cut her and I'll blow your fuckin' head off!" yelled one of the men.

"It's the only way to save her," Floyd snapped. "She's suffocating."

"Let 'im do it," said another of the guards. "We can always kill 'im later."

"Hold her tight!" Floyd shouted, and made his first incision through the skin, revealing the tough muscles of the trachea. The moment he cut between the muscles, air whistled in and the convulsions stopped.

Floyd reached behind him. "Give me the bottom of the pen and a clean handkerchief." Both were shoved into his hand. He tied the cloth around the middle of the plastic and inserted the empty body of the pen into the cut in the trachea, where it formed an airway for her to breathe. He raised her head to keep her from swallowing more blood. "Somebody, phone 911."

"Already done," Kula shouted back. "There's the siren."

"That's cops," the third man said. He patted Floyd's shoulder. "We owe you one," he said, and then took off running after the other two.

RIDGEWOOD HOSPITAL

"Why so glum?" Jill asked. "You're the hero of the day. Perfect timing for the ceremony. Your picture's in all the papers."

"I got hell from Georgee for putting his daughter in danger. We didn't get home until five in the morning, and the whole family was waiting. They wanted to kill me."

"Did the cops say who the White gang was?"

"The Brothers' Circle: Russian Mafia."

"I thought the big gangs worked together."

"The police think it was a bad drug deal that hadn't been settled," said Floyd. "The Crowns didn't get permission to enter Brighton Beach. There's a rumor that the Black Mafia thought it was beneath their dignity to ask permission from anybody White, and the Crowns bought it."

"So now there'll be a gang war. Brilliant!"

"How will that affect us?"

"The shit's going to hit the fan while we're out in gangland observing and trying to improve EMS in their territories. The devil's going to show up in his motorboat."

"That's the second time I've heard that phrase. What's it mean?"

Jill heaved a sigh. "Let's go out and look at our new ambulance."

Floyd followed her out of the ER, but at the entrance door a young Black man stepped in front of him. "You the doctor who saved the lady in Luna Park?" he asked.

"I'm no doctor, just a medic."

"But you him?"

"Yes."

"My boss, he Michael Leissner. He say, he owe you big time—and my boss always pay what he owe." The young man slipped away.

Floyd caught up with Jill. "Whc is Michael Leissner?" he asked.

Jill stopped so short he bumped into her. "Didn't you read today's papers?"

"I've been too busy apologizing to Kula's famiy."

"The woman you saved is Lucille Leissner. Her son Michael is the leader of the Crowns. It's said that he, along with the Crips and the Bloods, control most cities and towns from New York to Washngton DC—and some of the politicians."

"Interesting." Floyd relayed the message the young Black man had given him.

Jill looked up at him and said: "The drug business in Brooklyn alone is three hundred and twenty million dollars a year. If you're asking my opinion, stay away from the gang-bangers. If you're not asking my opinion, stay far away from them. If the Russian Mafia thinks you're tied to Michael Leissner, they'll turn you into a blivit."

"What's a blivit?"

"Two pounds of shit in a one-pound bag."

The team from International Trucking were experienced and methodical in their instructions. The ER crew were impressed, and took copious notes. At lunchtime Mac suggested they eat at the Greek's, but

Floyd tried to excuse himself. "Kula isn't there, but Georgee and his family are. They'll kill me."

"Then we'll make it the Brooklyn Spaghetti House. We can walk there."

The instructions on the ambulance continued until five in the evening, whereupon the crew went to dinner at Cohen's Deli. When they returned, they took the new ambulance out on two emergency calls. When they came back from those shakedown trials, Mac had a last announcement.

"Tomorrow morning," she told them, "Be here at 9 AM. Floyd, the Secret Service team will pick you up here, so bring a spare uniform just in case. You'll pick up the Undersecretary of Finance at 10 AM in the VIP lounge at Kennedy Airport. Be especially nice to her; she controls the purse strings."

The two Secret Service men who pulled up before Floyd reminded him of the movie *Men in Black*. They were little older than he was, physically fit, wore immaculate identical black suits with white shirts, blac ties, and black spit-shined shoes. The stretch limousine was silky black, with dark one-way windows. It sported a fully-stocked bar, television, telephone, and fold-down computer in the rear seating section. Floyd raided the bar for a Schweppes and relaxed on the scenic drive up Grand Central Parkway, over Van Wycke Expressway, and into Kennedy Airport.

The medallion on the limo's license plate gained preferential treatment from airport security and a parking space in front of the VIP lounge. One of the black-suited men accompanied Floyd inside. The plane was delayed fifteen minutes, and the Secret Service man said absolutely nothing while they waited.

Finally the passengers disembarked, and a tall statuesque woman in her fifties, wearing a beige skirt-suit, strode into the lounge and walked directly toward Floyd. She had the figure of a twenty-year-old, a beautiful mature face, and bright red lips. Her silver hair was swept back like the mane of a lion, and she scrutinized Floyd with intense and calculating gray eyes. He shivered involuntarily as she boldly undressed him with those visceral eyes. *Be especially nice to her*, he remembered.

"This is the first time I've been greeted by a *bona fide* hero," she said, holding out her hand. Floyd took it, and was surprised by the strength of her grip. She hooked her arm into his, pointed to the Secret Service man and commanded: "Lead on, MacDuff."

Once inside the limo, she pressed a button and a screen rose up to separate the front seats from the rear. She tapped another button, and *Music For the Love Hours* wafted in through hidden speakers. "What are you drinking?" she asked, pulling the mini-bar open.

"Er, I don't drink," said Floyd.

"I do, and they stock my favorite." She poured a mini-bottle of pre-mixed Bloody Mary into a long-stemmed glass, turned right and faced Floyd with a predatory look. She sipped her drink with her right hand, then reached out her left, jammed it into his crotch and squeezed his scrotum.

"Yow!" he shouted, leaped up, slammed his head on the ceiling, collapsed and doubled over with his head on the bar in front of him. *Be especially nice to her?!* was all he could think.

"You seem quite well endowed," she purred, manipulating his balls. "How many inches are you with a hard-on?"

"I dunno," he gasped, as waves of passion and pain shot through him.

"Every boy measures." She squeezed harder.

"Owww. That hurts." Floyd managed to pull his face out of the bar.

"Yet you're getting an erection. Now tell me how long it is."

"Ten. Ten inches. Please don't squeeze any more." *Be nice to her?!*

"And your girth?"

"I never measured, honestly. I don't know!" His voice cracked. "Please, you'll kill me!"

She released her grip and hunted down his trouser leg to his stiffening erection, and massaged it, purring like a tigress. "Stop!" he groaned. "Stop! Stop!"

"But you're enjoying it."

Nice? To her?! "I'll stain my uniform. I've got to stand before the cameras with you and the mayor. Owww, stop!"

"Surely you have a spare uniform at the hospital." She tightened her grip on the throbbing shaft until it went limp.

The driver's voice came over the intercom: "Arrival time, two minutes."

The Undersecretary finished her drink.

Bill deBlasio, Mayor of New York City, was first to address the crowd of more than five hundred people in the schoolyard of Public School #75. He stood before the new ambulance and praised the federal government and Dr. MacKenzie, and awarded the city's Medal of Bravery to Floyd Sorenson, who looked a little flushed as he accepted it. The following five speakers were mercifully brief, since the school needed the yard for lunch period and the medical staff had duties to perform.

"You'll see the government representative to the airport," Mac told Floyd.

"Uh, okay," he mumbled, looking a bit sheepish.

"Is there something wrong?" Mac asked. "She specifically requested you."

"Hmmm, no. No problem."

In the rear of the limousine, as soon as the door closed the Undersecretary reached as if for the medal around Floyd's neck, then went to grab his scrotum. He caught her wrist. "They're still very tender," he whispered, and then stuck his tongue in her ear.

She shivered, saying: "It's blue balls." That purr was back in her voice.

"I don't care if they're sky-blue-pink," he growled, unzipping. "I'm going to shove my cock into you. Take off your panties."

"Not necessary. They open up." The Undersecretary pulled open his fly, reached in and grasped his stiffened shaft. She pulled up her skirt, stretched her leg across his thighs, and with her hands on his shoulders she raised herself to sit on his lap. He burrowed his cock through the lace of her split-crotch panties and into her slick vagina. They both moaned. Their lips met and their tongues touched.

The limo driver grinned to his partner. "They're getting pretty frisky back there."

"Does she do this every time?" his partner asked.

"Damn near."

CHAPTER 8:
DISCOVERY

BUSHWICK HOSPITAL EMERGENCY ROOM

Mayzie greeted Mac and her staff with open arms. Her own staff was less welcoming. Mac asked Mayzie why as soon as they were alone.

"They're pissed that you sent Floyd to spy on them."

"It was only for a week."

"That's part of the problem. The ladies were plotting how to bed him."

"They can't have it both ways," Mac chuckled.

"How did we hold up in his report?"

"Quite well. With only ninety hospital beds, your ER is overcrowded."

"I could use half a dozen more ambulances on the weekends."

"Floyd came up with an alternate solution; have taxis transport your less seriously injured to other hospitals."

"I tried it." Mayzie made a face. "The administration got on my case, and the hospital drivers' union pulled a wildcat strike.”

“What if I can get Congressman Waters and the Borough President on our side?”

“Then I'm for it, in spades. What else did Little Lord Fauntleroy recommend?”

“Why do you call him that?”

“My girls do. He's so intent on doing his job, and the girls are trying to get his attention...”

“...And he's unaware it's happening,” Mac finished the sentence for her. “I have the same problem. He also recommends that you post a qualified person at the ER entrance to evaluate the walk-ins.”

“If you can swing the congressman to our side and get the taxis to transfer the lightly injured, I'll find a nurse to evaluate the incoming. Are you and your staff taking the first call tonight?”

“Yes.”

“Then you're on. That buzzer is the alert.”

Alphonso and Percy were in the front of the ambulance. Mac joined them. Jill, Martha and Bill were in the rear. Percy gunned the engine and drove out onto Monroe Street. Jill slid open the dividing window from the rear. “Where are we heading?” she asked.

“It should be on your computer screen,” Percy answered. “Possible broken leg. A ten-year-old girl dancing, got too enthusiastic.”

“Where did you get those dungaree hats?” Jill asked.

“The Army and Navy store on Broadway,” Alphonse answered. “They're our protection.”

“We've arrived,” said Mac.”Made it in less than

five minutes."

The house was an old one, with green tar-shingles. A distraught Black woman waited on the steps, lighting a fresh cigarette from the butt of one she'd just finished. Bill carried his bag and Jill's up the sidewalk as a police car pulled in and angled its wheels toward the curb. Two officers got out and a third locked himself in. The police told Mac to wait while they made sure that this was the woman who had made the 911 call, and went to chat with the woman on the steps. After a moment, they waved all three EMTs into the building. Martha stayed at the rear of the ambulance for a moment, then went over to the police car to chat with the driver.

Neighbors opened their doors to peek out at the police and the ambulance. Someone shouted: "Lock the bastard up!"

"Throw away the key!"

"Deport the son of a bitch!"

Mac followed the two cops into the kitchen and looked around. The floor was worn but clean, as was the kitchen table, on which sat a bottle of gin, a glass, and a saucer full of burnt-out cigarette butts. Two young boys cowered near an old refrigerator. The mother limped forward and led the crowd past two bedrooms and into the front room, where a man sat facing the TV set, holding a ten-year-old girl on his lap. One policeman shut off the TV. "Mr. Sloan," he asked, "What's the problem?"

"Sissy was dancing on that hammock in front of the TV," he mumbled. "She fell off and broke her leg."

"May I see?" Jill asked. Without waiting for an answer, she pulled away the blanket covering the girl's leg. A shin bone poked out of the girl's skin some three inches above the ankle. A little blood stained the blanket. "That must hurt," Jill commented.

Sissy nodded, and tears poured down her cheeks. Bill had already opened one of the ready-bags and was preparing a syringe.

"Give her half a dose," said Mac. "Then put on a blowup plastic cast to immobilize the break. She'll need surgery to repair the break and prevent infection."

"I've got no money..." Mr. Sloan began.

"You lying bastard!"the mother screamed.

She lunged for Sloan and tried to snatch her daughter out of his grasp. Sloan howled and held on. They struggled as the girl cried. The policemen separated them, and Bill neatly caught the child.

Jill promptly applied a gauze bandage and the inflatable cast to the girl's injured leg.

The father wailed that he wanted to go with his daughter in the ambulance, and the police insisted that the mother ride in the squad-car. Martha volunteered to ride with the mother.

On arrival at Bushwick Hospital the ER team immediately sent Sissy Sloan for a CAT-scan and X-rays, and scheduled the emergency room for her.

MacKenzie took Martha aside and asked her: "Why did you insist on riding back with the police? There was room in the ambulance."

"I wanted to talk to the mother alone. We've got

another case of spousal abuse, plus child molesta-tion."

"Sissy was being raped by her father?"

"That's why I requested a bone-density test. In all my years of nursing I never saw that kind of break in a youngster, except a fall from an extreme height or a car accident."

"...Did the mother confirm it?"

"Oh yes. Definitely rape. The child was resisting. The mother tried to stop him, and got the shit kicked out of her. The father was drunk, and is still drunk now."

"I'll order a blood-test on him."

"He won't give permission. The driver of the squad-car has been sent to the Sloans' place several times. He knows how to avoid jail, and has a friend in Child Protective Services."

"Then we'll get a statement from the mother. Will you talk to her?"

"My pleasure."

Mac and the ambulance went out on two more calls. The first was the minister of the Bedford Baptist Church.

"I keep falling over," he complained. "I open my eyes, and the room spins."

Mac took her hand off his shoulder, where he sat on the bed. He promptly keeled over. She asked: "Do you always fall to your right?"

"Huh, yes. I never thought about it before."

Mac held up her forefinger before his face and said: "Don't turn your head, but follow my finger with your eyes."

The minister toppled again, and laughed. "I feel like Humpty Dumpty."

"Well, I'm going to try to put you together again. Stay down and put your feet up on the bed." Mac came around to his left side and crossed his hands over each other on his chest.

He chuckled: "This is the way I lay them out when they're dead."

"You're not going to be dead today. I'll help you sit up.—Remove his pillow, please—now, sir, I'm going to throw you backwards. Keep your hands across your chest, and I'll turn your head to the left. Ready?"

"Yep."

Mac put her face close to his so she could watch his eyes, and threw him backwards. She saw the immediate change in one eye; now they looked the same. His expression changed from resignation to confidence.

"I can feel it!" he said. He sat up so quickly that he almost bumped heads with Mac. "It's like one of the miracles I preach about. Doctor MacKenzie, you are a blessed healer. Blessed be the Healer! Please pray with me."

After the second emergency call, Mac sat down with Martha and Mayzie over a cup of coffee. "Sissy Sloan is in the operating room," Mayzie reported. "They're concerned about infection. The blanket her leg was wrapped in belonged to the cat; it was full of urine and bits of feces.

Mac turned to Martha. "Did you get a statement from the mother?"

"Not yet. While waiting for the daughter's CAT-scan, the mother started coughing up blood. The doctor scheduled X-rays and a full-body scan."

"Let me know when they're evaluated. Mayzie and I have work to do."

An hour later Martha came into Mayzie's office. "Mrs. Sloan died of internal bleeding," she reported. We pumped four liters of blood into her: didn't help. Sissy is out of the OR, but running a fever."

"Infection?" Mac asked.

"We'll know for certain when the lab tests return, but I'd say it's a good bet."

"Where's the... husband?" Mayzie asked.

"He just finished telling the cops how his wife was drunk and fell down the steps before the child was injured. That, he says, explains the broken ribs and body bruises. Her spleen was also ruptured."

"Bullshit!" Mayzie bellowed. "The bastard beat her to death."

"Martha," Mac said slowly, "Ask your detective friends to sign off on an autopsy and question Sissy about being raped. Tell them we consider it a potential homicide."

"I'd rather have Social Services question Sissy, and the police interrogate the husband."

Floyd was on his way to Flatbush when his cellphone rang. "Hey, Siri," he called to it, "Who's calling?"

"You are receiving a call from Kula."

Floyd pulled to the side of Eastern Parkway, put down the kick-stand, shoved up his visor, put the phone to his ear and said: "Kula?"

"Where are you?" her voice came through the phone.

"Near Prospect Park on my way to the Flatbush Medical Center. Are you alright?"

"Yes, I'm fine. You want to meet?"

"Your father wants to kill me."

"All is forgiven. I explained to him and my brothers. My father framed the news photos and articles about what happened, and hung them near the cash-register."

"Your family wanted to murder me."

"They're a bit overprotective."

"Understatement of the year."

"Have you been to the Nine-Eleven Memorial?"

"No."

"Would you like to go?"

"With you? Of course."

Kula and Floyed walked to the elevated line on Broadway and took the train into New York. "This will be my first time in the city proper," he said.

"Then we'll get off at the station before Ground Zero, and walk in. It'll give you a sense of the Big Apple. We're going over the East River."

"That's where the gangsters dumped all the bodies, right?"

"You've seen too many old movies. To the right is the Queensborough Bridge and the Queens Midtown Tunnel. To the left are the Williamsburg, Manhattan, and Brooklyn Bridges.”

“Isn't that Delancy Street?” Floyd pointed. “It doesn't look like it did in the movies. The signs are all in Chinese.”

“Actually, that's Korean,” said Kula.

“Isn't the Bowery nearby?”

“A couple of blocks to the left, but we get off here at City Hall and we'll walk to Park Place. That's Ground Zero.”

They emerged from the subway into a stream of people of all kinds, shapes and colors. They flooded the sidewalks so that some of them were forced to walk in the street, where cars hooted at them. The noise matched the crowd.

Kula took Floyd's hand and pulled him forward until they joined a stream of humanity heading in her choice of direction. He held onto her hand even when it was no longer necessary.

“That's Gracie Mansion,” Kula pointed out, “Officially the mayor's residence since 1942. Fiorello La Guardia was mayor then, and the city bigwigs forced him to live there.”

“Why?”

“He was living in a tenement in Harlem, and they felt it wasn't in keeping with his position as mayor. My grandfather tells of listening to La Guardia reading the funny-pages on radio, Sunday mornings, to the children of New York.”

“Why didn't they buy the papers?”

“It started at a time when the delivery-workers were on strike, and continued thereafter because a lot of people simply couldn't afford the papers. The

Sunday papers cost five cents, and the dailies two cents. Rent was twenty dollars a month, but my grandmother cleaned the house and put out the garbage, so we paid only twelve dollars."

Floyd realized the people around him were walking less aggressively, and spoke in whispers. No car horns blared. "Is that it?" He pointed to a pair of reflecting pools and a man-made waterfall.

"Ground Zero," Kula replied.

"Where were you when it happened?"

"At the university. Security put the school in lockdown, and we watched it unfold on TV. I can't believe it's been almost 20 years."

"I was in Afghanistan. We watched it on TV."

"What did the soldiers think?"

"One guy said it was like sitting on a three-legged stool, and someone kicked out one of the legs. Most of the men were furious about being there, defending people who didn't want us, when we could have been defending our own country."

Inside the Memorial Museum few words were spoken. The twisted metal of a shattered staircase, shards of glass and plastic, told the story of three thousand people who had lost their lives and the thousands more injured.

"At Sloan-Kettering we have survivors with cancer from the blast," Kula murmured. "Powdered asbestos got into their lungs."

They exited by the reflecting pools, reading the names of the fallen written on bronze plaques to the sides of the pools. Kula realized Floyd had stopped. He was staring at a plaque and weeping. "What's wrong?" she asked.

He waved his hand and tried, but couldn't speak. She handed him a handkerchief, saying: "Take a deep breath." Then she guided him outside, where she ordered coffee for both of them. "Did you know that man?"

"I knew Carl was dead," he whispered, "But I forgot when and where. How could I forget?! He saved my life so many times... One time he covered me in a sniper's duel for two hours. I was tending a wounded Marine. Carl was no sniper, but he won the duel. Then he went home, and I thought he was safe."

"What was he doing in the Twin Towers?"

"He worked in a brokerage firm. Tried to convince me to change my major to Business Administration. He said it was an excuse to print money."

Kula saw that as long as Floyd was talking, he was less shaken. "So why didn't you go into finance?"

"I said, with a rich friend I can always borrow money from him. And he would have given it."

"That's a real friend."

"More like my brother. How could I forget that he died here?!"

"Because God built that into us. Try to remember pain; you can't. No one can. We're not supposed to carry around all the painful things that happen to us. Mental hospitals are full of people who do."

"You're smart, Kula."

They didn't speak on the train ride home. It was on

the walk to her house that Kula asked: "Why is it that veterans, like you and my brother, don't speak about the war?"

"As a medic, I thought about it. We want to talk, but it doesn't make sense telling you here what happened over there. Everybody's trying to kill each other. It doesn't matter if you're a soldier or a child or a pregnant mother. Any one of them can kill you, or be your target."

"And did you?"

"Kill? Yes. At first I refused to carry a weapon, but they kept shooting at me—even when I was tending their own wounded—so I shot back."

"Who were they?"

"No idea, but they shot first. Did I feel bad about shooting them? Hell, no. They didn't care who they killed, so I didn't care about them. One time three rag-heads bolted at us out of a bunker, and I took them down one at a time, each with a single bullet, and it felt... damned... good."

He saw the shock register on her face as she pulled her hand from his.

"There, I've talked too much," Floyd sighed. "Tell your father you didn't get shot at tonight."

CHAPTER 9:
FAMILY ABUSE

BROOKLYN VA HOSPITAL

"I thought you were an angel," Rosie said.

"It was the morphine," Floyd soothed.

"But I saw your picture in the papers. You're a real hero.

"Did Dr. MacKenzie put you in touch with that plastic surgeon?"

"She said I could have any shaped nose I want. She gave me these pictures of noses. Which one do you think is better?"

"Do you have a photo from before the accident?"

"It was no accident," said Mac, coming into the room. "Rosie, I'm glad to see you're sitting up. They've given you a wheelchair. Are you having any trouble?"

"I got in trouble because of the wheelchair." Rosie rolled her eyes. "A week ago Saturday morning, an old lady came behind me and pushed me to the elevator. I thought it was one of the vets fooling around, until she got me onto the elevator and I got a look at her. She took me to the Jewish prayer service."

"Are you Jewish?"

"No, but she wouldn't listen. She had to leave, and called the ward to send an aide to take me back when the service was over. Reuben came down early. I was the only woman patient, and the youngest person there. Everyone took pity on me. They kept giving Reuben and me wine. They kept refilling our cups, and we kept drinking. Yesterday was Saturday. I stayed in bed so the old lady couldn't get to me. The next thing I know, I'm being lifted up—pajamas, cover and all—and put in the wheelchair. It was Reuben. We got drunk again. Then I heard that the rabbi called the ward and uninvited me."

Mac bit back a laugh. "Are your feelings hurt?"

"Oh no. I don't really care for their sweet wine, and I didn't understand a word they were praying."

"Er, when I asked if you were having trouble, I meant over the death of your husband."

Rosie held two hands over her mouth and giggled. "It was like being able to breathe again. I'm free! I'd forgotten how it was. If Big Bill would let me, I'd give him a big hug and kiss. I wanted to kill my bastard of a husband. Dr. Mac, would you help me pick out a new nose?"

"No way! You could be looking in the mirror and cursing me for the rest of your life. No, no, you ask the surgeon. There's what they call the Dimensions of the Golden Mean; it has to do with measurements of the forehead, eyes, cheekbones, mouth, and jaw. The surgeon knows."

"It would be best to ask," said Floyd. "Does that surgeon take private patients?"

"Yes," said Mac, "But she's very expensive. Who were you thinking of?"

"Mrs. Leissner, the lady I helped. She was shot in the face."

Mac wrote a number and handed the note to him. "Telephone her office. She works privately by recommendation. Use my name."

Floyd rode his bike to Flatbush Hospital, where he found Mrs. Leissner in a private room. The nurse who directed him whispered: "Be sure to ask her bodyguards' permission."

There were several people in the hallway, all Black, some with wild afros and some with shaven skulls. They sat on benches and on the floor. All wore black leather vests, and their bare arms were tattooed. On the backs of their vests THE CROWNS was printed in large white letters. Somewhere in the crowd someone was coughing persistently. Nobody spoke.

Two large muscular Black men stood on either side of the room's closed door. All eyes fastened on Floyd walking toward them. When he stopped in front of the two guards, everyone in the hallway came to their feet.

"Fool," one of the guards growled, "What you stoppin' here for?"

"I came to visit Mrs. Leissner. How is she?"

"Only family. With that Whitey face an' blond hair, you sure as hell ain't Lucille's brother."

"He's the guy what saved her," a girl volunteered. "I seen his picture on the TV."

All of a sudden Floyd was surrounded by a crowd of well-wishers, patting his back and trying to make intricate handshakes. One of the guards phoned Michael Leissner; the other pushed the well-wishers back and opened the door for Floyd.

The room was full of flowers. Lucille's head and the left side of her face were covered in bandages. Thin plastic tubes ran into her nostrils, a larger one into her mouth, and an even larger accordion tube into her throat where Floyd had inserted the ballpoint pen section. Over the upper part of her body was stretched an oxygen tent. He glanced at the monitors; heartbeat, blood pressure, and temperature appeared normal.

A well-dressed Black man entered the room, and the guards stepped back. His hand-tailored suit, four-in-hand tie, shoes and socks all matched. He waved a manicured hand toward the door, and the guards exited. He held out a hand to Floyd and announced, "I'm Michael Leissner."

"You're too young to be her son."

"Lucille was fifteen when she birthed me. She said the pain wasn't worth it, and she'd never have another child."

"You dress and speak like you've done well for yourself."

"I control the drugs, prostitution, and gambling in this section of Brooklyn."

Floyd accepted that without so much as a blink. "Did you attend university?" he asked.

"I took public speaking courses, and played the father in a local production of *All My Sons*. I owe you big time for saving my mother. How did you know what to do for her?"

"I served a couple of tours in Afghanistan as a combat medic. We had to improvise."

"One tour was enough for me," said Michael. "I enlisted to learn about weapons. But I'd rather talk about my mother. She was a beautiful woman; now she talks about killing herself."

"It's not unusual for a deforming injury to depress a patient. That's why I brought this." Floyd handed Michael the note with the surgeon's name and phone number. "She's expensive."

"Is she the best?"

"She does Broadway stars, some from Hollywood, some from abroad."

Michael drew a handful of bills from his jacket pocket and held them out to Floyd. "For saving my mother," he said.

"I can use five hundred," said Floyd. "More than that, and I'll get in trouble. Please."

Michael shrugged, peeled off five one-hundred-dollar bills and handed the over. "Thank you," he said, got up and left the room. He returned a moment later, saying: "I told the guards you can enter any time. I'll call this plastic surgeon."

"I have another patient who's busy choosing her nose. Bring some photos of your mother, and I'll send her a nose chart. Your mom can pick whichever she wants. Lips, too. Hopefully, that'll encourage her."

In the hallway outside, the young toughs crowded around Floyd as he left, patting him on the back and wishing him well.

RIDGEWOOD VA HOSPITAL
CONFERENCE ROOM

Dr. Elizabeth MacKenzie adjusted the podium microphone and announced: "Please call me Mac. Everyone does. Now rumors abound, concerning this pilot program to create more efficient use of ER staffs, but before you leave, everything will be made clear. I invited the off-duty staff of each of the five hospitals involved in this plan. You were each given paper and pens; at the top of one sheet of paper, write the name of the hospital you work at. Without discussion, each of you write three things you believe are most important to the improvement of your ER procedures. Please do that now."

It took less time than she'd expected. Next, Mac set an order of priority for each hospital group's recommendations. These were collected and examined by Mac and Martha while the participants went to lunch. After the meal they all re-gathered, and Mac went on.

"All right. The ER functions on the cutting edge of technology, while surrounded by raw emotional pandemonium."

"Amen!" said Big Momma.

"I want to address the most prominent item on all your lists: higher wages for ER staff."

"It's logical," said Mayzie. "We operate on the

edge of chaos. The burn-out rate for ER workers is higher than all other departments combined. We gotta work shorter shifts and make enough to live on; so you want better service, you'll have to pay for it."

"I agree," said Mac. "I remember when New York City had a similar crisis of qualified teachers leaving for the suburbs. The city raised teachers' salaries, and in one year reversed the outflow of qualified educators. Student learning levels rose across the board. I'll personally champion this suggestion with Congressman Elijah Waters. Martha will now lead the discussion on the rest of your suggestions."

BICKFORD'S CAFETERIA, FLATBUSH, BROOKLYN

Congressman Waters, in his wheelchair, was pushed through the cafeteria doors and immediately surrounded by a dozen men at the first two tables. The smiling Black Congressman smiled, pointed to where Mac sat at a rear table, and was promptly wheeled to her.

"Since when the wheelchair?" she asked.

"Since I fell on my Black ass because of arthritic knees. Anyway, I took the opportunity to order meatloaf and mashed potatoes. Specialty of the house."

"What was all the commotion when you came in?"

Elijah flashed his straight white teeth in a broad grin. "They're horseplayers, and they sit closest to the entrance so they can see the latest race results coming in to the newsstand across the street."

"...Horseplayers?"

"A few weeks ago, when I was still walking, I went to their table and snatched up a paper and pointed to a horse. I showed everyone. They looked at me, I looked at them, nodded and returned the paper without saying a word. The horse won, and paid off at seventeen to one. Now they want another tip. I told them only one per year."

"Did you really know about the horse?"

"Lady, I never gamble." He flashed his white teeth again. "All I know about horses is that there's a front end and a back end, and if you bet on them you're looking up the wrong end. I just picked that horse because I liked the name: 'Anthracite'. I only bet on myself, and that's a sure thing."

"So why come to a horseplayers' den like this?"

"Because my constituents—from winos to super-businessmen—eat here. No matter how wealthy or brain-dead, they each have one vote. By the way, your taxi-ferry problem may be solved. Do you know Dr. Mel Moskowitz?"

"I know of him. He's been called to the VA on consultations a few times."

"He may be able to solve the insurance problem for cabbies transporting patients. He owns shares of Brooklyn's largest insurance companies."

"That's great, but..."

"You have another problem? Let's hear it."

"Special pay raise for ER workers. We must maintain the ER team dynamics to deliver the best care. We can't do that with an annual fifty-percent turnover because of burn-out. We'll never reach peak efficiency this way. They opt out for less stressful positions at the same pay, or even less. We've got to shorten the shifts for a living wage, and that means more money."

"Hmmm. How are the salaries computed?"

"By education, seniority, and specialization."

Mac could almost see the wheels turning behind those sly dark brown eyes. "Explain specialization."

"Nurses qualify for Critical Care, Pediatrics, Hospice, Mental Health, and so on."

"So... your problem's triangular: staff, management, and union. If you raise wages for the ER staff, won't the other nurses demand their pay go up too?"

"That's the problem. Now, I've heard you say that every problem presents an opportunity..."

"Mac, you're adding to a long list of my opportunities."

"Out of the goodness of my heart, I brought it to you."

"Careful with that ketchup; it's spicy. Hmmm, consider a specialized pilot program qualifying ER staff for higher wages. You can keep it within the five hospitals, use the funds allocated for your project. Collect statistics for a year. If they warrant it, bring them to me and I'll try to get a bill through Congress supporting you."

Mac leaned over and kissed the Congressman's cheek. "Thank you. And thanks for the meatloaf. I'm heading back to the seminar." She made a sandwich of the slice of meatloaf and pointed with it to the group of horseplayers. Why don't you give them another winner?"

"I don't want to ruin my reputation."

"The ER," Mac addressed the conference, "Is defined by the people who staff it. We dictate the initial level of care. If we reach the patients in sixty minutes, they usually live. It's called the Golden Hour. So what makes a good ER nurse? At first glance, there doesn't appear to be a common denominator: not race, religion, family background, education, age or gender. Then it struck me; the one thing all great ER nurses have in common is that patients *matter* to them. The patient takes precedent."

Mac held up a paper. "Your recommendations show me a group of dedicated people. Your first suggestion to be implemented is the assignment of a staff member, in each ER, responsible for ordering the priority of those waiting for care—in short, a Triage specialist. I don't want anyone dying on a bench in the waiting room. The person selected must be experienced, and cannot be overruled by any of the nursing staff, including myself.

"This brings me to a subject often missed, ignored, or swept under the carpet in the ER. We wring our hands, shed tears, and say prayers when ten, twenty, or thirty children are murdered. Yet ten times that many children die, each year, in the United States from parental abuse. Every day, fifteen children are killed in America. Their average age is two years.

"The same Triage Nurse will be responsible for

identifying victims of child or spousal abuse.

"Most battered children and wives will have been treated in the ER on previous occasions. Eighty-five percent of child abusers are the parents, in most cases the mother. Conversely, in spousal abuse cases, eighty-five percent of the victims are women."

Mayzie asked: "Are you correlating wife-beating to motherly abuse of children?"

"No, I'm not," said Mac, "And neither is this report." She held up a sheaf of papers. "These handouts will explain what to look for, where and how to seek help. Your individual ER departments have reported an extreme increase in spousal abuse. Statistics indicate that of the one hundred women sitting here, forty have suffered some form of spousal abuse."

She paused to let that sink in before continuing.

"If you feel endangered, please speak to your supervisor. If you would rather relate the problem to me, my personal phone number is on this handout. The ER is in a unique position to identify abuse cases. Since I've been collecting information from the five hospitals, abuse has reached epidemic proportions. Seventy percent of child and spouse abuse goes unreported."

"How do we know when to call in the police?" a Flatbush nurse asked.

"If you suspect abuse, contact your hospital social worker. Their office will determine the appropriate action. If the abuse is happening under your very nose," Mac carefully did not look at Bill, "Then of course you must summon the police directly.

There are more details in the handout."

"Dr. MacKenzie," a Red Hook nurse noted, "You failed to mention Granny Dumping, or other elder abuse."

"You're right." Mac flicked her fingers across her forehead. "I thought it too much for one meeting. "Thank you for bringing it up. Please explain it to the uninitiated."

"In New York," the nurse went on, "Over forty thousand elderly are cared for at home. Many times that number are in nursing homes and hospitals. Granny Dumping refers to abandoning old people at the ER entrance without identification or money. Often they have Alzheimer's. By law, the hospitals must take them in. This often happens around major holidays. Many families don't want their holidays burdened by a feeble elder, so they dump Granny."

"You appear well informed about elder abuse," said Mac. "Would you consider being interviewed for a place on this committee?"

"Damn right I would."

"Your name?"

"Joyce Murphy."

CHAPTER 10:
THE WIDOWMAKERS' SOCIETY

Jill watched Joyce Murphy enter the ER and thought: *She's the spitting image of Mac at that age.*

Joyce was twenty-four years old, 5'10" tall, slender, with red hair and green eyes. Her shoulders were squared, her arms relaxed, as she took in the layout of the VA Emergency Room and then followed Jill to her office.

"We don't have as much traffic as your Red Hook hospital," Jill said. "Mac asked me to interview you. Are you married?"

"Yes. Two children: a boy and a girl, four and five."

"What does your husband do?"

"Heavy equipment operator, bulldozers and cranes."

"Where did you study nursing?"

"Saint John's University. I have a Bachelor of Science, with six credits toward a Master's degree."

"How do you manage a family and a nursing career?"

"By the most efficient use of my time. I love learning."

"You graduated *cum laude*. Were you that good in high school?"

"No. In junior high school my teachers told me I was stupid. In high school they proved it. I was dyslexic."

Jill raised an eyebrow. "How did you overcome that?"

"A twelfth-grade teacher introduced me to the Davis System for dyslexics, and it worked. In three months I learned the required subjects to qualify for my high school diploma. In fact, I took the GED instead."

Jill grinned. "I've noticed that GED grads are generally better-educated than regular high school grads."

"That's because we seriously work at it," Murphy smiled back.

"How did you become interested in Granny Dumping?"

"...My father-in-law developed Early Onset Alzheimer's."

"Was his wife helpful?"

"She'd divorced him several years ago. He was an alcoholic and a wife-beater. Taking care of him, and my initiation into the ER, put me in touch with families who abandoned their elderly."

"Yet you're compassionate..."

"Nobody else was paying attention. Everybody passed the buck. One hospital sent them to another until they died or went comatose. By redirecting the hospital's outside security cameras I was able to identify the offenders—by their license plates. The police are very cooperative in locating and confronting the perpetrators."

"Would you share this camera technique with the other ERs in our project?"

"With pleasure."

"Where's Joyce Murphy now?" Mac asked Jill.

"At lunch with Bill and Martha."

"What's your impression of her?"

"She reminds me of you twenty years ago."

"Heh! That bad?"

"Mac, from the day you walked into this hospital, you were our shining star. And now you're Dr. MacKenzie."

"Hmph. Anyway, I got a disturbing call from Big Momma in Bed-Stuy. During the last two years she's treated a mother and her children several times. They were obviously beaten by the father: a twenty-nine-year-old alcoholic and druggie. Last night he beat the children and the wife; now they're all on the orthopedic ward with multiple fractures."

"How are the children now?"

"They'll be discharged today from Pediatrics to Social Services. Mama says they'll be sent home— with the father."

"Shit!"Jill snapped.

"That's why Big Momma called. The mother refuses to press charges."

"She's probably scared, and has a right to be."

"Is there any way we can help those children?"

"Kill the damned father."

"I'd do it if I could get away with it," growled Martha, from the doorway. "How old are they?"

"One, two, and three," said Mac. "The courts give preference to the parents rather than a foster home."

"I'll have the police look in on the father," Martha promised. "It might make him think before he acts."

"Incidents like this," Jill muttered, "Make me want to kill bastards like that."

"Let's return to Joyce Murphy," said Mac. "Take her, or leave her?"

"Take! Definitely a take."

"Ditto to that," Martha added.

"What about her family situation?" Mac asked.

Jill hesitated. "According to Murphy, home life is hunky-dory. She lives in Greenpoint, twenty minutes by bus."

"No car?"

"...Husband won't allow it."

"I sense a red flag there."

Jill pointed to the handout flyer on the desk. "Your profile of a battered wife fits Murphy. Her father-in-law was a wife-beater, is an alcoholic, and beat his son. The son, her husband, seems to resent his wife's higher education. Did you notice, all of us wore our sleeves rolled up in the conference room? Murphy wore hers buttoned all the way down to her wrists. Her left cheekbone was heavily powdered. I assume her husband is right-handed."

"You think he punched her in the left eye?"

Jill shrugged wordlessly.

"I'll see her after lunch."

"Come in," Mac said. "Sit down. How did you like my people?"

"They're very professional," said Joyce. "There was very little small-talk, none from Martha, and Jill is... quite perceptive."

"Think you can work with them?"

"I do."

"What are your children's names?"

"Joel is five, and Lorraine four."

"Unusual names for a good Catholic," Mac smiled.

Joyce rolled her eyes. "Back in parochial school, when a nun called out Patrick or Mary, half the kids turned around. I decided my children would have distinctive names."

"And your husband...?" Mac asked softly.

Joyce's face was still. "As long as the children are quiet, they're my responsibility."

"...And when they're not?"

Joyce remained poker-faced. "That's something I'd rather not discuss."

Mac sighed. "You're being interviewed because of your experience with the elderly, but you'll be dealing with the normal influx of ER patients. As a good Catholic, what's your reaction to a pregnant fourteen-year-old asking for an abortion?"

"I'm...not a perfect Catholic."

"I'd still like to hear your answer."

"In the first trimester, I'd schedule her a consultation with a social worker."

"What if you knew the social worker was pro-abortion?"

Joyce shrugged. "The patient made that choice when she came to this hospital. She can always leave."

"So you're pro-choice?"

"More or less."

Mac nodded. "What if she was starting the second trimester?"

"I'd explain the health risks of a later abortion, and tell her that she'll begin to feel better soon. In most cases the morning-sickness and fatigue are no longer an issue, and she should reconsider."

"Suppose the patient is frightened, and knows she's incapable of raising a child without a father?"

"I'll mention adoption and other alternatives, but I'll also tell her that all new mothers feel incompetent. When the doctor handed me my firstborn, I said: 'What do I do with him?' The doctor said: 'In spite of you, he'll grow up'. That's what I'd tell any young mother."

"What if he grows up to be a bad person?"

"That's the parent's responsibility, but not hers alone. A social worker would be better equipped to answer that."

"Umhm. Would you mind rolling up your sleeves?"

For the first time, Joyce Murphy appeared shaken. "Why?" she asked.

"It's not unusual to find drug addiction among hospital staffers." Mac kept her voice neutral.

"If you think I'm an addict, why the interview?"

"I and my staff want you," Mac said gently, "But not if you're drug-dependent."

Joyce stood. "Is this a requirement for the position?"

Mac likewise stood, and met the younger woman's eyes. "Yes," was all she said.

Joyce turned around, went to the door, and opened it to leave. Then she stopped, shut the door again, turned around again with tears streaming down her cheeks, unbuttoned her sleeves, and held her arms out. Her arms bore purple welts from wrists to elbows. "I need help," she sobbed.

"You were right," Mac complimented Jill, "She's a battered wife. That was a black eye she covered up. The sleeves hide a whipping with a car antenna."

"Why doesn't she call the police?"

"She did, once. He took it out on the kids until she dropped the charges. She has no family, and the husband never allowed her to form close friendships. She has no support network, and nowhere to go."

"His sort has to resent Joyce's success in school," Jill considered. "I've seen it happen time and again; supposedly happy married couples separate when the wife becomes more educated than the husband, let alone gets a better job than his."

Mac pointed to a woman and her husband carrying a baby into Cubicle 3. "At first I thought that was a case of child abuse. The husband assured me that his wife is the gentlest soul he's ever known. But the baby boy just will not sleep. The husband works nights, comes home and finds his wife trying to sleep while rocking the child in the baby-buggy. She's punch-drunk from lack of sleep. It's a happy child, but the husband is afraid that the wife could do harm to the baby."

"So what did you do?"

"First, I prescribed half a phenobarbital for the baby. When that didn't work, I told him to make it a whole pill—but he called and told me that the child was as active as ever."

"You handed them over to Pediatrics?"

"I told the husband to give his wife the phenobarbital."

"Ah, they've spotted you. Here they come."

"Dr. MacKenzie," the husband enthused, "It worked. Just look at my Julie! She's got color in her cheeks again."

The wife stepped forward and held out her hand, which Mac took. "Jimmy still doesn't sleep," she said, "Not as far as I know, anyway, but we're happy."

"Thanks to you," the husband went on, "Julie gets enough sleep, and Jimmy greets me with a smile when I come home."

"Ah, then why are you here?"

"Purely to thank you."

"That's very thoughtful," said Mac, with a bemused look. "I really appreciate it. Ah, but they're calling on the loudspeaker, and I have to go. Excuse me." And she made her escape.

Jill hurried after her. "That's not your number they're calling," she chided. "You've got to learn to accept compliments."

"I know, I know. Will I see you and Bill at the folk-dancing tonight?"

"Yes, but Kula won't be there. She said she didn't like Floyd calling the Muslims 'rag-heads'."

"I don't care for it either, but that seems a bit oversensitive."

"It's just the way these ex-combat guys talk. They don't mean anything by it."

"Well, I imagine it's hard to feel kindly toward people who are shooting at you."

"I think it was really something else Floyd said," Jill considered. "He mentioned shooting three attacking Arabs in a row, and feeling 'damned good' about it. Kula had trouble accepting that."

"Ah, it's called 'ecstatic relief'," Mac explained. "I've heard that story before. Some stranger is trying to kill you, so you shoot him; now he's dead and won't come after you again, and you're alive and safe from him—and yes, that feels good. That's what veterans have such a hard time explaining, and gently-raised civilians have trouble understanding."

"I'll try to explain it to Kula."

"See you at the dance."

Thursday morning, Martha made a point of catching MacKenzie in her office. "You missed an interesting conversation at the Gay Greek's after the dance," she said quietly.

"What was the subject?" Mac asked.

"The Widowmaker's Society."

"...And what's that about?" Mac suspected she

wouldn't like the answer.

"Killing spousal abusers before they can kill the wife or children," Martha said, all in a rush "it began as a joke, but then it got serious."

"You should have cut them off. Killing is no laughing matter."

"The subject came up when Big Momma called. That... husband, who put his kids in the Pediatric ward and his wife in Orthopedics, took his children home—and drowned them in the bathtub. Then he returned to the hospital and stabbed his wife to death."

Mac took care to breathe slowly. "Did they catch him?"

"Big Momma almost killed him. He'd gone to the Emergency Room. He was so drunk, he thought he was bleeding. It was his wife's blood."

"Momma should have buried the bastard," Mac admitted. "He'll get off with Involuntary Manslaughter."

"He could get five years."

"Not before an election, he won't. He might serve a year."

"He killed three babies, and his wife!"

"Our judges are elected, and from what I heard, the husband is Black."

"So were his wife and children."

"They can't vote, or influence those who can." Mac's face was very grim. "Bed-Stuy is predominantly Black. Any judge who sentences a Black man to the full extent of the law won't get elected in that district."

Martha pulled a ten-dollar bill from her pocket. "This says you're wrong."

"You'll lose," said Mac. "Put it away. One of the papers I wrote for my Ph.D. dealt with medicine and the law. The identity of the victim is the most important predictor of the severity of sentencing. Who was Mary Joe Kopechne? You never heard of her? Senator Edward Kennedy left her to die in a car-crash that he caused. Do you know the names of the woman and man killed by Patty Hearst? You remember O.J. Simpson, but can you remember the names of his victims? Those three got away with murder because their victims were almost completely unknown. This mother of three was probably anonymous even in her own community and neighborhood. She's dead. The husband is alive, and can be used by politicians to rally voters to their flag."

"You should have stayed last night. You would have voted with the majority to form the Widowmakers' Society."

"Who voted against?"

"Not one. A couple abstained because they couldn't figure out how to get away with it."

"What about you?"

Martha repositioned her nurse's cap and said: "Any bastard that would drown three babies and stab his wife to death—I'd kill the son of a bitch whether he was White, Black, or sky-blue pink."

"If you could get away with it, you mean?"

"That's easy. Eighty-five percent of murders are committed by someone who knows the victim. Forty percent of murders aren't solved. The odds favor the anonymous killer."

"Are you proposing a group to carry out street justice?"

"More like expert witness justice. I never regretted what I did, Mac. Besides, the others insisted that a vote had to be taken after someone pleaded in defense of the abuser. No action can be taken unless the vote is unanimous, just like a jury."

"Jesus Christ, Martha! I don't want to hear another word!"

CHAPTER 11:
PAYBACK

RIDGEWOOD VA HOSPITAL

"I know who put the money in my acccunt," Floyd puzzed. "What I can't figure out is how he did it."

"Simple," Jill smiled. "The Crowns picked your pocket and got your wallet."

"No, I've got my wallet..." Floyed reached in his hip pocket and checked it. "And there's rot a dollar missing."

"Specifically," said Jill, "When Leissner left his mother's room that first time, he gave orders. When you came out, his boys all crowded around you, slapping you on the back, wising you well—and slowing you down. One of them scarfed your wallet, took out your bank credit-card or debit-card and your driver's license. They took pictures of the cards, both sides, with a cell-phone. Then they put the cards back in the wallet and the wallet back in your pocket before you got out of the hallway. Leissner used that information to get your account number and make a five-thousand dollar deposit. It should only happen to me."

Floyd shook his head in amazement. "I'll return it somehow."

"Not if you want to keep your head on your neck! That would insult the leader of the Crowns, and you don't want to do that—especially with what's going to happen in Brighton Beach tonight."

"Is there a party at Coney Island?"

"Not exactly. That's why we called you in. It's Friday night, and Michael Leissner is going to pay back the Russians for shooting his mother."

"How do you know?"

"Floyd, Brooklyn is like a large village, and I'm ninth generation here. Change your *gotchkas* in Flatbush, and by evening they'll tell you what color in Red Hook."

"What are *gotchkas?*"

"Yiddish for winter underwear. Anyway, the word gets around."

"Jill, did you inform the police?"

"If they don't already know, the Crowns will tell them."

"Why would they do that?"

"So the cops are warned to stay away and not get hurt. The police are quite willing to stand back and let the gangs kill off each other."

"Won't the Russians find out?"

"Probably. Both sides have cops on their payroll. But the Russians won't know in time to bring up reinforcements."

"Sheesh! It sounds like a war."

"That's Brooklyn. Every few years, something

like this clears the air—and culls the less intelligent."

"No wonder you wanted a combat medic here. So what's our role?"

"Ever see the movie *Bringing Out the Dead*? On nights like this the police keep the dead; we bring out the wounded. Prepare the ambulance. Add ten more infusion bags, sets and tourniquets with bandages for high-impact injuries. Remember, someone always stays locked in the back of the ambulance. Alphonse and Percy will be there to help. You'll be given a helmet and a bulletproof vest; wear them at all times."

The Bunker Bar and Grill on the corner of Gates and Bedford Avenues was unusually crowded for so early in the evening. Men huddled at the bar in groups, whispering. Two of them were coughing. Drinks were on the house.

Michael Leissner was buying. He sat in the rear with six cell phones and a laptop computer and his chief lieutenant, directing the attack on the Russian Mafia in Brighton Beach. Computer printouts bearing the addresses of businesses, bars and gambling halls operated by the Russian mob were being distributed. "Every address is confirmed, connected to the Russian bastards," he said quietly.

"How did you get the info?" his lieutenant asked.

"Paid a Tong from the New York triad." Michael handed a simple cell phone to each of the five men sitting nearest. "At eight thirty PM, you call the only number on your phone. The Chinese scouts will say 'all clear' or else explain what the Russians are preparing for. In either case, you attack. Your targets are on the printout."

"We could be ambushed."

"I'll take care of that. When you hit the places, don't hit the civilians."

"Are all the guys at the bar here comin' with us?"

"Oh yes," said Michael. "There are five moving-vans outside. Pick up your men and follow your written instructions. Attack at nine PM exactly, and blast those mothafuckers to hell. This is for shooting my Mama."

Mister G's real name was Laurence Garfinkel, and he was a Russian Mafia enforcer from Odessa. He'd been sent twenty years earlier to organize and expand the mob on America's east coast.

He established himself in Brighton Beach, made significant contributions to local synagogues and churches, sponsored CYO and Salvation Army basketball teams, bought baseball equipment for the Police Athletic League and started his own semi-professional soccer team. Having proved his community credentials, Mr. G negotiated permission from One-Eye Pete Gotti of the Gambino family to take over gambling, prostitution, drugs and cigarette smuggling in the neighborhood. Through Gotti Mr. G negotiated with the head of the Genovese family for Russian entry into various New Jersey, Connecticut and Pennsylvania rackets.

Mr. G also provided hitmen on request. It was these Russian ex-Special Forces men whom he called on to defend Brighton Beach.

"Last time the Niggers invaded, they used moving-vans to ferry their men," Mr. G was saying. "They'll probably do the same this time."

"One of my scouts in Bed-Stuy reported moving-vans picking up men and distributing weapons," a lieutenant confirmed. "I'd say, set up roadblocks into Brighton and Coney Island, but be careful of some trick."

"What are you thinking?" Mr. G asked.

"I don't know, but Leissner is a rare kind of nigger; he thinks a lot. Who do we hold back at the roadblocks?"

"Anyone going into Coney Island. Those who have addresses to the end of Brighton can't go any further than Gravesend Bay. Let them pass. They're trapped; either they swim across the bay or they come back through us."

At eight thirty Mr. G received his first phone call. "There are five empty moving-vans," the scout reported, "Heading to the Golden Mandarin restaurant. The vans are empty except for moving blankets and stuff. The drivers and helpers are all Chinese. I checked their wallets and IDs. They look okay."

"You say the trucks are empty?"

"Yeah. They even have a freezer truck to keep the food fresh."

"My inclination is to send them back, but if I do the Crowns may be tipped off... What the hell is that noise?"

"We're on Brighton Beach Avenue, under the elevated. A train just passed overhead."

"As I was saying, the Crowns might be tipped off that we're setting ambushes. You're certain the trucks are empty?"

"Yeah."

"The crews are all Chinese?"

"Yeah."

"Let them through," said Mr. G, and answered another phone.

"Mr. G, this is Arthur in Bed-Stuy," another scout reported. "The Crowns have disappeared from the streets. Some were spotted getting out of a moving-van and up to the B & P elevated trains."

"They've come to Brighton Beach?"

"Right, but they can't escape by train; we've got them blocked."

"Make certain."

Mr. G the looked up a number in the phone guide and dialed it. "Golden Mandarin restaurant," answered an accented voice.

"I'd like to reserve a table for ten thirty tonight, please," purred Mr. G.

"Yes sir. How many in your party?"

Mr. G clicked off the phone and re-dialed the roadblock. "Did those moving-vans go through yet?" he asked.

"Yes, around five minutes ago."

"Send out two cars with armed men, and find those trucks. Find those Chinks and beat the truth out of them. Find out why there are five empty trucks in Brighton with no work for them."

Twenty minutes later a lieutenant reported in. "Mr. G, we found the trucks parked along the high school baseball field. Not a Chinaman in sight."

"Find the Chinks!" Mr. G retorted. "Interrogate any and all Chinese in Brighton Beach. Why were five empty moving-vans, driven by Chinese, abandoned by the high school ball field?!"

At eight thirty PM, along the B & P transit lines to Brighton Beach, small groups of Black men boarded. They carried shotguns, M16s and Kalashnikovs, displayed their weapons and ushered all the passengers off the train. They traveled one stop beyond the Brighton Beach station and then went down into the street. They checked in to report, and Michael made sure that each group-leader was oriented with a street map. Then he sat back and grinned widely; he had inserted his troops, unobserved, behind the Russian defensive line of roadblocks.

The Crowns then divided into five groups. The two largest moved down the north and south sides of Brighton Beach Avenue, followed by two smaller groups fanning out north and south behind the commercial district. The fifth group Michael held in reserve, deploying them between him and the Russians manning the roadblocks.

The first shops vandalized were a laundromat and a dry cleaner's. The staff and customers were chased out to safety, and the machines were shot up. Cash registers were rifled, slot-machines broken open for their cash, and then both shops were set on fire. Cars outside were smashed open and searched for valuables.

The third place of business on the south side of

the street was the Diamondback Casino. The guard/doorman called in: "Mr. G, they're letting the civilians go and are coming for us next. They've got automatic rifles, and I saw a shoulder-held rocket launcher. We can't stop them."

"Keep calm," said Mr. G. "Retreat into the club. Separate out the civilians from our men, and have our guys escape out the back. No shooting with civilians around. Escape to the pre-selected rallying point."

The roadblock cell-phone called in. "Mr. G," the lieutenant said, "There's shooting in the street behind us."

"Anything in front?"

"No, not yet."

"Leave a couple of automatic weapons and face your men to the rear. Be careful of crossfire. The Black bastards think they've got the initiative, but they're trapped. We'll bury every fucking one of them in Gravesend Bay."

"Mr. G, the fire trucks just pulled up."

"Shit! Tell them there's too much shooting for them to come in. Tell their chief to call Police Captain MacDonald, and call for ambulances too. Don't worry, reinforcements are on their way. We'll flush them into the bay."

Crown gunmen moved in on the Diamondback gambling den. It had once been a double-windowed department store, which made it easy to breach, but the six men protecting the place were former Russian Army Special Ops. They separated themselves from the workers and customers, who ducked under tables, to slip out the rear entrance.

There they were met with a hail of gunfire—inaccurate—from the Crowns' second group moving down the alley. The Russian return fire was so quick and accurate that the Crowns fell back and took cover. The Russians, though outnumbered, intensified their fire and drove the Crowns further back. When there was enough space, the Russians retreated in disciplined order to the rally-point.

Inside the casino, the Crowns ignored calls for help from their men in the alley; they were busy breaking into every slot machine and drawer that could hold money.

A duplicate scene took place on the opposite side of Brighton Avenue, at the Golden Nugget Poker Parlor, where again Michael failed to control his men. They looted thoughtlessly, tore mirrors from the walls, stuffed liquor bottles in their shirts, and grabbed money and jewelry from the patrons. While the Crowns stripped the clubs, the Odessa troops escaped to the Roller Dome.

The rally-point was an abandoned roller-skating rink, where Mr. G sat in the rubbish-filled office sketching with a marker-pen the movement of the attacking Crowns and muttering: "Smart general, lousy troops."

"Boss," his chief lieutenant said, "Those trucks at the high school can only be for one thing: to escape."

"You're a fucking genius," Mr. G acknowledged, "But escape to where? They can only drive into the bay or back into our hands. Michael Leissner is smarter than that."

"Maybe you give him too much credit."

"Destroy those trucks."

Michael Leissner stood in the middle of Brighton Beach Avenue at the roadblock, watching his men ransack every shop, car, and person they came across. The two groups in the alleys behind the main street had slimmer pickings as they joined the groups in front, and it took all of Michael's efforts to keep the reserve group from joining them in looting.

"Michael," one of his men said, handing over a cell-phone, "The Russians caught two Chinks and tortured them to death. The trucks are on fire."

"Shit. I'd hoped to drive us down to the bay," Michael growled. "Now we'll have to leave earlier and walk the mile and a half."

In the Roller Dome, Mr. G took the phone. "Who's talking?" he asked.

"Alexander. I have eight men in two cars by the trucks. The Chinks abandoned them when we pulled up. They scattered into the tall grass on either side of the road toward Gravesend Bay. I caught two."

"What did they say?"

"They didn't know shit. They were told, if we showed up, to run toward the road and they'd be led safely out of Brighton Beach."

"You burned the trucks?"

"Right. Now what?"

"Get your asses back to the Dome .. No, wait! Place two of your men on either side of the road, off in that tall grass. They are to avoid a firefight, but report to me when the niggers show up for the trucks."

Michael used his reserves to force, cajole, and threaten his men down Brighton Beach Road to Gravesend Bay. On the way, they passed the burning moving-vans.

On Brighton Beach Avenue, three blocks from the Russian main roadblock and out of the line of fire, twenty ambulances and as many firetrucks awaited permission to enter the war-zone. Police cars were everywhere, and nobody passed their barricade until the shooting stopped.

New York's Mayor DeBlasio pressured the police to send in SWAT teams. New York's Fire Marshall argued to allow the firefighters in. The police department, City Hall, and 911 lines were inundated with calls.

The police cordon and the emergency vehicles also blocked the Jersey-sourced Russian reinforcements from entering Brighton Beach.

Jill returned to the ambulance crew with news. "My cousin on the SWAT team says the Crowns are running in the direction of Gravesend. The police expect the Russians to trap them and wipe them out."

"Why don't the police go in?" Mac asked.

"After the loss of hundreds of police and firemen on 9/11, the mayor won't take chances. That's the official story, anyway."

"What's the real one?"

"Primarily that the Powers That Be would be just as pleased if the gangs wiped each other out. They don't want to waste police and firemen on scumbags, so they hold off until things sort themselves out."

"You mean they're going to let the gangs shoot it out?"

"That's pretty much it."

At the Roller Dome, another call came in. "Mr. G, you won't believe it. The Blacks just passed the burning trucks, and didn't even stop to look. It's like a carnival. They have music blasting. They're dancing and carrying off all kinds of shit. One guy is wrapped in the Golden Nugget's velvet stage curtain. They're all drunk. One guy's got a refrigerator on a loading dolly. Two others are carrying a washing machine, and there are several slot-machines being carried away."

"They're disorganized?"

"Most of them are, but Michael Leissner is leading a group driving the crowd toward Gravesend. They're well-armed."

"When it's safe, come out of hiding. You and the other pair will act as scouts. We'll be there in ten minutes."

Twenty cars and three trucks, packed with armed men, roared out of the Roller Dome parking lot.

At the police barricade on the outskirts of Brighton, Mac informed her ambulance crew. "Police will escort us in. Wear the helmets and bulletproof vests. Our destination is the Diamondback casino. Martha stays in the back: Alphonso, you in the cab. Percy, you and Bill and Floyd accompany Jill and me. Confirm and cover the dead. I'll set priorities for treatment of the wounded. Helicopter evacuation is available from the high school football field."

Police escorted or helped the walking wounded out of the burning casino to the middle of the street. Jill and Floyd attended an elderly man suffering from a heart attack. Mac and Big Bill found a man semi-conscious. A nearby cop said: "He looks in bad shape, but he was only shot in the foot."

"Did you find the exit wound?" Mac asked.

"Didn't look." The cop shrugged.

"Uh-oh."

In a flash, Bill and Mac used their scissors to cut away the trouser-legs and search. "Nothing!" they both said aloud. They cut away the shirt and undershirt, and still found nothing. "We're losing him!" Mac snapped.

"Internal hemorrhaging," said Bill. "Some bruising on the left ribcage..."

"He's losing a lot of blood somewhere. Set up a double IV, under pressure. Now!" Mac shouted.

Bill Schmersal didn't move.

"Hurry!" she ordered.

"Too late," said Bill. "He's dead."

"Damn! Where the hell did that bullet go?!"

Bill lifted the man's arm to fold it over his chest,

and a bloody bullet fell out of the armpit.

Mac leaned close, lifted the arm, and among the bloody hairs of the armpit she found the exit wound.

"That's why the ribs were bruised," Bill deduced. "The bullet entered just above the ankle, followed the leg bones up, over the hip, up to the ribcage and out the armpit. It must have torn up blood-vessels all the way. We couldn't have helped him. I'm just wondering what position he was in for the bullet to hit him that way, with enough velocity to go that far."

"You want me to bag this one?" Jill asked.

"Go ahead. How's your heart patient?" Mac said.

"Worried about his money. He was on a winning streak."

"What's happening across the street?" Bill wanted to know.

"Not the bloodbath we expected," Jill replied "But there's more to come. The Russians have the Crowns trapped at Gravesend; that's where the real shootout will take place."

"What are the police going to do?" Mac asked, already guessing the answer.

"My cousin says they'll wait to pick up the pieces. Ambulance and Rescue will put Humpty Dumpty together again. You can follow the advance of the Russians down to Gravesend by the streetlights being shot out along Brighton Beach Road."

"Mr. G, the flankers are out on both sides of the road."

"Advance slowly. I want prisoners. I can't believe the Crowns would be so easily trapped."

The Russians advanced unopposed through the tall grass on either side of the road. Cars rolled quietly through the dark behind them. The only sounds were the booms of shotguns shooting the overhead streetlights. Ahead, two bonfires lit the vacant beach. A shot rang out on the right flank, but it was only one of the men killing a rabbit. Three hundred yards from the beach, Mr. G ordered: "Scouts out!"

The men waited in the darkness. To their left, passing traffic lit up the Belt Parkway. Ahead, the lights of the Marine Parkway Bridge hovered over the bay. Behind, the Verranzano Narrows Bridge spanned the waters and lit the night sky.

"They're gone!" the scout reported.

"What the hell do you mean?" Mr. G demanded.

"There's nobody on the beach but two white guys surf-fishing."

"Where the hell did all those niggers go?!"

"Both guys said five charter boats from the Sheepshead Bay fishing fleet pulled up to the beach, lowered ladders, and took all the drunken coons aboard."

"Son of a bitch!" Mr. G roared. "He pulled a Dunkirk on me! That bastard Leissner used the trucks as a diversion. Now here I am with my dick in my hands, like a monkey fucking a football."

"So what do we do now?"

Spittle formed on Mr. G's lips. He drew his automatic, fired into the sand, and growled: "Kill the Black motherfuckers."

CHAPTER 12:
THE DEFENSE

RIDGEWOOD VA HOSPITAL

"We're all going to the Gay Greek's," said Martha. "...We're going to hold a mock trial."

"For whom?" Mac asked cautiously.

"That son of a bitch who drowned his three kids and knifed his wife to death."

"Is this your Widowmakers group?"

"Yes, and we can't find anyone to defend the slime-ball."

"What's the purpose of this?"

"If it were real, it would be to punish the lowlife bastard."

"With death?"

Martha chuckled. "First we have a trial, and then we hang him."

"I really disagree with this concept!"

"That's why I brought up the subject. Would you defend that piece of shit?"

"Of course not."

"But we have no one else to ask."

"Because what you're planning is illegal and immoral."

"Good, then argue that. We need someone to defend him."

"Then you'll hang him."

"Oh it's a prejudiced court, all right, but most courts are. You'll have the opportunity to give the accused a fair chance."

"It's a kangaroo court, and against the law."

"The law is dictated by politics and big money. Just this week, thirty-five killings in Chicago, and who's even counting the family abuses? It used to be if a man beat his wife or abused his children, the neighbors would set him straight; if he was too much for the neighbors, the cops would do it. But now? No one gives a damn. You told us yourself, in your opening talk, about Patty Hearst and OJ Simpson and others who got away with murder because they had money and power while their victims were nobodies."

Mac was shaken by Martha's vehemence. "I'll defend the rule of law," she said, "On one condition: the Widowmakers must define their motives and objectives before the trial—and know that my only purpose is to dissuade you from taking any action."

THE GAY GREEK'S

Conversation at the table in the back corner was done in semi-whispers. Dessert was deep-dish apple pie and Jasmine tea, and everyone ate slowly. Silence fell as one after the other finished eating and waited. Jill tried to lighten the mood by joking about the Army dungaree caps that Alphonso and Percy were wearing, but it drew little laughter.

Finally Martha raised a hand. "Doctor Mac has agreed to act as defense attorney," she said, "And I will be the prosecutor. Everyone at this table will participate in any way you wish, but never in anger. We'll conclude with a vote. Jill, our secretary, will now read our collective answer to Dr. Mac's question: 'How do we define the Widowmakers Society, its motives and objective?'"

"Please do," said Mac.

Jill opened a school notebook and read: "We, the undersigned, are a group of concerned citizens whose motive is to eliminate those predators in our society proven dangerous to their spouses, their children, our neighbors, and us. It is further noted that all decisions for action must be unanimous."

"Is that all?" Mac asked.

For answer, Jill pulled the paper out of the notebook and held it up so that everyone could see the brief writing and all the signatures at the bottom. Then she crumpled the page, put a lighter to it, and dropped it into a teacup.

"Why?" Mac asked.

"For our protection against prosecution." Jill's voice was all business. "Can you imagine us trying to explain to the police about our taking out a wife-beater or child-molester? Agree with us or not, they'd at best be a wee bit uncomfortable about civilians doing their jobs for them. Think of what that leads to. Nothing of the Widowmakers can remain in writing."

"So you do understand the seriousness of this meeting?"

"Of course," said Martha. "Everyone at this table has a Bachelor's degree, and some a Master's. We know what we're getting into, but we're fed up with courts that send children and wives back under the same roofs with their abusers."

"Think hard. Are you doing this for revenge?"

"No, for prevention. You know that abusers who get away with it will only abuse again. Even if this... abuser goes to prison, he'll get out too soon—and go back to the same pattern."

"It's likely that the other prisoners will make that hard for him," Mac offered. "You know how long molesters last behind bars."

"That would be sloughing off the responsibility on someone else," Martha countered, "Someone we don't know and can't necessarily trust. We know the facts in the case, and we'll argue over every step. You know that."

"Do you think that eliminating a few abusers, one at a time, will stop the problem?"

Big Bill rocked back and forth like a religious Jew praying. "It couldn't hurt," he said. "And it'll save a few more lives."

"This is no joking matter. We're talking about taking a life."

"And the... man we're talking about has taken four lives. We've all seen women and children brutalized. I've taken several men into the parking lot, and would have killed them if I could have gotten away with it." Tears welled up in the big man's eyes and trickled down his ruddy cheeks. Jill handed him a napkin.

Percy Cook started to speak, but choked on his emotions. Alphonso spoke for him: "I've seen a lot of guys who needed killing. A couple of times I almost did it. But where do *we* the right to decide?"

"That's what we do," said Martha. "We're caregivers, sworn to saving lives. We give measles vaccinations to protect children; that's introducing a hostile element into the child's body in order to save children. We make that choice. Likewise, if we know of a predator with a history of spousal and child abuse, and the law—for whatever reason—is unable to stop him, isn't it our duty to protect that family, the community, and society?"

Mac could feel her resolve weakening. "Martha was my supervisor," she said. "From her I learned the Nurse's Creed: 'I solemnly pledge before God and in the presence of this assembly to pass my life in purity and to practice my profession faithfully'. Our profession is saving lives, not taking them."

"But aren't we saving lives by preventing a danger to them?" Jill asked. "If a proven history of abuse predicts lethal behavior, aren't we obliged to act?"

"Act, yes, but within the constraints of the law. Instead of a Widowmakers' Society, form a Family Abuse organization."

"They already exist," said Martha. "In extreme cases like this they're ineffectual. The majority of judges are male, the defendants are male, seventy percent of the legal profession is male, the laws themselves have a male bias, and so do the precedents. Centers for abused women are often concentration camps for families with dangerous mates."

"I concede the bias, but without the rule of law society would disintegrate."

"Society's disintegrating *with* the law," Bill growled.

"We're already making law," Martha went on, "Law by First Responders, to aid the injured and people abused by society."

"It should be done by the law of the land," Mac tried again.

"Everything Hitler did, in killing twenty million people, was legal," Bill said, "According to the laws enacted by the Reichstag in 1935. The democracies of the world fought against them. On winning, the allies had to create a new law—called Crimes Against Humanity—to prosecute the guilty. So why can't we fight against brutality and murder of women and children?"

"You're free to do as you wish," Mac conceded, "But you know you'll be held accountable for your actions. Besides, this is the wrong case to prosecute."

"Why not?" Jill asked, amazed.

"There's nobody left to protect," Mac pointed out. "His victims are dead, He never posed a threat to his neighbors, or the rest of society. He was dead drunk at the time, and he's going—for however long—to a place where he might be rehabilitated."

"Or where somebody else may take up this decision for us," Bill murmured.

"Thank God you aren't his lawyer," said Jill. "I want to kill the bastard, but you're right. Our business is to protect the living."

"Then help me," said a quiet voice from the corner. The others looked and saw Joyce Murphy dabbing at her eyes with a napkin. "He's going to hurt my boys."

"Who?" Percy growled.

"My husband. He stopped treatment for Post-Traumatic Stress Disorder two years ago. He was deployed seven times in Afghanistan, and now he's not the man I married."

"Where was he treated?" Jill asked.

"The Sandy Hook VA hospital. They immediately put him on paroxetine, combined with psychiatric counseling—but he never saw a doctor."

"How can that be?" Floyd asked. "You need a doctor's signature to get paroxetine."

"The consultant nurse probably told the doctor what to give him. Initially she was correct, but it should have been followed up with psychiatrist's visits."

"And he was getting that from the nurse?" Mac asked.

"Once a month. He'd come home worse than he went. He drank more, and finally refused to go back or take his pills. I convinced him to go one last time, and I went with him. That hospital is the most depressing place you'll ever find! Young men old before their time, unshaven, in dirty clothes, shuffling from one place to another carrying forms to be filled out. Many were obviously addicted to alcohol or drugs. The VA personnel hide behind bulletproof glass."

"We have that at Admissions," Mac recalled. "Some of the vets get violent."

"The way they're treated, *I* would get violent," said Joyce. "They're pushed around like bums. Complain, and they're shown the door. I filled out several forms and never heard a word back. I saw one young man given a gross of Maalox for his prescription. He tried to explain to the pharmacist that he couldn't carry the carton on the bus. The pharmacist called two guards, who escorted the man and his box out the door. When I left I saw him giving away Maalox bottles at the entrance."

"Did you speak to the Psychiatric nurse?"

"We saw a nurse. She had a Nursing diploma on the wall behind her, but no specialization in Psychology."

"Did you tell her you're a nurse?"

"No. Her attitude was hostile when we entered. She put her feet up on the desk, so we were looking at the dirty soles of her shoes. She said: 'I'm glad you brought your wife; now I can have her input on your behavior', but she didn't ask me any questions. She just criticized my husband's actions. She pontificated for thirty minutes, handed my husband a prescription for three months' paroxetine, and showed us the door. When I said I thought the session was supposed to be for an hour, she shouted at me that she was a professional, and she determined the length of visitation."

"Did you complain?" Mac asked.

"I demanded to see a doctor. There was more shouting, in which she informed me that doctors don't come down to the clinics; they only see cases evaluated by the nurses for admission. I did get to see the Head Nurse, and identified myself as a nurse. By this time my husband was across the street in a bar, drinking Johnny Walker."

"Did you get any satisfaction from the Head Nurse?" Martha asked.

"She was more civil, but only repeated what the first nurse had said. She explained that the hospital was grossly understaffed, and budget cuts made improvements impossible. She extended every professional courtesy, but suggested my husband be treated privately. We both make reasonable salaries, but the cost of private psychiatric care is beyond our budget."

"I would have demanded to see the hospital administrator", said Jill.

"I tried, but couldn't. I called the VFW and spoke with the Commander of the New York area. He said my complaints weren't unusual. They know that vets rarely see qualified doctors, and are often overmedicated for extended periods of time."

"Thank God our Ridgewood VA doesn't have that problem," said Mac.

"My patients on the Substance Abuse ward would say you've got your head up your ass," Martha snapped. "You've been so busy getting your Ph.D and running the ER, you haven't been out front in the day-to-day functioning of this facility. Joyce's husband should be admitted to my ward, but he'd have to go through the same nonsense first. Has your husband had a brain scan?"

"No," Joyce admitted.

"If you can get that done, and it shows characteristics of PTSD, then he would have to be admitted."

"He's not going to any hospital." Joyce shivered. "He's already an alcoholic, and I expect him to be fired soon."

"What work does he do?" Alphonso asked.

"Construction: heavy equipment operator, cranes, bulldozers and so on."

Jill said: "I think that's enough for tonight; we've strayed off the path and reached the point of anger."

She tugged Big Bill's sleeve. He gently took her hand and sat her on his knee. "I want to hear Joyce's story," he said.

"I'd rather Dr. Mac told it," Joyce demurred.

"I looked up the records," Mac sighed. "Joyce explained that her husband has PTSD; this is how we think he got it. On his last deployment he operated a super-bulldozer, among the largest in the world. A bus with twenty-seven civilians aboard had driven into an off-limits part of town in Ramadi—coincidentally, where my husband died. When the driver got out to ask directions, he was killed by a mine. A Marine patrol cautioned the passengers to stay inside. A bomb-disposal unit found that the bus was in the middle of a minefield. The mines, they thought, were small ones—anti-personnel. They called in the super-dozer to use its giant blade and carve a path through the minefield to the bus' rear door. Small mines wouldn't damage the super-dozer or its driver. Joyce's husband did as ordered. Sure enough, several small mines exploded while he was making the path. Everything went well until he reached the rear door of the bus. Unknown to the bomb-disposal squad, the bus was parked on top of an enormous explosive charge, which was triggered electronically from a nearby building.

"Yes, at this point in the story I wondered—as the Marines later did—how the bus came to be so precisely positioned. They deduced that the driver didn't get there by mistake at all; he'd been paid, or intimidated, to drive to that exact position, stop and get out. Obviously, whoever set the trap hadn't told the driver about the antipersonnel mines.

"When the main bomb went off, the explosion was so powerful that it demolished the bus. It killed all the passengers and flipped the bulldozer onto its side. Joyce's husband was protected by a steel cage, but the cage was bent out of shape and trapped him there. The noise ruptured his eardrums. The configuration of the blast drove most of the body-parts into the mesh of the cage. Blood poured onto him and blinded him, and fragments of flesh and bone dripped through the mesh onto him. It took six hours to extract him from the wreckage, six hours blinded by blood and fragments, unable to see or hear that help was coming."

"I've sent guys to hospital for far less than that," Floyd added.

"He spent five months in hospitals, getting his hearing restored and his physical wounds healed, but he went into a shell," Joyce took up the story. "Wherever you told him to go, he'd go, sit, and stare at the floor without talking. If the TV was on and someone stood in his line of vision, he never asked us to move or changed his position. Two months after his discharge, some of his buddies returned and took him out. For five days in a row, they got roaring drunk. I thought it might be good for him. He came out of his shell, but he wasn't the same man who went in. He has to control everyone and everything around him, and he drinks steadily. They say he's one of the best crane operators in the state, but he has no friends: not from the army, the neighborhood, or work. If he loses his job, I don't know what he'll do, or how I'll manage."

"According to what Mac told us about his beating you and threatening the children," Martha said, "You should get yourself and the kids the hell out of the house before he kills you. I can arrange a brain-scan for him."

"I haven't been able to convince him to go for any help," said Joyce.

Alphonso leaned over and whispered to Percy, who nodded in agreement. The both stood. "We'll be leaving now," said Alphonso.

"Do you accept my argument to acquit the killer husband?" Mac asked.

"You've changed our minds," Percy conceded. We came prepared to kill the bastard, and now we won't, but we're no closer to a solution."

Everyone left but Mac and Joyce.

"My husband is threatening to hurt the children if

I don't do exactly as he says," Joyce confided. "Most of his demands are petty, but every now and then he can be brutal."

"There must be a solution," said Mac. "I just can't think of it. Here's my personal cell-phone number; call me day or night. I'll walk you to your car."

CHAPTER 13:
INTERVENTION

PUBLIC SCHOOL 73

As Mac and Joyce walked across the school parking lot to Joyce's car, the younger woman stopped short and grabbed Mac's arm. "There are three men by my car!"

"Not to worry. That's Percy, Alphonso and Floyd. Hello, guys. What's happening?"

"We wanted to talk to Joyce," said Alphonso.

"Can I listen in?" Mac asked.

"We're glad you're here," said Floyd. "You know the three of us were combat medics; PTSD is something we saw and treated, in and out of the service. We have an idea of how to help your husband."

Bill, Jill and Martha stepped out of the shadows of the school building. "We have a plan too," said Martha. "Your husband's problem is in my sphere of expertise. The treatment will involve taking your children to live at Jill's for awhile."

"I have two private bedrooms and a private bath for the lot of you," Jill promised.

"Bring enough clothes for a week," Martha went on. "We're going to dry out your husband so he can make a rational decision to enter the program on my ward and get clean."

"Couldn't he go directly into your program?" Joyce asked.

"Without his cooperation it's not worth the effort."

"And if it doesn't work?" Joyce asked.

"Then we go to Plan B."

"What's that?"

"You get as far away from him as quickly as possible."

Joyce took a deep breath. "What do you want from me right now?"

"Take us to your house. The four men, go in Bill's car. Mac will help Jill set up the rooms for you and the children. I'll go with you. First we'll stop at the hospital for some supplies. Is your husband a very physical guy?"

"Very. Jack is six feet tall, with arms as thick as most men's legs."

"I'll bring a straitjacket."

"Is that necessary?"

"It may be."

The little convoy stopped in front of a duplex house with lights showing on the first floor. Reluctantly, Joyce led the way into the ground-floor apartment. The hall door opened on a foyer that led to the kitchen. On the right was the living room. In it, a man in boxer shorts and undershirt sprawled on the couch watching children's cartoons on TV. He was holding a can of beer, and an empty bottle of Jack Daniels lay on the coffee table.

He started up as the gang of nurses walked in. "What the hell?" he snapped, pointing at Joyce. "I told you not to bring anyone here. Are you crazy?"

"Don't shout," Joyce pleaded. "You'll wake the children."

Meanwhile, Alphonso and Percy and Bill and Floyd took up positions at either side of him.

"Who the fuck is she?" Jack yelled, pointing at Martha, who walked up in front of him.

"I'm the one who's here to answer your complaints to the VA regarding treatment for PTSD." Martha took hold of his arm, which felt like corded steel. Jack lunged to his feet but stopped there as the four men stepped closer.

Martha led him to a straight-backed chair, saying: "Sit. I need your vital signs." She stuck a thermometer in his mouth.

He pulled it out. "Who the fuck do you..."

Martha shoved the thermometer back in. "We're from the Ridgewood VA, the hospital where your wife works. We're here to give you the care you should have been given years ago, but we must have your cooperation. Now sit still, I'm going to draw some blood. You have excellent veins. Hmmm, you also have high blood-pressure. Do you sometimes feel as if the top of your head is going to explode?"

Jack nodded, glancing around.. Percy, Alphonso, Floyd and Bill stepped up beside him.

"We'll have to lower your blood-pressure," said

Martha, taking out a syringe. "I'm going to give you a shot for that."

"Who are these guys?" Jack mumbled around the thermometer.

"They're ambulance drivers and medics with our hospital emergency service."

"They look like Mafia enforcers. You're not taking me in any goddamn ambulance!" Jack exploded. He threw the beer can at Bill, who ducked it, and shoved Martha so hard that she flew across the room and hit the far wall. He lurched to his feet, biting down on the thermometer, which broke and cut his inner lip. Blood streamed out of his mouth as he pointed down at Martha and yelled: "You can shove that needle up your ass!"

The four men pounced on him and pushed him to the floor. Bill and Percy held him down, Alphonso held his head still, and Floyd pried his mouth open and swabbed the blood and broken glass out of his mouth. Jack struggled, cursed and yelled while Floyd and Alphonso slipped the straitjacket over his feet and pulled it up his legs. He howled louder as Bill and Percy forced his arms into the sleeves and buckled the wraparound straps. Floyd stuffed a gauze bandage into Jack's mouth, and Alphonse slapped tape over it. They both hauled him back to the couch and dumped him face-down on it. Martha approached, syringe in hand.

"So you were going to shove this up my ass?" she grinned. "Hold him."

Bill and Percy did so. Martha pulled down Jack's boxer shorts and stuck the needle in his right cheek while he screeched. "Roll him over," she said. "I want to talk to him. Where's Joyce?"

"With the children, in the car," said Floyd, rolling Jack face-up.

"Okay. Bill, you go with her to Jill's house."

"How long will you be here?"

"About a week. We'll take turns. Now I want to talk to him."

She pulled up the straight-backed chair and sat on it, facing the husband. "You can struggle all you want to," she said, "But you're no Houdini." Jack's muffled yelps and furious struggling earned him a hard slap in the face, which quieted him. "Look, you're suffering and it's not your fault. We came to help, but we can't do that if you won't help yourself. Now, you have a beautiful wife who cares for you, and two sons who need their father. But you? You're a disaster. You'll probably forget what I say, but it'll be repeated, again and again, until it gets through your thick head.

"If you don't get control of yourself, your wife and children will leave you. You're a threat to their lives."

Jack's eyes opened wide, and he struggled to talk past the taped gauze. Martha pulled it out. "Yes?" she said.

"Fuck you, lady!" he yelled. "Get the hell out of my house!"

Martha sighed, slapped the gauze back in, taped his mouth shut, and leaned her face close to his. "You smell like a pig," she said. "When was the last time you took a bath?"

He only struggled violently.

Martha asked slowly, "Do you want to die?"

Jack stopped struggling. His eyes looked beyond Martha, and after awhile he shook his head.

Martha slapped him on the shoulder. "Well, buddy, that's the first positive sign I've seen out of you. You may have a chance. You're at the bottom; the only way out is up."

Mac rearranged schedules for the following week, allowing the men to rotate Jack-watching. Floyd was relieved of all ER duties, and spent the most time with him. Martha looked in daily, and administered drugs to reduce the effects of chills, sweating, muscle cramps and delirium tremors. Kula, who heard about the arrangement from Jill, volunteered to bring food from the diner. She made certain to arrive when Floyd was on duty. She stiffly informed him that if she had been born two hundred yards to the north on the isle of Cypress, she would have been a 'rag-head' herself."

"The stork must have been Greek," he smiled. "That's just the way guys in the military talked. It was hard to be polite after being shot at a few thousand times."

The two lovebirds kissed and made up. They steamed the windows of Kula's car while making out. They went for walks, to the movies, and to a Broadway show.

Four days later, with the four men in the room, Martha ordered the straitjacket removed. The double dose of paroxetine had its effect; Jack was calmer, his vital signs close to normal, and he ate a full meal of meatballs and spaghetti. He even engaged Alphonso, Percy and Floyd in talking about their tours of duty in Afghanistan. He accepted, with relief, the news that the team had already talked to his boss and union about his taking a leave of absence for health reasons, and that he would have his job back when he returned. He kept insisting, though, that they had no right to come into his house and intervene in his life.

"It's not just your house or your life, you fool," Martha yelled at him. "You're forgetting the rights of your wife and children!"

To that he only responded with sulky silence. She considered that a troubling aspect of his rehabilitation. One positive aspect was his willingness to take his medications without a fight. Martha asked Mac and the crew to maintain Jack's schedule for another forty-eight hours, and everyone agreed.

On the evening of the ninth day of treatment Martha and Mac sat down with Jill, Bill and Joyce.

"Joyce," Martha explained, "We'll soon leave here to see your husband. He'll be free to go where he wants and do what he wishes. I'll take him to the Substance Abuse ward, and if he walks in it will be six months before you see him again."

"But I can help him..." Joyce offered.

"You may speak to him on the phone, but that's all. He'll be there to learn to help himself, and nobody else can do it for him. I'll partner him with the best on the ward, but he crawled into the bottle by himself, and must crawl out the same way.'

"What percentage of addicts are rehabilitated?"

"Your husband isn't addicted to drugs—yet; he's an alcoholic. I respect you as a nurse too much to gild the lily. You'll hear numbers of about twenty percent rehabilitation success, but it's bullshit. The average for alcoholics falling off the wagon in the first thirty days is ninety-five percent. That's why I keep them in the ward for six months. Because I keep them isolated for so long, we have one of the highest rehabilitation rates in the US and Canada. I use the word 'rehabilitation' because once an alcoholic, always an alcoholic. The only sure cure is death. My rate of success is eighteen percent.

"I see that you're shocked. Well, here's something that will grab you by the short hairs. In the US, a hundred and fourteen people die every day from opioid overdose. That's forty-four thousand a year—ten thousand more than die of all gunshot wounds. Two hundred and thirty die every day from alcohol abuse; that's more than eighty thousand a year. Unless we can get Jack into the twenty percent, he's a dead man in five years."

The three women sat in silence for a long moment. Finally Joyce looked up and asked: "What do I do if he refuses to enter the program?"

Martha pointed to Mac, who said: "You run."

"But where?"

"There's a position open in the ER of a Pennsylvania VA hospital," said Martha. "The hospital manager is a friend. The schools are good there, and the cost of living and taxes less than in New York. But let's not jump to conclusions yet. We'll take Jack to the Substance Abuse ward and give him his options."

At the house Jack showered and shaved and was given clean clothing: freshly pressed trousers, a sports shirt and jacket. Floyd hired a local barber to come to the apartment and trim Jack's hair. They rode together in the back of the ambulance to the Ridgewood VA hospital. Upstairs they waited outside the Substance Abuse ward until Martha came out with JJ Dougherty. "This is JJ," Martha said. "He and I are both alcoholics. If you decide to enter this program and dry out, you'll remain behind these doors for six months."

"And if I don't agree?" Jack hedged.

"You'll lose your wife, your sons, and your union card for work. When I called in about your 'leave of absence', I talked to your union boss. He granted you a year's leave to dry out, but you must return with a medical certification that you're able to perform your duties. All rights, benefits, and seniority will remain in place for a one year period."

"You told the union about me?!"

"The only thing I told them that they didn't already know was that you were taking the cure."

"You had no right to do that!"

"I had an obligation to. You're a danger to all you work with."

"Fuck you, lady! And fuck all your friends! You don't know diddly-shit about me. I can beat this by myself."

"No, you can't," said JJ. "You're making a big mistake."

"I've done that before," Jack snarled. He swatted Martha on her backside. "I owe you one syringe in the ass."

Martha pointed to the sign above the door. "You know where I live," she said.

Jack winked at JJ. "Want to join me for a drink?" he asked.

"Oh yes." JJ began to tremble. "But I want my family and my job back even more."

Jack shrugged, turned away and walked off toward the elevator.

"We lost that one," Mac sighed, watching him go.

"Death is the only cure," said Martha. "He'll be rehabilitated on the way to the graveyard."

"Want to join me at Jill's to help Joyce and the children get off to Pennsylvania?"

"What I really want is a double shot of bourbon. I'm going to sit in with JJ. I need some counseling."

CHAPTER 14:
STRATEGY

OFFICE OF E. MACKENZIE, RN, PH.D

"I studied so long and worked so hard to get to this position," Mac groaned. "I had everything planned out. Now I don't know which way to turn. Damn, all that time and effort we wasted on Jack Murphy, and we didn't even get to keep Joyce. Damn!"

"Define the problems, then we can assign an order of priorities." Martha pulled out a pad and pen. "Let's make a list. Start with the money."

"That's got to be the top. I never dreamed of being responsible for fifty million dollars! How do I control the money? Should I form a committee? Set up budgets? What government agency oversees my expenditures? When will they check my procedures or lack thereof? What will they be looking for? What should I be looking for?"

"Stop!" Martha held up a hand. You're trying to solve the problems before you've identified them. Let's make that list."

"All right," Mac sighed. "In no particular order:

the problem of vets being shunted back and forth, not seeing doctors, being over-medicated or self-medicated thanks to our VA bureaucracy."

"So noted," said Martha, writing.

"My authority to improve the EMs in Brooklyn."

"Noted."

"Violence in the community."

"Big one."

"The community's needs in relation to the ERs. Upgraded training for our staff. Parental abuse. Spousal abuse. Abuse of the elderly, both institutional and private..."

"Slow down, girl! I can't write that fast."

"And I can't think that fast. What do I do?"

Martha thought for a moment, and then smiled. "Ask our Black angel."

"Who?"

"Congressman Elijah Waters."

Once again the meeting was held at Bickford's Cafeteria in the Flatbush terminal of the Long Island Railroad. The horseplayers near the entrance crowded around Elijah's wheelchair, but he smiled and passed them by. He arrived at Mac's table at the same time as the meatloaf and mashed potatoes.

"Pass the ketchup," he said. "You mentioned a list of problems?"

"So many problems, I don't know where to start," Mac admitted.

"You have a list? Start at the top."

"I have fifty million dollars and don't know how to spend it."

"Spending isn't a problem. Getting more is."

"I don't know who I'm accountable to, or the guidelines for expenditures."

"As the late Rabbi Goldman used to say, 'If you don't want to hear the answer, don't ask the rabbi'. As a teenager, I worked in the office cf Congressman Adam Clayton Powell. Whew! He agreed with the rabbi. Spend it, and let the clerks run around trying to figure it out. But you *must* spend all of it; otherwise you'll never see another government dollar."

"What if they think I'm stealing?"

"Don't get caught."

"Oh, please!"

"Just keep track of everything you spend, maybe in a little pocket notebook. Loosen up, lady. You read that list while I eat, and then I'll respond while you eat."

Mac obediently read. The Congressman shoveled in mouthfuls of meat and potatoes, grunting every now and then to show he was listening. He cleaned his plate with a slice of bread, leaned back with a glass of iced tea, and said: "Alright, now you eat and listen."

Mac emptied the rest of the bottle of ketchup on her meatloaf.

"Wow! Woman, you sure do like ketchup."

"Not really. I just don't like meatloaf."

"I'll order something else."

"Not to worry: I need to lose a few pounds."

"Lose? You look like you were in a famine, and I look like I caused it."

"Please, I know your time is valuable, and I need

direction."

"Okay, look: you're going to make mistakes, and they may be big mistakes because you're now in a position of importance. As the saying goes, 'shit happens', and it will happen to you. For example, your purchase of that ambulance was a mistake."

"How so?"

"You failed to utilize your support staff."

"My ER staff has less knowledge than I do on that subject."

"But your secretary knows a lot. Why do you think your Chief Administrator assigned Ms. Basch to you? That woman knows the bureaucracies up and down. If you'd asked her, she would have referred you to the hospital Purchasing Agent, who knows all the shortcuts for buying. Hell, I would have introduced you to the purchasing office for New York City. They tell me they could have gotten that ambulance for $25,000 less. In addition, you would have had a Gotcha on the Purchasing Agent."

"What's a Gotcha, as opposed to *gotchkas?*"

"It's a favor. You'd be doing one for the Purchasing Agent by letting him choose the company you bought it from. When you need a favor, you grab him by the balls and squeeze. Gotcha! He owes you. I collect Gotchas; it's like money in the bank. Keep Ms. Basch in the loop on everything, and she'll keep track of the Gotchas for you. She'll also grease the wheels.

"So that's how the system works!"

"You don't have to steal money; use your power with discretion, and people will throw money at you.

Make sure Ms. Basch keeps track of it all. Now, back to your list."

"At this rate, we'll never get through it all."

"We won't; you will. Go through the list and cross out everything you're not officially responsible for. Go over it again, and cross out those things you're not morally responsible for—such as the bureaucracy in the VA and the violence in the neighborhood. Now circle those aspects of your job that relate directly to ER treatment in the Brooklyn community. Of those circled, pick the most important three. These will be your first objectives. You approached your job like a young hunter with a shotgun, trying to hit everything. You need to act like a sniper; pick a target, assess its value, get it in the cross-hairs, and POW!"

Congressman Waters leaned back, smiled, and nodded at the group of horseplayers. "You want to pick a winner? Form committees. They're like blankets, and cover a multitude of sins."

"Why are you convinced I'm going to be a sinner?"

"It's the nature of the public service beast. We all have good intentions, but we never satisfy everyone. Some people are just natural contrarians; they'll oppose and challenge anything and everything. That's why you form committees. Forming the committee is the most important part. You choose people who are influential in the field you're dealing with. Select those who agree with you on grand strategy, but are able to challenge you on tactics, without opposing your objectives."

"That's a tall order."

"It's worth the effort. You'll be pressured by different departments in the city, state, and federal governments. Civic groups will hound you, and so will politicians like me. Businessmen and realtors will try to bribe you."

"What do they usually say?"

"Let me give you a f'rinstance. My first bribe offer had to do with running a city water-pipeline out to the city garbage-dumps in Canarsie. The realtors had planned hundreds of condominiums on top of the garbage-heaps, and required the water-supply before they put in a bid for the city land. The real-estate people sent a beautiful young Black woman to make the pitch. She's now in Washington DC, by the way. I offered her a seat, but she preferred to stand. She opened the top button on her blouse, pulled out twenty hundred-dollar bills from her bra, spread them neatly on my desk, and said: "You can do one of three things. Refuse the money. Take this money and deny we ever met. Or you can take it and vote for the waterline into Canarsie—in which case I'll return with another five thousand dollars.'"

"So what did you do?"

"I put the money in my pocket, and took her to bed."

"And that didn't bother you?"

Elijah Waters smiled. "I didn't tell her that I'd already decided to vote for the pipeline. It was a great city investment. Those condominiums now sell for a million dollars apiece. The city collects taxes from each one, and Canarsie people stopped complaining

about the seagulls shitting on their cars and clothes-
lines because the garbage is gone."

"...You've given me a lot to think about. One
question: how do I turn down a bribe offer without
insulting the person making it?"

"Bring it to your committee."

Mac tapped her teeth with her pen for a moment,
then said: "All right, how does this sound? I already
have my financial committee to keep track of the
money. Now I'll create a managing committee, made
up of the ER chiefs of all five hospitals. For Ridgewood, I'll promote Jill to head of the ER and promote myself sideways into some meaningless title
that will simply keep me from being officially on the
committee. We'll tell the financial committee to divide up the money five ways and assign equal shares
to each hospital, specific spending being subject to
recommendations from the managing committee.
How does that sound?"

"Very good," Waters grinned. "Keep going."

"I know what my first recommendation to the
managing committee will be, subject to advice from
the brilliant Ms. Basch, and along the lines you've
suggested."

"Ah, and what will that be?"

"We buy nine more ambulances."

"Smart girl," the congressman chuckled. "Call
me anytime."

He turned his wheelchair and rolled it out past
the gang of horseplayers, one of whom had a persistent cough.

CHAPTER 15:
THE PROPOSAL

SLOAN-KETTERING HOSPITAL,
NEW YORK CITY

Floyd met Kula just outside the hospital entrance in the slushy parking lot, handed her a motorcycle helmet, and asked: "So how did the interview go?"

"I have the position, if I want it."

"Why wouldn't you want it?"

"That depends on you. If I take Mac's offer, we'll be working in the same place."

"Is that bad?"

"If we're married, it could be disastrous. Aren't you going to ask me to marry you?"

"Er...ah, yes."

"Then you have to help me decide."

"Why could it be disastrous if we worked at the same hospital?"

"Because there will always be gossip. I see how women look at you."

Floyd reached out, took the helmet from her hands and knelt before her on the wet pavement.

Passersby stopped to watch.

"My dearest Kula," he said, "I've finished sowing my wild oats. Will you accept me as your husband?"

The crowd clapped, then fell silent as Kula took both his hands in hers and raised him up. Then she kissed him. The crowd cheered.

Kula took the helmet back and led Floyd to where his parked motorcycle waited. "Let's go look at engagement rings," she said.

"First, I made an appointment with Mrs. Leissner at Bushwick hospital. I thought you might like to meet her."

"And afterward we can go look at engagement rings." She put on the helmet, and they got on the motorcycle. Kula wrapped her arms around his waist and giggled: "Let's go, Napoleon. Time's a-wastin'."

The two guards outside Lucille Leissner's hospital room jumped up from their chairs when they saw Floyd and Kula approaching. Otherwise, the hallway was empty.

"Hospital complained 'bout the noise," said the nearer guard. "Go right in. Lucille's waitin'."

As they walked into the room Floyd saw that Lucille's bandages had changed. Now they covered the top of her head, her left eye and the left side of her face, but her left arm was also bandaged over her nose. Nonetheless, she recognized Floyd as soon as he entered. "My hero!" she said, her voice somewhat muffled by her arm.

"Ah, is that a skin graft?" Kula guessed.

"Yes, and that plastic surgeon your boyfriend

recommended is top shelf. Says she'll make me better than new."

"Floyd isn't my boyfriend, he's my fiancée," Kula beamed with joy. "He proposed just half an hour ago. You're the first one we've told."

"Congratulations!" Lucille whooped. "Chowder, ger your big Black ass in here!"

One of the guards hurried in. "Yes, Miz Lucille?"

"Get that bottle of champagne from the fridge; we've got a celebration! When will the wedding be?"

"We don't know yet," Floyd admitted.

"Oooh. And what kind of wedding will it be?"

"Greek," Kula said firmly. "My father's been planning it since I was born."

"I've never been to a Greek wedding," Lucille considered.

"Me neither," said Floyd.

"You're both invited," Kula grinned, "Especially you." She patted Floyd's shoulder.

They laughed and accepted paper cups from Chowder. He struggled to uncork the bottle, and sprayed half the room when it popped, which inspired more laughs and jokes about baptism.

"That's the first time I've seen smiles and heard laughter in this room," said a voice from the doorway. It was Michael Leissner.

"Boy," Lucille crowed, "Grab a cup and toast the bride and groom to be!"

"Mama, are you allowed to drink?"

"To toast this beautiful couple, I am. Fill up my cup until it runneth over."

Michael Leissner shook Floyd's hand and kissed

Kula's cheek. "Is there going to be an engagement party?" he asked.

"First we want to buy a ring," said Kula.

"Michael," his mother commanded, "Call Ben Moshe in Jew-town. That's the Diamond Exchange in New York, 47th Street near 5th Avenue. He'll give them a fair shake. Girl, never buy a diamond without a lab certificate from GIA or AGS. You can judge a stone by looking at the four Cs: carat, cut, color, and clarity. Clarity is the least important."

"How do you know so much about diamonds?" Kula asked.

"Awww, smiling hurts my face. I've been engaged six times and still have the rings to show for it. Michael, you call Ben Moshe. They'll be there in an hour."

She waited until Michael closed his cell-phone, and then asked: "Where are your bodyguards?"

"In the ambulance parking lot."

"They should have come into the hospital with you. Those Russians are bad-ass motherfuckers. Have the guards pick you up at the main hospital entrance."

"Mama, you worry too much. I've got it covered."

"You worry too little, and I'll be covering your Black ass with a shroud. We laid a serious hurt on those Russkies, and they'll want payback in spades."

"We're ready for them."

"I want to talk to you about that. Let these two lovebirds go to the Diamond Exchange."

Kula held onto Floyd through the wet wind as they

drove over the Brooklyn Bridge, onto 5th Avenue and into 47th Avenue, where they parked the bike at the address Lucille had given them. They checked the number again, since Diamond Exchange could refer to the area as well as the particular building. The couple was immediately spotted by street hustlers and surrounded by hawkers who urged them into various shops, promising great deals on perfect stones. With Lucille's advice still ringing in their ears they ignored the crowd, went through the described door and up the elevator to the third floor. Two large men scrutinized them as they stepped out, and Floyd asked: "Mr. Ben Moshe's office?"

"Do you have an appointment?" one of them asked.

"Michael Leissner sent us."

"Second door on your left."

Ben Moshe was an affable Orthodox Jew in his sixties. He shook hands with Floyd but declined Kula's gesture, saying: "No, no touching beautiful women."

"What if I were ugly?"

"There are no ugly women; some are simply more beautiful than others. Come, sit down at my table. Now, you're here for a stone to put into an engagement ring, no? What is your budget?"

Kula and Floyd looked at each other and shrugged. "I've got twenty-five hundred dollars saved," said Floyd.

"I've got three thousand," Kula added.

"Five thousand can purchase a nice-sized stone," Ben Moshe smiled.

"I think the man should pay for the engagement ring," Floyd objected.

"We're going to be partners for life," Kula insisted.

"When we seal the partnership we can share the expenses," Floyd said firmly. "If it's acceptable, I'd like to see the stones in our price-range.'

Kula added: "But we have to remember the four Cs."

"I taught that to Lucille Leissner," Ben Moshe smiled knowingly. He spread a square of black velvet on the table-top and poured out a small canister of sparkling gems onto it. Then he handed Kula a pair of tweezers and a jeweler's loup. Her hand shook at first as she separated the finely cut stones.

"Pick them up and examine the four Cs," Ben Moshe said. "Put aside those that interest you, and I will then suggest settings that will appreciate their value."

"They're all so beautiful," Kula murmured, awed.

An hour later Kula was still examining, comparing, and evaluating the gems. Ben Moshe was leaning heavily on the table, and Floyd was dozing in a plush leather armchair.

"I think I like these five best," Kula announced.

"Good," Floyd muttered. "Can we leave?"

"I have to pick a ring for the setting. Mr. Moshe said he would help me with that."

"I will! I will!" Moshe swept the rejected stones back into the container and placed the five selected ones side by side on the velvet. "Of the five you have chosen, there are three different settings that will show them to the greatest effect. Two will make the stone appear larger, and three will reflect more light and be brighter."

"Brighter rather than larger," Kula pronounced.

Ben Moshe took away two of the diamonds and brought out a tray of golden engagement rings without stones.

"Let me have your hand," he said. He slipped a ring-sizer on her left ring finger, then selected three rings and had her try each one. Then he inserted the stones in each for Kula to select. She walked back and forth before the full-length mirror with each ring, posing so that the ring could be seen. "Let me know when you choose," Ben Moshe smothered a yawn.

"The one I'm wearing," Kula decided.

"Thank God. Wake up your fiancée." He handed her two cards. "You have one more thing to do; go to one of these two laboratories and get an evaluation of the stone. God bless, and good day."

"What about the ring?" Floyd asked.

"That's my wedding present to you. Any friend of Michael Leissner is a friend of mine."

"Are you going to just let us walk out of here with the ring? We didn't pay."

"Iron Mike will take care of it," said Ben Moshe. "He likes you, and I wouldn't want to be his enemy. Did you hear what he did to the Russians?"

"You mean the massacre in Brighton Beach?"

"He invaded their territory. There will be more blood in the streets, alas. I live in that neighborhood, and I know."

"How do we get to this laboratory?" Kula asked.

Kula and Floyd took a seat in the laboratory waiting room, and were soon called into a small office with a man sitting behind the only desk. He had a jeweler's loup attached to his eyeglasses, and he examined the ring under artificial light and in the sunlight streaming through the window behind him. He set it under a microscope and moved it about, inspecting the cuts and facets, then turned to a computer on his desk and typed. Handing the ring to Kula, he said: "You can pick up your evaluation at the front desk."

At the front desk Floyd opened the paper, did a double-take, and told the secretary: "There must be some mistake. The evaluation's too high."

The secretary asked the evaluator to come in and explain.

"I stand by my evaluation," the man said. "The stone alone is worth $4500, and the setting another $500."

"But I'm only going to pay $2500," Floyd puzzled. Kula gripped his arm warningly.

"If that's a problem," the evaluator shrugged, "I'll buy that ring for five thousand right now and sell it today for six."

"Thank you, but we'll keep it," said Kula, as she pulled Floyd toward the door. As they left the laboratory, she tugged his arm and explained: "It's Michael Leissner's way of thanking you, dummy!"

Once outside, Kula pranced down the street with her

left arm extended and the ring flashing in the cloudy sunlight, and she purposely put her left hand on Floyd's shoulder while riding behind him on the bike. She asked him to pull over near Prospect Park, and phoned her father at the diner.

"Daddy, I'm engaged!" she said.

"You mean you got the job at Sloan-Kettering?"

"No—Well, yes, I got the job...

"Congratulations!"

"But I mean, I'm also engaged to be married."

"Married? Without asking your father?!" There was a long silence. "So who is this man?"

"Floyd Sorenson, from the hospital. You know him."

"I don't like him."

"Come on, why don't you like him?"

"He's too good-looking. You should marry a proper Greek."

"I'm not in love with any Greeks. Don't complain, Daddy; you've been planning my wedding since I was born."

"I planned a Greek Orthodox wedding."

"So we'll have it." She put her hand over the phone. "Floyd, do you agree to a Greek Orthodox wedding?"

"Sure. I'm not a particularly good Protestant; maybe I'll be a better Greek Orthodox."

She pulled her hand back. "Papa, you've got your Greek wedding."

"When's the date?"

"We haven't set it yet; we just got engaged. We'll see you at the diner.'

"I'll make a small engagement party for you in the back."

"We'll be there about six. I have to stop at the hospital and tell Dr. MacKenzie I'm taking the position at Sloan-Kettering."

Floyd pulled into the diner's wind-lashed parking lot and noted: "Where'd all these cars come from? There's hardly room for my bike."

"Oh, no!" Kula wailed. "Papa said it would be just a 'small' engagement party, but he must have invited the whole family."

"The diner's packed," said Floyd, working the motorcycle between two cars.

"My father gets excited."

"How excited?"

"Not to worry. Papa has lots of friends. The neighbors remember my mother running a free soup-kitchen in the back of the diner, back during the bad old days. This was a dirt-poor neighborhood then."

"What am I going to do in there?"

"Just be Floyd Sorenson."

"What if they don't like Floyd Sorenson?"

"They won't show it."

"Thanks for the encouragement."

Just then Mac and the ER staff arrived, looking for parking spaces.

Inside the diner, Georgee burst through the crowd and embraced his daughter. "Mama would have been so happy," he chortled. "She loved you so. You were our darling little girl, and now you're going to be married." Tears filled his eyes.

"Papa, don't cry. This is the happiest day of my life."

"And it should be mine, but I can't imagine putting you into this big bum's care." He slapped Floyd on the shoulder and poked a forefinger at his face. "Remember, your wife-to-be got a very tough father and two tough brothers. If you give her trouble, oh boy! You don't give her trouble. That's the first rule. Now you and me and Kula's brothers sit down and discuss the dowry."

"...Dowry?" Floyd gave Kula a bewildered look as he was herded to a table in the center of the diner by a crowd of relatives. Kula was whisked away by friends who marveled over her ring.

Once they were seated, Georgee poured four glasses of Ouzo and raised his glass to Floyd. "May God bless your engagement and your coming marriage. When is it going to be?"

"I don't know yet," said Floyd., cautiously sipping the ouzo. "Whew! Licorice!"

"Kula will tell you. Her mother always told me." Georgee slugged down his glassful of Ouzo, and the two brothers did likewise, their eyes daring Floyd to do the same. He managed, without making a face. Georgee poured four more glassfuls, and went on. "I am now going to give you the most important advice, but first we drink to your health, because health is the most important thing. If my wife had her health, she would be here celebrating with us. Now drink."

"What advice do you want to give me?" Floyd temporized.

"First drink."

Floyd managed. As he put down the empty glass Georgee's oldest son said: "Ouzo will put hair on your chest, so don't let Kula drink it."

"Why not?" Floyd asked, checking to make sure he still had feeling in his tongue.

"Do you really want a hairy-chested bride?"

Everyone around the table roared with laughter. Georgee poured a third glass and pointed at Floyd. "Take up your glass and listen to what I will tell you."

"I'm listening."

"But you're not drinking."

Resigned, Floyd lifted his glass with the other men and drained it. His tongue felt as if it were on fire. "Now I can hear better," he wheezed.

"Good," said Georgee. "The advice is: don't answer the question."

"That's the advice? What does it mean?"

"It means, in days and years to come, sometime my daughter will ask you a question. You will say 'darling, do as you wish'. She will tell you she wants your input. You will say 'whatever you want is fine with me'. She will pout, 'oh, you never help me decide'. So you will answer her question and select this or that. Then begins the tricky part. She will ask very sweetly 'why did you pick that?'—and before you can reply, she'll give you give reasons why it's not good. You will try to change your mind and select the alternative, but your wife will accuse you of just mollifying her and demand that you defend your first choice, which she will shoot down again. Then you will argue, and you will have to apologize. You will be smart to buy her a gift, and lucky if she accepts it."

"...Uh, how do I avoid this?" Floyd asked.

"I don't know," Georgee said. "Married thirty-six years, and I never learned."

CHAPTER 16:
COUNTERSTRIKE

BRIGHTON BEACH

Flight 236 from Chicago-O'Hare arrived on time at
JFK Airport. Two tall Black men, dressed in dark
business suits with four-in-hand ties tucked into
starched white collars, carrying black briefcases,
ignored the passengers heading for the luggage car-
ousel and walked directly out of the receiving lounge
to the street. A waiting cab-driver greeted them and
took them in. The cab sped as fast as its driver dared
on the slick streets, onto the Van Wyck Expressway
to Southern State Parkway, and arrived at the
Brighton Beach Roller Dome in twenty minutes. The
men entered and submitted to a body-search.

"What do I call you?" Mr. G asked.

"I am Jamal X," the taller man answered, "And
this is Malike X. You want the Leissners eliminat-
ed."

"The sooner the better."

"Tomorrow night, then. We have return tickets
for Sunday morning."

"I don't have worthwhile up-to-date intelligence."

"Don't worry; our people in Bushwick have already done that."

"Do you need guns, explosives, or what?"

"Nothing. Send a wired cash payment to our Chicago office for half the amount agreed, and the other half when we're done."

Mr. G turned to his computer and sent the money via PayPal. Turning back, he asked: "Is there anything else I can do for you gentlemen?"

"Give us a reliable Black cab-driver to Bushwick."

"I wanta see Iron Mike."

"And who the fuck are you?" Chowder demanded.

"I'm the man what am, that can do what's gotta be done."

"Fool! You're high as a fuckin' kite."

Chowder grabbed the man by the scruff of the neck and was about to throw him down the stairway when the driver yelled: "I got information on the Russians!"

"What you got?" Chowder demanded.

"There's a reward?"

"Yeah."

"Then let me speak to Iron Mike."

"Only people get to see the boss."

"I'm a people, and I ain't tellin' you shit."

"Let him through," Mike called from his office.

After a pat-down, Chowder shoved the little man ahead of him into the office, to a space in front of

Mike's desk.

"You'd better shit information," Mike growled.

"Okay. I gotta call to take two Black Muslims from Mr. G's headquarters at the old Roller Dome to a Black Muslim house on Bushwick Avenue."

"Black Muslims? How do you know they don't live there?"

"'Cause they from Chicago."

"How do you know?"

"I heard 'em talkin. They got the accent, and they axed me questions about the neighborhood that everyone in New York knows."

"And why's that important to me?"

"Everyone knows you're payin' to keep an eye on Whites who come to Bed-Stuy. Now two Black Muslims come out of Mr. G's office and go to Bushwick? That gotta mean somethin'.

Michael stood and dropped four hundred-dollar bills at the man's feet. As the driver scrambled for them, Mike said: "Don't say anything. Now get out."

When they were alone, Chowder said: "They can't get close to you with White men, so they imported Black brothers from Chicago."

"I got to speak to my mother."

"You got lucky," Lucille said. "Double your bodyguards, and the rewards for information. Give that cabbie another thousand dollars."

"But Mama, he's happy with what he got."

"He'll be happier with more, and he'll tell everyone. Now you've got to be careful. Your daddy used to say the Muslims have the best killers, so you watch out. Never get into your car first; let it be driven to you. No restaurant, party, or theater reservations. If you must attend a scheduled affair, have a double take your place entering and leaving. And I want your office, home, and all phones electronically swept once a day. Your car must be eyeballed twenty-four seven."

"Mama, that all costs money."

"Boy, you've got more money than God. Spend the wealth to keep your health, because it won't matter how much you've got in the grave."

The two Muslim hit-men, dressed as doctors, arrived by taxi at the Bushwick hospital ER entrance. One used his cell-phone to issue the order: "Initiate". A van parked down the street pulled away from the curb and drove up to the Emergency Room entrance, where seven men and women spilled out trying to help an injured man. They carried him into the reception area of the ER, where a fight promptly broke out. The bogus doctors, in white jackets, stethoscopes around their necks, slipped past the angry crowd to a position near the elevators.

The lone hospital guard tried to break up the fight, and was knocked to the floor. The bogus doctors helped him up, and one of them said: "You need to call for assistance."

The guard, agreeing, called the 79th Police Precinct across the street. "I have a riot situation at the Bushwick ER. Send help!"

At the same time, the second Black Muslim called Michael Leissner's personal cell-phone.

"Is this Michael Leissner, son of Lucille Leissner?"

"Yes. Who's calling?"

"Dr. Barrett at Bushwick Hospital. Your mother had a violent reaction to the medications."

"Is she in danger?"

"We have her on life support. I suggest you come immediately."

In seconds, Michael was out the door with his bodyguards. Three cars sped to Bushwick Hospital, and arrived within five minutes.

The argument between the people from the van was still going on. The newly-arrived police had separated the two groups, but the situation was still potentially explosive. Police stopped Michael at the entrance.

"Let me through!" Michael shouted. "My mama's dying!"

A police sergeant recognized Michael and let him pass, saying: "Only family can go up. The others have to remain here."

Michael left his bodyguards behind, and ran to the elevators.

One of the hit-men dressed as a doctor pressed the elevator button. The car arrived promptly, and both the men got on with Michael. "What floor?" one of them asked.

"Two," Michael said.

"Are you Michael Leissner?"

"Of course."

"We're going to see your mother right now."

Automatically, Michael observed the two men.

Both had four-in-hand ties tucked into starched white collars. Their white jackets did not have the Bushwick name or emblem. Their shoes were spit-shined to a reflective sheen. Michael reached for his gun.

One man grabbed his wrist. The other whipped out an automatic with a silencer attached, pumped two bullets into Michael's stomach and two more into his forehead. He slumped to the floor.

The men exited at the second floor, pushed the button to send the elevator to the fourth floor, and walked down the corridor to Lucille Leissner's room.

The two guards at her door were shot before either of them could stand up.

Inside the room, Chowder was washing out Lucille's coffee cup in the sink when the door burst open and hit him. His three hundred and fifty pounds rebounded off the wall and came back swinging. He hit the door with all his weight, knocking both hit-men to the floor just as they were in the act of shooting at Lucille. One bullet grazed her right cheek and another puffed up white dust from the plaster cast on her arm. She grabbed for the pistol under her pillow.

Chowder reached around the door and fired blind. One of his bullets buried itself in a gunman's hip. The other hit-man emptied his gun through the door, hitting Chowder with four bullets. Lucille whipped up her pistol and fired blindly at the two gunmen. She missed, but the hail of shots drove them back out into the hallway. Lucille pounced on the emergency-caller button.

One gunman dragged his wounded partner down

to the stairwell and helped him stand. Together they limped downstairs to the ER exit.

There a security guard saw them, pointed to the wounded man's bloodstained trousers and asked: "Hey, doc, are you alright?"

The uninjured hit-man shoved his pistol in the guard's face and pulled the trigger. It clicked quietly. Only then did the man realize that the slide was all the way back, revealing the empty chamber and magazine. He growled: "I am a descendant of the prophet Elijah Muhammed. If you identify us, I'll kill you and your family."

The guard's eyes widened. Without a word, he pushed the door open to let the men out into the slush-coated parking lot, where a dark car waited with its engine running.

In the lot the police and the angry crowd were gone, but Michael Leissner's bodyguards were waiting near the exit. They saw the two men come out, one bleeding and the other with a gun in his hand, and rushed to cut them off. They surrounded the men, took away their weapons, and were yelling questions when the idling car spun its wheels and attempted to flee the parking lot. Eight men fired. Windows shattered and holes were punched in the car's doors as it went out of control and smashed into a pillar beside the open exit-gate. Michael's body-guards then turned their attention back to the two hit-men.

On the second floor, nurses and doctors rushed Chowder to the emergency operating theater. Within five minutes of being shot, he was being prepped for the table. The news was surprisingly good. The four bullets that had hit him had come from pistols encumbered with silencers; those muffled noise, but also reduced the bullets' velocity. Going through the door slowed them even more. One slug was lodged in his forearm, another two in his shin and knee, and the most serious in his spleen.

Lucille accompanied him to the operating room doors, and when he disappeared behind them she began to tremble. A nurse took her by the shoulders, led her back to her room, and medicated the cut on her cheek—but knew better than to try to get the gun away from her. The cast was only scratched.

Four of Michael's bodyguards filed into the room, avoiding Lucille's eyes, and the nurse prudently left. "What's wrong?" Lucille demanded.

No one looked up.

"Spit it out!" she shouted, shaking harder.

The biggest of them managed to say: "We caught them two hit-men. They're alive, an' on their way to Cheap Charlie's garage."

"I want to know everything they know. If they die before they tell you what the insides of their mothers' cunts look like, I'll have your balls for dinner. What else did they do besides come after me?"

No one responded.

Lucille's eyes went wide, and froth showed at the edge of her lips. "What're you not telling me, Raymond?" She pointed her pistol at him. "Say it, or I'll blow your fuckin' head off!"

"Lucille, shoot me, 'cause I ain't gonna be the one

to tell you."

She squeezed the trigger, to no effect, and then realized—like the hapless gunman, that her automatic was stretched open and empty. Still nobody spoke.

"Son of a bitch!" she shouted, understanding. "They got Michael? My baby's dead?! How could you let that happen?! You no-good rotten mother-fucker sons of bitches—"

Lucille collapsed. Raymond artfully caught her pistol and hid it in his shirt before hitting the emergency-call button beside the bed. A team of nurses and doctors rushed in. They converged upon Lucille and chased everyone else out of the room—all but Little Joe. He refused to leave.

Mayzie called Mac from the Bushwick ER for assistance. The shootout had added to the normal flow of patients dead and wounded, who had to be treated ot tagged and bagged. The largest number were suffering from opioid overdose; two were already in the morgue, and another was on the way.

"It was bad in San Francisco," Floyd noted, "But this overdosing rate is crazy. What are they all running away from?"

"Life," Jill sighed. "We've got fourth and fifth-generation welfare recipients. They get so much money from the government that it doesn't pay them to work. They sit in front of the boob-tube all day, until their brains turn to mush. They deaden the brain-pain with drugs. Then they need more money, so they take up selling the stuff. Meanwhile they make babies, and not just because they it's too much effort to use BC, but because each child brings an increase in welfare payments. More money, more drugs, and they leave the kids to grow up however they can. So they get knocked up, locked up, and the kids get sent to foster homes to grow the next generation of welfare recipients."

"Don't they care about their kids?"

"These are mush-brains."

"I can think of a few ways to change it..."

"I doubt if they'll take you up on it. Mush-brains on welfare have the same voting power as the citizens who pay for the system—not to mention marching in the streets waving signs, yelling, and throwing rocks. The numbers are about equal, and the welfare mush-brains will always vote themselves a raise in benefits, not change."

"How can something like this survive?"

"It can't. We're all playing musical chairs, here. Eventually we'll run out of chairs, and we'll all be sitting on the floor. Oops, here come some more."

They both pulled down their clear plastic facemasks to attend a man bleeding from several stab-wounds. Jill and Big Bill returned from an emergency ambulance call to the Bushwick ER, attending a nine-year-old girl with a broken ankle and a dislocated shoulder.

CHAPTER 17:
WINTER FOLLIES

RIDGEWOOD VA HOSPITAL

"Before you take off," said Martha, "You'd better set up an emergency schedule for the ERs you're in charge of."

"Why?" Mac asked, picking up a sheaf of papers.

"It's approaching Christmas, and you're going to a school Christmas ceremony with the Congressman. All the little shits will take the opportunity to prove their adulthood. They usually do it at the dance this evening. You'd better have the ERs ready for the surge."

"Damn, I forgot. Can you take care cf that? I'm running late."

"Which school are you going to?"

"Halsey."

"Wow. That was once the jewel in the crown of Brooklyn's schools. Jackie Gleason went there."

"I thought Barbra Streisand did."

"No, she went to Bushwick. Just keep your speech short, the kids got *shpilkas.*"

"What's that?"

"Bill told me. It's Yiddish for ants in the pants."

Halsey High School registered 612 students and 54 teachers. Most teachers were young women in their first year of work. The front of the old red brick building faced Evergreen Avenue, and was shaped like a giant U with its two wings stretching back to embrace the macadam playground and basketball courts. The two arms of the building formed an outdoor auditorium where row upon row of chairs were set up for students, teachers, and guests. So were microphones, loudspeakers, and a stage with a special ramp to accommodate Congressman Waters' wheelchair. Some students were already seated, and others were filing in. The senior class would arrive last, since their classrooms were on the fourth floor.

In Class 12-B Miss Greenberg was handing out grades and placement tickets for the upcoming Christmas ceremony.

Nineteen-year-old Dishan Jabar sat impatiently in the rear. He stood six feet two inches tall, and was captain of the high school's football and basketball teams. He was also the leader of the Cadet Crowns, whose boss, Iron Mike Leissner, had been killed just two days before. Dishan felt obligated to make a statement in memory of Iron Mike and was prepared to do so at the ceremony. The last name Miss Greenberg called was his.

"I'm sorry," she said, "But you will not receive a ticket."

"Why not?" he demanded, thinking of the speech he'd meant to make.

"You hardly attended any classes."

"A lot of other people don't never come to class."

"You didn't submit even one homework assignment."

"That's bullshit!" he yelled, standing up tall, broad in the shoulders, with visible veins snaking down his tattooed muscular arms. "I came to get a ticket, and you're gonna give it to me!"

The rest of the class let out an expressive "Whoooo!" and giggled.

At this point a more experienced teacher would have pulled out a stun-gun, but Miss Greenberg only pointed and said: "Dishan, take your seat."

"Fuck you, lady!" He marched to the front desk—at which point a more experienced teacher would have used the stun-gun —but Miss Greenberg only sat frozen, bewildered. Dishan stepped to the teacher's left, shoved his hand into her blouse and under her brassiere to grab her breast. "Sign that fuckin' form!"

He squeezed so hard that tears leaped to her eyes. She gripped the pen she'd been using, and stabbed his hand. He jerked it away and slugged her in the jaw. She fell unconscious to the floor.

"If I don' party, nobody does!" bellowed Dishan, as he swept all the papers off her desk.

The class erupted in cheers. Books and notes were flung about with abandon. The noise and blizzard of papers spread into the hallway and ignited the other four senior classes. Students jubilantly trashed the rooms and hallway. Chairs were thrown through windows, and fell dangerously close to those assembled in the courtyard below. The students on the top floor yelled at those below to join them, and the cry "Freedom!" was shouted everywhere.

The school principal shoved Mac and pointed at the congressman, shouting: "Get him out of here!"

A shot from an upstairs window echoed through the courtyard. Guests, students, and teachers fled in all directions. Mac unlocked the brakes of the wheelchair and almost overturned the congressman as she raced him down the ramp. His limousine waited in a special parking space with two police guarding it, and Mac rolled him up to it. "Get in there and stop the riot," Waters ordered.

"We can't do that, Congressman," one of the cops apologized.

"But there's gunfire!"

"Your city council passed a law last year that forbids any police from entering a public school without written orders from a judge."

"You think this is funny? People could be killed in there!"

A chair burst through an upstairs window and smashed on the avenue sidewalk. The policeman gazed at it and said: "Mr. Waters, you should leave now."

Gunshots rang out as the limousine pulled away from the curb. Sirens of fire engines, police cars and ambulances descended on the school. Brooklyn and Queens SWAT teams arrived in armored trucks.

The next day, in Mac's office, Jill read the local paper aloud.

"The riot at Halsey High School claimed three lives and left fifteen hospitalized. This was the Christmas gift from Dishan Jabar, a teenage gang leader who started the riot by molesting a teacher in front of her class. He broke her jaw, vandalized the classroom, and incited other students to join him.

"Jabar was killed when he engaged three SWAT teams in a shoot-out. Two more students died and fifteen were hospitalized. Numerous students and teachers were treated as out-patients.

"Congressman Waters, who was also forced to flee, asks: 'How did the gang members bypass the metal detectors with their weapons?' A dozen pistols and an automatic rifle were confiscated by the police. An officer was shot through the neck and another suffered a heart-attack. Both are in stable condition.

"Two ambulance drivers, Alphonso Constable and Percy Cook, are responsible for disarming and capturing four gang members fleeing the scene."

Jill stopped reading and asked: "How did the two of you catch four gang-bangers with guns?"

"Only two had guns," said Percy. "Salute, and we knocked them out."

"Salute?" Martha asked.

"These dungaree hats you guys have been making fun of," he explained. "When I say 'salute' we whip our hands up to the peaks as if to salute. Then we whip the hats off and slap the guys with the three-ounce lead sinkers sewed into the back of the hats."

"Like a blackjack," Floyd explained.

"Even better," Percy chuckled.

"Read on," Mac said.

"There's not much more." Jill resumed reading. "The weapons had been slipped into the school through the Eldert Street ground floor widows. Committees are being formed to investigate."

"That means," Mac considered, "That the guns were planted beforehand. Jabar and his friends had meant to shoot up the ceremony. I'm sure the police reached the same conclusion, but nobody wants to talk about that. The congressman told me that if you want to bury something, you form a committee."

"There's an interesting addendum from the reporter," said Jill. "He asked the high school principal how public education had drifted into this state of affairs. Mr. Sweeting replied that John and Robert Kennedy had said, and I quote: 'If we cannot clean up and promote inner city education within five years, it will be impossible to achieve'. He left the reporter to say how long ago that was.

"Now note that during the Vietnam War college grads could get a deferment from the draft by signing up for a teaching license. This led a generation of flag-burners to infect our students' minds with self-righteous victimhood and corrupted morals."

"That's a bit different from the serious peace-marchers," Floyd amended. "They made a big point of being absolutely non-violent, so as to keep the moral high ground. Also, they were fighting for other people's lives, not just to save their own skins."

"How would you know?"

"My mom was one."

"Well, now that the Kennedys' deadline has long passed, what would you do with these inner-city kids?"

"Revive the WPA and the CCC," said Floyd, "Only with a lot less corruption, paperwork, and bureaucracy this time, and let kids join as early as sixteen. In fact, cut off welfare at sixteen for anyone able-bodied enough to work unless they're in school and keeping their grades up. Provide safe and reliable day-care for parents with small children, so they don't have baby-tending for an excuse. If they don't want to learn in school, they can learn on the job— actual work-skills, the habit of collecting a paycheck, and how to springboard a basic job into a better one. It'll also keep them too busy to hang out on the streets, and going out into the boondocks to plant trees will get them out of the 'hood' altogether."

"Nice theory," said Jill. "Do you have any solid evidence that it would work?"

"It did for my grandpa."

"Bill, you've been very quiet," said Mac. "What are pondering?"

"I was thinking, we formed the Widowmakers but the street kids have taken it over and redirected it."

No one spoke for a long moment.

The office door opened, Crazy Mayzie came in and looked around. "I never saw so many articulate people being so quiet," she said. "What's going on?"

"We're practicing for the three wakes after the shootout," said Mac.

"There's more to come," Mayzie promised grimly.

"What do you mean? Did Lucille's bodyguard die?"

"No, he might lose his spleen, but none of the bullets penetrated far enough to be lethal. One even popped out of his leg on the operating table. But Lucille has gone bonkers. She's declared war on the Russians and the cops."

"She always was the brains behind her son," Jill considered.

"But why the police?" Floyd asked.

"Her troops captured the Muslim hit men. From what they said, she believes that the cops were paid by the Russians to keep her son's bodyguards from going upstairs with him."

"That's possible," said Jill, "But Mayzie's right; there's more to come. The other big gangs will test Lucille to see if she can hold her money-making territory, and the smaller gangs will try their wings against her. Meanwhile she'll be after revenge."

"And where do the cops come into it?" Floyd asked.

"They sit on the sidelines and take their payoffs, so long as no police get hurt. That's the Golden Rule."

"And what if Lucille breaks it?"

"Awhile back, two Harlem boys broke it," said Jill. "They held up a Brooklyn bar where two off-duty policemen having a beer after their shift. The Harlem boys put the cops on their knees and then blew their brains out. Every cop on the east coast went looking for them. Eventually one of their brothers sold them out. They were holed up in a cheap hotel in New Jersey. The New York police were informed and two senior detectives were dispatched, even though they had no legal authority in Jersey. They found the two guys, made them kneel, and shot them twice in the back of the head.

"Both detectives were retired two weeks later, with honors."

There was a long silence again.

"...Martha," Mayzie broke it, "Did you work that nine-year-old girl with the broken ankle and the dislocated shoulder?"

"She was my last patient. I handed her over to your staff."

"Why?"

"Over the last couple years I've seen the mother three times. This is the second time with the daughter."

"I never saw the mother, only the father."

"Neighbors brought the mother in after you finished work. Her front teeth were knocked out, bruises around the head and shoulders, and her body looked like it was used for a punching bag: three cracked ribs on one side, and one broken into the lung on the other."

"Spousal abuse," Mac spoke up, "Again."

"I almost got the husband locked up last time," said Mayzie. "Some young do-gooder from Welfare recommended leniency, and the bastard got off."

"I'll go over there now and talk to the mother and daughter."

"I already did. The child dislocated her shoulder

trying to pull away from the father. He had a baseball bat. That's how he broke her ankle."

Martha looked around the room. Nobody spoke, but everyone was looking at her expectantly. "I think it's time," she said, "That I talked to Big Momma about the Widowmakers Society."

"I thought you guys gave up on that."

"Not exactly... maybe... but I'd still like to talk to her."

"I'd like to know what comes of that conversation," said Mac.

"All of us would," added Big Bill. "There's got to be some justice in this world."

"Not enough to notice," growled Alphonso, coming into the room.

"What's bugging you?" Jill asked.

"Come down to the ER and see, all of you."

The group followed Alphonso to the elevators and down to the ER. There the new intake nurse was helping an old man in a wheelchair drink from a container of coffee. The old fellow wore pajama pants, bedroom slippers, and a World War Two Eisenhower jacket with four rows of ribbons. The stripes and shoulder patch declared the wearer a sergeant of the 82nd Airborne.

"He's got four Battle Stars and two Purple Hearts," Floyd noted. "The Greatest Generation, come down to this."

"He's a vet, for sure, and he belongs here," said Jill. She leaned down, put a hand on his shoulder and asked: "Sarge, what's your name?"

The old man raised his gray head, looked into her eyes with rheumy pale-blue eyes, and smiled vacantly.

"He doesn't know," said Alphonso, "Not his name, address, age, or anything."

Jill choked, and turned away.

"Where did you find him?" Mac asked.

"In the ER parking lot."

"Did he have any papers? A list of prescriptions? Any ID?"

"Nothing."

"Have the doctors give him a thorough exam. Sign him in as John Doe—Sergeant John Doe. Martha, how old do you think he is?"

"Second World War vet? Mid-nineties."

"Bill, you look after him. Martha, use your police contacts to find out who he is. Jill, set up a meeting of the Widowmakers at the Gay Greeks for Wednesday."

"Include me," said Mayzie. "I want a part of this."

CHAPTER 18:
STRATEGY AND TACTICS

ROLLER DOME, BRIGHTON BEACH

"Mr. G, it's one of the X's, calling from Chicago."

"Put him on the speaker-phone. ...Hello, this is Mr. G speaking. How can I help you?"

"Pay the remaining half of the hundred-thousand-dollar contract," said a raspy voice.

"Finish the other half of the contract. She's still alive."

"We lost two of our best men."

"You knew the risk."

"Their bodies were desecrated in the most obscene way."

"I hear they were tortured to death, the bodies sewn into the bellies of pigs and left on Bushwick Avenue."

"We recovered the bodies and will bury them properly. Pay what you owe."

"If they'd done their job properly, they'd be alive and we wouldn't be having this conversation. You can get the other fifty thousand by eliminating the existing threat."

"You are being unreasonable. How can a woman be a threat to you?"

"Immeasurably, you Arab jackass. She was always the brains behind Iron Mike, and she controls a large part of Brooklyn. Fulfill your half of the bargain, and I will fulfill mine. Good day."

Mr. G turned off the phone and turned to address his lieutenants. "For now, the target is no longer Lucille Leissner. She's hiding behind a fortress in Bushwick Hospital, and the police are also protecting her, thanks to that idiot Jabar getting those cops nearly killed."

"Mr. G, how about we poison her food? I have connections in the hospital kitchen."

"And I've got spies there, too. Her food is all catered in from the Bed-Stuy neighborhood a different restaurant for every meal, and her drivers are untouchable.

"No, we go after her organization: drugs, whores, gambling, protection, stolen cars, and especially the docks. We'll have help from the Irish in Red Hook, but don't step on their turf. The only thing we share with them is the docks."

"Sooner or later, we've got to take Lucille out," one of the lieutenants said.

"We cut into her business, and sooner or later she'll have to come out to protect it. Then, *bam!*" Mr. G slammed his fist into the palm of his other hand. "We kill the bitch. She started this by coming to Coney Island without an invitation."

Kula and Floyd would meet for lunch when he had the night shift, and for dinner or a movie in the city when he worked days. They often rented a hotel room and didn't leave it until work began. Floyd didn't tell her about the Widowmakers until her father told her about a heated discussion at the diner on Wednesday evening. She questioned Floyd and, contrary to her father's advice, he made the mistake of answering. He explained about Rosie, and how the group came about through casual discussion, and he'd thought it was abandoned when Joyce Murphy and her husband became involved.

"Why didn't you tell me about this before?" she demanded.

"I thought you'd disapprove of us even talking about it, and after the failure with Murphy, I didn't think anything would come of it."

"Well... my first reaction was negative, but after hearing about the effort you made not to kill anyone, I realized that you're a serious and moral group, dealing with issues not appropriately addressed by society. No, I guess I don't disapprove."

"Whew!" Floyed wiped his forehead with the back of his hand. "I was worried about that."

"At Sloan-Kettering we deal with life and death moral issues every day."

"As a dietitian?"

"Of course. We have people who give up and try to starve themselves to death. Others try to starve themselves into better health or some bizarre ideal of beauty. Then there are those who think that overeating will make them stronger. They really believe these things, and we have a hard time convincing them otherwise."

"I thought you personalized meals."

"That too, definitely. My father said there was a heated discussion Wednesday...?"

"Two cases that we thought required the Widowmakers.

"One was a Grandpa Dumping of a decorated World War Two vet from the 82nd Airborne. It turns out that he'd been living with his nearest relative— his daughter, sixty-eight years old, on Social Security and recently widowed herself—and they'd both been thrown out of their apartment. She was living out of her car, and there was no room in it for the old man and his wheelchair. She'd parked the car near a private-mailbox company, where she was waiting for the checks to come in so that she could get another, cheaper, place to stay. She'd parked her dad with us in hope that he'd get help until she could find a home and come back for him. Her own children moved out of state years ago. She'd lost the old man's ID and papers during the eviction. We learned we could solve that one the next day by finding her social worker and getting the woman into some cheap housing in another part of the city. That was the easy one."

"And the other?"

"That was a battered wife and nine-year-old daughter. We all agreed that if we found a consistent history of spousal and child abuse, we'd take it to the next step."

"Which is?"

"Voting on whether to take action or not."

"Action? Killing the husband?"

"I think so."

"Who would do it?"

"That's what the argument was about. None of us wanted to kill anyone. Martha said she had a couple of detective friends that could break some of the husband's bones and put the fear of God into him. Others said that would involve other people learning about us, or doing for us what we didn't have the guts to do ourselves."

"So how did you vote?"

"We didn't."

CHAPTER 19:
MOBILIZATION

BUSHWICK HOSPITAL

Lucille brought in Little Joe's sisters, Ida and Camille, to attend her twenty-four seven. They both took after Little Joe in height and physique, being over six feet tall. They had played basketball since childhood for the Saint Barbara's Catholic Youth Organization, and now they were Tri-State champions. Little Joe was twenty-five years old, seven feet tall, and had signed a contract with the New York Knickerbockers.

The contract was annulled after Little Joe was caught carjacking.

It took half the 97th Precinct with nightsticks to bring him down. Then he challenged the police in his cell, and the second beating caused brain damage. His speech was slow and his thoughts slower. He could follow an idea if it was presented slowly enough, and once he had a task in mind he never wavered. Neighborhood Jews called him Golem—a mythical humanoid creature who could perform only one task at a time, but would do that to perfection. He never deviated from a task, and destroyed anything hindering his orders.

Now he was Lucille's bodyguard.

"Ida!" Lucille bellowed, "Get me some coke."

"The doctor said none o' that stuff," Ida insisted.

"Girl, who's your boss?"

"You ain't got a nose to sniff it up with, anyway."

"I'll have one next week. Right now I want to mainline."

"You never did this shit that way."

"I haven't slept since they killed Michael. Oh, give me sweet dreams; I feel like I'm surrounded by wolves, all trying to tear pieces out of me. And when you finish, find out how Chowder's doing."

"I brought him a pot of clam soup, and he's happy as a pig in shit. Doctor says he'll keep his spleen, and be up and around in two days. If you want sweet dreams you want smack, not coke, an' if you haven't taken it in awhile you want to lick it, not shoot it."

Lucille acquiesced, grumbling, and Ida went to fetch the eyeglass case that held a tiny plastic zip-lock bag nearly filled with white powder. The leader of the Crowns then slept for thirty-six hours. Ida and Camille worked double shifts and took turns sleeping on a cot in the corner. Messages and messengers piled up outside the hospital room, while rumors flew and tensions rose.

It was the plastic surgeon who woke Lucille to remove the cast and clear the skin graft. Then followed an hours-long operation to insert a titanium cast of Lucille's lower jaw and implant teeth. Meanwhile, pressure outside the sickroom grew to near-hysteria. No one took charge of the Crowns, and while they waited for news or direction, the smaller gangs did not. They filtered into the Bed-Stuy turf from all five boroughs, unopposed. The Crowns were in danger of total collapse. The sisters reduced the heroin and, with the discreet help of the surgeon, brought Lucille back to the real world.

Lucille woke to find her head bandaged, with slits for the eyes, mouth, and rebuilt nose.

"No, I won't allow you to see your face yet," said the surgeon, who had been fully briefed by MacKenzie, and had no illusions about her patient. "Not until the stitches come out and the swelling goes down. You're healing well, but if you were to look at yourself now, you'd be back on full doses of heroin. So cut the shit and be a good patient; the worst is over."

"From your mouth to God's ears," Lucille managed to say.

"Then lie back and let Nature takes its course. No drugs but what I give you, which will be mostly vitamins and protein supplements. Let yourself heal."

"Now you're shittin' me," Lucille mumbled between swollen lips. "Every gang in New York, and some from Jersey, are tryin' to take over my territory."

"Attend to the things you can change, and ignore the ones you can't."

"Layin' here, I can't do diddly-shit."

"You can think, can't you? And any orders you

relay through your, uh, attendants will be obeyed, right?"

"I guess so."

"Then use your mind to think your way out, and then give orders. Remember, every problem presents opportunities; think about the opportunities. Other than that, concentrate on healing. With any luck, you'll leave here in maybe two weeks."

"Without the bandages?"

"They'll come off."

Jill recommended that Mac move her team headquarters from the battleground at Bed-Stuy to Red Hook Hospital while the formidable Ms. Basch dealt with bureaucracy in Ridgewood. Red Hook was a very old and stable Irish neighborhood, where the hospital treated mostly children's injuries and car accidents.

The Gaeilic gangs dated back to the Civil War, and allowed no intrusion. They were quietly active, and on good terms with their cousins on the police force. They were more interested in maintaining public peace and control of their neighborhoods than in expansion or drug money and the trouble that comes with it. Their income came from the piers, container shipping, illegal liquor, untaxed cigarettes, protection rackets and loan sharking. The violent-crime rate was very low, and the streets were quiet.

Red Hook had third and fourth generation Greeks, Jews and Poles; together they outnumbered the Irish, but they rarely organized new or younger gangs. What gangs they had morphed into cultural societies based around churches, synagogues, and sports teams. The neighborhood suffered a normal accident rate, which increased on the weekends, since bar-fighting was an old tradition among the Irish. Other than that, the Hookers were a hardy and independent lot, and Mac's crew were kept busy but not overwhelmed.

"Wake up!" Big Bill shouted. "House fire! Multiple firemen and civilians with smoke inhalation. Possibility of contaminants."

The main ambulance, followed by three others, raced up Lormier Street to the new five-star McCarren Hotel. Behind the tall beautiful building with trimmed lawns and landscaped grounds were rows of tar-papered, three-story, hundred-year-old buildings. It was from one of these houses that firemen came stumbling into the street, guiding a group of civilians. They held their own oxygen masks over the faces of men, women and children.

Mac was almost knocked over as Bill, Floyd and the crew ran by, carrying oxygen masks and tanks. The firemen refused aid until the civilians were taken care of. Mac found and approached the chief. "Is it asbestos?" she asked.

"Don't know," he said, "But I think they're all contaminated: seven of my men, and six civilians."

"I'll farm out the civilians to Bushwick and Flatbush hospitals. Your men will remain in Red Hook."

"Appreciate that. I have a forensic team coming to identify the contaminant."

"The sooner the better."

Smaller gangs moved first against the Crowns. From Flatbush, Queens, New York and the Bronx they infiltrated Bed-Stuy's lucrative drug trade at street level, moving in their own dealers and pushing Crown dealers off the corners and out of the alleys. Scattered gunfights broke out on contested streets, keeping the ER busy.

Then came Iron Mike's funeral.

Twelve flower cars and ten limousines followed the hearse. A line of vehicles a mile long, accompanied by a police honor-guard and stuffed with celebrities—most of whom had never met Michael or Lucille—blocked traffic throughout Brooklyn. In the first limousine, Lucille with her bandages hidden behind a thick veil sat between two stars in the first limousine. Others followed in a Cadillac convertible. Speakers at the graveside included Congressman Waters, the mayor of New York City, Brooklyn's Borough President, and the Archbishop of the First Abyssinian Baptist Church of Harlem. They praised Michael Leissner as a "community activist", a "champion of youth employment", and a founder of "local athletic teams". A bugler from the local National Guard armory played "Taps", and the church choir sang "Steal Away To Jesus" in four-part harmony. The floral donations covered Michael's grave to a height of seven feet.

The sheer spectacle halted gang activities for the whole day.

Lucille fainted when Michael's coffin was lowered into the grave, and she returned to the hospital by ambulance with Percy, Alphonso, Jill and Floyd tending her.

"Now the shit will really hit the fan," Jill said as they left Lucille's room.

"How do you mean?" Floyd asked.

"The smaller gangs have already moved into Bed-Stuy, and the larger gangs will come next. There are bound to be more than enough casualties to keep us tied up."

"So what can we do?"

"For ourselves? Just keep working. For everyone else in town? Go to a basement corner with concrete walls on every side. Sit on the floor with your knees up. Bend forward, put hour hands behind your head and your head between your knees, and kiss your sweet ass goodbye."

After the funeral, the smaller gangs moved more cautiously into Crown territory. Housing projects and neighborhoods of Bed-Stuy were targeted by two-man teams. Once promising sites were chosen, five cars carrying five men each drove up and set a safety perimeter with twenty armed men, and then opened for business. At first they made no further attempt to force Crown dealers off their corners; they simply lowered prices and sold a better-quality product. Only after a week did they start using their now superior numbers to slowly push the Crowns out. The uncoordinated response from the Crowns encouraged the smaller gangs and whetted the appetites of the larger ones. The Crowns lost territory, money, and respect.

The Mafia watched and waited. Cheech, the new

Italian consigliore, held the larger gangs back predicting that the small gangs would get greedy and over-extend themselves. The more territory they occupied the fewer men they had for protection; then Cheech would unleash the larger gangs and take the territories.

Mr. G and the Russians waited on tenterhooks for a revenge attack. Every Black man or woman entering Brighton Beach was suspect. The strain took its toll on the Russians, and nerves were frayed. Mr. G, waiting to see what the Crowns would do, wasn't yet ready to go on the offensive. Tension in the police precincts and on the streets was thick enough to taste. Police, firemen, other First Responders, and their families living outside the city kept the radio and TV news turned on, anticipating the war in Brooklyn.

Thus passed Christmas, not very merrily.

Finally the Gambino family summoned the Brooklyn gangs to a meeting at the Hombre House, on Myrtle Avenue in Brooklyn. The area was controlled by Three-Finger Brown, a Gambino under-boss, and his restaurant was considered neutral territory. The meeting was chaired by Cheech—a.k.a. Charlie Giambavlo—forty-five years old, six-foot two, dapper consigliore to the New York City Mafia families. He had inherited his position from his father; he was comparatively young, but had a Big Belly—Italian for a lot of guts. He brought senior Police Inspector (retired) Jim Moran with him as a safety measure.

Outside the restaurant, FBI agents walked

through the freezing parking lot, recording license numbers.

Cheech opened the meeting by recognizing the Mafia leader and then the five major gang leaders, by name, in their order of importance. The Crowns were listed third, after the Crips and Bloods, but well ahead of Black Lives Matter.

Lucille sat in a wheelchair, hands folded, head swathed in bandages. Cheech added his wish for her speedy recovery, and added: "Lucille, at my request, Mr. G is absent. He is represented by the well-known Russian arbiter, Taguir Abazov."

"What the fuck is an arbiter?" the Flatbush crew leader demanded.

"It's English for consigliore," said Cheech, not batting an eye. "He is here, as we all are, at the request of Don Lorenzo Manino, Capo di Tutti Capi. The Don's absence is regrettable, but he is busy with... other affairs." He didn't mention that the particular affair today was a colonoscopy. "His message is: 'Business, blood and bullets don't mix'. If you want to make money, then no fighting. If you want revenge—" he glanced at Lucille "—or someone else's territory, we Italians will step aside and let you go at it. But—"

Cheech slammed his fists on the table so hard that glasses jumped, drinks spilled, and men flinched.

"—don't touch Mafia territory or our people. Those are sacrosanct." He glared at the Flatbush gangster and added: "For this stupid son of a bitch, 'sacrosanct' means Mafia money, territories, businesses and people are holy. So are civilians. They are so fucking holy that we have commitments from Italy, Canada, Mexico, Puerto Rico, South America and fifty American states to back us in a war of obliteration against anyone who violates them. For you other dumb cunts, 'obliterate' means to wipe you out. Got that? Okay, then I now open this meeting for discussion of our problem."

"First we should define the problem," Inspector Moran noted.

"To be sure, that's easy enough, boy-o," said Frank MacClenny of Red Hook. "Little Miss Lucille, sittin' so quiet with her head covered in bandages, wants to kill Mr. G and every fuckin' Russian alive..."

"Right," said Lucille.

"...And while she goes about murderin' the Jew, we take over—lock, stock, and barrel."

"Wrong," said Lucille.

Russian mobster Abazov raised a hand, and Cheech recognized him. "You first put the horse in the cart," he said.

"You fuckin' Russians have got to learn English," MacClenny laughed. "It's 'the cart before the horse'."

"I meant what I said. The horse is the small gangs moving into Bed-Stuy. How do we get them into the cart and push them out of the neighbor-hood?"

"Keep your fucking ideas to yourselves," Lucille growled, her voice surprisingly strong. "That means all of you. I'll take care of the small gangs—and any one of you motherfuckers who tries to take my turf.

If civilians get hurt in Bed-Stuy, that's my business. No Guinea goombas ever ran Bed-Stuy, and you're not going to tell me how to run it now. Anyone sniffing for weakness in my organization will have his head cut off and shoved up his ass."

She jumped up from the wheelchair and pointed at Abazov. "You appear to be a reasonable man, but I'm going to kill you and that Jew bastard and all of you fucking communists for what you did to me and my boy. It's war." From the slits in the bandages her eyes seemed to glow like burning anthracite as she gazed at each man at the table. "And it's war with any of you who support these commie bastards."

She strode toward the exit, stopped, turned and pointed at the wheelchair. "That's for Mr. Abazov," she snapped. "He's going to need plenty more."

Lucille left the Hombre House surrounded by bodyguards and entered a bulletproof Cadillac. Once inside it she whipped out her cell-phone, pushed the pre-dialed number, and asked: "Is the microphone working?"

"It's perfect," Ida answered. "The wheelchair must be near the middle of the table. I can hear everyone."

"At least I got their attention. What are they saying?"

There was long silence while Ida listened and made notes.

"According to Cheech," she reported, "You're one mean mother. He claims its war between Bed-Stuy and the Russians. The others will have to choose sides. They're arguing that now."

There was another long silence before Ida had news.

"They've pretty well all sounded off," she said.

"What does Red Hook say?"

"The Irish want no changes or invasion of their territory. They'll stay neutral unless attacked."

"I can arrange that."

"Why? Let them stay neutral."

"I've had time to think. What do Bushwick and Flatbush say?"

"Nothing."

"No answer is still an answer."

"And what's that?"

"War. It's logical. They border our territory, and together with the Russians, they outnumber us four to one. What do the Italians say?"

"Cheech repeated his warning about businesses and civilians. Moran added cops to the no-hit list."

"That's a given."

"The Russian, Abazov, admires your figure."

"What did he say?"

"He said: 'We may have fucked up her face, but she surely has a sweet ass. Put a barrel over her head, and problem solved'."

"He's got good taste. Remind me of that barrel joke when I kill him."

CHAPTER 20:
MANEUVERING

MADISON STREET

The old Salvation Army building on the corner of
Madison and Bedford streets now served as the
Crowns' headquarters, and there Lucille plotted her
campaign. Ida and Camille were left waiting in he
outer office.

"What the hell is she talkin' to Little Joe about?"
Camille fretted.

"She's planning strategy," Ida answered.

"Our bro doesn't understand shit. Little Joe ain't
got enough smarts to wipe his ass. Our people wanta
take out the small gangs, and Lucille's askin' Joe for
advice?"

"She's talking to Little Joe to hear herself think."

"She'd better find someone else. Our bro's a dollar short in the brain department."

"Girl, Lucille is really listening to herself."

"Why?"

"'Cause she's the smartest one around."

"You shittin' me?"

"Nope. In junior high school she tested at a hundred and fifty IQ."

"What's that?"

"It measures how smart you are. The highest ever in our school was one hundred and twelve. She was smarter than the teachers."

"Don't they have special programs for kids like that?"

"Yeah, but she got knocked up with Michael."

"If she's so smart, didn't she know 'bout condoms and the pill?"

"She liked to fuck. Still does, and that cocaine she's shooting don't help."

"The bandages come off next week. If she's got her nose back, she can sniff again."

In fact, Lucille had already decided to quit cold turkey. In her one-way conversations with Little Joe, she ordered him to stop all drugs from coming into her presence. He was to prevent her from using, even if he had to hold her hands to stop her. She then followed the plastic surgeon's advice and listed her problems in order of priorities, and discussed them with herself through Little Joe.

"Little Joe, from now on, call me Lucille."

"Yes, Miz Leissner."

"Lucille!"

"Miz Lucille.

She accepted the compromise and went on, pacing back and forth. "Now, you sit and listen. We talked before about my face, the operations, my recovery, and stopping drugs. Next week the bandages come off, and I have to lead the Crowns. That requires discipline. I must show power. I have to be swift and decisive. It will take the maximum amount of discipline to win this fight. I must put the fear of hell into my people. They have to fear me more than the enemy. In the end I get my revenge on the Russians, hold my territory, and take over the Flatbush and Bushwick turf. Then I negotiate better terms with the Mafia for their police protection."

Little Joe grunted. He hadn't understood any of that, but whatever Miz Lucille said was okay with him.

"You're a good listener. Heh! I'm a real Leissner, but a better talker. The plan is to take out the small gangs without fighting, and tear the larger gangs a new asshole. I must keep the Irish and the Mafia neutral until things fall into place. Yes."

For the first time since Michael's death, Lucille felt in control again. She went to the door, opened it, and shouted to the outer office: "Camille! Order in Peking duck, pork friend rice, and wonton soup, from Ming Wong's this time. I'll give my new teeth a real workout. Ida! Arrange a meeting of the Crown's leaders for Wednesday evening."

Camille darted for her phone, but Ida paused to ask: "Isn't that the day your bandages come off?"

"That's right." Lucille ground her teeth. "I want them to see what a real monster I am."

"It's too soon!"

"It's not soon enough. I don't have to look at me; they do. They have to obey me, or we'll all be in deep shit."

"How the hell can we win?"

"By copying Napoleon and Sam Austin; play both ends against the middle. Also arrange for a photographer to take pictures on Wednesday night. Some of us will be dead before this is over."

"The way the street's talking, everybody will be dead."

At about the time that Mac and the Widowmakers were finishing dinner at the Greek's, the Crowns' street-captains gathered in the gymnasium of the old Salvation Army building. Folding chairs were lined up on the dusty basketball court, which was so narrow that the foul-line on one side was three feet up the wall. Older men told stories of how they'd beat better teams there because it was legal to dribble and bounce-pass off the wall; by the time the visiting teams got used to that, they were too far behind to catch up.

Lucille stood in the shadows of the balcony, looking down at the crowd, going over her meticulous plans for every possible scenario. She watched men set up the head table beneath a broken blackboard. She watched Ida and Camille spread a four-by-eight-foot sheet of clear plastic on the floor between the head table and the first row of seats. She watched men below swapping jokes and friendly insults despite the thick tension. Since Michael's death there had been a general sense of desperation to sort out the leadership of the Crowns: now men stood in groups, eyes darting back and forth, searching for signs of alliances or betrayals. Lucille allowed the tension to build. Everyone in the room knew it was decision time: war or capitulation. The smaller gangs were openly challenging the Crowns. So far, except for a few incidents, Lucille's orders had held—self-defense, but no retaliation. It was time to change that.

She had selected Greco as her second in command. An ex-Marine sniper with thirty-three confirmed kills, six feet four inches tall and a fitness-freak, he had muscles in his ears and intelligence between them. She summoned him now.

"You see Bucky Walters and his lieutenant talking to the crowd around him?" She pointed them out.

Greco nodded. "He's been agitating since he came in."

"When I call him up front, see that his lieutenant comes too. Now you and Little Joe escort me downstairs to the head table."

Earlier that morning the plastic surgeon had removed the bandages, allowing Lucille for the first time to see her rebuilt face. As much as she had prepared herself, Lucille had almost fainted. The grotesque face staring back from the mirror was unrecognizable; the eyes and cheeks were swollen, the lips distorted, and the jaw tracked with two hundred stitches and metal staples. Most of the stitches had dissolved in the skin and the remains were easily brushed away, but the staples had to be plucked out one by one by one, painfully. Surprisingly, her nose appeared closest to normal. Ida and Camille had wept at the sight of her, and that had stiffened Lucille's spine.

"You girls stop that, now," she'd said. "You're going to bandage me up, and then unwrap me at the meeting tonight."

Lucille marched to the stage, pulled a chair out in front of the table and sat smoothly, Ida and Camille flanking her, Greco and Little Joe beside them. The chairs on the basketball court were full of men, teen-age boys and a few girls, and others slouched against the old painted brick walls, all of them watching intently. Lucille signaled to Ida and Camille, who began unwrapping her bandages. Everyone in the hall fell silent, watching. As instructed, just before Lucille's face was exposed the two women stepped in front of her, blocking everyone's view. Then they removed the last piece of gauze and stepped away, revealing her face.

Many of the toughest men gasped. Others shuddered and looked away. Lucile remained silent and motionless for long seconds, watching their reactions, before she spoke.

"For this," she said, pointing to her face, "And for killing my son, I want revenge."

A great sigh went up from the crowd.

"The doctors replaced my left cheek with skin from my arm," she went on. "That's why I had a cast that made it look like I was saluting. My jaw was blown away, so they took the fibula bone from my right leg and made me a new jawbone. Into that they put false teeth made of titanium. My eyes weren't injured, so I can see what's going on. My brain wasn't touched, so I know what's been happening and what to do about it. But I need to be certain there are no traitors here tonight that'll try to stop me from guiding us to victory."

Most of the men stopped looking at Lucille's scarred face and glanced around for signs of danger or alliance.

The danger came soon enough. Bucky Walters' voice boomed: "An' we got to know if you got the balls for this fight."

Lucille was surprised that Bucky had challenged her so early in the meeting. He must have been planning this since the day of Michael's death. She looked to Greco and Little Joe, who were frowning wordlessly. Yes, they'd be loyal. "Bucky boy," she called, pointing to the plastic sheet on the floor in front of the table, "You come forward, and share with us your point of view. Go ahead and speak your mind."

Bucky and his lieutenant, with no urging from anyone, stood up and swaggered to the plastic-carpeted section of floor, where Bucky took a preacher's pose.

"We're the Crowns!" he shouted. "We don't take shit from on one, but since Michael died there ain't no respect on the street, in the neighborhood, or in all Brooklyn for the Crowns. We're coastin' on the reputation of bein' the baddest mo'fuckers around, but that's wearin' thin. Even the Chinks from the city helped the Russians against us. The cops complain because our business is fallin' off, so they're getting' less payola. An' the reason business is off is because of the little gangs! Those fuckin' little bastards invaded our territory, an' you told us to back off! The Bushwick an' Flatbush guys are droolin', waitin' to jump us. You all know that!

"An' now we got what the Guineas call a vendetta with the Russians. Miz Lucille says the Irish an' the Wops will stay neutral, but when they see our money flowin' into other pockets, they'll want some of that action. We're gonna get hit by the Russians, Bushwick an' Flatbush together, that's for sure. We gotta show strength! In one night we can clean the little pissants out of Bed-Stuy. It's the only way to get back our respect, and we gotta have that to beat the odds against us. Miz Lucille, she's not Iron Mike. She done suffered greatly, an' I respect that, but she can't lead the Crowns."

Lucille stood and pointed at Bucky. "And just who," she asked, her voice laced with sarcasm, "Would you like to have lead us?"

"You sure ain't doin' it!"

"You think you can do better?"

"Yeah!"

Lucille reached behind her back, under her waistband, pulled out an old .38 Combat Masterpiece revolver and shot Bucky between the eyes. Blood and brain-flecks spouted out the back of his head, spattering his lieutenant and a dozen people in the front two rows. She turned the gun on the lieutenant and fired. He collapsed on the plastic sheet beside Bucky.

"Does that answer your question about whether I've got the guts?" she asked the crowd.

Nobody said a word.

She pointed to the bodies and turned to Greco while shoving the pistol into the front of her waistband. "Wrap them up," she said, "But leave them there for now." Greco and Little Joe hastened to comply.

"Bucky Walters was right," she said, turning back to the stunned crowd, "But I'm not wrong. Yes, we're in deep shit, but I can get us out, and we can make money doing it. Bucky was right when he said I was no Iron Mike—but neither was my son. That was a name and reputation that I built for him. You senior captains know: I was the brains that brought the Crowns up from a handful of hubcap-stealing glue sniffers to the multi-million-dollar organization we have today. Every move Michael and the Crowns made was dictated by me. Every alliance and every fight was approved by me. I brokered the deal with the Italians, the Irish and the Muslims. My plan is for the Crowns to come out on top again, and I know how to do it. Anybody who doubts me is free to leave."

Nobody did.

Lucille patted the revolver in her waistband. "If you don't take the opportunity to go that means you're prepared to fight to the death. This battle is for your lives, your families, and their futures. Make no mistake about it; people are going to die, and get hurt. Now Bucky said I've got no balls. In one sense he's right, and that's why I love to fuck. But if he meant courageous balls, then let me tell you, I've got balls of brass—and in stormy weather, when they clang together, then lightning shoots out of my ass."

She waited for the nervous laughter to finish.

"I'll share with you most of my plan. If you leak any of this information, you'll be killing yourself—if I don't kill you first. Bucky was right about another thing when he said the little gangs are challenging us, and we do nothing. Well, consider why I held you back. Consider that the more they spread out, the thinner they're spread. The smaller fish are taking our territory, but who else wants our money-makers? That's right: the Bushwick and Flatbush boys, and the Russians. If we let the smaller fish in, the bigger fish will be forced to stop them. Why not let them do the work for us?"

An older captain raised his hand to be recognized before he spoke. "That still doesn't solve our problem," he said respectfully. "Those three big gangs still outnumber us."

"By five to one," Lucille agreed. "Still, I have a plan to even the odds. We can win this fight—but only if there's strict discipline. We have to be a real army now. You get an order, you do it: no questions or hesitation. That was Bucky Walters' mistake. If you follow me, we'll take the prime territories and have those gangs working for us. Then we cut into the Mafia's construction, garbage, trucking and banking businesses." She clenched her fists, raised both hands and shouted: "The Crowns will rule! The Crowns will rule!" The crowd took up the chant.

That was the signal for men to enter the gymnasium carrying buckets of fried chicken, sliced watermelon soaked in gin, and ten cases of canned cold beer. The crowd plunged into the feast with a will.

Lucille took Greco aside and whispered: "Use half a dozen of your most trusted men. Have them circulate in the crowd and get me the names of those who side with Bucky. My rule must be like steel."

Then she took Little Joe aside and quietly told him to drag the plastic-wrapped bodies out into the alley and shove them onto a waiting truck.

Little Joe faithfully did as he was told, and didn't notice that the driver had a persistent cough.

The table was cleared in the rear of the diner. The meal had been splendid, but the usual banter was lacking. Mac, understood; they had to make a serious decision, to continue or disband the Widowmakers. She raised her glass to bring the meeting to order.

"Correct me if I'm wrong," she said, "But in reference to Rosie, Big Bill decided the outcome. Regarding the Grandpa Dumping, given the situation, the family is not to be punished. The man is a veteran and deserving of respect, and he'll be admitted to our hospital. Ms. Basch has contacted trustworthy public services to get the family, such as it is, into decent housing and provide care for the father once he's discharged.

"The next case comes to us from Mayzie. It concerns a wife and daughter severely beaten, and this is the third time we've been made aware of this man's abuse of his wife and child. Martha will give us more details."

Martha peered briefly at her notes. 'The subject,

referred to as John Doe," she said, "Is thirty-nine years old, born in Tijuana, Mexico, abandoned as a child, grew up on the streets working for drug cartels and as a male prostitute. He fled Mexico to San Francisco. Mexican police have two warrants on him for murder of women, and a third for trafficking minors for prostitution."

"If the San-Fran police know that," Big Bill asked, "Why didn't they deport him?"

"San Francisco is a 'sanctuary city'," Floyd sneered. "I lived there. The city authorities won't assist in immigration enforcement and deportation."

"Why?"

"It's politics—local rights against the federal government—and harvesting lots of immigrant votes. It's wonderfully easy to register to vote in San Francisco. All you need is a driver's license, and nobody checks to see if it's faked. My question is why Mr. Doe left San Francisco."

"He was caught trafficking minors," said Martha, "Young White girls and boys. It seems it was alright for him to deal in Korean, Chinese, and Latino kids. The local authorities knew, but did nothing."

"Why didn't they lock him up?" Bill seethed.

"They would have had to turn him over to the federal government, which is currently run by the wrong political party." Martha smiled grimly. "So the San Francisco city council simply voted him persona non grata, and told him to get out of town. They didn't inform the FBI, or ICE, or anyone in Washington."

"He probably hitched his way three thousand

miles to New York," Jill guessed. "Thanks loads, Frisco."

"And is New York a sanctuary city?" Floyd asked.

"You bet your sweet bippy it is," Jill growled. "Our dear mayor is courting the Latino vote. He believes that in another ten years Latinos will outnumber all the other races and creeds in this country."

"Unless the Arabs beat them to it," Floyd chuckled.

"Return to the subject," Mac insisted.

"This sounds like one bad character," Alphonso piped up. "Do we vote now to kill?"

"That's up to everyone here," said Mac. "I haven't yet decided how we should do the voting."

"We just raise our hands," Percy offered.

"That's not proper. One person might be influenced by others."

"A secret ballot, then," said Jill. "All agree?"

"There's another problem," Floyd pointed out. "If we vote to kill this lowlife, just who is going to bell the cat?"

Everyone lowered their eyes.

"We'll worry about that if we get there," said Mayzie.

"The vote must be unanimous," said Mac, "Just like with a jury. One vote against, and we have no more to say on the matter."

Jill went to the cashier and brought back a handful of business cards. Nine of them she marked with an X. Then she handed each person one marked and one unmarked card. Finally she spread a napkin over an empty bread-basket. "If you put in the card with an X, it means John Doe dies. I'll go first. I'll palm my card so that no one can see it, put my hand under the napkin, drop the card, and pass the basket to my left."

"Before we go any further," Mac cut in, "I have a question. We haven't asked the wife. What if she says she doesn't want her husband killed?"

"We off the bastard anyway," Martha said grimly.

"I agree," Mayzie added. "Nine times out of ten, the wife defends the bastard who kicked the shit out of her."

"You're right," Mac sighed. "I've seen it."

"I agree too," Jill added. "And we don't tell her about it, lest she tries to stop us."

"What about the child?" Bill asked. "We can't tell her either."

"That's the real question," Percy said. "The mother's not protecting her own daughter. We have to do it for the kid's sake."

"Should we vote on that too?" Jill asked.

"Not separately," Mac decided. "The X card will represent both death and not informing the mother. That should make it harder to arrive at a death sentence."

She took the bread-basket, put her hand under the napkin and pulled it back empty. No one said a word as the basket passed around the table until it came to Jill. She placed her card, then removed the napkin, reached in the basket and pulled out a card. She held it up, and everyone could see the X marked on it.

She laid it on the table, reached in and took out another card—likewise, bearing an X. At each card, the intake of breath was audible. Every card showed an X.

Jill reached for the ninth and last card, scratched the bottom of the basket, then stood up and looked. "We're missing one vote," she announced.

"We didn't consider abstaining," Mac noted.

"Will the person who abstained," Mayzie said, "Please stand up and vote now?"

The other Widowmakers eyed each other and shifted in their seats, but no one spoke.

"What do we do now?" Alphonso asked.

"Take another vote," said Martha.

"No," Jill groaned. "The first was too nerve-wracking."

"Does the abstention mean they agree or not?" Bill asked.

"It means what it is," Floyd explained. "The abstainer is noncommittal, according to Robert's Rules. It doesn't affect a unanimous vote."

"How many agree with Floyd?" Percy asked, "And how many against?"

Hands went up around the table.

"The ayes have it," Jill announced. "We uphold the death penalty."

"Now, who's going to do it?" said Bill.

Everyone slumped in their chairs. Mac didn't raise her head for fear she would see her own guilt in someone else's eyes.

"It can't be anyone from our group," Alphonso insisted. "If we did, then we could only do it once.

Nobody with any connection to the ERs."

"Why don't we do what the Russians did?" Percy offered. "Hire hit-men."

"The Russians paid a hundred thousand dollars for Michael Leissner," Jill recalled.

"I heard it was fifty thousand apiece for Michael and Lucille," said Mayzie, "And the Russians paid only half."

"Ether way, it's out of our reach," said Mac.

"There may be another way," Jill considered. "Floyd has an important friend."

"...You mean, Lucille?" Floyd asked.

Jill nodded.

"I have a meeting with her next week."

"Would you... bring up the subject?"

"How?"

"Ask her straight out," said Jill. "What would it cost to kill this wife-beater and child-molester?"

"What's your meeting with her about?" Mac asked.

"I'm introducing her to a friend I worked with in the San Francisco VA hospital. She was a makeup artist for the San Francisco Play House, and she volunteered to help veterans with severe facial injuries. She's been with *The Phantom of the Opera* in New York for two years now."

"What's the relationship between a makeup artist and our request?" Mac puzzled. "Jill's right; just ask Lucille straight out."

"And she'll ask me why."

"For the Crowns, it'll be just another business deal," said Jill. "What do we have that they want?"

"How much do you think it'll cost to hire gunmen?" Mayzie asked.

"Assassination of a nobody like this abuser?" said Jill. "In Bed-Stuy the going rate is a thousand dollars."

"About a hundred dollars apiece," said Martha.

"Enough for tonight," Bill concluded. "Let Floyd talk with Miss Lucille. We'll meet next Wednesday to hear what's happening."

CHAPTER 21:
OPENING SKIRMISHES

THE ROLLER DOME

"Mr. G, how long before we move on the Crowns?"

"Soon. I thought that by this time Miss Lucille would have kicked out the smaller gangs, but she seems more interested in her plastic surgery than business. Get her wheelchair out of here and call in our captains for a meeting tonight. Tomorrow I'll meet with the leaders of the Bushwick and Flatbush gangs; we'll coordinate our move on Bed-Stuy with them."

"What about the Muslims from Bushwick?"

"What about them?"

"You owe them $50,000."

"That's the Chicago Muslims, and only when the job is done. There aren't enough rag-heads left in Bushwick to make a difference. Tell our captains to bring a list of their men, the weapons they have, and those who need weapons and ammunition. We're going to war."

THE SALVATION ARMY BUILDING

"It was smart to plant a microphone in that wheel-chair," Greco said. "Too bad they're gonna ditch it."

"That's all right," purred Lucille. "We learned what we needed."

"So they'll go after the smaller gangs for us?"

"That's all who'll be out on the streets when the Russians come. I want our men only close enough to watch. I want to know what numbers and weapons the Russians have. Our people aren't the brightest bulbs in the box, so you'll have to tell them—probably several times—if fired upon, back off: no retaliation. It should appear we're retreating. Keep an eye on the Russians, especially Abazov and his people. Once they've shown what they can do, and they've driven out the small gangs, I plan on taking our territory back, with interest, before they can re-organize."

"Before I took this job, guys told me you were smart," said Greco. "I see they were right."

"Thank you kindly, Greco, but you're going to be doing the work. Tomorrow's Tuesday. I have a meeting at 3 PM, and I don't want to be disturbed."

"I want to suggest something, if ya don't mind. When you speak to our gang captains, be careful of your language?"

"What the fuck are you talking about?"

"That's more like it. Since you've been in the hospital, you talk to us like you do to the doctors and nurses, and it makes the guys nervous. Throw in a few shits and bitches and motherfuckers.'

"Stop," said Lucille. "It hurts my face when I laugh. My mama washed my mouth with soap for using that kind of language."

"What about your father?"

"He taught me."

The Bushwick and Flatbush gangs scouted Bed-Stuy turf because they were paid to, not out of any love for the white-skinned Russians. On a Brooklyn street-map they pin-pointed for Abazov some twenty-three locations where five or more members of the smaller gangs were operating. Mr. G then rented no less than fifteen limousines with dark one-way windows.

At 6 PM on Monday evening the limousines, carrying five men each, descended on the smaller gangs' locations and overwhelmed all resistance with maximum force and speed. There were only two brief gun-fights. For the rest the Russians used metal bars to punish the intruders, very specifically breaking their right forearms and left shins before darting away into the dusk. Unseen observers took notes.

RED HOOK HOSPITAL

Mac stormed out of the Red Hook office and into the ER, demanding: "Why is everyone running around, and where are all the ambulances going?"

"The shit hit the fan," Jill reported. "Bed-Stuy has gone crazy; the Russians invaded."

"Gunshot wounds?"

"Mayzie got two. Mostly it's beatings requiring hospitalization."

"Get Mayzie on the phone."

"She won't answer. She's got patients in all the beds, on the floor, and under the beds."

"Tell someone in Bushwick to send the overflow to Big Mama."

"Mama's full up already. That's why our ambulances are scrambling."

"We'd better get ready, then."

"That's why we're running around."

"Okay. Good job," Mac admitted, pleased to see how her organizing work had progressed. The taxpayers, she judged, were getting their fifty million dollars worth of improvements. She phoned the hospital operator and reported: "Put the 911 operators on notice; all our ambulances are occupied for the next six hours. Call in doctors to all Brooklyn hospitals. This is a Class One emergency."

The first Bushwick ambulance arrived at Red Hook with two patients, and Mac heard the medic shout: "Multiple cuts to the head, broken right elbow and left ankle. The patient is in shock." A moment later his partner reported the other patient with almost identical injuries.

Through the night Brooklyn's streets were lit by the flashing lights of ambulances and police cars, and loud with the sound of sirens. Mac opened ten beds in the Ridgewood VA for patients, and till had to transfer others over the bridge to Bellvue Hospital in the city.

During a moment's respite Mac asked Jill: "You

said this happens every few years?"

"You can practically set your clock by it."

"How can politicians and police allow it to go on? New York is the greatest city in the United States; how can people live with this?"

"It's just part of the scenery." Jill shrugged. "It's been going on for centuries. Even Peter Stuyvesant and the Dutch had to deal with gangs. The citizens will get up in a couple hours, have coffee, listen to the news about gang-battles in Bed-Stuy, and then walk through and around the wreckage to get to work as usual. The mayor may think he runs this city, but all he and his cops do is direct traffic, pick up the garbage, provide clean drinking-water and transportation. He also has a pretty good fire system. The money is controlled by gangs, and not only street-gangs. I mean Wall Street, private businesses, manufacturers, and the fur trade. Everything is controlled by some group. If you're not getting paid off, you're paying for protection."

"Is it just New York, or other cities?"

"Other cities, certainly. In 1962 President Kennedy, and his brother who was Attorney General, did a study of America's largest cities. They concluded that if the corruption, mismanagement, and gang control of the cities wasn't rectified in five years, it would be impossible to improve conditions. That was in 1962. The teacher who told me that believed that JFK and his brother were killed because they went after the Mafia. She said it was hired guns from New York."

"Wait a minute. Sirhan Sirhan, who shot Robert

Kennedy, was a Palestinian.”

“Half the patients brought in tonight weren't born in America. My teacher said money has no nationality. And remember, JFK won against Nixon only because Illinois went for Kennedy. Now, who controls Illinois?”

“I don't know.”

“The Mafia owns Chicago. Chicago controls the state and everything in it. The Italians had a long-standing agreement with JFK's father, dating back to Prohibition.”

“But Obama was the junior senator from Illinois...”

“That answers your question.”

“Nice conspiracy theory, Jill.”

“Floyd, there are always conspiracies going on, great and small. It's just a question of which ones are successful. Most of them aren't, but a few of them are—very successful.”

“Let's get back to work,” Mac cut in. “Do the police expect more casualties?”

“No, it's over for now,” said Jill. “But they're trying to figure out the strange pattern of things.”

“You mean the broken right arms and left ankles?”

“No, that was a clear sign from the Russians not to 'cross' them again. The real mystery is the lack of Crown gang members among the injured. There wasn't a single one.”

“What does that mean?”

“It means that none of the Crowns were there when the Russians hit,” Jill explained. “Now Miss

Lucille and the Crown boys are among the ugliest gang-bangers you'll ever meet, and the Russians spilled Crown blood—Lucille's and Michael's—and as long as Miss Lucille lives, she'll pay back in blood. Yet she held her troops in reserve while the Russians ran around in her territory beating up minor punks from the small gangs. Why do you think that is?"

"She was studying the Russians' tactics," Floyd guessed. "Now that she knows precisely how they work, she's planning a major counterstrike."

"In that case," Mac sighed, "We'd better clean up, restock, and prepare for the next battle."

SALVATION ARMY BUILDING

Six-foot-tall Floyd Sorenson stood in the doorway of the office next to a five-foot-tall woman with flaming red hair, a freckled face, and mischievous green eyes.

"Who's the leprechaun?" Lucille asked him.

"Miss Lucille, allow me to introduce Amazing Grace. Grace Webb is in charge of makeup for *The Phantom of the Opera* on Broadway."

"And what is little Gracie doing here?"

"She'll teach you how to make up your face to cover the scars until they're fully healed."

"Does little Gracie have any questions."

"Yes, ma'am. How's the back of your belly-button?"

"What?"

"You wanted me to ask a question, so I did. What

I'd like to do first is test you for allergies." Grace limped forward, took Lucille's right arm, and cleaned it with an alcohol swab. "Oooh, you have nice-colored skin."

"We don't call it colored anymore. It's black."

"More like walnut color," said Grace, dabbing the cleaned skin with six different moist Q-tips.

"Black is Black. Did you ever work on a face as messed up as mine?"

"Several of them. Your doctor must have told you that the swelling and scars will eventually go away. You've been treated by one of the foremost plastic surgeons in the world. Her work impresses me, and so does your attitude. You aren't hiding or feeling sorry for yourself." Gracie stood back. "We'll wait five minutes to see if your skin reacts to any of those creams."

"How did you get into this line of work?" Lucille asked.

"I was a dancer, and a good one. I wanted to be a Rockette, but you had to be at least five-foot-six inches tall to be considered. Still, I had steady employment, and loved the theater. Male dancers liked me because I was small, and easy to throw and carry. One threw me a bit too far, and broke my knee."

"So that ended your career in the theater?"

"It would have, but a makeup artist friend who knew how much I loved the theater gave me part-time work with her. It came naturally to me, so she encouraged me to go to school. I completed the course, and the school hired me as a teacher.

"That's where Floyd came in. He had several severely disfigured burn patients in the VA hospital. I helped some of them, and the *San Francisco Chronicle* put me in their weekend centerfold. The manager of the San Francisco Play House read it, and hired me."

"What can you do with a mess like me?"

"You can call it skin camouflage. It's the application, by a specialist, of highly pigmented creams and powders which reduce the appearance of a mark, scar, or skin condition."

"You've got your work cut out for you."

"It seems you have no allergies. I'll mix several colors you can choose. I hope you don't mind, but I have to take photographs so I can plan just where and how to apply the makeup."

"That's alright as long as no one else sees them. Can I have a lighter shade of Black?"

"Any color you want, but I suggest you stay with what you have. Your skin is a rich walnut color, and naturally beautiful. I'll show you how to apply the different shades of makeup, and where."

"I have your answer," Lucille smiled.

"To what?"

"The back of my belly-button. It's playing tag with my liver."

CHAPTER 22: MAINTAINING THE PEACE

THE ROLLER DOME

"It's a problem, Mr. G. We took over the Bed-Stuy locations easily enough, but it takes three eight-hour shifts, twenty-four-seven to cover them. Our white skins stand out among the natives. Some restaurants refuse to serve us. Our people are attacked by adults and kids from the rooftops."

"By the Crowns?"

"No, not so far as we can tell. They're mostly kid gangs, but they throw rocks, bottles, and Molotov cocktails from the roofs. We need more men."

"I thought the color difference would be made up by the Bushwick and Flatbush gangs."

"They're part of the problem. They want a bigger piece of the pie: the prime drug-selling areas, the loan-sharking operation, and twenty percent of the docks, piers, and trucking."

"Impossible!"

"We may have to give it to them, Mr. G. My men are pulling eight hours on and eight off. They can't park their cars except in a guarded lot. They can't find rooms to sleep in, not anywhere in the neighborhood. The markets and liquor stores won't serve them."

"But you've heard nothing from Lucille Leissner?"

"Zilch. Nada. Not a peep."

"I never thought she would roll over and play dead."

"It's getting on everyone's nerves, but maybe that shotgun blast to the face scared her off."

"I'm not so sure. Keep everyone on their toes; she's a tough broad, and may have something planned. I'll try and talk the Black and Latino gangs from the Bushes into relieving our men, for a more reasonable price."

"As quickly as possible, Mr. G. My men aren't used to selling on street-corners all day and night. They're falling asleep standing up."

"Not while I'm paying them!"

THE SALVATION ARMY BUILDING

Days later Grace returned alone, toting a wheeled metal case as tall as herself. "This is my makeup department," she said, patting the case. "I have a problem."

"Spit it out," said Lucille.

"I'm afraid to come here."

"I'll send a limo and a couple of guys to pick you up and take you home. You'll be paid for your travel-time."

"That won't work. People in the city are talking about an upcoming battle in Bedford-Stuyvesant."

"They're right. So?"

"I've got another idea. What if you send Camille with me, and I teach her how to apply the creams, color and powder? In the beginning, someone will have to help you apply the stuff anyway. As you heal, each makeup session will take less and less time."

"Say, what happens if I get caught in the rain, or have to take a shower?"

"With the ointments I use, tears or perspiration or water won't affect your makeup. You'll have to remove it with a solvent cream."

"How can Camille learn to make up my face if I'm not there?"

Grace stood her cabinet on end and clicked open the latches, revealing shelves with rows upon rows of makeup creams and powders, brushes and mirrors. On the bottom was a towel-covered object which Grace struggled to lift and set on the table before Lucille. "Is Camille available?" she asked.

"Camille!" Lucille shouted, "Get your booty-ass in here! Gracie, you gonna tell me what's under that towel?" Camille hurried in and stood watching.

"Take it off and see," said Grace.

Lucille whipped the towel away, revealing a plastic bust.

"Oh, shit! That face is uglier than mine!"

"It *is* yours. Our theater prop-man made it from the photos. Now I'm going to work on you. Camille will work with me and on this bust. She'll have to visit me five days a week for a month—"

"Say what?" Camille yelped. "Where?"

"On Broadway," Lucille snapped. "You're gonna get a new education, girl. Go on, Gracie."

"By that time," Grace went on, "You'll be using half the makeup we put on today. I'll visit once a week to see how you're doing, and maybe take more photos as you heal."

"For a little red-headed leprechaun, you're an impressive lady. Let's get started; there's an important meeting tonight."

Grace began rummaging through her supplies. "Before there was the world's oldest profession, men and women were putting on makeup. Everyone wants to improve on what God gave them. I make a very nice living doing just that. Camille, I'll be talking to Lucille but I'm also talking to you, so listen carefully. I brought a pad and pen for you to take notes." She handed them to Camille. "You'll be doing the same thing over and over, but you'll apply fewer cosmetics as she heals. It's very important that Miss Lucille doesn't appear one day with pitch-black skin and the next day as a creamy mulatto. Consistency is the key; there must not be the slightest color or tone variation. I'll give you a color chart. Right now..." Grace handed Camille a small pink sponge. "We're going to clean the skin so we can lay on a strong foundation. I use soda-water with the sponge to clean the pores of the skin. Notice that I don't rub but dab gently, and not too many times in the same place. You'll see the dried blood around the stitch and staple marks fall away. It leaves a pinkish dot that will disappear. Now soak your sponge and try the right side of the face. Dab gently. Lucille, did you say that you had an important meeting tonight?"

"I did, and I do."

"I can make you up for the meeting. It won't be perfect, but—"

"Whatever you can do will look better than that." Lucille pointed to the bust.

"Then let's get cracking," said Grace. "The eyes frame the face. "I'm going to form an upside-down triangle with this ointment under each eye. Using the tip of your forefinger gently spread the cream in a circular motion down to the cheekbone until the cream is absorbed into the skin."

"Camille," Lucille warned, "You stick me in the eye with your long fingernails, and I'll have your ass for supper."

"Heh! Always thought you were part cannibal," Camille snickered.

"Enough of that," Grace went on. "Camille, you duplicate what I do on Lucille onto the plastic bust. The face will look fuller, since certain areas are swollen and puffy. Try to keep up with me. Use the same powders, colors, and greasepaint I do. Now we lay on the foundation, and then the eyelashes and liner. Hmmm, you have beautiful almond-shaped eyes... Close your eyes, now. I want to apply this yellow cream to the lids."

Little Gracie worked for a full hour and a half, her green eyes shining with intensity. She applied various tones to the ears, nose, and throat, then applied rouge to the cheeks, forehead, and chin. Lucille's face took on a form of normality. The transformation shocked Camille into silence. She stared, amazed, as Lucille's scars disappeared with each application. Now the ravaged features were gone, and Gracie took exceptional care in applying the lipstick.

Suddenly the scarred face was no longer there. Gracie dusted the forehead, nose, chin and cheekbones, and Lucille Leissner's face glowed. Not a sign of a stitch, staple-mark, or scar was visible. In her intense concentration Gracie had moved the mirror, so Lucille had no idea of the transformation. Camille was crying. She reached out and hugged Lucille so tightly that Gracie had to pry her away, singing: "Teardrops are falling on my art. You two both are taking part... in the rebirth of Miss Lucille Leissner."

Grace pulled the mirror over to where Lucille could see it. On viewing her reflection, Lucille looked behind her to the right and left, then at the half-worked plastic bust, and finally stared back at the face in the mirror. "Oh, my Lord! Jesus Christ sent you to redeem me from hell!" She stood and hugged Grace. "Can I touch it?"

"Certainly. Act normally. Just don't leave it on for more than two days; your skin has to breathe."

"Wait 'til they see me!"

"You really want to impress them?"

"I most certainly do."

"Wear a veil, and pull it off at the most dramatic moment."

"Camille, get down to Grandma Bailey's store.

Tell her I'm wearing a black silver-sequined dress with silver around the bust and a diamond necklace into the cleavage. Tell her I want a big hat with an opaque dark veil. She knows my size."

The meeting of the Crowns was called for eight o'clock, but it was close to nine when Lucille arrived. She sashayed into the rear of the crowded basketball court, a mysterious gorgeous figure in close-fitting silver and black, whose face was hidden by a black veil, followed by her two tall bodyguards. The balcony at the far end had standing-room only, but the people on the court parted before their leader like the Red Sea before Moses, all of them staring.

Grandma Bailey had used a broad-brimmed Panama hat to carry the veil. The form-fitting silver-sequined dress accentuated Lucille's body. Her full breasts looked ready to burst free of her bodice. As she passed she reveled in the adoration of her troops, the smell of their masculinity, and their heated whispers.

"I love my wife, but that woman am sleek and fine."

"She's built like a brick shit-house, sure 'nough."

"Good thing she wearin' that veil, 'cause the rest of her could knock your eyes out."

Lucille walked to the front table, flanked by Greco and Little Joe, but instead of taking a seat she stood before it, took up the microphone and said: "Look to your right. Shake the hand of the man next to you. Ask him where he's from, even if he's your blood brother. Ask where he lives, who's his under-boss and neighborhood boss. If you don't know him or he answers wrong, point him out to Greco. Do it now."

A man bolted for the exit, and was stopped by a baseball bat in the face. After another few minutes' scuffling, five men were brought forward. Two were verified as true-enough Crowns, just too high on drugs to remember their addresses, and they were taken out into the alley for some corrective punching. The other three were frog-marched to the sheet of plastic in front of the head table and forced to kneel facing the crowd.

Lucille walked behind them, jerked up the head of the man with the smashed face, and announced: "We're about to go to war. This is going to be a fight to the end. If we lose, we're dead. Our families are dead. There's no future.

"If we win, Brooklyn is ours for generations to come. Eventually New York will be ours, the Russians will be nothing, and the Mafia will be history. We no longer take orders from the spaghetti-benders. We are the Crowns!"

The building shook with the roar of approval, and the wood floor trembled under the stamping feet. Lucille waited a moment, then silenced the crowd with a gesture.

"If you want out, leave now." She pointed at the kneeling men. "Because I'm going to kill these spying motherfuckers. If you're here when I do it, you're accessory to murder. But if you decide to leave, get clean out of the state. If I find you, I'll kill you. Sneaky Pete, give me your razor."

The three men struggled frantically, to no effect. A tall thin man came forward and offered Lucille a pearl-handled straight barber's razor. She took it, flicked it open, tested it's sharpness on the ball of her thumb, and stepped closer to the smashed-face man. She pulled his head further back and slashed his throat in a single deep stroke, then held him upright until his twitching ceased and dropped him on the plastic. There wasn't a sound in the hall as she went down the line until all three lay still on the bloody plastic mat. The front row of men stepped back to avoid the pool of blood spreading across the basketball court. Lucille flicked blood off the razor and handed it back to Sneaky Pete.

"We're at war," Lucille repeated. "Like this veil I'm wearing, I've hidden my plans from those who want to steal from us. Well, those cocksuckers will learn they've got a wildcat by the tail. Yes, I purposely kept you from attacking the Russians and the small gangs. That forced the Russkies to clear the little punks our of our territory for us. Now the Bushwicks and the Flatbush boys are holding the Russians up for a bigger part of our territory than they bargained for. My aim is to get them fighting each other."

"Amen!" shouted a few voices in the crowd.

"How?" one of them asked.

"By surprise," said Lucille. "Like this one." She whipped away her hat and veil.

The crowd was stunned into silence. Lucille reveled in the effect for a long moment, and then ordered: "Captains, line up to get your orders from

Greco. You've been reporting on the Russians, the places they took over, and their defense teams. Now you'll get detailed instructions on how, where, and exactly when—to the minute —to attack each spot. You'll notice there's an avenue of escape left for each Russian target. If possible, I want them to run. If they don't, just kill them."

"What about the cops?" another voice asked.

"If you don't bother them, they won't bother you. We have until dawn, when the police patrols return to duty on the morning shift. Make yourselves scarce by then. Later, go back to your corners and sell, but don't carry weapons; just have them stashed nearby. Any of our wounded, take to Red Hook medical center or the Ridgewood VA hospital. We have a working arrangement with them."

CHAPTER 23:
OPENING SALVOS

RIDGEWOOD VA HOSPITAL

"Decision time," said Mac. "Big Momma wasn't with us when we took the vote. I gave her the opportunity to opt out of the Widowmakers."

"And what did she say?" Bill aked.

"She wants to be part of the group."

"Is that why you called this meeting?" said Alphonso.

"No. We have to keep our priorities in focus. As first responders we exist to serve the public, and a gang war is about the break out. Bed-Stuy will be the battlefield, and Big Momma's hospital will get most of the wounded. From what Floyd tells me, Red Hook will remain neutral. If you receive wounded from Brighton Beach, Brooklyn ER or Flatbush, treat them as quickly as possible and send them to their neighborhood hospitals. Should Big Momma's ER become overcrowded, send the Bed-Stuy people to Red Hook. If there's a dire emergency, send them here to the Ridgewood VA."

"The VA will treat them?" Percy insisted.

"It's the deal I made with the politicians to service the community... and to solve our problem of just who would terminate John Doe."

"You mean the abuser is part of the deal?" Martha almost whispered.

"Correct," said Mac—and warned Floyd with a stern glance to keep silent about the arrangement with Lucille.

"Isn't that dangerous?" Mayzie asked.

"I took that decision for the Widowmakers."

"Well, I agree. The less we know, the less we're responsible for. I meant transferring patients according to their gang affiliation instead of their types of injuries."

"It makes sense," Jill put in. "In the past, gangs carried their feuds into the hospitals. I once caught a couple of guys sneaking down the halls to kill a member of an opposing gang."

"So," Mac finished. "Are we all ready to roll?"

Everyone answered in the affirmative.

The clock on the Williamsburg Savings Bank closed in on midnight, and the streets were abnormally quiet. Here and there a car sped by, or an ambulance siren caused a dog to howl, but few pedestrians walked the streets. Buses and trains were empty.

In the Roller Dome Mr. G listened on the intercom as his captains reported in. Repeatedly he was asked: "What do you make of the quiet?"

To the last one he answered: "There's a storm coming; I feel it in my bones."

"But nothing's happening."

"That's not normal, and my informants in the Crowns are late checking in."

"Maybe there's nothing to report."

"Bullshit!" snapped Mr. G. "There was a big meeting, and I can't find out what happened. The Crowns must know we couldn't get the Bushwick and Flatbush gangs to help us, and our men are over-tired. They're up to something..." He was beginning to sweat.

It was twenty past twelve when he dropped into his desk chair, pressed the conference-call button and announced: "All captains, hear this. I expect you'll be attacked. Protect yourselves, but do not initiate action. If it's a determined action to dislodge you, withdraw—I repeat, withdraw—with as little gunfire as possible."

He was certain of only one thing; his men were more disciplined than the street gangs. They came from elite units of the Russian army and navy. Most were combat veterans of Iraq, Syria and Afghanistan. They might be outnumbered in hostile territory, but he could move them like chess pieces. His gut told him to be on guard. He had underestimated Lucille Leissner once before.

Lucille and Greco were perfectly aware of the Russians' capabilities, and the lack of discipline and training among their own troops, which was why they'd decided to attack now. The Crowns had the advantage of knowing the territory—the alleys, streets, roofs and basements. They weren't disciplined fighters, but the survivors of a hundred street-fights; finally released to fight the Russians, the Crowns lusted for vengeance on the White Europeans invading their turf.

At 2 AM groups of men in Bed-Stuy made their way into specified tenement houses and up onto the roofs. There, they lined up bottles of half-frozen kerosene with rag wicks soaked in gasoline. Others filtered into the streets. Cars moved to predetermined locations mapped out by Greco, carrying instructions on how and when to attack, and at least one man in every group was literate enough to read them. At every target Greco left a corridor for fleeing Russians to take, for he knew that they'd fight to the death if so ordered. He'd also insisted: "Do not fire unless fired on."

He took personal command of the largest group, whose targets were all four corners of the intersection at Gates and Nostrand Avenues. Each corner hosted a bar. From each of those bars, in addition to alcohol, drugs, gambling, and prostitutes were supplied. Tonight no drinkers, gamblers, dope buyers or johns graced any of those bars, and the silence of the street pervaded them.

At 2 AM those inside the bars heard a popping sound outside, and the glow from the streetlights went out, one after the other. Four flaming Molotov Cocktails arched down from the roofs, and each exploded before the entrances Lights in the four buildings went out. The Russians grabbed up their weapons and took up positions inside the bars. All they could see were vague shadows of armed men moving into the streets. Quickly-dispatched scouts reported no blockage of the back-door exits, just clear avenues of escape. Similar scenes took place throughout Bed-Stuy.

The attacks would have caught the exhausted Russians off-guard but for the warning from Mr. G. They soon saw that the Crowns were offering them safe passage back to Brighton Beach if they didn't fight. The Russian captains recalled their orders, and began to withdraw.

One captain sent two men to extinguish the flames engulfing the front door, A Crown fighter, high on meth, cut them down with a burst of automatic fire. The Russians' return fire killed him at once. Other Crowns opened fire *en masse*, but most were poorly aimed shots. The Russians replied with a deadly fusillade by expert marksmen.

The sounds of battle spread through Crown Heights and triggered sporadic gunfights up and down the avenues. At Four Corners, though outnumbered five to one, the Russians' response was so well coordinated, accurate and quick to reload that they forced the Crowns to retreat.

Once the shooting stopped, the Russians followed Mr. G's orders and withdrew to Brighton Beach.

The Roller Dome rink was swept clear, and two hundred mattresses, pillows and blankets lay side by side on the floor. Mr. G set up a defensive perimeter outside the building, and then sent out for a hundred pizzas and twenty cases of Smirnoff vodka. Only after the food and drink arrived did he go back to his office and to make a report to his superiors in Odessa. He ended it with the smug note: "The bitch is ingenious, but her troops are lousy shots."

He didn't mention that despite their losses, the Crowns had effectively chased his money-makers out of Bedford-Stuyvesant.

The ER team crowded into Mac's office as Jill folded the copy of *The Brooklyn Eagle* in half, then in half again. "Read it aloud," Martha urged, as soon as the door was shut. "Let's hear what Goldberg says about last night."

"Who's Goldberg?" Floyd asked.

"I think it's a nom-de-plume, but he knows more about the gang scene than any three other reporters," Percy explained. "He's either got a very good source in the police department, or he's secretly a cop himself."

"So read it aloud already," Alphonso said.

"Okay," said Jill. "The headline is: 'WAR IN BROOKLYN'. The sub-head says: 'Americans may be fighting enemies in Afghanistan, Beirut and Syria, but it's Americans versus Americans in Bedford-Stuyvesant'."

"Not with artillery at least," Bill chuckled. "Read on."

"Okay. 'Last night's crime wave was the opening salvo in a multi-sided gang fight. The prize is the drug, prostitution and protection rackets up for grabs in Bed-Stuy.

"'It began with the unexplained shooting of Iron Mike Leissner's mother at the amusement park in Coney Island. The Russian mob maimed Ms.

Leissner, but failed to kill her. Iron Mike, leader of the powerful Crowns gang, swore vengeance.

"'The Crowns then pulled off a raid in the Russian mob territory of Brighton Beach. The invasion tricked the Russians and made them look weak.

"'The Russians retaliated by killing Iron Mike in an elevator of Bushwick Hospital while on the way to assassinate his mother. Again they failed to kill her.

"'Ms. Leissner proved that she really is one tough mother by organizing last night's attacks on Russian drug dealers who had infiltrated Bed-Stuy after Iron Mike's death. According to police observers, it was a cleverly conceived plan but poorly implemented. The Crowns made well coordinated attacks on Russian drug-dens throughout the neighborhood, but faltered at a site on Gates Avenue. Some of the Crowns were high on drugs, and fired at the Brighton Beach mobsters while they were withdrawing peacefully. This made the Russians dig in and fight. Though fewer in number, the battle-wise Russians responded with sufficient force to drive the Crowns back. They then evacuated and returned to Brighton Beach, leaving the Bed-Suy territory in Crown control. It appears that both sides originally tried to avoid casualties, but drugs, nerves and inexperience caused the shootings. Known battle losses are:

"'Crowns: 24 wounded, 7 dead.

"'Russians: 8 wounded, 5 dead.

"'Several of the wounded are in critical condition. Funerals for the Crowns dead will be announced later this week. The bodies may be viewed at Wick's

Funeral Home at the corner of Bedford and Flatbush Avenues, Brooklyn. Of the Russian dead, three will be transported to their homeland for burial in family plots and two will be interred locally.

"'The police are investigating the conflict, and arrests are imminent. Police refuse to speculate on why the Bushwick, Flatbush and Red Hook gangs held back from the battle, but street wisdom says these three wanted to see who was stronger, and then make alliances accordingly. Since the Crowns succeeded in taking back their territory, but suffered greater losses, that's a serious question.

"'A trusted source claims that the Bushwick and Flatbush gangs will honor an agreement to support the Russian mob, but the Red Hook faction will remain neutral.

"'This raises more questions. If the three mobs defeat the Crowns, how will the territory be divided? Will the Red Hook gang be included in the spoils? How will the Crowns' share of the protection money from trucking, construction and drug-smuggling be apportioned? The Crowns drove out the Russians because they outnumbered them, but that was on their own turf. Now the Crowns will face three times their number, unless they can gain allies fast. Will Red Hook stay neutral? If not, which way will they ally? The Russians have better troops, but Crowns have more to lose and therefore more to offer. Brookynlites got up this morning wondering what tonight will bring.

"'The one killing last night which seems unconnected to the war was in Brownsville, where Mr.

Julio Diaz was found dead in the street. He was apparently the victim of a robbery gone awry, shot twice in the head, his pockets turned inside out, and his wallet gone. Police had difficulty identifying him, as his wife and two children are presently in Bushwick Hospital with serious injuries. Mr. Diaz, who had a history of spousal and child abuse, was considered the cause of those injuries. Police speculate that the robbery may have been payback by his wife's family, who have not been found.'"

A moment's silence followed the reading.

"You're right about Goldberg," Floyd murmured.

"Diaz!" Martha burst out. "Was that our John Doe?!"

Mac only nodded.

"Hallelujah!" Martha shouted. "Thank God, the bastard got what was coming to him! Oh yes, there is justice in the world. I invite you all out for a drink on me."

Jill tugged Martha's sleeve. "Marty," she almost whispered, "You don't really want to go there."

"I'm allowed one drink," said Martha standing up, "And I can't think of a better occasion. See you later, at the Greek's."

"Not me or Bill, you won't," Jill sighed.

Mac only sighed, watching Martha leave.

No one else showed up at the diner. Martha drank alone. Kula and Floyd came in from a late movie to help Georgee close the diner and found Martha there. She was in no condition to drive, so they took her home.

Seven Crown warriors rested side by side, on plush white satin, in polished mahogany coffins. Their bodies were dressed in new blue jeans and Crown jackets open at the neck, with gold pendants on gold chains resting on their bare chests. Many of the mourners, both men and women, kissed the dead as they dropped black and white scarves—the Crown's colors—on the corpses. The seven families sat to one side, nodding quiet acknowledgment to words of sympathy from other mourners. While the rest of New York celebrated New Year's Eve, Bedford-Stuyvesant was grimly quiet.

On the second day of mourning an eighth body was brought in and another family added to the mourners. He had died in Red Hook Hospital from wounds received in the battle. Crown guards were doubled, and renewed every two hours, with no lack of volunteers for the duty. The flow of visitors was constant, orderly and respectful.

The visitors stirred when Little Joe led Lucille and Greco to the mourners. Lucille lifted her veil, and only those whom she hugged could discern the jagged scars on her face. It served to remind them that she too had just buried a son. She then went to each coffin in turn, knelt, prayed, and left a black-and-white kerchief on each body. She returned to the mourning families and asked: "Would you allow me the privilege of sitting with you? When my son died I was in the hospital, and couldn't go to properly mourn his passing."

The eight families promptly made room for her, and a wave of grief and anger swept quietly through the room. A lust for revenge flowed through all the Crowns present. Lucille felt it, and before she took her seat she announced: "Fear not, my brothers in Christ. We will have... satisfaction."

The funerals took place the next Tuesday, which was cold but unusually bright and sunny. The eight coffins were carried by forty-eight Crowns wearing their jackets and bandannas, and went across the street to the First Baptist church where the minister and entire congregation were out on the steps to receive them. The caskets were placed end to end down the center aisle leading from the entrance to the pulpit. The sobbing of women and the muttering of grim-jawed men accompanied the eulogies from New York's mayor, Brooklyn's Borough President, Congressman Waters and the minister.

After the service eight hearses led the way to the cemetery followed by eight flower-cars. After them were two hundred private cars and ten buses packed with neighborhood mourners. The New York City police, FBI, ATF and other special anti-crime units anonymously trailed the entourage, checking license plates and using photo-recognition equipment to identify any with outstanding warrants. New York's mayor had ordered no interference unless a blatant crime was being committed, for everyone knew that all the Crowns were carrying illegal weapons. The cortege proceeded slowly and quietly to the cemetery.

A problem ensued when two of the cars in the funeral cortege were identified as having been stolen the night before. An argument followed, between the mayor and the police, over whether to make an arrest; they compromised by planting tracking devices on both cars, with the intention of picking them up after the burial.

A platoon of fifty police in riot gear was stationed just out of sight at the cemetery, since it wasn't unusual for rival gangs to attack during funerals. The church supplied ushers who directed the parking of cars, placement of flowers, and seating of families and important guests. The service flowed smoothly and speeches were kept to a minimum.

Lucille was last to speak. She lifted her veil, and people gasped as the purple and blue scars on her face were revealed. She had cleaned off her makeup during the drive, and the revelation had the desired effect.

"A man is many things," she began. "Men come into this world as sons and brothers, and grow into friends, husbands and fathers. Most of these eight brothers were too young to be husbands or fathers, but they will always be our friends. We shall keep them alive in our hearts, talk to them in our prayers, love them forever—and exact retribution for them."

Her voice rose and fell, sliding into the pattern of an old Southern preacher, and the audience responded with Amens and Hallelujahs. She clutched the audience's hearts, and her voice trembled with passion. She spoke of the personal backgrounds of the eight martyrs, and her voice lowered to a deep fury as she spoke of the enemy. The crowd was riveted.

Few noticed the sleek six-door black stretch limousine that rolled past the parked cars and into the cemetery. Its windows were tinted black and its engine purred like a leopard.

It paused near the funeral party, and all six doors flew open. Three men on the near side crouched and automatic weapons. Three men on the far side got out, stood up, and fired over the car's roof at the crowd.

Little Joe shoved Lucille to the ground. Everyone else ducked, scattered, screamed, ran or fired back. Ignoring his own danger, Joe stood head and shoulders above everyone else, aimed carefully, and emptied his clip. Everyone else was firing by the time he reloaded. The Russians dived back into the limo, slammed the doors and sped off with bullets tearing holes in the vehicle and smashing its rear and near-side windows. Little Joe stood straddled over Lucille and wouldn't let even Greco help her up until he was certain the shooting had stopped.

"We can't ignore this," Greco shouted over the noise from the crowd.

"I know," Lucille growled.

The three of them watched while the police swept in with guns drawn, followed by three ambulances, sirens whooping.

Doctor MacKenzie led the three crews through the crowd, looking for the injured. To their amazement, they found no bullet wounds though easily a hundred rounds had been fired. There were only sprains, contusions, scrapes and other minor injuries caused when the crowd bolted, and they were easily treated at the scene.

Floyd asked Jill: "What's going on here? The attackers probably took more injuries than their targets."

"My cousin is in the police contingent," Jill said putting back a roll of tape. "I'll go ask him."

By the time Jill returned the crowd had broken into angry clusters, the biggest of them centered around Lucille, who was speaking fast but quietly.

"My cousin," Jill reported to Mac and Floyd, "Says that police intelligence thinks the Russians who shot up the cemetery were under orders not to hit anyone."

"Why?"

"To insult the Crowns in general and weaken Lucille in particular. They made it onto national and international TV news. Intelligence expects Lucille to come out fighting, but they also think this shows that the Bushwick and Flatbush gangs are siding with the Russians."

"I hope it won't disrupt our wedding," Floyd sighed.

"You and Kula are definitely getting married?" Mac asked. "No second thoughts?"

"Her father made it mandatory. He said something about bringing his 'Lupo'. What's that?"

"Bad, bad, bad," said Jill, shaking her head theatrically. "Very not good. It's Italian for a sawed-off shotgun, used for settling vendettas."

"Vendettas?" Mac puzzled.

"We've been staying out overnight," Floyd admitted.

"Worse!" said Jill, rolling her eyes.

"So when's the wedding?" Mac asked.

"Three weeks. Georgee's family is coming from overseas."

"Congratulations!" Jill and Mac said together.

"Do you think Bill will act as my best man?"

"If you survive the Lupo," Jill grinned.

"Mac, will you take the place of my mother in giving me away?"

"What about your parents?"

"...They passed, some years ago."

"Do you have siblings?"

"None."

"All right. It will be my pleasure, but I won't be giving you away; We'll be accepting you into our ER family."

CHAPTER 24:
STRANGE BEDFELLOWS

SALVATION ARMY BUILDING,
BEDFORD-STUYVESANT

Firefights, drive-by shootings and neighborhood gun battles erupted all over Brooklyn—but particularly in Brighton Beach, with secondary fights in Bushwick and Flatbush. The battles intensified at night, and now there were few sanctuaries. Churches, bars, and shopping centers were targeted. Schools, hospitals, and public service centers became no-man's land. Only First Responders—emergency rooms, firehouses, and police stations—were off limits. Even those were attacked by children's gangs from the rooftops, with Molotov cocktails, bricks, and sporadic gunfire.

The drive-by shooting was the Crowns' favorite mode of attack. Two or more cars, never predictable, swooped by spraying gunfire, and the targets were always important. With the war going on, distribution of street-drugs became dangerous and supplies dwindled. The Crowns having large reserves, Greco was exceptionally good at getting intelligence through the many addicts on the street. At the Crowns headquarters in the old Salvation Army Building he questioned informers, evaluated reports, and briefed Lucille.

He was in the middle of reporting his plan to trap an attack at Four Corners when she got a phone call and signaled him to be silent. She listened intently for a moment, then said: "There'll be five of us." She hung up and said to Greco: "Give that ambush plan at Four Corners to somebody else. You're coming with me."

"Where to?"

"Out of state."

"Both of us gone for even a short time is dangerous."

"We have to risk it. We're outnumbered and outgunned. This is the only way I can think of to win this war."

"What are you gonna do?"

"You know the answer to that."

"Well, everybody—including me—has got to keep this one. Little Joe and Chowder will be with us. You and Ida should have automatic pistols with lots of loaded extra magazines."

"How long we going for?"

"We leave in fifteen minutes."

"Dammit, Lucille..."

Three limousines pulled up to the loading dock behind the Salvation Army building, and three groups of five people, dressed in identical clothing, entered each one. One limo drove north to LaGuardia airport, another went east to MacArthur airport, and the third—with Lucille and her group—went to Kennedy.

"Where do I go?" the driver asked.

"International departures," said Lucille. "Shut off your radio and hand me your cell-phone."

He did, and she threw the phone out the car window.

"You'll be paid for that," she promised, "And for being detained at the airport. It'll be worth your time. Now go to the El Al departure lounge."

"Why El Al?" Greco asked.

"The best security in the world, especially against Muslims."

"You expect the Black Muslims to come against us?"

"I'm going against them. They killed Michael."

"I understand revenge, but you're just adding another enemy to a long list."

"I have a plan to turn that around."

She took a white handkerchief and waved it out the window at an Israeli security guard near the lounge entrance. He signaled back, and two men appeared at the driver's door. They motioned the driver out, one man got behind the wheel and the other escorted the driver into the building. They drove to the end of the lane and turned right, into an underground parking lot where another limo waited. There were two suitcases resting on the trunk, and Lucille gestured to have them put inside. All five got into the new limo, and were driven out onto the tarmac to a private jet. They all got in, with Little Joe carrying the suitcases. As soon as they were seated, the hatch closed and the jet taxied into position for takeoff.

"If we're going to some sort of meeting," Greco ventured, "You ought to prepare us."

"You're here because the Irish in Chicago want to meet you. Ida keeps me looking pretty. Chowder and Little Joe keep me safe."

"What the hell do we want with the Chicago Irish? We can't even talk to the Brooklyn Micks."

They landed at O'Hare airport and taxied to an old and dusty hangar on the outskirts. There the five were bundled into a shiny stretch limousine and driven straightaway to Cicero. The meeting took place at a roadside inn along old Route Sixty-Six. A short barrel-chested man with red hair, a freckled face and a sweet Irish smile came forward, hand out-stretched.

"Miss Lucille," he said, "I'm Mike Murphy. I've heard about you. I expected something different after the description of your injuries, but colleen, you're a rare beauty."

Lucille took his hand in a firm grip. "If you want to fuck me and change your luck," she said, smiling toothily, "I'm sorry, but I haven't got time."

"My luck is just fine. What's in the suitcases?"

Lucille waved to Little Joe, who put one suitcase on the table and opened it, revealing cash.

"There's five hundred thousand dollars," said Lucille. "You can do one of three things with it. One, refuse to touch it, and we go our separate ways.

Two, take it and say you'll do what I ask, but not do it. Three, take it and do what I ask, and get another suitcase with the same amount."

"And if I refuse?"

"You lose a friend."

"And if I take it, but don't do it?"

"You gain an enemy."

"You've got enough of those in Brooklyn. Why should I make your enemies mine?"

"For a million dollars."

"Sweet darlin' you've got my interest. What is it you're askin'?"

"Send a crew of your men to Brooklyn. They must be obviously Irish. They're to attack specific targets owned by the gangs opposing me."

Murphy clasped his hands together as if in prayer and pressed his fingers to his lips. "You're a wicked woman," he murmured. "You want my men to appear as the Red Hook boys attacking the Russians and the Brooklyn gangs, so they'll get into it with Red Hook and take the pressure off your Crowns, eh?"

"Does that present a problem?"

"I lost me morals at me Confirmation, but I'd not care to betray me Irish cousins."

"They're distant relatives, and I'll make it a million two."

"A million and a half sounds better."

"A million and a quarter."

Mike Murphy took his hands from his lips, spat in the palm of his right hand and held it out to Lucille.

"What the hell's this?" she puzzled.

"Now you spit in your hand, and when we shake it means we're puttin' our souls on the line."

Lucille spat in her hand and shook his.

Murphy gripped her hand and asked: "What would you've done if I'd taken the second option?"

Lucille freed her hand from his grip. "Pay the other half-million to those who'd kill you and your family."

"Not to worry. What's in the other suitcase?"

"I had my people cruise the bars, restaurants, movie houses and bowling alleys in Red Hook, to pick up matchbooks, napkins, swizzle sticks and the like, for your men to drop at the targets."

"Clever girl. Do ye have time for a Chicago steak?"

"Sorry, our plane is waiting. But you wanted to meet Greco? Here he is."

Murphy shook Greco's hand and said: "I did a bit of research. You worked for the Jannazzo Mafia in Shreveport, Louisiana. A contract hit man. You don't look Black."

"I'm what they call High Yellow: one sixteenth Black on my father's side. The rest is true."

"How the hell did you wind up in Brooklyn?"

"Iron Mike hired me for a specific job. He liked my work and gave me two more contracts. Then he made me an offer I couldn't refuse. Mr. Jannazzo agreed, and I've been there ever since."

Murphy turned to Lucille. "Me first name is the same as your son's," he said. "I am sorry for your loss."

"Me too. When your men complete the job, I'll give them the remaining seven-hundred and fifty thousand dollars. The sooner, the better."

RED HOOK MEDICAL CENTER

"Mac, this is Mayzie. We need all the help we can get. Three cars of Russians drove into Bed-Stuy and machine-gunned the bars at Four Corners, but it was a trap. There are at least six dead, four wounded, and still counting. Send what help you can."

Mac hit the panic button and three ambulance crews rushed to their vehicles. She pulled on her ER jacket and called Big Momma, to learn that her crews were on the way.

At the scene, the ambulances were lined up on Gates Avenue awaiting safety clearance from the police. While the crews pulled on bulletproof vests Mac went up to the police captain to ask: "Why can't we get in there?"

"Oh, darlin'," he explained, "You can get in there, but getting' you out alive again would be a real problem."

"You mean they're still shooting at each other?"

"No, m'dear, they're shooting at us and the firemen. If your ambulance people want to become targets, Mayor DeBlasio won't allow it."

"Who are they?"

"Kid gangs, and it's anyone's guess who they're allied with. We control the streets, but they control the rooftops. Worse, they broke into a gun-shop and have more weapons and ammo than they know how to fire. The SWAT team snipers refuse to shoot kids."

"Thank God for that, at least."

"Look, lady, I've got three policemen down, one in serious condition with a bullet through his neck. I don't appreciate your prayers on the little bastards' behalf."

"Who's treating their wounded?"

"Who cares? Fuck 'em."

"If I can get in there, maybe I can persuade them to back off or go away."

"I don't agree, and I doubt the mayor will either. I'd have to clear it with him.'

"Call him—and say that Dr. MacKenzie, from the newly-constituted Board of Brooklyn ER Manpower is making the request."

The captain gave a deep sigh and pulled out his phone. "What the hell," he muttered, "I don't have anything else to do."

Mac waited.

"...Yes, Mr. Mayor; she's standing right here."

She could hear the reply: "Put her on."

Mac grabbed the phone and said in a rush: "Mr. Mayor, I accept full responsibility. I'll take two volunteers with me. They're both combat medics. Yes, I'll follow the police instructions to the letter."

"Put the captain back on."

Mac handed back the phone, but could still hear the speaker. "Captain, what I'm telling you now I never said. Understand?"

"Yessir," said the captain, much subdued.

"If possible, let the little bastards disappear back

into the woodwork."

"You mean, let them get away?"

"Exactly."

"My men shed blood, and they want blood."

"And the media will have *my* blood for it, if you kill kids. Let 'em run."

"That's a tall order."

"You weren't hired as a short-order cook. I gave you the menu."

"And if I serve the meal the way you want?"

"You'll be promoted."

"Thank you, Mr. Mayor."

Mac called to Percy and Alphonso: "Have you got your hats loaded?"

"Yes," they both answered.

"This is strictly volunteer, and it's dangerous," the police captain warned.

"We understand."

"You three must make the little bastards understand that if they threaten you in any way, my men will shoot to kill. The SWAT team negotiator will tell you want to look for. Dr. MacKenzie, step over here a moment with me."

Mac did, making a good guess what this was about.

"Look," he said, "What I say to you now is in the strictest confidence. I'm up a tree here, and don't know what to do. I can't shoot the little bums, and if I arrest them the public will riot. Bad publicity for the police. I'd say a coffin or jail time for the little assholes, but what can I do? The mayor says to let them slip away. Can you think of a better solution?"

Mac shrugged. "I can't think of one."

"You agree the kids are in danger?"

"That's why I volunteered."

"Okay. Here's what to do. Figure out who the leader is and make this offer: I'll have three Board of Corrections buses at the southeast corner of Gates and Nostrand; they'll take the little bastards anywhere they want to go. They won't be followed, identified, or photographed. I want them to disappear. All their weapons and ammo must be handed over before they board the buses. Make sure they know what the alternative is."

"Phew! I've studied for every role I ever sought in life, but not for this."

"Truth be told, I'd advise you not to go. The younger they are, the less compassion and sense they've got."

"But if I don't go in, who will you get?"

"Someone else from the First Responders who can treat bullet wounds."

"I won't oblige someone else to do what I'm afraid to."

"You're afraid?"

"I can scarcely keep a tight asshole."

"Captain, sir," the SWAT negotiator shouted, "They're prepared to let in three ER people to treat their wounded. We've got to move now. Are your people ready to go in?"

Mac nodded, and she and Alphonse and Percy went up to the door of the building.

Two fifteen-year-old girls came out, searched the

three, and poked through their duffle-bags of equipment. Percy asked: "You want some pizza?"

The girls didn't answer, but exchanged glances. They led the ER crew into the building and up two flights of stairs.

On the third floor landing eleven youngsters were lined up, seated on the floor with their backs against the wall. Some were in shock and covered in blood. One boy, whom Mac thought was perhaps nine years old, was sucking the blood from his bullet-shattered hand. Mac signaled for Percy and Alphonso to evaluate and treat the most serious cases, while she went to the nine-year-old and clamped her thumb over the artery in his wrist to stop the bleeding. "Why are you drinking the blood?" she asked.

"If it goes on the floor, I'll lose it," he mumbled.

"Damn," Mac snapped. "We need stretchers and more ambulances. These children need to be hospitalized."

"We ain't no fuckin' children!" shouted a young male voice behind her. "Agreed to let you three ambulance people come in and patch them up, and then get the hell out of here."

"Who said you could let them in?" snapped a tall thin boy with an Afro haircut and three rifle-armed youngsters behind him. Several more youngsters moved up behind them, rifles raised.

"I don't even know your names," said Mac.

"That little son of a bitch you're talkin' to is Small Change," said the thin boy. "I'm Prince."

"Call him shit for brains," sneered Small Change. "I hear you asked if we wanted pizza?"

"Hell, yes," said Percy, bandaging a bullet-gouge in a girl's leg. "This is a lot of work, and we're hungry."

"You think you're gonna put sleepin' powder on it, to knock us out?" Prince growled.

"Just plain old pizza," said Alphonso. "If you don't eat it, we will."

Immediately, the youngsters started shouting orders for different pizza toppings. Prince and his crew drove everyone back to their places with kicks, curses and punches. Small Change shouted: "Forty pizzas, half pepperoni and half onions, and forty large bottles of Zero. We're thirsty."

"Forty," Mac agreed. She'd been instructed by the SWAT negotiator to make the pizza offer so as to estimate the number of gang members in the building. She bandaged up the injured boy and moved on to another gunshot wound.

"Here's the deal," she explained. "The cops are willing to let you sneak out the back door, and onto some waiting buses on the southeast corner of Gates and Nostrand. The buses will take you wherever in the city you want to go, but you have to leave your guns and ammo behind. We'll stay behind and take your wounded to the hospital. That's the deal."

An argument broke out between Prince and Small Change. Their factions line up behind them in the hallway with guns drawn. Mac noticed that Small Change's right hand was bent inward, as if he had suffered a stroke. He stepped closer to Prince and straightened his hand. A stiletto shot out of his sleeve and into his hand. He moved so quickly that

Prince never had time to touch the pistol in his waistband. He staggered backward with the steel blade embedded in his chest, and collapsed into the arms of his gang members—encumbering their hands so they couldn't shoot. Small Change's faction pointed their weapons. Small Change pointed at Prince, who was gasping and bleeding from the mouth.

"We can fight each other," said Small Change. "That's what the fucking cops want. Then they come in and bust our ass. Or we can work a deal through this Dr. Mac. But *I'm* the boss."

"Don't touch him!" Mac shouted. "Leave the knife in. Alphonso, Percy, help me intubate him."

"I've done a few," said Alphonso, "But these wounded need immediate hospitalization."

Mac looked at Small Change. "You heard," she said.

She took off her jacket and placed it under Prince's head, rolled him on the side where he was stabbed, pulled his arm out straight, set the jacket on his arm and his head back on the jacket so that the blood drained from his mouth.

"He'll die in an hour if we don't get him out of here," said Mac. "All these people need hospitalization."

"We ain't takin' no deal," Small Change snarled. "We gotta gets guarantees."

"Only the police captain can do that, and he guarantees just what I told you."

"I'm talkin' to you, bitch!"

"If Prince dies, all bets are off and you'll be charged with murder. I witnessed him arguing that with the mayor's office."

"You think you're getting' out alive?"

"If I or my men are harmed, everyone in here is dead. I heard him arguing that, too."

The gang members began shouting and challenging Small Change.

"If one hangs, we all hang!" he shouted. "We all get saved or die here. The cops made us an offer; we sneak off quietly and disappear. They forget about us and we become invisible."

"Take the deal," said Percy.

The crowd shouted: "Take the deal!"

"Fools," Small Change snarled. "How we gonna guarantee the cops keep their word?"

There were mutterings and more shouting: "Yeah! Lyin' buncha blue-bellied pigs."

"Miss Lucille," a timid girl's voice piped up. "I trust her. Did you see her face at the funeral?"

There was a moment of silence, and then the group started murmuring: "Yeah, she got it right." Soon the youngsters began chanting: "Miss Lucille! Miss Lucille!"

"Alright, we'll ask Miss Lucille" Small Change shouted. "Anybody got her fuckin' phone number?"

There was silence in the hall.

"I do," said Mac.

Small Change ground his teeth for a moment, then said: "So call her, and I'll talk."

"I'll call her, and I'll talk," Mac insisted.

"Why you?"

"Because I'm older and smarter than you, and I'm not betting my life and everybody else's here on your twisted little brain."

"You shut the fuck up, lady! I'll carve your ass!" He pointed at Prince, who was gasping for air, and asked: "Is he gonna live?"

Alphonso, who was inserting a tube down Prince's throat, only shrugged.

"If Prince doesn't make it to the hospital in an hour," Percy explained, "He'll die."

"Call Miss Lucille!" Small Changed howled. Foam formed at the corner of his mouth, and his hands trembled.

Lucille Leissner's stretch limousine was pulling out of Kennedy airport when her cell-phone rang. She recognized the caller's number. "Dr. Mac," she said, "Good to hear your voice."

"Very good to hear yours, Lucille," said Mac. "I'm in trouble."

"How can I help?"

"Do you know what's going on here?"

"You mean the war?"

"The standoff between the police and the kids at Four Corners."

"My driver was just telling me. Dr. Mac, you tell the cops to give me an escort there. I'm in a black stretch limo on the Van Wyck Expressway, breaking the speed limit. Call Congressman Waters. He writes something about letting the kids off, and I'll do what I can."

"Will do," said Mac, handing over the phone. "Please talk to Small Change so he knows it's really you."

Two NYPD motorcycles escorted the limousine to the barricade outside the factory building. The police captain met Lucille and her entourage with a large envelope. "It's a copy of a guarantee from Congressman Waters. If the kids come out peacefully, everything will be swept under the carpet."

"No charges?"

"None."

"And if I have to break a few heads?"

"Break all of them." The captain shrugged. "Then you'll have to deal with Black Lives Matter instead of us."

Lucille laughed briefly. "Those commie fools only know how to extort rich White guilty liberals. How many kids are inside?"

"We estimate forty. That's how many pizzas and drinks they ordered. Yes, if they leave their hardware behind, the kids will be put on the buses with no strings attached. If you can help us out here, the department will owe you, big time."

"Chowder, you and Little Joe and Greco come with me. Ida, you stay, and keep your phone open."

The four walked between police cars into the old factory building and up to the second-floor landing. Mac, Percy and Alphonso stepped back from the wounded to greet Lucille. Most of the watching youngsters were awestruck.

"Jesus H. Christ!" bellowed Lucille, running her gaze over the wounded. "It looks like the railway station scene from *Gone With The Wind!* Did you kids try to take on the whole New York City police department?"

Small Change stepped forward and announced: "We ain't kids."

Less than a second after the last word left his mouth, Chowder backhanded him across the face, knocking him two feet back and flat on the floor. The other youngsters did nothing but stare.

Lucille pointed down at Small Change. "Don't speak unless I ask you a question. You the leader of this cluster-fuck?"

"Yeah." Other kids helped him to his feet with warning pinches on his arms. "Yes, Miz Lucille, I axed for you."

"I'll give you credit for knowing the right address." She held up a printed page. "This is a written guarantee from Congressman Waters, the Police Chief and the Borough President that you'll be safely escorted to the Salvation Army building—which is under my control. Before any charges can be brought against you, you'll escape. Everything that took place here will be forgotten. You'll leave the hardware here; Little Joe, Chowder and Greco will check you out as you leave."

"How can we trust the cops?"

"You can't, and I don't." She took out a pen and signed the paper. "You're trusting me, Congressman Waters, the Borough President and Mayor DeBlasio. If they renege, they'll lose the next election. That I can guarantee."

"I'm hungry," one of the younger kids said.

"There's a whole pizza and soda for each of you on the buses."

"Let's take the deal," the crowd mumbled. "Take

the deal. Take the deal!"

Seeing control slip away from him, Small Change waved four of his followers forward so they faced Lucille and the medics, Little Joe, Chowder and Greco. "I wanna see that paper for myself," he insisted.

Alphonso shouted: "Salute!"

He and Percy snapped their hands up to the brims of their caps, whipped them off and cracked the two heads in front of them. Chowder and Little Joe jabbed their hands out and grabbed the other two of Small Change's goons by the throat—and throttled them until they collapsed. Greco got Small Change by the throat and just held him, squeezing slightly.

Lucille stepped up to Small Change and whispered in his ear: "Get down on your knees and beg forgiveness or you're dead."

Small Change began to tremble. He sank to his knees and tears trickled down his face. He tried to speak, but choked on the words.

Lucille kicked him in the face with the pointy toe of her high-heeled shoe."Chowder and Little Joe," she said, "Send the wounded out first. Then get the rest of these assholes on the buses."

CHAPTER 25:
AMENDS

RIDGEWOOD VA HOSPITAL

JJ Dougherty stepped to the podium in the Substance Rehabilitation Room and glanced around him. There was standing room only. "Some of our outpatients traveled a hundred miles to hear tonight's speaker," he said. "This lady has touched the lives of everyone in this room and many more who aren't with us tonight. I take no pleasure in presenting a lady whom I respect, admire, and try to emulate. I present the former Charge Nurse of this rehabilitation ward, Martha Dowd."

JJ had gotten Martha's hair done in the hospital beauty salon. He'd personally ironed her dark green hospital pajamas and provided clean stockings and slippers. When she stepped onto the stage, everyone in the room stood at attention. Men and women choked back tears as she took the microphone and said: "My name is Martha Dowd, and I'm an alcoholic."

A number of men and women wept. Those who

had faced death on the battlefield choked back sobs and averted their eyes.

"I didn't want to see you," Martha pressed on. "I dreaded having to say those three words: 'I'm an alcoholic'. I betrayed you. How could I face you? I tried to practice what I preached, but I failed. I held myself up as an example of getting dried out and staying off drugs or booze. JJ cleaned me up so I could appear before you; otherwise I would have looked like an old bag lady who just rolled out of the gutter. I thought I was better than you. I taught you the Twelve Steps of Alcoholics Anonymous. I thought I was Wonder Woman of the AA brigade. So what made me agree to bare my sotted soul?"

She pointed at JJ.

"He pointed out something that I knew and preached, but didn't believe applied to me. That is, the only time you're cured from addiction is when you're dead. My answer is the same that many of you gave me: 'so I'll commit suicide'."

She waited for the effect, and it came as the audience bent forward to hear.

"If death is the only way out, then why not take it? The answer I gave you is that death is permanent. It cuts you off from life on Earth. Six of the Twelve Steps refer to making amends to those whom we've wronged, and you can't do that if you're dead. Death is a cop-out on a debt you owe in life. Once you're dead it's *finito, compadre*. You get only one chance on this wheel of life."

"For what purpose?" a woman asked.

"You asked the right question of the wrong person," said Martha. "I'm here to ask for your help. You see, the other six tenets of the Twelve Steps is a belief in God—and I've lost my faith."

"And you think we can help you restore it?'

"I need a miracle!"

"I'm also a Protestant minister, and an alcoholic. We may help you on the path of reconciliation with God, but only you can make it happen."

"I don't know how," Martha wept.

The woman stepped to the center aisle and walked to the podium. She placed both hands on Martha's head and pronounced: "May the Lord bless you and keep you. May He make his countenance to shine upon you, and direct you in the path of right-eousness for His name's sake." Then she turned and addressed the audience. "Would everyone who feels disposed to offering a blessing for Martha Dowd come forward and place your hands on her head? Pray for moral strength to flow from God to her, and may she find his holiness in the house of the Lord forever. Amen."

A line formed, and one by one the members of the audience came forward to give Martha their blessing. A tall elegant woman in a nurse's uniform waited at the end of the line, and was the last to place her hands on Martha's head. When she spoke, Martha recognized her voice and looked up.

"Mac?" she whispered, amazed.

MacKenzie smiled. "I am your sister in Christ, and an alcoholic."

Kula stood just outside the Gay Greek's Diner, waiting for Floyd to roll up on his motorcycle. As she thought about him, her heart melted. She was surprised at how deeply in love she was, and in some ways it was beautifully disturbing. She had to think for two. They never discussed children. She was the only girl, and the princess, in the family. Her father couldn't deny her anything. Her brothers were almost comically overprotective. Her mother less lenient and more experienced in family matters, had also been a beauty and pampered while growing up. She anticipated Kula's manipulation of her father, and this brought them into conflict, but it was a conflict of love.

Kula chuckled as she remembered her first adult date after high school. A boy two years older, whom she'd known in high school, had just returned from the war as a Marine sergeant. Prior to entering the Marine Corps, he'd been arrested for fighting in a local bar. He'd suffered several stitches, and it was the talk of the neighborhood. Her brothers had cautioned her about how to walk with him, which arm he should hold, and not sitting with her legs crossed. Her father had warned her about hugging and kissing. Her mother was silent, dead set against Kula dating in general, and especially set against dating with an American combat veteran. Kula remembered that her mother's silence as the loudest voice in the room.

When she returned home that evening, the family was waiting.

"So what happened?" her brothers asked. "Where did you go?"

"The movies."

"Which one?"

"*Foot Locker*. He said that every time they showed it on base in Afghanistan, they were attacked, so he never got to see it all the way through. Afterward we went to dinner."

"Where?"

"A new Chinese place in Borough Park."

"You could have eaten for free at the diner," her father grumbled.

"What, with you and Momma sitting there, and she looking like she just ate a barrel of lemons? Ho, ho! Besides, we'd neither of us had Chinese for a long time."

"Now don't talk like that. Your Momma loves you; she wants what's best for you."

Momma raised a finger, and Papa fell silent. She asked: "Did he try to kiss you?"

"He asked," Kula said.

"Right!" her brothers laughed. "The big tough Marine asked your permission?"

"More important," her father said, "What was your answer."

"No."

Kula saw her mother's eyebrows raise, and knew she didn't believe that answer. Her father raised a bottle of Ouzo and said: "That's my girl."

Her mother kissed Kula's forehead and whispered: "Don't make a habit of lying."

Momma wanted an arranged marriage with a young man from the old country. She definitely would have opposed Kula marrying Floyd, at least until she got to know him. He was naturally good-hearted. Though his motorcycle definitely had power, he never showed off with it. He might not have been born Greek, but he looked like one of those Classical Greek museum statues—especially when he was naked...

The loud purr of an approaching motorcycle announced Floyd's arrival, and Kula smiled.

They rode off to Holy Cross Greek Orthodox Church in Bay Ridge, where Father Joseph was waiting for them. Georgee had asked specifically for him to administer the conversion, and the church was happy to oblige. The Podromakeos family name was carved into the church's cornerstone, Georgee was chairman of the Board of Trustees, and a major contributor.

Floyd pulled the motorcycle up onto the sidewalk in front of the church, noting that it was a large building with a long-peaked red tile roof. The walls were tan-colored brick and the entrance consisted of three pure-white stone entrances which, as Kula explained, stood for Father, Son, and Holy Spirit. "The sixteen steps leading up to the entrance," she went on, "Are for each of the saints."

"It's pretty, anyway," said Floyd.

He was more impressed by the interior. The walls and ceiling were covered with sculptures and paintings in the most vivid colors. The pulpit was a single lectern with a microphone. Behind it hung a large ornate red felt tapestry of the cross, embroidered in gold and silver thread. On either side stood eight alcoves, holding statues of sixteen saints. Above them was a massive exquisitely painted mural of the Last Supper. A gigantic cut-glass chandelier lit up the center over the oak wood pews, and smaller identical chandeliers hung in the corners.

A tall bearded man in his late forties, wearing a white silk robe decorated with gold filigree, strode up the aisle. He offered a hand to Floyd and the other to Kula, saying: "You're even more beautiful than I remember. It's been a long time. Hello, Floyd. I'm Father Joseph." He took off his glasses and polished them, asking: "Do either of you know the meaning of the term 'Protecxia'?"

"Hmm, a person with Protecxia," said Floyd, "Can influence others to his own benefit."

"Excellent," said Father Joseph. "Your wife-to-be's father has Protecxia up to the gates of heaven." He adjusted his glasses. "Kula my dear, I respect your family's contribution to our church, but your father requested that the six-month indoctrination period for acceptance into the Greek Orthodox church be waived. So..." He looked to Floyd. "You were baptized?"

"Yes, in the Episcopal church."

"Good. Kula, your father contacted the bishop in New York, and I was instructed to teach you our religion until you marry. When is the wedding date?"

Kula and Floyd answered together: "Sunday, the seventeenth of February."

"Excellent. You must lock pinkies and make a wish."

"Why?" Floyd asked.

The priest shrugged, so Kula explained. "It's something we grew up with. We don't tell each other our wishes." She locked pinkies with Floyd.

Father Joseph checked his pocket computer. "Sunday the seventeenth is good," he said. "We have an opening between ten and eleven AM. Put the date and time into your computers. Until then, four evenings a week we meet here for religious instruction. You must attend together."

"But you were my teacher," said Kula. "You taught me everything. What else is there?"

"Then you were a child. Now you are a grown woman, about to accept the holy bonds of matrimony. The divorce rate in America is over fifty percent. That means a divorce every thirteen seconds. That comes to 277 divorces per hour, 6646 divorces per day, 46,523 per week, and 2,419,196 per year. That means there were nine divorces in the time it took me to say this. The divorce rate in the Greek Orthodox church is only eighteen percent. I do not intend to waste my time. Floyd, I have some questions."

"Ask away."

"You, in turn, may ask any question but one."

"Which one is that?"

"The one I don't have an answer for. Now, this is the first time you entered a Greek Orthodox church, yes? What's your reaction?"

"Wow, it's gorgeous! You've got more saints statues and murals than any ten Catholic churches, fewer stained-glass windows, but the matching chandeliers are magnificent. How do you keep them so sparkling?"

"That I don't have the answer to. As a Protestant, are you put off by all the imagery?"

"A few years ago, it might have."

"What made you change?"

"The war."

"In what way?"

"Well, I felt closer to Christ, but thought less about God. I came to the conclusion that God doesn't give a damn. He created everything and then left it to us to make do."

"In what way did you feel closer to Christ?"

"I could talk to him in my heart. He once walked on Earth in the body of a man... I haven't been to church in years."

"Did talking with Christ help?"

"I slept better. But neither God nor Christ helped those who were killed and maimed in war, or for that matter here in Brooklyn."

"Are you angry at God and/or Christ?"

"Absolutely! I definitely am angry at God."

"Good!"

"Father!" Kula gasped. "How can you say that? You taught us to love God!"

"Now you will hear the grownup answer. If you have found the love of the Holy Trinity, then you are fortunate indeed. To be angry at God means you believe He exists. Your young man is a fervent believer; for him, God is real. I'm heartened by his response.

"Floyd, what if I were to tell you that, although Mary the mother of Jesus is held in the highest regard, she too was guilty of Original Sin?"

"Huh?"

"She didn't become the mother of Jesus until later in life. And did you know she had other sons and daughters?"

"Yes. It came up in discussion once, during a beer party. A deacon's son explained it."

"And now I will try to explain a most peculiar aspect of Greek Orthodox religion; it is a blending of faith and culture. Thus far I am heartened by your attitude and forthrightness; you have expressed your faith in the most cognitive way. Never be afraid to question, and always be patient evaluation the answers."

"What's so different about the culture?"

"Your first exposure to the Greek culture was Kula's family. They and most Greek kinfolk are overprotective."

"My family's the perfect example," said Kula, rolling her eyes, "And not unusual in modern era families."

Father Joseph went on: "Siblings often move long distances from nucleus families, and lose contact. People worry about this, so my parishioners try to keep together. We still pray in Greek, and most send their children to learn the language of their ancestors."

"I know of Orthodox Jews who do the same thing, but the language you use today isn't the same as ancient Greek."

"Ah, you've been talking to someone."

"Not me," said Kula.

"I searched the internet," Floyd explained.

"A useful tool when done properly," Father Joseph conceded, "But what I meant about culture is that eventually you'll become culturally acceptable to Kula's family. It will take longer to integrate into the religious community. They will refer to you as Xeno, which can mean guest, friend, outsider, foreigner—anything but being born a Greek."

"Father," Kula asked, "Do you have to be religious to be happy?"

Father Joseph pondered the question. "In most cases, yes," he admitted. "Religion gives people a moral compass to guide their faith and actions in life, as well as a community of like-minded people. As Rabbi Goldman used to say, it couldn't hurt.

"So, tomorrow night at seven. And bring your motorcycle inside. Once it gets dark, the punks will steal the railing it's chained to."

CHAPTER 26:
THE NEXT WAVE

BEDFORD-STUYVESANT

Two large men lumbered along the upper balcony walkway of the Bedford Motel, grumbling about the weather. They stopped and knocked on door number seven. A voice from inside shouted: "Who's there?"

"Cheap Charlie from Red Hook sent us. He said we could score."

"Are you cops?"

"Are you nuts? Bejaysus, wouldn't my own mother disown me if I were! She's doing five to ten in Lexington. I talked to you on the phone. I'm ready to pay for half a kilo."

"Describe Cheap Charlie."

"A fat slob in his fifties, almost bald, and has two red Chow hounds chained to his rocking chair."

"Okay."

The door opened.

The two men reached in, grabbed the Black man behind it by his shirt, hauled him out and hurled him over the railing into the parking lot twenty feet below. They drew their pistols and broke into the room, firing. Finding no one else there, they ransacked the room for drugs, cash, and weapons. As they left with their booty, one of the gunmen dropped a book of matches on the floor. The ad on the cover read: Shanrock Bar and Grill, 333 Lornier Street, Red Hook, New York.

Throughout Bed-Stuy the Chicago Irish masquerading as Red Hookers hit seventeen locations taken by the bigger gangs from the smaller ones. The sight of White men rampaging through Black neighborhoods was a call to arms, since the Red Hook Irish were supposed to be neutral.

The Russians were the first to react. Mr. G phoned the leader of the Hookers and bellowed: "Frank, what the fuck do you think you're doing? Why get your boys involved in this war?"

"What the fuck are you talking about?"

"Your men are raiding our money-makers in Bed-Stuy, the Bushwick's and Flatbush boys' too. Have you gone over to the Crowns?"

"What kind of bullshit are you giving me? The Hookers don't move unless I order it, and I haven't."

"Somebody's tearing up the neighborhoods, and they've got Irish faces and Irish accents. We killed one who had a wedding invitation to a church in your district, and a parking ticket in Greenpoint."

There was a long moment of silence before Frank McKenny spoke, in a slow distinct tone. "Mr. G, I smell a rat. A large Black female rat."

"Well, do something, and fast. Two of my men

are dead, and several wounded. They want blood—Irish blood."

"You've got the wrong address. Give me forty-eight hours, and fax me that wedding invitation, the parking ticket, and the fingerprints of that dead Irishman."

"What you want is on its way. Twenty-four hours. Have an answer for me, or I'll cut off your balls and make your wife eat them after I kill your children."

"Yeah, yeah. Make it thirty-six. I gotta make a lotta phone calls."

Mac called in off-duty ER people from all over Brooklyn to handle the onslaught. The night was filled with sirens and the flashing lights of ambulances. Emergency teams, firemen and police raced in all directions. People stocked up on food, lining up at the bodegas and supermarkets in anticipation of a long-drawn-out street war. Playgrounds were empty. Feathery snow fell as the temperature dropped and tempers grew short. Police patrolled three per car, and on foot in pairs with matching pairs across the street. They always carried extra ammunition, wearing metal helmets to protect against rooftop attacks and bulletproof vests against shooters. All first responders were similarly outfitted.

Through her cousin in the police department Jill learned about the Irish hit-squads roaming Brooklyn, and she advised Mac to move her headquarters back to the Ridgewood VA hospital. "The other four gangs will attack Red Hook," she warned.

Mayor DeBlasio refused to call an emergency meeting. Congressman Waters demanded that the National Guard be activated, which the mayor likewise refused. The FBI sent a hundred agents to infiltrate the neighborhood. They failed, but they did verify the information provided by Mr. G.

Frank McElhenny called personally. "Mr. G, you were right. The dead guy was an Irishman, but not one of mine. His name is Patrick 'Gummsy' O'Donnell, thirty-four years old, has five arrests, served seven years for manslaughter. The parking ticket was a sham. The wedding invitation was bought from the printer and doctored. The book of matches is authentic; it came from the Irish Pub. It could have been picked up any time and given to him. Me and my boys are being set up."

"So what do we do now?"

"We all go to talk to the Cyclops."

"Just who are 'we'?"

"You, me, and the other Black and Latino gang leaders. Aye, the Black bitch from Bed-Stuy is behind this, and I'll have her head for slanderin' me good name."

Smothering a snicker, Mr. G asked: "How can you be sure?"

"I can't, but Pete Gotti can. Greco, Lucille's second in command, worked for the Wops in Louisiana."

Mr. G silently ground his teeth. He didn't have any such direct contact with Pete Gotti. "Okay. Set it up with my lieutenant, Arbuzov."

"Sounds Arabic. He an Arab?"

"A crazy Cossack."

CHAPTER 27:
HOT TIMES IN THE OLD TOWN

RIDGEWOOD VA HOSPITAL

New York City froze. Homeless people slept in subway tunnels and storm-drains, often starting trash-fires to keep warm. Those who could afford it fled to the southern states and even as far as Arizona. The hospitals became refuges for the elderly poor, since most medical facilities had private backup generators. Mac used the police, Boy and Girl Scouts, and church groups to seek out the elderly needing assistance. In addition to those seeking relief from the cold there was the normal flow of ER patients, and on top of that was the war in the streets complete with its dead, wounded, and hysterically frightened. Hospital wards, hallways, and storage areas were at maximum capacity.

Mac ordered: "Break out the old mattresses and put them under each bed. That way, we can accept three hundred and fifty more."

"Thanks a lot," said Jill. "What happens when there's no more room on the floors?"

"Have the police open the movie theaters."

"Well, stick a broom up my ass, and I'll clean the floor while I'm at it," Jill grumbled. "We're going to have to feed them, you know."

"Get Martha and JJ to help with that."

"Uh, can she handle that?"

"If not, give it to JJ. Tell him to solicit restaurants."

"How will we pay them?"

"Issue IOUs. I'll redeem them from the ER fund. Congressman Waters will back me up."

"You hope."

"You're right, and I'm not wrong. They're sending the overflow from Bushwick and Flabush to us," said Mac, fielding a phonecall. "Hello? ...Just a moment please."

"Why not to Red Hook?"

"According to your cousin, the shit's about to hit the fan there. ...Yes? What's your emergency?"

"Why not send the walking wounded to the New York City hospitals?"

"I've been doing that. Try to keep the corridors open and a trauma team always at the ready. ...Yes, we are accepting cases of hypothermia. Use hot water bottles during transportation."

"I'm on it," said Jill, getting up to leave.

Georgee Prodromakeos bought an auxiliary generator to power the diner and the heating. People lined up for tables. He had to require reservations for seated customers. This was good for business, but he had to hire and train new help, oversee his staff, and increase foodstuff purchases. On top of that he was preparing for Kula's wedding. He had an appointment with her and Floyd to look at an apartment for rent. If they liked it, he had a surprise planned for them.

As Floyd rolled up through a light dusting of snow, Georgee took Kula outside with him and pointed to where to safely park the motorcycle. Then he led them to a shed behind the diner, opened the large Yale safety lock and swung the doors open wide. Revealed was a shining four-door luxury sedan that looked like a cross between a Rolls Royce Phantom and a 1930 Chrysler Air Flow. The reflection of its bright yellow exterior forced Floyd to squint. "What is it?" he breathed, awed.

"A 1972 F8000 Bicine, made by Norieon in Greece," Kula sighed. "My father went to Chicago to buy it. There were only two ever made."

"In the whole world?" Floyd marveled.

"And mine is in better shape than the other one," Georgee grinned.

"I love odd cars! I once owned a 1958 Saab."

"So why do you ride a crazy motorcycle?"

"To find parking spaces and save money on gas. Are we going to take a ride?"

"Not today. I just wanted to show it to you before we go see this apartment."

"Can't we drive there?"

"It's just down the block. We'll walk."

"My father rarely drives it," Kula explained,

"Except on Memorial Day, Fourth of July, and church parades."

Georgee pulled the doors shut and locked them, then led the way down the street past neat four-family homes built of red brick, each two stories high, with porch fronts and rear entrances overlooking walled spacious back yards. He stopped in front of one modestly labeled 373 Central Avenue. "This is it," he said.

"From the outside, it looks beautiful," Kula marveled. "Can we go in?"

Georgee dangled a set of keys. She took them and dragged a dumb-struck Floyd up the stairs to the entrance. The door was of polished walnut with a full-length oval of etched glass set in the center. The cut glass doorknobs and brass work were highly polished. The smell of the interior foyer was distinctly clean and old.

"One apartment of four rooms and a bath on the right," Georgee explained, "The same on the left, and two more upstairs."

"It's immaculate," Floyd noted.

"The owner was a builder. He put in modern baths and kitchens."

"Why is he leaving?"

"I like this boy," Georgee chuckled, "He's intelligent. Look, the owner lived here with his wife and children. The kids moved to Long Island. He can't manage a house this large by himself, and winters are worse for him. He's moving to Boca Raton, Florida. There's a finished basement with a workshop, office, lounge and bathroom down there."

"Daddy, can we walk around?"

"You must. The owner is in a rush; he wants to get himself and his wife to Florida before the snow gets worse. Me, I'm going to watch TV; I want to see the squabble over the impeachment hearings."

"And no doubt laugh yourself silly. We'll be back soon."

An hour later Kula burst in on her father, with Floyd trailing close behind. "Daddy, how much is the rent?" she practically gibbered. Can we buy some of the furniture? When is it available? We love it!"

"Then it's yours."

"But how much a month?"

"You two pay the taxes, utilities and upkeep. That's all."

"For which apartment?" Floyd asked.

"You and my daughter get the two upstairs. I and your unmarried brother get the two downstairs."

"You're renting it for us?"

"No, I'm buying it—lock, stock, and barrel."

"But-but—" Kula stammered, "It must cost over a million dollars!"

"Two million, and I've got it covered."

"...How?"

"I've got an offer of a million two for our house, and half a million for the car."

"But Daddy, you love that car."

"I love you more. Besides, the steps in our house are getting hard for me. I need a walk-in shower, and I can't keep up with the repairs or snow in winter. Your brother and husband will handle that in this place. You take the two upstairs apartments; we'll break through the walls and make one big apartment for you."

"What are we going to do with eight rooms?"

"Fill them with kids for Grandpa Georgee to spoil."

Floyd blushed. Kula beamed, embraced her father, and rained kisses all over his face.

Following Lucille's instructions, the Chicago Irish rampaged through Bushwick and Flatbush, breaking heads and driving the gangs off the streets with gunfire. When she judged the time was right, Lucille sent five truckloads of Crowns into Brighton Beach with orders to go after the Russians directly—and take vengeance for Michael. The police stayed away from the troubles, leaving shops unprotected from opportunistic looters. Assorted political took advantage of the situation to "protest", and add to the looting.

Coney Island hospital was full. The walking wounded were sent by cab to New York City hospitals. At Ridgewood VA, Mac's ER teams were sleeping on army cots beside their ambulances. Mayor DeBlasio finally activated the National Guard—to erect tents on streets bordering the hospitals. Fortunately, the tents came with cots, blankets, large heaters and generators to run them. Old Brooklynites who had retired to Florida sent two truckloads of blankets. The Los Angeles Dodgers, remembering that they had once been the Brooklyn Dodgers, donated two truckloads of warm team jackets. Ex-

Brooklynites in Long Island donated to children, the elderly, and the infirm seeking relief from the cold and chaos.

The ERs and ambulance teams treated more cold-related cases than battle wounds, though there were fewer deaths, and they seriously feared going into the war zones.

In Brooklyn alone thirty-six people died from the cold, and forty-two from gunshot or knife wounds. Police, firemen and ER crews were placed on 24/7 duty and forbidden to leave the city. Panic set in, complete with mob looting, daylight car-jacking, and disruption of traffic over the Brooklyn, Triborough, and Williamsburg bridges.

Charlie "Jumbo" Giambavlo, *consigliore* to the Gambino crime family, put in a personal call to Mayor DiBlasio, saying: "Mr. Mayor, I am speaking for Mr. Gotti."

"And what," said the mayor, "Does the Don want with me?"

"To help you."

"In what way? ...And at what cost?"

"He asks three Gotchas."

"What's a 'gotcha'?"

"It's a request under duress."

"And what might these three Gotchas be?"

"We don't know until we need them."

"Just how do you propose to earn them?"

"Stop this war in Brooklyn."

"How soon?"

"Immediately, but we need police escorts to and from New York's Little Italy."

"What about the mobs and the rioters?"

"That's why we require the escorts. The civilians are your problem; we'll take care of the gangs."

"Heh. Can you do anything about this weather?"

"My mother says it will break soon. She feels it in her knees."

"From her knees to God's ears."

The five police escorts, consisting of three motorcycle outriders and two police cars, crunched through the latest snow heading over the bridge to Little Italy in New York. The Brooklyn streets were deserted, but traffic on the bridges was chock-a-block. Only the police sirens cleared a path for the convoy.

Finally the motorcade pulled into Mulberry Street. Police cars sealed off both ends of the street, and the motorcyclists covered the rear entrance of Joe La Rosse's Ristorante.

Inside, four square oak tables were placed in the middle of the empty dining room. Jumbo nodded to each of the gang leaders as they entered, and left them to sort out among themselves where they sat. Once they were seated Jumbo walked behind the four men, reached over their left shoulders and placed a silver dollar and a forty-five caliber bullet in front of each man. He returned to his own seat and said: "Now we vote."

Then he pushed forward his silver dollar.

One after the other, the rest followed suit.

"You voted for peace and prosperity," Jumbo announced. "It comes with a price."

He was interrupted by the Flatbush leader. "Before you tell us what we're gonna pay, I wanna know why this Irishman is sittin' here while his people are shootin' up my men!"

"'T'isn't us." Frank McElhenny tossed down a shot of neat whiskey and announced: "These are Chicago Micks, paid for by Miss Lucille, to make us fight each other." ...*And a fine job she's done of it, too*, he thought, but didn't say.

"Exactly how do you know all this?" Mr. G insisted.

"I have an Irish lad in the FBI."

Mr. G ground his teeth again.

"They workin' for you?" the Bushwick leader demanded.

"More like with me," said Jumbo.

"The hell you say!" Mr. G burst out. "How can the FBI help us get rid of Lucille? She's the problem!"

"Correct," said Jumbo. "Mr. Gotti will see to it that she dies. Then I will divide her territories between you four. In return, each of you remits twenty percent of those profits to Mr. Gotti."

"Too much," Mr. G grumbled. "Fifteen percent."

Jumbo stared at Mr. G for a long moment, and said: "Seventeen and a half, and nobody sells fentanyl. Mr. Gotti will eliminate those who sell it and those who allow it to be sold in Brooklyn. That stuff kills more people than this war."

"And how do you intend to end the war?"

"Cut off the head of the snake."

"We tried," said Mr. G. "None of us got close to Miss Lucille."

Jumbo gave him another long and unreadable look. "Mr. Gotti has that answer. Is it a deal?"

After a short silence, every man at the table pocketed the dollar and passed the bullet back to Jumbo. He hefted them in one hand. "Each bullet has a name on it," he said. "Your name. Default on this bargain and the bullet will be returned in the back of your skull. Now it is time to eat the best Italian food ever made: spaghetti, calamari, veal parmigiana, lasagna, fresh garlic bread, oysters, and a special red wine I personally imported from Sicily. Cannolis and Turkish coffee for dessert."

Greco hadn't slept for thirty-six hours. Lucille ordered two of her men to take her lieutenant home and see him to bed. When they stopped in front of his house he ordered: "Take off. I can get to bed without your help."

"Miss Lucille said…"

"When she's not around, who's your boss?"

"We don't want to lie to her."

"So walk me to the front steps."

"The front door."

"Come on."

Greco unlocked the door, walked through, turned and said: "Now get the hell out of here."

The men shrugged and turned away.

Greco shut the door behind them, turned to lock it, and was promptly hit on the head with a blackjack.

He fell to his knees against the door. A cloth sack was pulled over his head. Two men turned him around and pulled him to his feet. A third man stepped in front of him and kicked him in the groin.

Greco awoke in pain, on the floor of a limousine, under the shoes of two men pinning him to the floor. The anguish in his groin precluded all thoughts of escape. He retched into the bag covering his head and got several kicks in response. He heard the driver being challenged and an electric gate opening, then the limo moving up a path, crunching gravel. It eventually stopped, and he was dragged out. The hood was whipped off his head, smearing the puke across his face. Two men held him upright, and he saw that he was at the entrance of a mansion. One of several guards at the front door picked up a garden hose, turned on the water and washed Greco down. When the water turned off, another guard threw him a large beach towel and said: "Don't wet the carpets."

"You guys have done this before," said Greco.

One of his captors slapped him hard on the back of the neck. Greco saw stars and his knees started to buckle. Two guards held him up, patted him dry and tossed the towel over his shoulder. Then they dragged him through large delicately-carved oak doors, into a white vaulted ante-room, through a magnificently furnished salon with rich tapestries covering the walls and cut-glass chandeliers sparkling above. Then he was shoved through another door, into a library, where no less than Pete Gotti sat waiting.

The Mafia don looked Greco up and down, and

said: "Break his fucking nose."

Gotti's bodyguard stepped forward and smacked a large calloused fist into Greco's face. Before the blood could gush out, he used the wet towel draped over Greco's shoulder to staunch the flow. The nose swelled to twice its normal size.

"Now that I have your attention," said Gotti, "Do you know who I am?"

Greco nodded. Oh yes, he knew; this was the top of the crime-industry food-chain in New York. If Gotti wanted Lucille dead, she was doomed. She might fight off the other Brooklyn gangs, and she might fight off the Russians, but there was no hope against the classic Mafia.

"Good. You worked six years for the family in New Orleans, on contract."

Again, Greco responded with a nod.

"You are now working for me and the Gambino family."

Greco knew what was coming, and understood that he had to convince Pete Gotti of his sincerity, so he didn't nod. He met Gotti's eyes, but remained silent.

"Do you have a problem working for me?"

Greco didn't answer, but continued to stare into Gotti's eyes.

"You're an arrogant bastard," Gotti sneered. "I should kill you and get this over with."

"Then you'd have trouble implementing your plan," Greco spoke up.

"And how would you know what that is?"

"From your current position, it's the only way to

stop this war."

"And how's that?"

"'Cut off the head of the snake'."

Gotti lunged out of his chair as if fired from a cannon. "Those are my exact words!" he shouted in Greco's face. "Who's the spy in my Family?"

I'm sorry, Lucille, Greco thought. "Not who: what," he said. "It's the wheelchair."

"What the hell are you talking about?"

"When Lucille left the wheelchair at the consigliore's meeting it had a listening device in the armrest. Someone brought it here for your mother."

"She doesn't use it."

"I saw it in the anteroom. It picks up all your conversations in the salon. That's where you hold your meetings."

"You mean she's listening right now?!"

Greco thought of answering yes, thought of what that would lead to, and reluctantly told the truth. "Somebody is, but they can't hear in this room."

Gotti motioned to his bodyguard. "Bring the fuckin' thing in here."

"I wouldn't do that," said Greco. "That's a method of feeding Lucille information we want her to have."

"But she must know we've got you."

"You haven't mentioned my name, and anyway, they can't hear us in this room."

"You said 'us'?"

"As you said, I'm working for you now. So I'll do it."

"Do what?" Gotti demanded.

"I'll get rid of Lucille."

Gotti's eyes narrowed. "And what do you want?" he asked.

"The wheelchair," said Greco, "And men loyal to me to operate the listening device. You want me to work for you. I want to work for myself. I get rid of Lucille, and you support my takecver of the Crowns."

"You want to replace Lucille?" Gotti took a cigar from a humidor, went through the ritual of lighting it, and puffed a blue cloud at the ceiling. Greco, you're smart. Get too smart and you may wake up dead."

"My ambitions are modest, and you can help me get rid of Miss Lucille."

"Precisely how?"

"Mr. G has a special, Russian Army, battery-operated, digital bomb that can be set off from a hundred yards."

"How do you know that?" Gotti knew about it, of course, but he was interested in Greco's intelligence system.

"He used one against us last week on Nostrand Avenue."

"If he's got it, you'll get it."

CHAPTER 28:
WHEN THE WIDOWMAKERS
MEET AGAIN

RIDGEWOOD VA HOSPITAL

Mac brought two containers of coffee into the day-room, where Martha was holding a table for them. She accepted the coffee, saying: "It just shows to go ya; you can't tell the players without a score-card. I would have bet anything that you were clean as the driven snow. Why didn't you come to me?"

"It would have become known." Mac sat down and sipped her coffee. "I would never have received this appointment, nor my doctorate."

"Tell Aunt Martha about it."

"I never told anyone. After my husband's death I set my sights on a doctorate, and continued as head nurse of the ER. There weren't enough hours in the day, so I tried not sleeping."

"Thomas Edison almost went bonkers doing that."

"I started with black coffee and Coca-Cola, then

high-potency vitamins, speed, ephedrine, and anything else to stay awake."

"What about your love life? You're a good-looking woman..."

"Nonexistent. The minute I got into a bed, I fell asleep. I think one guy screwed me while I slept."

"How did you get clean?"

"I knew I was in trouble. On completing the doctorate I had two months vacation, and went to a rehabilitation center in Colorado."

"Again, why didn't you come to me?"

"My entire career has been in the VA. Again, it would have become known."

"But I could have recommended a place, or reduced the cost."

"It was my secret. I kept it until the other night, when I heard you speak."

"...I didn't say what I really needed to."

"What's that?"

Martha bowed her head and scrunched her shoulders. "I crawled into the bottle after killing the mother of that frozen child. I fell off the wagon voting for the Widowmakers to kill the man who murdered his family. He deserved to die, and me too. I can't go on with it."

"You mean the Widowmakers?"

"Yes."

Mac heaved a sigh. "I came to speak with you tonight because I was again tempted to do drugs. Rebuilding the ERs, servicing a community at war, and taking an active position on spousal abuse—it's too much. I'm ashamed."

"Of what?"

"The Widowmakers. Floyd and Kula expressed their misgivings. Alphonso requested a private meeting. I'm certain it's the same subject."

"Call a meeting."

"And do what? Street violence is outstripping domestic violence. Both affect all levels of society. The social, racial, or economic status doesn't matter; emotional violence precedes physical abuse."

Mac spread her hands and asked: "How can we change that?"

"We can't," said Martha. "Since I signed myself in here, I've had time to think. The psychological trauma of domestic violence seems to be a force of nature. It's found in every level of society and education. It fosters a system of control of a woman's life, resulting in injury and even death."

"We must stop it!"

"No," said Martha, "We can't. That's why I'm in here and you're asking me what to do about it. That's why you're on the verge of doing drugs again."

Mac bowed her head. "I thought that when I got my doctorate and was appointed to revamp the ERs in Brooklyn, that my dream had come true. Rabbi Goldman used to say: "Be careful what you wish for; you just might get it."

"Mac, you took on the Widowmakers in addition to your ER organizing and rebuilding. Let the Widowmakers go."

"How can I face the group and say that I'm backing out? I'm responsible for the death of a man."

"Continue, and you'll be responsible for your

own death and that of others.”

“So what's to do?”

“Tell the truth. Hold the meeting here. JJ and I will help.”

The loudspeaker came to life. “Dr. MacKenzie, please call Station 43.”

Mac dialed, and heard Jill report: “We're on stand-by. There have been drive-by shootings in Coney Island, Bushwick, Flatbush, and Bed-Stuy. The Irish are loading street-fighters into trucks. The police will let us know when and where it's safe to go in.”

“I'll be there in a minute.”

Mac entered the ER in time to see her crews suiting up with bullet-proof vests and metal helmets. Jill helped Mac into her vest, and said: “Four Corners, Gates and Nostrand Avenues. At least three dead and nine wounded.”

“Has the shooting stopped?”

“Except for the kid-gangs being chased off the roofs.”

Mac's emergency phone rang. Through it, Crazy Mayzie announced: “I've sent two ambulances to Coney Island. The Crowns invaded, and there are dead on both sides. Multiple wounded. Can you send a refrigerator truck to store the dead?”

“Can do. Anything else?”

“A couple more hands, a cold beer, and a broom.”

“What's the broom for?”

“To stick up my ass, so I can clean up while doing my job.”

"Hang in there. It's got to get better."

"Bullshit."

At Four Corners, all the plate-glass windows of stores, shops, and apartments were shot or blown out by bullets or explosives. Mac stepped away from the ambulance, and ducked back as a flaming bottle arched down from the roof and exploded near a police officer. Fellow officers covered him with their bodies and rolled him on the ground to extinguish his burning clothes. Mac rushed in and applied medicated bandages to his face and hands. Alphonso and Percy cut off his smoldering jacket and trousers.

"Can you see?" Mac asked him.

"Yes," panted the cop.

"Are you married?"

"Yeah, with five boys. Why?"

"They're going to laugh that your eyebrows are singed off."

"...Am I alive?"

"Definitely."

"That's all that counts."

Mac covered him with an aluminum blanket, tagged him for evacuation, and went to oversee her group. Overhead, a police helicopter buzzed the roof, driving the vicious kids away.

Next, she called in a Medivac helicopter to take out the wounded from nearby Lincoln Park. There had been a brief but fierce gunfight there. The police suffered casualties, and began using semi-auto rifles and shotguns. The Crowns retreated. The Bushwick and Flatbush boys melted away. The Chicago Irish, having caused havoc in three neighborhoods, returned to the airport and Illinois.

The police had had enough and took charge. With the aid of civic and church groups, a semblance of order returned to Brooklyn. For the first time since the Civil War, martial law was declared in the borough. The Marine contingent in the Brooklyn Navy Yard was put on stand-by. A six PM to six AM curfew was ordered. Local police captains put out the word: "The war is over. Anyone with a weapon who is not a law enforcement officer is the enemy."

Greco got his nose repaired at the ER, passing off the injury as a mild encounter with an irritable cop. He gave the same excuse to Lucille. He also made arrangements with Big Momma for Lucille to visit the Crowns' wounded at Bed-Stuy Hospital. He, Chowder, Little Joe and Ida accompanied her into the limo that would take them there. Greco carried a leather briefcase holding a hundred thousand dollars in hundred-dollar bills.

Buried under the bills was the Russian explosive device.

Greco's phone rang as he was about to enter the limo. He listened then said: "Send a car for me at Madison and Evergreen. Don't make me wait."

"What was that about?" Lucille demanded, leaning out the limo's door.

"A fight between families at the funeral parlor." He handed her the briefcase. "There's the hundred-thousand for the families of the wounded. I'll catch up to you as soon as I straighten this out."

"Maybe you should take half the money and pay off at the funeral home."

"Nah, there aren't that many of them," said Greco, sweating as he refused the briefcase. "I'll give them an IOU for twenty thousand each. You go on."

Lucille placed the briefcase between herself and Ida. "See you at the hospital," she said, and closed the door.

Little Joe pulled the limo away from the curb and on down the street. Within thirty seconds another limo drove up, with three Mafia men inside. The rear door opened, and Greco entered.

The driver handed him a small control box with a blinking red light and a telescoped antenna. "As long as the light's on," the driver said, "You're in range of the detonator."

"Keep their car just barely in sight," said Greco, as he pulled up the antenna. He held the blinking control box in his lap and leaned forward for a better view of Lucille's limo as the car began to move.

Lucille pulled the briefcase into her lap and tried to open it. "Damn, Greco forgot to give me the key," she grumbled. "Chowder, give me your knife."

Chowder reached into his pocket.

The briefcase exploded.

All six of the limo's windows blew out, followed by fire and smoke. The gas tank ruptured and exploded. A large fireball formed and hovered over Madison street, incinerating the limo and the remains of its passengers.

Greco closed the antenna, saying: "That's that."

The man in the passenger seat up front turned around with a silenced pistol in hand, and put a bullet into Greco's forehead. As they drew up beside the still-blazing fireball, the man in the seat beside Greco retrieved the control box, opened the door, spit on Greco and shoved the Cajun's body out beside the burning wreck.

"You'd betray her, you'd do the same to us," he said.

He pulled the door shut, and the car rolled on.

CHAPTER 29:
AFTERMATH

RIDGEWOOD VA HOSPITAL PARKING LOT

In the rear of his limousine Congressman Waters answered his cell-phone, listened for a moment, then interrupted Mac, opened the intercom and ordered his driver: "Put on the news."

Mac fell silent as the announcer's voice came through the rear speakers.

"This is Lewis Miller reporting for WINS. A powerful warm front is barreling up from the southern states. It's over Virginia right now and is expected to slam America's northeast coast this evening. It will bring great relief to those millions suffering from the longest unbroken cold spell in forty years. You might say that New York Mayor DeBlasio's prayers are answered: the cold will break. That's the good news.

"Now the not so good news. At four PM in Brooklyn a car-bomb went off, killing five people. That in itself is no surprise for New Yorkers; there have been bombings, shootings and drive-bys since the Brooklyn gangs went to war this winter. But those killed in this incident were Lucille Leissner, leader of the powerful Crowns gang in Bedford - Stuyvesant, her second-in-command Toledo Greco, two bodyguards and personal friend Camille Lehe.

"Police intelligence believes that the death of Lucille Leissner will end the war on the streets of Brooklyn. From private sources I've learned that the Mafia called a halt to the fighting; apparently, it was bad for business.

"The cease-fire came at just the right time. People are fed up with the bloodshed and violence that revealed the corruption in our police department. Former Mayor LaGuardia is quoted as having said: 'No bookie, loan-shark, pimp or protection racket could exist without the compliance of the police.' The citizens' rage was fanned to an inferno by the cold spell, and there were worries that the citizens might take the law into their own hands if the war didn't stop. Both factors seem to be negated by to-day's events.

"The northeast electronic grid shows a ten percent reduction in power as rain sweeps into New York State. Have a warm, wet one. Enjoy! This is Lewis Miller for WINS."

"Shut it off," Elijah Waters said, and closed the intercom. He turned to Mac. "I don't want to hear another word about the Widowmakers. Distance yourself from them.

"As for your problem of being over-extended, welcome to the club. Your doctorate gave you entry into the harshest facet of public service."

"What's that?"

"The more you accomplish, the more you'll be expected to do. As sure as shit draws flies, you'll come under pressure to do things beyond your knowledge or reach. When you fail to deliver, you'll be ostracized by your former supporters who want your position. You can see that in politics all the time."

"What can I do?"

Waters chuckled. "I already told you."

Mac thought for a moment. "Form a committee!"

"Atta girl. That's the way the game is played. Spread the blame and collect the fame." He poked the intercom once more and told his driver: "Call a cab for Dr. MacKenzie. I've got to go meet the mayor."

THE ROLLER DOME

Taguir Abazov sat behind Mr. G, who answered one of the five phones on his desk while he scribbled replies to notes Abazov handed him. Abazov lit a large Havana cigar and puffed a stream of blue smoke to the cloudy ceiling. The special phone in his breast pocket vibrated, but he made no move to answer it. Only one man had that number, and he was in Odessa: Boris Yakabovsky, leader of the Russian Mafia. Abazov leaned forward and tapped Mr. G's shoulder, simultaneously exhaling another cloud of smoke. "I'm going out for fresh air," he said.

Mr. G waved him away, and put another phone to his ear.

Alone in the parking lot, Abazov answered the quivering phone. "Yes, Boris?"

"Brooklyn sounds like an American cluster-fuck crossed with a Chinese fire-drill. It's making international headlines. That's bad for business."

"It should cool down while the weather warms up, now that the Crowns' command staff has been cut off."

"We need to prevent this sort of stupidity from happening again. Kill Mr. G."

"When?"

"Yesterday."

"Do you want to send a message?"

"Make him disappear. That's the message."

"Who takes over?"

"You."

"What are my marching orders?"

"Rebuild your section of Brighton Beach by the springtime opening of Coney Island. I want quiet, lots of quiet. Have your casinos, drug trade and the rest up and running by the first of May, or you too can disappear."

"Understood. Thank you for your vote of confidence."

Abazov switched to his second cell-phone and had four of his own men meet him in the parking lot. Two he sent to the hardware store, and two brought up Mr. G's limousine. Back in the office, he informed Mr. G of a meeting with the Mafia consigliore.

"Why didn't he call me direct?" said Mr. G, putting down his phone.

"The Wops have a big thing for respect. I'm your consigliore."

"Then I'll be meeting with Gotti?"

Abazov shrugged. "It is what it is. Jumbo is already traveling to Dead Horse Bay."

"Shit, he could at least pick a decent restaurant. Give me my jacket, and let's go."

Outside, they entered the limo. Mr. G noticed that his regular driver was absent. "Where's Nikita?" he asked.

"Went out for a pastrami sandwich."

"I could use a couple of them," Mr. G said, and slapped Abazov's knee. "Things are beginning to look up. Already the pushers are back on their corners, the whores back on their parades, and the poker games up and running. Soon we'll get our share of the Bed-Stuy action. That extra money should make Boris happier."

"Amen."

"Look there: they haven't hauled away the burnt-out trucks from the high school."

"Too busy ducking bullets, I'd guess."

"I'm glad that's over with. Now I want you to get close to Jumbo. One day we'll have to wipe out the spaghetti-benders."

The limo stopped and parked on a wet sand dune overlooking Dead Horse Bay. A cold damp wind swept across the water and up the lonely beach. Mr. G, Abazov, and his two men got out. Another car pulled up behind them, and two men got out and came forward, carrying a heavy length of chain.

"Did you get an air mattress?" Abazov asked,

sliding a hand under his coat.

"From the Army-Navy store," one of the men answered.

"What the hell is this about?" Mr. G demanded, pointing to the chain. "Where's Jumbo?"

"He's not coming," said Abazov.

Mr. G whipped out a Beretta automatic, shot one man in the leg and began to run. The damp sand sucked at his shoes, and he lost one. Abazov's men fired repeatedly. Mr. G ran in circles to evade the shots. The men emptied their guns and Mr. G absorbed half the shots, but he still didn't die. He fell to his knees at the water's edge, gasping for breath. Abazov walked up to him, gun drawn, and put a bullet in each eye. He turned to his men, scowling.

"I swear, you couldn't hit the side of a barn, from the inside. Wrap him up in the chain, blow up the air mattress, and float him out with the tide. The crabs and eels will take care of the rest."

"Won't someone find him floating around?"

"Not if you can shoot out the air mattress at a hundred yards off the beach. You need the target practice."

RIDGEWOOD VA HOSPITAL

"I called this emergency meeting of the Widowmakers," said Mac, "Because this will probably be our last meeting. I'm glad to see Big Momma and Mayzie could make it. Kula and Floyd couldn't. They're making arrangements for the wedding, and want to end association with the group."

"Did they say why?" Alphonso asked.

"They believe it's morally wrong."

"And I agree with them," Martha added.

"But you were the most pro-punishment of us all," said Bill.

"It's no secret I fell off the wagon and signed myself into rehab. I became an alcoholic again because I did on my own what the Widowmakers are only contemplating. I don't want that to happen to any of you. Taking another person's life is a terrible thing. The responsibility is too much for me."

"So what are we here for?" Jill asked.

"To vote on whether or not to continue the Widowmakers," said Mac.

"It's a foregone conclusion," noted Big Momma. "Kula, Floyd and Martha are opting out. If you were for continuing, you would have found a different way to approach us. All you need is one more vote."

"They've got it with me," said Mayzie. "I'll wade knee-deep in a patient's shit to save him, but to take a life is something I never did and never want to do."

There was silence in the office.

"So, do we wish to take a vote?' Mac asked.

"Not necessary," said Jill. "The Widowmakers are disbanded by consent."

"Does this mean we wash our hands of obvious spousal abuse cases and child molestation incidents?" Percy asked.

"The opposite," said Mac. "Based on the recommendations of the ER workers in our first general meeting, those two subjects will have the highest priority. I'd like to see Martha and JJ take personal charge of this element in our new program. All of us can participate in making their efforts successful."

"Will you still call yourselves the Widowmakers?" Percy asked.

"Only among ourselves," Martha answered. "We won't make any more widows. The widowmakers' club is officially ended."

Alphonso and Percy looked at each other. "Officially," Percy mouthed silently.

CHAPTER 30:
SHOWERS

RIDGEWOOD VA HOSPITAL

"Did you hear that thunder" Kula's voice came over the phone.

"Listen." Floyd held his phone close to the window. "It's closer to me than you."

"It's pouring buckets."

"Here too. Do you want to call it off?"

"We can't. The stuff must be delivered by the seventeenth, and we've got to order now. Both places are friends of my father. We're getting a special price."

"I don't want to use the motorcycle in this weather."

"I'll meet you at Gates and Evergreen, and we'll take the bus to Myrtle and a train over the bridge. Do you have an umbrella?"

"Yes. See you in twenty minutes."

Floyd held the bus door open as Kula ran from across the street. The wind turned her umbrella inside-out. He slapped the metal frame back into place and helped her up the steps, where they kissed.

"Even lovebirds have to pay," the bus driver chided.

On the train it was obvious who had been home before the rain struck; those who hadn't were muffled up in winter clothes. The wind rocked the train on the elevated line over the Manhattan Bridge.

Floyd and Kula got off in the factory district a block from Rabinowitz's Furniture, where an old man awaited them. He was tall, heavy, wearing a small yarmulke on his bald head, and glowed with a bearded smile. He held his arms wide and embraced Kula, saying:"It's been twenty years since I last hugged you. How you've changed!"

"I was very young then," Kula giggled. "How did you come to know my father?"

"It started with your grandfather, then your father and mother. Saints, all of them."

"What did they do?" Floyd asked.

"What didn't they do! We were a group of poor, scared, half-starved Jews in a strange country. Your parents learned the rules of kosher food to help feed us. Your mother took the ladies and children to the Goodwill store and the Salvation Army and Saint Barbara's Church to get clothes for them. I remember your father leading a group of fifty of us men and boys to the public bath-house on every Shabbat, every Friday afternoon, like clockwork. He and your grandfather would shower with us. We had coal and wood-burning stoves, and in winter they gave us wooden crates to burn. When we left the neighborhood you were just beginning to walk. I made your parents promise that when you got married they would tell me. Your father remembered.

"Now it is my turn to remember. Please turn around. I would like to introduce you to my wife Janet, my daughter Barbara, her two daughters Anav and Loriel, and their three daughters Shira, Yara, and Bara, and this is my son Jeff. They're Israelis. I wanted them to meet the daughter of the man who has my respect as a most exceptional human being.

"Ah, but you came to select a bedroom suite and a living-room set. Go through those double doors and you'll find the finest display of modern and traditional styles to choose from."

Floyd and Kula shook hands all around, then let themselves be led into to the double doors. Floyd pushed them open to reveal a long well-lit room with two thousand feet of floor-space. One thousand feet on the right were used for bedroom suites and the other thousand were filled with living-room furniture. Every set was color-matched and coordinated in style and design.

Floyd had to trot to keep up with Kula. She moved down the aisle pinching pillows, slapping mattresses, caressing bureaus, dressers, mirrors, and lifting lamps. She lay down on one of the beds, then hopped out as Floyd jumped in. He caught up to her as she reached the living-room furniture.

"I thought you had a plan drawn up," he grumbled.

"Isn't it all so beautiful?"

"So are the prices."

"My father will help us."

"He's already committed to the house. Didn't you say you made a plan for the upstairs, so you'd know what furniture you want?"

Kula dove into her handbag and pulled out several pages with room sketches. She held up three of them. "These are for downstairs, where we'll be staying until they finish the apartment upstairs. All non-bearing internal walls will be taken out, and the two apartments will become one. There are two bathrooms that have to be modernized. Don't you agree?"

Floyd made his first mistake; he answered the question. "I kind of liked the older fixtures with the brass handles and white porcelain."

"How can you say that? Look at the modern chrome and ceramics. I envision etched-glass shower doors..."

Forgetting Georgee's warnings, he plunged on. "Plenty of people like the old style. It brings back childhood memories."

Kula pulled out a captain's chair at the head of a table, and sat down hard. "You're ruining what should be a lovely time," she pouted. "These are moments we'll never forget."

"Why are you getting so upset? You asked, and I answered. It's no big deal. Just choose what you want, and I'll agree."

"That's not an answer. If you think the old stuff is better, stand up for yourself."

"It's something I like, but I can live without it."

"We're only engaged a few weeks, and you're already talking about living without?"

"Kula, you're taking this all wrong. Can we get back to selecting furniture?"

"We're here, so we might as well." Kula pulled out a tape-measure and a small notebook from her bag and began writing down model numbers.

Floyd pretended intense interest in the choices, prices, and placement of pieces in their new home. He was careful not to be too earnest in agreeing, yet accepted every choice Kula made. It was a mental balancing act that strained his patience.

Finally the entered Mr. Rabinowitz's office. "Have you decided?" he asked.

"We made several choices," said Kula, "But it'll depend on the cost and how we can make the payments."

"Let me worry about the payments. Now give me your first choices of bedroom and living-room sets." He took the paper Kula handed him, and smiled. "You have good taste." He wrote up a bill for the sets, took out a rubber stamp and ink-pad, and stamped the bill, in red ink: PAID IN FULL.

"B-but Mr. Rabinowitz," Floyd marveled, "That's a lot of money."

"Yes, it is," the old man smiled. "And I wouldn't have a penny of it without your future bride's family. Nor would I have raised so fine a family in this wonderful country of America. I've been waiting and praying to stay alive long enough to do this. The only thing you'll have to pay for is the delivery and set-up costs to the truckers for putting the bed together. I understand you're going to Mel Springer's factory for kitchen furniture and supplies, yes? Tell him... No, never mind. I'll call him. My son Jeff will drive you over. Lots of rain, but we need it. Give my regards to Sylvia." He took Kula by the shoulders and kissed her forehead. "Every day I count you and your family in my prayers."

Mel and Sylvia, another vigorous old couple, met Floyd and Kula at the factory entrance. They too introduced the couple to their children, grandchildren and great-grandchildren. "What a pleasure, said Mel. "We always remember your family in our prayers. My children know all about you. We left the old neighborhood shortly after you were born. Ah, what a celebration your parents made for you! It overflowed from the diner into the parking lot. They even opened the school across the street for toilets and parking."

"Oh, let them catch their breath," old Sylvia chuckled. "I made cups of hot tea, and have a nice piece of Edinger's sponge cake. Sit, sit, you two. We have a thousand chairs."

"I remember my grandfather telling about Mr. Springer," Kula smiled. "He said you could whistle like the birds."

Mel pursed his lips and emitted a series of beautiful bird-calls. "Your grandfather made me whistle while I was cutting fruit or cracking nuts," he said. "If I stopped whistling, he knew I was eating."

"Your grandfather hired Mel," Sylvia went on, "Even though he had a limp from polio. Mel had no family. They all died in the camps."

"I lived with the Rabinowitzes," Mel explained.

"Your grandfather gave me to cut onions and potatoes. Then I graduated to fruit and nuts, and whistling. Did you know your parents co-signed a loan so that I could start a lamp business? Then I went into furniture, and finally specialized in kitchens. So, come into the showroom. Sylvia will take you; she knows more about my business than I do."

Springer's Kitchenware Products was similar in size and layout to the Rabinowitz furniture warehouse. At the far end of the showroom were the factory machines for cutting, sizing, and shaping glass, plastic, marble, and metal. Appliances were separated by function: cabinets, tables and chairs by style.

It took two hours for Kula to make her selections, and all the while Sylvia paced beside her and Floyd telling how Kula's family had helped feed and clothe the poor of Ridgewood.

In his office, Mel Springer took another large red stamp and inkpad, and stamped PAID IN FULL on Floyd and Kula's receipt. With tears in his eyes he handed it to Kula. "Thank you for letting me do this," he said. "Steven will drive you back to Brooklyn."

"I thought we'd go eat at the Chinese restaurant near the bridge," said Kula.

"Nie, nie," said Sylvia. "A lot of people have gotten the flu eating there. And isn't your father waiting for both of you at his house? He wants to discuss the wedding with you."

Kula looked at Floyd, who shrugged. "Your dad told me he might call."

"Okay," she laughed, "Then it's to Daddy's house

we go."

Steven pulled the car into Bleeker Street and noted: "There are no parking spaces."

"That's unusual," said Kula. "Oh, there's my father on the left, with the big colored umbrella. You should find parking down the block."

"I'll drop you off. I have to get back home."

"Thanks," said Kula. She ducked out under her father's umbrella, peeked back into the car and said: "You have very special parents."

Floyd joined her, and she noticed a man standing in the downpour taking pictures. He ran ahead of them to Georgee's house, turned in the doorway, and snapped more pictures. "What's that about?" she asked.

"A crazy neighbor," said Georgee. "Don't worry. Now, into the house."

The photographer opened the front door, opened it, disappeared inside and shut the door behind him, which affected Georgee not at all. Puzzled, Kula opened the front door—and was greeted by a hallway full of women, young and all, shouting: "Surprise! This is your bridal shower!" They crowded close to hug and kiss her.

Shocked, Kula looked to her father, who was grinning widely, and Floyd, who shrugged. "You deserve it," he said.

So many women came forward that Kula and Floyd were separated. The hallway was lined in bouquets of flowers with blue and white streamers. American and Greek flags hung side by side along the walls. Kula was led into the living-room, where a long white table extending into the dining-room was set with white plates and blue napkins. "The colors of the Greek flag," Georgee chuckled. "The theme is Vegan. The wine is from your cousin in Athens. Your family from abroad is coming to the wedding."

"Who arranged this shower?"

Georgee shrugged. "Me, your brothers, Floyd, and the nurses from his Emergency Room staff. I sent the men. Sloan-Kettering sent the flowers."

"How many people are here?"

"Forty ladies. The men will leave soon." Georgee pushed Floyd toward Kula. "Give your girl a kiss. My little girl is getting married..."

He began to weep. Kula hugged him and Floyd at the same time, raining kisses on them both. "Oh Papa, don't be sad," she said.

"I'm not. I'm so happy it makes me cry. Look, I made black bean chili, falafel burgers, linguini with vegetables and tomato sauce, okra and curry with vegetable meatballs, Singapore noodles with salt and pepper tofu, and for dessert butternut and chestnut cakes with cool mint yogurt. Lemon tarts to finish."

"Oh Papa, thank you!"

"Now your brothers and I are going to put some hair on your husband's chest."

"He's already got hair on his chest."

"How do you know?—No, I don't want to hear." Georgee herded his sons and Floyd toward the door.

Mac and Martha came up to congratulate Kula and lead her to a high-backed armchair at the head of the table surrounded by gifts. Once she was seated, the first box opened and the last thing Floyd saw as he was shoved out was a matching pair of Prisoner of Love pajamas—white with black stripes and red felt hearts over the left breast. The ladies laughed, clapped, and made jokes. After that came a sheer pink nightgown followed by a skimpy black lace bra and panty set, then towels, linens, cooking pots and pans, and a sixteen-piece setting of Corel-ware from her mother' sister.

"Auntie," why so many settings?

"Because you'll take over from your mother and me for hosting Sunday family dinners."

"But there aren't that many people in the family, at least not here in America."

"You wear those skimpy panties and bra, and there will be."

The evening was completed with a Bingo game. Every person got one card, and only one game would be played. "The entire card must be filled," Kula's aunt explained. "The winner receives two round-trip tickets to Florida, by the grace of our host, Georgee Prodromakeos."

CHAPTER 31:
BACHELOR PARTY

GEORGEE'S DINER

Huddled under the large umbrella, Georgee led his sons and Floyd to the rear of the diner, where they ducked under the garage overhang. The door swung open to reveal Alphonso, Percy and Big Bill smiling at them. Further back from the door stood four older men, who raised paper cups in a toast to the groom.

"We can have our own party," said Georgee, slapping Floyd's shoulder. "You can eat Vegan if you want, but that's a lamb roasting, and over there are Greek meatballs, flavored rice, and salads with good Greek bread and wine."

"If you don't tell Kula about the meat, I'll join you."

"It'll be our secret."

Floyd looked around the garage, and noticed what was missing. "Where's the car?' he asked.

"Gone," said Georgee. "I sold it."

"Did you get your asking price?"

"I was hoping he would argue, but he paid without thinking twice."

"I know what that car meant to you. My father had a '35 Cord that he loved."

"Did it run?"

"Smooth as a sewing machine. It would pass anything but a gas station. It had chrome exhausts coming out of the hood and into the fenders to ventilate the engine."

"Ah, I understand completely."

Georgee hustled Floyd into the garage, introduced him to the four older men and sat him down at the table. The men kissed Floyd on both cheeks, wished him well in Greek and English, then took out instruments and began playing old Greek melodies. Alphonso and Percy made a line and started dancing. Floyd, guessing what would follow, plowed happily into the food. The lamb with jellied mint sauce was delicious. Georgee's sons hustled about between drinks, setting up an amplifier system while Floyd filled his stomach.

One of the sons passed Floyd another paper cup, but this time instead of wine it held Jack Daniels square-faced bourbon. Yes, they were going to make this a drinking contest. Well, before becoming somewhat Vegan, he'd been a Marine medic and could drink with the best of them.

Floyd swallowed his last mouthful of lamb, slugged down the shot, got up and joined the line-dance. He didn't know the steps, but everyone—including Big Bill, Alphonso and Percy—were wrong-footed too. They'd been drinking before he got there, and it showed. There was more enthusiasm than coordination, and the older men gave up trying to correct him. Georgee began singing along with the music, matching each gesture to the chord-changes of the instruments, projecting his melodic voice to invigorate the dancers.

Suddenly there came a banging on the corrugated metal door. Everyone stopped. The banging continued, and the reverberations were like the inside of a metal drum. The youngest son staggered to the door, shouting: "What the hell do you want?"

The door swung open, revealing a short young woman with her fists dug into her hips. The man staggered back. "Annie, it's you!" he gulped.

"You're damned right it's me," she said, marching into the garage.

"Uh, let me introduce you to my new brother-in-law."

"He's going to marry Kula?" Annie looked Floyd up and down, apparently approving of what she saw. "Well, boy, you're getting a wonderful girl, but a crazy family."

"What's the problem?" asked Alexi, closing the door.

"You! You're the problem."

"What did I do?"

"You're drunk! It's not yet six o'clock, and your amplifiers are all the way up. My daughter is trying to take a nap, and the music sounds like a bunch of sick goats with the shits."

"Aww, you shouldn't say that. We're making America great again."

"Grating, you mean. Are you telling me you're

for that low-life Trump?"

"No man better!"

Annie's fist and caught Alexi under the jaw. The young Prodromakeos went down like a sack of potatoes.

The men with their arms around each others' shoulders gaped at her in stunned silence. Annie pointed at them and snapped: "Shut it down!."

Georgee watched her march away toward the door. "Better do what she says," he admitted. One of the men hastened to comply.

Floyd was the first to reach Alexi, and checked him over. "You're okay," he announced.

"Wha' happen'?" Alexi mumbled, shaking himself awake.

"That woman cold-cocked you."

"Little Annie knocked me out?!"

"A right uppercut to the jaw."

"She used to walk me to school."

"You didn't learn how to duck a punch."

"This is terribly embarrassing." Alexi grabbed the front of Floyd's jacket and whispered fiercely: "You mustn't tell anyone. Decked by a lady! ...Ohhh," he groaned as he realized that behind Floyd stood his father and friends, his brothers, Big Bill, Alphonso and Percy. "My reputation's ruined. Decked by a little woman!"

One of the older men began to sing. The others joined in. Alexi winced.

"I don't understand Greek," said Floyd.

Giggling, Georgee took his son in his arms and translated the words. "Alexi, Alexi, pudding and pie, kissed the girls and made them cry. When the girls came out to play, they kicked the shit out of Alexi."

Alexi groaned again.

Eventually Georgee brought the party back to his house, where the bridal shower was just finishing.

Kula pointed to the boxes and presents, which were many, "Oh Papa," she crooned, "Thank you for the lovely shower."

"Ah, your friends from the VA and Sloan-Kettering did it," he demurred.

Floyd played along with a straight face. "I had no idea," he said. "Your dad is taking me to a final meeting with Father Joseph before the wedding."

"This time the priest will explain the ceremony," said Georgee.

"How is it going with plans for the wedding food?" Kula asked.

"It's become a problem."

"Why? What's the problem?"

"You and your mother."

"Mama's gone, and I didn't do a thing."

"Sweetness, from the moment you were born you were beautiful. Your mother and I were standing at the glass partition, waving at you, when a little old lady in a black dress and a stiff white lace collar came up and asked if this was our first child. Mama said: 'It's our first girl. Isn't she beautiful? Look at those darling ears, the button nose, the little pink lips.' With a twinkle in her eyes, the old woman said: 'Welcome to the bull shitter's club.'"

Kula smothered a burst of laughter.

"Your mama and I had been planning for this

wedding since the day you were born, but it's not only you who is drawing people. Many have been waiting to thank your mother, your grandparents, and even your great-grandparents for the help they gave during hard times. These people are coming, with or without invitation. It's going to be an old-fashioned Brooklyn block-party. The precinct captain is closing off the street for it."

Kula shook her head, imagining that. "How can you feed them all? Where will you put them?"

"The school across the street is letting us use their toilets, and their parking lot. I ordered a hundred tables and ten times as many chairs to be placed in our parking lot. We'll have an outdoor reception."

"Papa, that's a thousand people!"

"I'll feed the wedding party and our family; that will be negan. Everybody else, as I've said on the invitations, bring your own and everybody shares. That's a block party. Ahhh, the last one we held was at the end of the Vietnam War. Your mother and her sister made fifteen hundred pocket-breads, and it wasn't enough. The Jews' food was eaten first, by everyone who wanted to know what matzoh-balls tasted like. Chopped liver was the biggest hit. That's why it's on the diner's menu now."

"I'd wondered."

Georgee stepped back and rubbed his chin. "Last night I dreamed of Momma. I swear, she really came to see me. She opened the door to my room, dressed in the old-time Greek style, complete with babushka. She looked beautiful."

"What did she say?"

"Nothing, but her eyes said it all. She approves of the marriage."

Kula embraced her father and wept on his shoulder.

Georgee hugged back. "Your mother could say more with a look than a politician can with a twenty-page speech."

Kula stepped back at the sound of an approaching motorcycle. "That's Floyd. We have an appointment with Father Joseph."

Georgee held his daughter at arm's length and smiled at her. "Since Momma passed, I've been hoping she'd visit me. I know in my heart she would want me to tell you and Floyd to use the car. Motorcycles are dangerous."

BAY RIDGE, CHURCH OF THE HOLY CROSS

Kula closed the visor on her helmet and climbed onto the seat behind Floyd. She hugged him around the waist as they drove up Gates Avenue, past Bushwick, past Broadway, and took a right on Atlantic, on to Flatbush, then Fourth Avenue up to the Holy Cross Greek Orthodox Church. Father Joseph was waiting for them at the entrance.

The priest was dressed up today, wearing a black hat similar to a college graduation cap, but round. His robe was black from the shoulders to the toes of his Gucci shoes, he had exclusive Mascot coral-blue-framed glasses, and his handlebar mustache flowed into his white beard that stretched halfway down his broad chest.

At his side a good-looking younger man in casual clothes was taking notes. He introduced himself to Floyd and Kula as: "Mark Goldberg, editor of the *Brooklyn Eagle*. Your wedding will be Brooklyn's social event of the year. I'd appreciate your permission to write about it. Yes? Excellent. Your families have been a pillar of strength in Brooklyn, outstanding in the Ridgewood community. The *Eagle*, founded here in 1841, wishes to thank you."

"Er, that's Kula's family," Floyd chided.

"Could you include the story of Floyd's family's trek to Oregon?" said Kula, batting her eyes.

"My pleasure," Goldberg agreed, jotting notes.

"Don't forget to mention my mother."

"A fabulous lady, and your father is a man among men. Now I'm going to stay quiet and listen in while Father Joseph explains the ceremony."

"It begins here, at the top of the steps leading to the entrance of the church," Father Joseph boomed, slipping into his professional oratorical style. I will be standing here, with Floyd and the Kimbro."

"That will be Dr. MacKenzie," Floyd explained. "She agreed to act in place of my family."

"Mr. Prodromakeos will escort the bride up the steps. Kula will extend her right hand, to be taken by Floyd's right hand. She will step away from her father and closer to the groom. This is the beginning of the Betrothal ceremony. The Greek Orthodox church binds a couple in faith, oneness of mind and truth. This symbolic ceremony reflects the elements of marriage: love, mutual respect, equality and sacrifice. The Traditions have special significance; most symbolic actions are repeated three times, accentuating the Holy Trinity. The Betrothal, or Engagement, ceremony is completed at the altar inside, where you will exchange rings. Then the Wedding ceremony begins."

"...Elaborate..." muttered Goldberg, scribbling furiously.

"I'm getting nervous," Floyd admitted. "I can't possibly remember everything."

"Me neither," said Kula.

"Fear not, my children," Father Joseph smiled. "I will whisper instructions in my beard. This is preparation for the most joyous and important day of your lives. Relax and enjoy it."

He led them into the church with its magnificent cut-glass chandeliers, beautiful paintings, and simple icons on ceilings, walls, and fluted marble columns. The altar in front of the pulpit was a simple oak table covered by a white linen cloth on which rested a Bible, a candle, a cup of wine, and two bejeweled crowns.

There the couple enacted the exchange of rings, and the Engagement ceremony was concluded with prayers.

The sound of people approaching distracted them. Mac and others of the wedding party entered the church to join the practice session. Father Joseph had a hard time speaking above the excited group and placing them into position for the wedding ceremony. The reporter took more notes.

Mayzie arrived early at the KFC restaurant, and she

set up two tables so the Widowmakers could sit together. Mac and Martha were not invited. Neither were Kula and Floyd.

"There's a problem," Percy announced.

"Which one?" Big Momma asked.

"It's that none of us are really killers. I think that was the reason for our breakup. No one's against killing this monster who raped his daughter and killed his wife, but none of us wants to do it. Of the four remaining men, only JJ has had that experience. We can't put it all on him, or he'll follow Martha back into the bottle."

"You got a solution?"

"No."

"I may have," Jill spoke up. "I feel as Percy does. "The bastard needs killing, but I don't want to do it and I don't want Bill to do it either. It would eat him up."

"So are you saying we abandon the idea?" Mayzie asked.

"No." Jill cleared her throat. "I hope you'll forgive me, but I talked to someone about the Widowmakers."

"Who was it?" Alphonso asked.

"My cousin."

"The one on the SWAT team?"

"Yes."

"Holy shit! She talked to a cop!"

"Listen to what she has to say," Bill snapped.

"I'm all ears, and getting ready for twenty years in prison," said Big Momma.

"Would it surprise you to know," Jill asked,

"That the Brooklyn SWAT team has been discussing something similar to the Widowmakers for awhile?"

"What held them back?" Mayzie asked.

"Getting correct information about the target, in such a way that it couldn't be traced to them," said Jill. "In spousal and child abuse cases, they're only called in on hostage situations. They too want the right to judge whether the death penalty or just a good beating is required."

Two buckets of Kentucky Fried Chicken were brought to the table, along with salad, chips, and diet Zero. The discussion grew more animated as the chicken bones piles up.Mayzie rapped the table for order and asked: "Jill, how did you leave it with your cousin?"

"I said I'd broach the subject and tell him our decision."

"And what do you think that should be?"

"We have to decide as a group, but as an individual I think we should explore it further."

"Isn't it strange," said Percy, "That we and the SWAT team come up with the same idea at the same time?"

"At first it did," said Jill, "But I just had a patient who directs three different TV shows, and he told me that back in the '80s there were many lawsuits, initiated by TV and Hollywood people, for infringement of copyright laws. It was proven in court that similar ideas were generated in different places influenced by the news, TV, movies, radio and newspapers. Now these last few weeks everyone in Brooklyn has been fed up to the gills with street violence and these spousal abuse cases."

"If we open up to the SWAT team," said Big Momma, "We'll be exposing ourselves."

"If my cousin and his cronies listen to what we say, they'll be just as liable."

"We don't seem to have any other options," said Bill. "We aren't killers; we're healers."

There was silence for a moment, then Mayzie said: "As long as we have the veto power, to stop an assassination..."

"We'll decide who deserves... disciplining, and make recommendations," said Jill. "My cousin says his people must have veto power to stop any action voted on by our group."

"That makes me feel better," said Alphonso. "It'll act as a double check on our decisions."

"Everyone, speak for or against Jill's proposal. "We'll go around the table and take a vote."

"By the way," Big Momma remembered to say, "Maybelline's shop has the dresses for the brides-maids and the tuxedos for the men. Be extra nice to the lady; she's giving us a big discount. See you at the wedding."

CHAPTER 32:
THE VIRUS AND THE WEDDING

DISTRICT CONGRESSIONAL OFFICE

Mac took a seat at Congressman Waters' desk. "Have you finished with that society business?" he asked.

"By mutual agreement, we disbanded. But something *must* be done! Women are being beaten, tortured, even murdered. Parents are raising children who'll become the next generation of wife beaters or beaten wives."

"The children learn from their parents, obviously."

"Absolutely. Social workers and church people are little help. The wife stays subservient for the sake of the children. She hopes the husband will mellow as he ages, but it rarely happens."

"Why can't the social workers solve the problem?"

"If they tell the wife to leave the house, her options are severely limited. In most cases she has no job, and the family is living hand-to-mouth. The wife rarely has access to money. The husband limits her involvement with family or friends. If she were to move in with anyone, she couldn't hold up her end of the financial burden. She has nowhere to go."

"What about the women's shelters?"

"Inadequate. You helped found many of them; you must know that they're overcrowded, often pre-booked months in advance. We need ten times as many."

"You've got me there. No matter how much money I throw at the problem, it's never enough."

"This is how the Widowmakers came about."

The congressman winced. "Don't even think that name. If the story came out, your meteoric rise would splash down in a sea of shit." He sat back and changed the subject. "I heard you're representing the groom's family at the Prodromakeos wedding. I wasn't invited."

"Half of Brooklyn is coming without an invitation. You'll be totally welcome."

"When I started my political career Georgee and his father introduced me to the Greek communities in Bay Ridge and Red Hook. I haven't forgotten."

"How about you escort me to the wedding? We'll enact the Koumbaros together."

"But I don't know what to do."

"Do what I do. The priest will guide us. Can you stand from your wheelchair?"

"If required."

A clerk entered the office to say: "Congressman, your 2 PM appointment is waiting."

Waters waved the clerk out, saying: "Mac, I perused the figures for the expansion of ER rooms in the five hospitals. One question. Do you think the Bushwick hospital can handle the growth?"

"I'll raise that subject with the administrator. He's a straight shooter."

"And I'll collect you Sunday morning for the wedding. ...By the way, don't you have a team of Chinese nurses studying at the VA hospital?"

"Yes, half a dozen of them. Why?"

"Any of them from the city of Wu Han?"

"I don't know. Is that a village?"

"A city of eleven million people. A friend of mine returned from there recently—obliged to leave, really—and says that there are strange goings on in the medical field. Could you ask your Chinese guests if they know anyone from there?"

"I will. See you Sunday."

Floyd picked up the phone, and instantly recognized the voice on the other end. "Kula, why are you crying?" he asked.

"I can't find the marriage license," she moaned. "Oh, I'm fed up with all the preparations. Can't we just get married and run away?"

"Please don't cry or I'll join you."

"We aren't supposed to see each other until we meet at the church."

"I meant I'll join you in crying. Where do you think you put the license?"

"If I knew, I'd look there. I put it someplace where I wouldn't forget it."

"I suggest you hang up the phone, sit down with your eyes closed and envision where you were last night. Where did you prepare your gown and other stuff?"

"Yes, I see them."

"Remember them and think backwards. That might remind you of where the license is."

"I love you."

"I love you too. Now hang up and call me back when you find the license."

The phone clicked off. Floyd stared at it, willing it to ring. In five minutes, it did.

"I found it in my shoes!" chirped Kula. "What you said worked. Who would forget their wedding shoes? I've got to get dressed. See you later."

"Have you been practicing writing to Mrs. Sorenson?"

"I've got it down pat."

"Good. Let's get married."

Six Chinese nurses entered Mac's office entered Mac's office and listened to her brief questions about Wu Han city and any health problems there. As she said "Any information you can give me will be greatly appreciated," she felt an invisible wall spring up between her and the nurses. She waited, but was greeted only with silence. That puzzled her, since on all previous occasions she had found these nurses, male and female, to be super polite and gregarious. "If any of you have a friend, relative or colleague who might know of any medical abnormalities in Wu Han, please ask them what's happening," she finished. "Now I must be off to a wedding. Have a good day."

On Monday morning Jill came trotting into the ER, waving a copy of the *Brooklyn Eagle*, morning edition. "Goldberg did a really lush job of reporting on the wedding!" she chirped.

"Read it," JJ implored. "Let us all hear it together."

"Amen," said Big Bill, still nursing a bit of a hangover from Sunday's festivities.

"Here we go," said Jill. "Ahem...

"Brooklyn's Wedding of the Decade, by Mark Goldman. The groom's entourage set off from Ridgewood. Neighbors cheered the cortege on their way to the Greek Orthodox Church in Bay Ridge. The groom's car was driven by his Best Man, William Schmersal, who works with the groom as an Emergency Room nurse at the Ridgewood VA hospital."

"As if we needed advertising," Bill snickered.

"The groom is a twenty-seven year old ex-Navy combat veteran who served in Iraq and Afghanistan, where he earned the Silver Star and Purple Heart. His great-grandparents made the trek to Oregon in the late 1800s. Floyd stands six feet tall, with blue eyes and blond hair, Although a quiet young man, he attracts attention Dr. MacKenzie and Congressman Elijah Waters represented his parents, who are deceased."

"Hey, they left out his last name!" JJ objected. "Floyd oughta sue."

"Don't worry, they got it in the announcements column. Let me finish this," said Jill.

"The bridal entourage was a far larger motorcade, including friends and family from Greece. In 1911 the senior Prodromakeos settled his family in Brooklyn, where he opened the Gay Greek diner. He helped the people of Ridgewood during the Great Depression while supporting families in Greece and Cyprus, and helped establish the Greek Orthodox church in Bay Ridge."

'Naturally that's why they held the wedding there," said Bill.

"Upon arrival at the church, we were positioned outside at the top of the steps until the bridal party arrived. They joined us, forming a double line from the curbside up to Father Joseph and the groom at the church entrance. The bride's father, Georgee Prodromakeos, escorted his daughter by her right hand and led her through a shower of flower petals to the top of the church steps. There he placed her hand into that of the groom, who drew her to his side.

"I've described the groom as handsome, but the bride was dazzlingly beautiful. She positively glowed, and seemed to float up the steps. Her gown was a simple long Greek tunic of white linen, belted at he waist. She wore sequined sandals that revealed elegant ankles and long aristocratic toes. Her raven-black hair and tan Mediterranean skin glowed in the sunlight, and her dark eyes sparkled like anthracite. The aquiline features of both Greek bride and Nordic groom were a sight of classic beauty."

"Oboy, lush isn't the word," Bill hooted. "He sounds in love with both of them."

"Quit interrupting," said Jill. "It's just getting to the good part. Ahem...

"Father Joseph led the bride and groom inside the church to a simple table, covered with white cloth, before the pulpit. On the table were two crowns made of gold filigree, two rings, a silver cup of wine, a Bible and two white candles. Father Joseph began the betrothal ceremony in his melodic voice singing a prayer to bless the couple. The rings were exchanged three times. The actual marriage ceremony began with more prayers for the couple. The crowns of marriage were taken up by Dr. MacKenzie and the Congressman, and placed three times on the couple's heads, switching each time to symbolize the intertwining of two souls. After the crowns were replaced, the common cup of wine was shared by the bridal couple. The ceremonial march, led by the heads of the families, circled the altar table three times. Double wedding bands were used, as an official act indicating that an agreement is reached between two parties."

"How did Congressman Waters manage to walk three times around the altar?" J. J. wanted to know.

"Didn't you notice that Mac was practically holding him up?" said Bill. "Go on, go on, Jill."

"At the conclusion of the ceremonial march the couple returned to their places. The priest blessed the bride and groom as he removed the crowns from their heads and implored God to grant the newly-weds a long, happy and fruitful life together. He then lifted up the Bible and separated the couple's joined hands, reminding them that only God can separate the couple from one another: 'What God has joined together, let no man put asunder'.

"Father Joseph then did something unusual. Being a friend of the family, he offered the couple gifts from the Bishop of Nikolaos and expressed the gratitude of the birthplace of the Prodromakeos family. He gave blessings for the family's support over the decades for the community, then kissed Georgee and his sons on both cheeks.

"The congregation formed two lines from the church entrance to the cars festooned with silk ribbons and flowers. The long cavalcade of automobiles pulled away from the curb blowing horns while pedestrians cheered and waved, and wound its way through Brooklyn on its return to Ridgewood and the wedding reception."

"Oooh, how much of that does he tell in detail?" Bill groaned.

"I couldn't imagine the reception being more spectacular than the wedding, but it was. On arrival we found Menahan and Bleeker Streets closed and filled with folding tables covered with food and drink, tended by families who came to thank the Prodromakeos family by offering their own culinary delights to one and all.

"The largest number of tables served Greek dishes. Georgee Prodromakeos said there were twenty-two different salads, and I saw mounds of falafel balls and piles of pocket-bread. There were four yard-long barbecues, each with a chef to slice the fifty-pound racks of lamb for gyros. Another table held dozens of roasted chickens stuffed with dried fruit and tabooli. On a fourth table were gallon jugs of Greek wine. On a fifth were platters of honeyed baklava cakes stuffed with chopped almonds, flanked with two urns of Turkish coffee."

"Oh, I'm getting hungry again," JJ sighed.

"The second largest display was presented by the Italians, who had several tables loaded with strings of sausages, mounds of pasta in different shapes and colors, bubbling pots of tomato sauce, bowls of assorted cheeses, loaves of warm garlic bread, and delicate sweet pastries served with rich espresso coffee. The Irish contingent marched in carrying cases of beer and bottles of Irish whiskey, accompanied by slab on slab of corned beef and platters of soda-bread ready for slicing. Not to be outdone, the Poles and Germans brought in salamis, sausages, wursts, pig knuckles, sauerkraut and three barrels of beer.

"Two of the most crowded tables were staffed by the Spanish Pentecostal and Ethiopian Baptist churches. The Latin families each brought small aluminum grills with glowing coals on which they barbecued seven different flavors of skewered chicken served with white rice, pine nuts, and sweet or hot roasted peppers. The Ethiopian church had slaughtered two four-hundred-pound hogs, and from the intestines they made long strings of sausages, as well as meat barbecued in a large mobile cooker. Children and adults alike were given large paper towels to wipe the barbecue sauce off their faces and hands, and they needed them.

"A family of twenty Chinese people quietly set up a table which they covered with platters of eg-grolls, dipping sauces, pot-stickers, and dozens of crisp Peking ducks. I saw Georgee break away from a conversation and hurry to the Chinese family, where he was greeted warmly. I questioned him later, while he cradled a plate of Peking duck, and he told me this story.

"'We used to live in the back of a store on Evergreen Avenue', he told me. 'My mother would sell tea and coffee. Next to us was a Chinese laundry. They came on hard times. My grandfather fed the poor from the rear of the diner. He called it his private soup-kitchen. They are here to say thank you. They opened a Chinese restaurant on Broadway and Palmetto Street. Now they have five restaurants in New York and San Francisco, and the father just returned from China where he opened a new restaurant in the city of Wu Han. I'm glad my grandfather was able to help them.'

"We stopped talking as a haunting melody from a hundred voices floated toward us. Orthodox Jewish men, in black from head to toe, came into the parking lot, followed by their womenfolk wearing long sober dresses and bandannas covering their hair. I recognized the tune they were singing, since I had my Bar Mitzvah at their synagogue, and had studied there.

"'I didn't expect them,' Georgee said. 'Our food isn't kosher.'

"I asked what he knew about kosher food, and he explained what his father and grandfather had taught him. The ancestors of those Jewish people came out of the concentration camps and badly needed help, but they couldn't eat at the family soup-kitchen because the food wasn't kosher. 'So my father took in a *mashgiach* to kosher the food for them,' he said. 'Now those folk are going to entertain the bride and groom. They see it as their religious duty to make the couple joyful. It's their way of saying thank you to the Prodromakeos family.'"

"Wow," Bill marveled. "I never knew that about Georgee."

"It gets better," said Jill. "To go on…

"Four women came forward and escorted the bride to a chair set out in front of the diner, and four men escorted the groom to a chair beside her. In front of the couple four rows of ten bearded men threw their arms over each other's shoulders and began to sway back and forth in time with the soft lullaby they sang.

"Suddenly the song changed to a rousing, hand-clapping, Hassidic melody. The lines of men opened and three dancers came forward, balancing bottles on their foreheads as they hopped, skipped, and jumped around the bridal couple. They were followed by two dancers with wide hats whose fedora brims were rings of fire, and they danced before the bride and groom. The whole wedding crowd closed in to watch, for they'd never seen such expressions of joy from these dour-looking Hassidic men.

"They pulled the groom from his chair and brought him into a wild circle-dance. They whirled at such speed that Floyd was pulled off his feet and stayed upright only by holding onto the shoulders of the men beside him. The women came forward and drew Kula into a circle of their own that whirled as fast as the men."

"I remember that," laughed JJ. "I thought Georgee was going to have a heart-attack, but he was just laughing his ass off."

"When the dancing slowed, the two chairs were brought forward and the bride and groom seated again. The chairs were lifted into the air, and a slower ritual dance began winding through the crowd. The Greeks ran forward and threw money into the laps of the bride and groom. Bills fell to the ground and were swept up by ushers with push-brooms. The Hassidim retired and Georgee's Greek musicians led the procession with the theme-song from 'Zorba the Greek', and everyone joined in. They danced in the parking lot, in Bleeker Street and in the school-yard.

"The Prodromakeos family took over carrying the couple, and danced onto Bleeker Street, down the block to the house of the bride and groom. The couple were deposited at the entrance to the house, and the Greeks sang a sweet lullaby as they entered. The rest of the crowd returned to the reception party, which lasted for hours longer."

"Mostly because we were too stuffed and exhausted to move," Bill snickered. "The on duty cops came and joined us."

"There's more that you didn't see," Jill chuckled. "To go on...

"Georgee and his sons waited quietly in the street

outside while the lights went on in the upstairs living-room and then the bedroom. I heard Georgee ask: 'Are you certain you loosened the screws enough?'

"The living-room lights went out, and then the lights in the bedroom. There was a moment of dead silence inside and outside the house, then a crash and the bride's scream. The little crowd outside roared with laughter, and then began chanting good wishes to the bride and groom which almost drowned out the burst of swearing from inside the bedroom. I heard one of Georgee's sons claim: 'I told you, we rigged the bed to collapse just right.'

"In a few moments the curses from upstairs died down to giggles, then silence.

"Thus ended Brooklyn's wedding of the year."

"And the feast of the decade," J. J. added. "Good God, what a party!"

When Mac entered her office she found an unsigned note on her desk, saying: "Please meet me in Number Three X-Ray room at 9:30 AM". A quick call to Ms. Basch confirmed that the note had been dropped off by one of the Chinese nurses. "It was Dee Woon," the secretary noted. "She was very quick and discreet about it."

"Hmmm. Can you give her a cover-story for about 9:30?"

"Easily done," Ms. Basch chuckled. "If anyone asks, I took my coffee-break with her in the far corner of the crowded lunch-room, and we both had tea."

The X-ray room was dimly lit when Mac entered. She heard a click at the other end of the room, and the interior and exterior warning lights came on. No one would come in now. A slight figure stepped into view. "Dee Woon," Mac recognized her. "If anyone asks, Ms. Basch will swear that you are having tea with her right now in a dim corner of the crowded lunch-room. But I heard that your name means 'down to earth' and 'practical'. Why all this secrecy? It hardly suits your name."

"For me it must," the little woman said quietly.

"Please explain."

"Kindly Doctor Mac, in every group sent abroad by the Chinese government there are always spies. We have at least one, Liang Chao, and there may be more."

"What could you possibly reveal in the medical field that could interest your government? We share information; American and Chinese doctors pick up the phone and question each other."

Dee Woon shook her head. "In China, secrets are treasure. Foreign information is important, whether it is about crops, industry, military or medical. All must go in, but nothing must come out. Chinese authority projects its own image. No one is to go outside of channels."

"Or what?"

"You disappear. Sometimes there is a trial to show the public what not to do, and then you disappear."

"I see. Hmm, and if you should choose to disappear into America, it could be arranged. Now what is it you wanted to tell me?"

"I have a cousin who is chief pharmacist at Wu Han's largest government hospital. If special medications are being used, he will know."

"Can you contact him?"

"If I may use your telephone."

"What's the time difference?"

"Twelve hours. He will go off duty in twenty-five minutes."

"We'll go to my office, and you can make the call there."

"I don't wish to be seen by anyone. Wait a little, and then meet me up there. And... Is there a way to make my cousin disappear into America also?"

"I'll see what I can do."

Forty minutes later, Mac emailed Congressman Waters.

"Dear Elijah:

"I was privy to a conversation between one of my Chinese students and her relative in Wu Han. He's a chief pharmacist in the major hospital in that city. For purposes of security, the conversation was held in English. The following is a summary.

"There have been an exceptional number of orders for an anti-corona-virus vaccine developed in Israel, and inhalation equipment. This recently changed to requests for an anti-bird-flu medication used twenty years ago, plus enormous numbers of face masks. This disease is known as H5N1, or bird flu, and is related to SARS. A doctor at this same hospital identified the virus as coming from the Wu

Han wild-animal market. He went on Chinese TV to warn the public about a corona virus outbreak, but it seems he didn't have the permission of the politbureau. It was before Chinese New Year, when hundreds of millions of people travel to be with their families, and the Chinese economy needs that travel money. The doctor was arrested. After a short detention he went on TV to recant all that he'd said. Soon thereafter, he died of complications from the virus he had warned about. He had claimed that this strain was sixty times more communicable, and twice as deadly, as the bird flu.

"None of this information has appeared in our medical journals. I searched the internet and found nothing. If you receive more information, please let me know. I will do the same.

"PS: please put me in touch with someone who can make a nursing student disappear safely, without a trace, into the US.

"Thank you."

After sending it, she called Ms. Basch on the intercom and said: "Ms. Basch, I need to talk to someone who can discreetly arrange for one of our students, Liang-Chao by name, to become infected with something that will keep him quarantined for as long as possible, something infectious, that looks like flu but isn't."

Ms. Basch chuckled wickedly. "How does 'severe mononucleosis' sound?"

CHAPTER 33:
DIVIDING THE SPOILS

ROLLER DOME, BRIGHTON BEACH

Two Black men dressed in suits sat in a rented convertible across the street from the Roller Dome, watching the entrance. The man in the passenger seat held a small black box with a button and a flashing red light. The driver said: "Wait until those two guys go inside."

Two men who had just parked nearby got out and disappeared into the Roller Dome, and the driver said: "All clear." The passenger pushed the button.

The explosion rocked the convertible on its wheels, and shook the Roller Dome.

"Make the call," the driver said.

The passenger did.

"Mr. Abazov, this is a representative from the Muslim Brotherhood. The fact that I've got your private phone number and just blew up a car in your parking lot shows that I know enough to kill you. You owe us a hundred thousand dollars."

"You made the deal with my predecessor, who

has disappeared," said Abazov.

"And now we're dealing with you. The bitch is dead, so pay up."

"You didn't kill her; the Mafia did."

"What does it matter who killed her? We lost two good men in the attempt. You gotta pay."

"I can't authorize that amount without approval from higher up."

"So get it."

"As I said, the guy who made the deal has disappeared. Give me something to negotiate with."

"Like what?"

"Twenty-five thousand instead of a hundred. You guaranteed the job and didn't complete it."

"We took out Michael Leissner and his bodyguard."

"The bodyguard died with Lucille in the explosion. That was the Mafia's doing."

"All the better. We'll settle for seventy-five thousand."

"Call back in an hour," said Abazov.

He hung up, called the Black Sea number and explained the situation.

Boris answered: "See if you can Jew him down to fifty thousand, but if you have to, pay the seventy-five—out of your pocket. I don't want any further trouble from goddamned Brooklyn. Have you been paying attention to the news? If half of what they're saying happens with the FBI and CIA, we'll be in a shit-storm. And then there's this Chinese clap or something."

"What are you talking about?"

"Our intel says they've got an epidemic in Wu Han, and it's spreading. Knowing how things spread from China, a lot of people are going to die."

"What does the World Health Organization say?"

"They're so full of shit their eyes are brown. The Chinese have them in their pocket, anyway, and they're keeping quiet about it. Send your people home and have them quarantine themselves. Don't tell the other gangs about it yet."

"I may already have trouble. A couple of my guys have the flu. One of them was taken to the hospital and is on a respirator."

"Damn. Doctors and scientists aren't sure how it spreads, but it's nasty. The contagion rate is ten times that of normal flu. Your president did a smart thing by quarantining all visitors from China and stopping Americans from going there, as well as kicking the car companies into making ventilators, but you can bet the democrats will roadblock him. Soon Russia will announce restrictions on nonessential travel to China."

"It sounds serious. We haven't heard anything on the news."

"Like you could trust those bozos. And it gets worse. I want you to consider investing in gold. Today's price is fifteen hundred and fifty-six dollars an ounce.

"Understood," said Abazov, realizing that Boris had dumped the burden on him. If this speculation worked, Boris would take the credit; failure would be Abazov's responsibility.

"And close that deal with the Black Muslims,

quick, before the Chinese nail them down.

"The Chinese? But they hate Muzzies and the niggers."

"But they're hoping to rent them out to the biggest gang in the country."

"The Mafia? But they hate Muzzies and niggers, too."

"Not the Mafia; the Democrat National Committee. They're planning to use them for another big campaign against Trump. This is a campaign year, and they're throwing everything they can think of at him, hoping something will stick."

Abazov hung up, thinking about how gold-speculation could be used to pay seventy-five thousand dollars quickly. Income from drug sales, he calculated, would cover immediate costs.

Ten days later Mac received a large envelope from Congressman Waters. In it were several files and a long letter that read:

"Dear Dr. Mac:

"I said I'd look into the rumors your nurse mentioned, and here's what I've found. Wu Han has a population of eleven million, which makes it bigger than New York City. Within the city is the University of Wu Han, and within that is the medical college, and inside that is the Wu Han Institute of Virology, which has been studying the SARS virus but hasn't published anything about it for some time.

"Let me caution you not to show this to anyone. Doing so could reveal my sources and betray a confidence. One of them reminded me of a Chinese curse: 'May you live in interesting times', and this story is downright fascinating.

"The medications requested from the Wu Han pharmacist appear to be related to a Corona-type virus similar to SARS and MERS which were so devastating twenty years ago. The story about the Chinese whistleblower doctor is factual. He went public, was jailed, and soon died of what is now called Covid-19. The World Health Organization was called in, and claimed that the transference was from animals (specifically bats) to humans, not human to human, thus negating the possibility of an epidemic.

"The WHO had to reverse their claim when a case linked to Wu Han appeared in Thailand a few days later. This was independently confirmed by the CIA and the Taiwanese secret police. President Trump is ordering recent arrivals from China put under quarantine, and the democrats are already decrying this move as 'racist'. I wish the DNC would once in awhile ask me what I think is racist or oppressive, instead of assuming they already know what I think.

"There is no known cure or vaccine for this virus. The Israelis, with their large poultry industry, came up with a vaccine for the bird-flu years ago, but it only applied to birds. The WHO still refuses to label this a potential epidemic, most probably so as not to interfere with the Chinese New Year celebrations, which are as big a moneymaker for the Chinese economy as the Christmas season is for us.

"Both the CIA and the Chinese secret police believe the virus first infected a female laboratory worker in Wu Han, but the stories diverge there. The Chinese claim she got it from a boyfriend who operates a large shop in the wild animal market, and he got it from his livestock. The Taiwanese secret police have a darker theory; the woman got infected at her work in the lab, which has a bad history of sloppy safety procedures. There have been a lot of such careless escapes over the past twenty years, and the Taiwanese believe these releases are not accidental. They point out that the Republic of China has been trying fiercely to reduce its population for the last thirty years, and would not cry hard if the country lost a million, or ten million, or even a hundred million of its subject; after all, it has a billion more. And of course China would not cry at all if the rest of the world lost a hundred million people. Possibly these rumors of 'germ warfare' are what prompted the WHO to form an investigating committee.

"I called President Trump and we had a brief conversation. He is going to order a halt to travel to and from China, despite fierce opposition from Congress. As I'm dictating this CNN News is reporting the outbreak of Corona Virus in Wu Han. Cases have also appeared in South Korea, Japan, Spain, Italy and Iran. My sources say China has fudged the number of deaths. At present it seems that this is twice as deadly as common flu, but less than a quarter as deadly as the Spanish Flu of a century ago, which now turns out to have been another form of the SARS virus.

"The symptoms are a dry cough, temperature, flu-like aches and pains. It weakens the immune system and exacerbates pre-existing conditions. People with severe cases have died of pneumonia. The largest organs affected are the lungs. Ventilators to help them breathe are in short supply. The disease is extremely contagious, transferred very readily from person to person, from objects to people, and possibly from humans to animals and back.

"China has locked down the entire city of Wu Han. No travel is allowed in or out. Everyone must wear masks and no gatherings are allowed except in houses with permanent family members.

"Iran has one of the highest death-rates, though their government has attempted to cover it up. They just canceled public events and Friday prayers. Schools, universities, shopping centers, bazaars and holy shrines are closed, and festival celebrations are banned, though the news media are forbidden to say anything about it. Multiple government ministers and senior officials have been diagnosed as positive for the virus. Twenty-three members of the parliament (about 8% of all MPs) and at least twelve sitting or former Iranian politicians have died as a result of the virus.

"The Taiwanese Secret Service estimates of the number of Covid-19 deaths are much higher than those from Chinese sources. The Beijing government has been accused of cover-up, censorship, and mismanagement. However, the WHO says it has no problems with China's or Iran's reported figures. We've had no reports at all from India.

"As I learn more, I'll share it. The international

press is finally beginning to look into the situation. All I can suggest is to prepare for an epidemic.

"Respectfully Yours,

"Elijah Waters.

"PS: You'll soon be visited by a nondescript gentleman named Thornberry. Please introduce him to your nurse who wants to disappear."

Mac put the letter down and sat back to think. How would an epidemic affect her ER services in the five hospitals? Finally she reached out and picked up the telephone. "Martha," she asked, "Is it true that during the SARS epidemic you were in charge of the emergency room at South Shore hospital?"

"Yes. Why?"

"Can you get down here now?"

"I'm in a counseling session..."

"Leave it, say nothing, and get down here."

A few moments later, Martha entered the office. "What's the rush?" she asked.

"Close the doors and pull the blinds shut."

Martha did so, then took a seat. "Does this have anything to do with those Chinese nursing students?" she asked. "Or that Chinese virus they mentioned on the radio?"

"I can't tell you all I know. Suffice it to say you're not to repeat this conversation."

Martha pulled her chair closer. "Understood."

Mac took several minutes to explain the contents of the congressman's letter, omitting the parts that could have revealed his sources. "There you have it."

"How can I help?" Martha asked.

"I have no experience dealing with an epidemic. You do. What we do know is that the virus is extremely contagious, more than the SARS epidemic was. How do we prepare for this?"

"If the death-rates from China, Italy and Iran are true, then go down to the deepest room in the hospital, sit down in a corner, pull your knees up, put your head between your legs, and kiss your sweet ass goodbye."

Mac nearly choked on her coffee laughing. "We don't have that option. So where do I begin? How do we prepare for an epidemic before it starts?"

"I'm glad you recognize the seriousness. Bill Gates has been warning us for three years about the possibility of a pandemic, and no one's been listening."

"So what do you recommend?"

"I have my notes from twenty years ago. Let me consult them and write up my thoughts."

"Could you do that as soon as possible?"

"I'm on it as of now."

The Black man seated in the front of the Bed-Stuy Salvation Army basketball court looked uncomfortable and out of place in his suit, bow tie, shined shoes and rimless glasses. Those who crowded into the hall wore Crown colors and jackets with bandannas as headgear or smooth-shaven skulls that reflected the overhead lights. The man stood to speak, but it took several minutes before the crowd came to order.

There was more coughing from the group than

usual, often a dry rasping cough. Several people appeared unwell, and were seated on the floor with their backs against the walls.

The man announced: "My name is Franklin Delano Roosevelt, but some of you may remember me as Rosie from the Saint Albans all-Black football team."

There were a few chuckles of recognition, then one voice saying: "You gonna be playin' with yourself if you don't get quick to what we're here for."

"I'm the accountant and treasurer for the Crowns," Rosie said. "There is thirty-five million dollars in five banks, and one million five hundred-thousand dollars in debts owed to your organization."

The crowded room went dead silent for a moment. "Shiiiiit!" somebody called out. "Miz Lucille was a good ol' girl!"

The gymnasium erupted in hoots, shouts, and clapping. The predominant question was: "How do we get the money?"

"That's the problem," said Rosie. "The accounts are all in Miss Leissner's name. She's dead. Her only heir, Michael, died first. Miss Lucille never got around to changing her will."

"The Crowns are a legal organization," someone shouted. "We're incorporated."

"I'm aware of your club's legal status. But you would have to file in probate court to have the money released. The first question the judge will ask is proof of how you earned the thirty-five million dollars."

"None of his fucking business!" someone shouted. "Selling crack cocaine!" yelled another voice. Someone else added: "If the judge doesn't gimme the money, I'll blow his fucking head off!"

"The probate court," Rosie plowed on, "Will then oversee the process of distributing the deceased's assets to the proper beneficiaries. The court has the authority to compel an executor to give an account of their actions and source of the money involved. Illegitimate and untaxed funds will revert to the state."

Arguments broke out. Push turned to shove, then to knives and guns. A shot was fired. Everyone crouched and ran for the exits. Rosie tried to slip away, but was grabbed at the exit and pulled aside. Having also been captain of the Stony Brook wrestling team, he quickly dispatched the two men, got out to the parking lot, jumped in his car and drove away.

He drove for three blocks, then pulled into a parking lot and stopped. "Okay, Ida," he said. "You can come out now."

Ida threw off the blanket that had covered her and sat up in the back seat. "How'd it go?" she asked.

"As bad as expected," said Rosie. "Now we go to Plan B."

"All right," Ida sighed. "How do I become Miss Lucille's next of kin?"

"We use the DNA samples the cops collected at the explosion," said Rosie pulling out a cigar. "What they found were remains of two women and four men, too badly burned to identify, except for Greco. All they know is that one of the women's bodies belonged to Miss Lucille. They know nothing about Camille."

"Nothing about my sister," Ida whispered, grinding her teeth.

"So if your DNA matches one of those female bodies, you can claim to be Miss Lucille's sister. Iron Mike's body has been a-moldering in the ground long enough that that cops aren't likely to dig him up and check. We order samples of the DNA, establish that you're Lucille's bastard sister, and take that into Probate Court. As for all the other paper-dancing, leave that to me.

"Point is, you get the money—and you become queen of the Crowns. Then we start making alliances with the other gangs, and get the Mafia to accept it."

"Everyone but the Russians," said Ida, baring her teeth. "They killed Lucille. They killed my sister, and I want them dead."

"So do I, honey," said Rosie, lighting the cigar. "So do I."

Somewhat different meetings were held in Bushwick, Flatbush and Red Hook, to sort out the new priorities of the Brooklyn gangs. At each of those gatherings could be heard dry rasping coughs. Several people came with flu-like symptoms and a few with high temperatures. They were given little attention, as everyone focused on the new priorities of Brooklyn's gangland.

The Mafia, represented by the Gambino family,

watched with amusement as large and small gangs jockeyed for position and shares of the Crowns' turf. The Red Hook Irish, under the leadership of Frank McKenny, made it clear that they wanted nothing to do with the drug trade, and would be satisfied with inheriting the Crowns' share of illegal shipping and trucking in New York's port. After that the other gangs began sorting themselves out. When necessary, Pete Gotti would smooth out the process with money, bullets, or well-placed words. Little by little, the dust settled and the violence died down.

As Valentine's Day approached, families considered it safe to send their children out to the parks again.

One group conspicuously not invited to the turf-sorting was the Russians. Abrazov noticed, and began investing seriously in gold futures.

CHAPTER 34:
PLAGUE-STRIKE

RIDGEWOOD VA HOSPITAL

"I looked in on you a couple of times," Mac said to Martha. "You were in deep conversation with a couple of men."

"One is a South Korean doctor," Martha explained, "And the other's a political science professor whose specialty is China. Both are drying out with me."

"Have you been listening to the news?"

"That's why I spoke with them. The 'Chinese virus' is out of the bag. That's all they're talking about."

"It's spread so quickly in China, Iran, Italy and Spain. The death-toll is unbelievable."

"Don't believe it. Some health departments are padding the numbers in order to get more money—"

"How do you pad the numbers of a plague?"

"Claim that anybody who dies that also tested positive for the virus is a Covid-19 death—even if they actually died of cancer, heart-attack, or even by traffic accident. At least 90% of the reported deaths fall into that category. And then there's the under-reporting. The political scientist said the Chinese government is lying, and the South Korean doctor concurred. He said the 'totalitarian socialist government of China' would never take responsibility for so many deaths, because then it would have the responsibility of the health and welfare of all the victims. That might be enough to remove the current regime from power.

"In any case, both men believe that the death-toll in China is much worse than anyone is saying. The doctor says the reports on contagion are sketchy and conflicting. They aren't certain if the contagion is entirely airborne or if the virus can survive on inanimate objects for days or more. Contagion also seems to depend on the physical condition of the host. Some of the infected have symptoms so mild they don't even know it, yet they can pass the virus to others who keel over and die of it. Random facts: social isolation seems effective, 80% of those who need respirators die of pneumonia, 90% of the elderly with previous medical conditions die."

"Age and previous conditions," Mac considered. "Sounds typical of flu. How can we stop it?"

"Without testing, we can't."

"Then we have to test everybody who comes in here."

"First we have to get enough reliable tests, and those are in short supply. There are a billion and a half Chinese. America has three hundred and thirty-five million people. I've heard that Trump has been going around goosing American medical-supply companies to turn out more tests, but it will be a long time before they can catch up with the demand. Iran, Italy, Spain and France are yelling for tests. Population movement will require new testing. People could possibly be re-infected; we don't know if surviving the virus makes you immune or to what degree. Only testing can tell—and, for obvious reasons, we can't use tests made in China."

"What can I do to prepare for the onslaught?"

"You're too late; it's already in Brooklyn."

"But we haven't had any rush of patients."

"Not here, not yet—but Bed-Stuy and Bushwick have. In the seventy-two hours since we last met, lines have grown outside the ERs and into the parking lots. All elective surgeries have been canceled. Big Momma, Mayzie and their crews are working double shifts without PPE."

"Without what? You lost me."

"Proper Protective Equipment—it has a title already. Both hospitals are filled to capacity. Patients with the virus are sent home to quarantine themselves, unless they need the immediate service of a respirator. Rumor has it that the doctors are telling the ambulance crews with a patient over sixty-five to not even bring the patient to the hospital."

"Final selection!" Mac snapped. "Just leave the old folks to die. Unbelievable."

"So that the young will live."

"And no guarantee of that. What can I do?"

"I've done my best with these three pages of recommendations," said Martha, holding out some papers. "This hospital is a ticking time bomb."

"Us? Why?" Mac asked, taking the pages.

"The age of the average patient in this hospital is sixty-seven. The rooms, wards, toilets and eating facilities aren't designed for infectious cases. We got one case of Covid-19 and we could lose all our patients."

Mac took off her glasses and wiped tears from her eyes. "What do I do first?"

"All I can advise is think about what's right, not how your superiors might judge you when this is over. It will end, though just how badly I can't guess."

"Give me your worst estimate."

"Privately, Governor Cuomo says it could be two hundred thousand dead in New York alone."

"Good God!"

"It could be better or worse; think of the politics. Cuomo has reason to exaggerate, but he's also clueless as to how to handle a pandemic. Without tests, there's no way to estimate."

Mac thought for a moment, then asked: "Will you drive me to the federal building downtown? The big-shots from Washington have called an emergency meeting. I can read your report and question you on the way."

"Let me change out of my scrubs."

"We haven't time."

Mac and Martha arrived just in time to hear one of the men from Washington make his opening statement.

"In response to the Corona virus, the federal government must cancel all public events, including religious services. Schools, universities, shopping centers, sports events and bars must be closed. Meetings of ten or more people must be banned. We're working on economic measures to help businesses that must close and families that won't have jobs. We rejected plans to quarantine entire cities, but the large outbreak in New Rochelle, New York, may revive that order. The federal government will immediately limit travel between hot-spots. We must have a national order to wear masks and keep social distancing in public, but to stay home as much as possible. That's the only way to stop this plague." He took his seat, wearing a defiant look.

An older woman went to the podium, shaking her head. "The federal government does not have the Constitutional authority to shut down the entire country like that," she said, "Not without declaring martial law, and we're nowhere near any justification for that."

"Go ahead and declare martial law," the man snapped. "Anything less is a failure of leadership! We know that unofficial estimates of Covid-19 deaths are much higher than those from official sources. Our government, China and Iran have been accused of cover-ups and censorship to keep the numbers secret, and we haven't heard anything out of India. The reality could be much worse than we know. You can't believe everything put out by the media or official sources, including ours."

"We know there's been under-reporting," the

woman sighed. "President Trump has charged the World Health Organization with dereliction of duty and mismanagement, and he'll cut off funds to that organization. Specifically—"

"Oh, brilliant!" the man shouted. "Cut off the WHO in the middle of a pandemic!"

"Specifically," the woman plodded on, "The president requests that the Director General of WHO—Tedros Adhanom Ghebreyesus—be fired. He's an Ethiopian put up for the presidency of the WHO by the Chinese. He's the first non-physician ever to hold that position. Trump believes that Tedros is protecting China—and Iran—by underreporting the number of deaths and infections. Since the WHO cannot be trusted, we have no use for it and should stop wasting money on it. Quite simply, yes, you can't trust anything put out by the media or official sources, including our own. We really have no idea how far the virus has spread or what to do about it. That's why I've requested Dr. MacKenzie to address us on the state of affairs in the five ER facilities under her direction. They'll be our first line of defense in this war."

Mac took the podium and saw that, aside from those first two speakers, the people seated around the long table were quite relaxed. Some were busy in private conversations while others helped themselves to platters of mixed donuts. A waitress poured coffee for her, asking: "Sugar or cream?"

Mac picked up her coffee and flung it down the length of the table. Half a dozen people were splashed. She followed that with a platter of donuts.

Jelly, cream, and chocolate donuts rolled into people's startled laps.

"Now that I have your attention," Mac announced, "I'm going to give you a history lesson about the future."

"You could have been a little less dramatic," Congressman Waters muttered.

"Hear what I have to say and then tell me that. Look, it's far too late to talk about containing the virus. *The plague is already here!* It's been here for awhile, perhaps since early winter, and we don't know how far it's spread. In years to come we'll be asked: 'Where were you when the shit hit the fan?' The more important question is: 'What did you *do* during the pandemic?'

"You've asked for the assent of our ER facilities to fight this war. Yes, this is indeed a war, and we know almost nothing about the enemy. The nearest comparison we have is the Spanish Flu of a century ago, and if that pattern holds, the future looks very grim. We have to assume the worst. Governor Cuomo's estimate of deaths in the state of New York alone is four hundred thousand. We can assume that the plague has reached California, which houses one in nine of all Americans. Where will you bury the bodies? The crematorium in Maspeth can't keep up with the demand. Are the bodies of the dead infectious? We don't know. How long can the virus survive in the air, or on surfaces? We don't know. There's too much we don't know about this plague, and we need reliable information fast."

"What about the use of malaria medications?" a

hospital administrator spoke up.

"Results so far are idiosyncratic; they seem to work for some patients, and not for others. We need more anti-viral medicines, and we need to test them thoroughly. The virus seems to be an artful dodger; it ducks, hides, bobs and weaves, only to pop up and kill where you least expect it."

"Can we assume that younger, healthier people are in less danger than the elderly?"

"We don't even know that. The Center for Disease Control just announced that three French aircraft carriers have been struck with the Covid-19 virus; a third of the six thousand men on those carriers have been infected, and where can you find a healthier group of young people? The carrier *USS Theodore Roosevelt*, with a crew of five thousand, reports seven hundred sailors infected. One sailor to date has died in the Guam hospital. The ship has been deactivated, and the captain was relieved of command because he used an unsecured line to inform his superiors. The news was leaked, and you'll hear about it on tonight's news."

Mac's cell-phone vibrated. She read the text message and looked up.

"One of my ambulance drivers just informed me," she said, "That at Brooklyn's Cobble Hill Health Center, a nursing home, they found fifty-five dead patients. There are four other nursing homes, in the Bronx, Queens, and Staten Island. The driver asks: 'Where do we put them all?'"

"In the city morgue," someone said.

"It's overflowing," Mac replied. "The mayor ordered refrigerator trucks to store the bodies, at least until we can find enough crematoria to handle the surge."

The Brooklyn Borough President and Congressman Waters pulled back from the table. "Order more refrigerator trucks," said Waters, "From wherever you can get them."

Another man stood, pecking furiously at the buttons on his cell-phone. "I'm the CEO of Autar Trucking," he said. "I'm donating two refrigerator trucks for the duration of the crisis. They're on their way to Cobble Hill right now."

A middle-aged woman raised a hand. "I'll donate two refrigerator trucks too. Tell me where to send them."

"The city morgue for now."

"And I must leave for Cobble Hill," said Waters.

Others stood, preparing to leave, just as a secretary entered carrying copies of Martha's report. Mac held them in place, announcing: "Before you leave, take a copy of our recommendations compiled by Nurse Martha Dowd. I require your agreement on a particular problem right now."

"Get on with it," said the congressman.

"Aggressive testing, quarantines and social distancing have shown some promise in slowing the spread of the virus in hot-spots like New Rochelle, Hong Kong and South Korea, but it's too late to employ a similar strategy in New York. We can spread the word to wear protective masks and keep social distancing in public, but there's really no way to enforce it. Neither will closing the schools; it's hard enough to keep masks on wiggly children, and almost impossible to keep them on lively teenagers and college students who are passionately devoted to partying and public: protesting.

"The number of cases has overwhelmed the city's ability to test, let alone trace the contacts of those infected. We have no idea how many respirators will be needed. Each hospital must declare the number of respirators they have and how many are in use—and in any case we'll need more, as fast as we can get them. And of course we'll need more tests, likewise fast."

"Is that your major problem?" the Borough president asked.

"No. We need massive amounts of protective gear for the hospital personnel, and then for the patients."

"Why not the patients first?"

"Because our personnel meet so many patients in the course of a day, and are more likely to contract the virus. In Cobble Hill there were one hundred and twenty-five patients, and fifty-five of them died. In this VA hospital we have close to a thousand patients. The Fort Hamilton and New York veterans' hospitals have far more. Their average age is sixty-seven; they're prime targets for the virus. If Covid-19 gets into these hospitals, they'll become slaughterhouses."

"Then keep it out," said Waters. "Isolate the Covid patients as soon as you find them, and send them somewhere else."

"How do we do that?"

"Petition the President and the Governor to give you permission to exclude Covid patients from entering the VA hospitals."

"Would they consider it?"

"They already have. There's an emergency hospital being set up in the New York Javits Center, and the Navy hospital ships *Mercy* in New York and *Comfort* in San Francisco. The tests are coming as fast as we can turn them out. Test your patients before they get into your hospital, and separate them."

"All right. Now, what about the hospital staff?"

"What about them?"

"We don't have enough protective gear to safeguard the doctors, nurses, and caregivers. We're using plastic bags to cover our smocks, and bandannas folded over coffee-filters to cover our noses and mouths. Our workers are pulling double shifts, but they go home to their families, who might be infected. That means our own staff could be bringing the virus to or from the hospital. How fast can we get the protective gear?"

Waters shrugged in defeat. "I can only tell you to do the best you can. Now I'm off to Cobble Hill. Good luck."

As Waters rolled toward the door two men from New York's garment district came up to Mac.

"You should have a lot of *mazal*," one of them said. "If you'll give us correct specifications for the masks, Sam and I will donate a million of them."

Sam added: "I know a guy who'll donate a million smocks."

"Izzy? He won't give away spit."

"He will when I tell him what she said."

"Nah, he won't."

"I'll tell my wife to nag her brother until he does. Include the specifications for the smocks."

Mac leaned down and kissed each man on the forehead. "Do either of you work with plastic, or gloves?"

"Sam's brother-in-law handles rubber gloves."

"He's a cheap son of a bitch."

"Sam will call him. What do you need in plastic?"

"Clear plastic face-shields. The virus can infect through the eyes."

"Call Rabbi Wolff from the Great Neck Jewish Center," Sam said. "He administers a trust for the synagogue, and it includes a big sunglasses factory. You call him."

"I'll have to let him win at our next pinochle game."

"*Nish gefelt.* Doctor Mac, give us a couple of your cards. We'll see what we can do."

She gave them the cards, and they hurried off.

Martha came up to Mac, who was wiping tears away. "Why are you crying?" she asked.

"I got support from the group. I expected to leave here without a job."

"No fear of your being fired, at least until it's over. Then the politicians will need somebody to blame, but now they need you for when things get worse."

"How much worse can it get, really?"

"Well, look on the bright side. We've been treating this as if it were as bad as SARS or the Spanish Flu; it could be a lot less lethal than those. With everyone alerted, we can slow the spread—hopefully until the lab-boys come up with vaccines and treatments."

"You saw I printed up your recommendations at the secretary's desk and handed out copies to everybody."

"Give me one of them; I want to see how bright and humble I really am. Thanks. Ahem. Can I have your attention please?' she said to the remaining visitors. As they stopped to listen, she read aloud:

"Advisory to emergency rooms, by RN Martha Dowd, Ridgewood VA Hospital, Brooklyn, New York.

"Screen patients, visitors and employees for symptoms of respiratory illness before they enter the healthcare facility. Examine for fever, cough, and difficulty breathing. Personnel who come in close contact with confirmed or possible Covid patients will utilize proper Personal Protective Equipment.

"Conduct an inventory of available PPE (at this time there is an acute shortage).

"Encourage sick employees to stay home. Personnel who develop respiratory symptoms should be instructed not to report for work.

"Protect your patients and your staff.

"Be certain your staff is properly equipped and informed. Separate patients with respiratory symptoms so that they are not waiting among other patients seeking care.

"In mild cases the virus patients who can be

cared for at home should not be hospitalized. There is a shortage of healthcare personnel, beds, medications and respirators.

"Use telephones, local TV and radio to inform incoming callers about where, if and when to seek medical or emergency care. Provide callers with home-care advice. This should be a doctor-approved paragraph read by the telephone operator.

"WHO officials meeting per regulations (HR 2005) to assess whether this outbreak constitutes a public health emergency of international concern could not reach a consensus. They will reconvene in ten days. It is my opinion that this outbreak is a global pandemic of epic proportions. The most stringent precautions should be employed to protect healthcare workers and the public. The WHO's postponement of such a decision is irresponsible. Thousands have died in Italy, Iran, France and Spain. More will die in the United States.

"Prioritize homecare for the ill. Because of the lack of equipment and the unpredictability of the virus, the hospital is a dangerous place to be. In accepting patients extremely ill and unable to recover, the patient should be made as comfortable as possible at home and not brought to the hospital. This last suggestion is born from experience with the MERS epidemic. It does not apply to nursing homes and health-care givers in New York. State law requires nursing homes to bring any patient they cannot treat to another care facility or public hospital.

"Martha Dowd, RN"

"Your paper saved me," said Mac, as they walked toward the parking lot. "I couldn't have done anything as good. Let's get back to the VA.'

"No," said Martha. "I got a call. We're heading for Bushwick Hospital."

"What's doing there?"

"Big Momma is down with the virus."

"Why is she in Bushwick?"

"When Mayzie found out, she went over with an ambulance and kidnapped her."

"Kidnapped... Why?"

"So she could take care of her without interference. When word got out that Big Momma had the virus, half of Black Brooklyn came to pray and pay their respects. They crowded into the Bed-Suy parking lot. The hospital lounges and the street were jammed with people crying and praying. They broke the police cordon and crowded into Momma's hospital room. There was a riot when they found out that Mayzie was taking her to Bushwick."

"But she got her there?"

"There, and on a respirator."

"Not a good sign. Does she know where she got the virus?"

"Oh yes. There was a large meeting of the Crowns that got a little rowdy. When the meeting ended, three were passed out of the floor—from the virus, not injuries. Those who could talk told about some forty Junior Crowns teenagers hiding in an abandoned warehouse. Many of them had high temperatures, and difficulty breathing, and were coughing."

Martha pulled the car into the ER's crowded parking lot.

"Momma went to help the children. Now she's in a private room on the second floor. I'll find a parking space."

CHAPTER 35:
ONSLAUGHT

BUSHWICK HOSPITAL

An anxious crowd blocked Bushwick Hospital's elevator, where two beleaguered policemen were trying to maintain some semblance of order. Mac took the stairs. She found Mayzie in Big Momma's room, pushing people out while the crowd tried to push in. Mac got in behind Mayzie, and together they managed to push the door shut. In the ensuing quiet the ventilator wheezed loudly. Big Momma lay still, an enormous hump under the sheet, her hands bound to the railings.

"Why did the nurse tie Momma's hands?" Mac panted.

"She kept trying to pull the ventilator tubes out of her throat," said Mayzie, "But she's quiet now."

Mac went to the bedside, leaned over and kissed Big Momma's forehead.

"That's a no-no," Mayzie snapped. "We don't need you down with the virus too."

"Damn it, I love this woman."

"Me too." Mayzie wiped tears from her cheeks.

"How did she get it? Do you know?"

"A former army medic, a member of the Crowns, found these kids squatting in an abandoned factory. He got the virus from them. He told Big Momma. She realized no hospital could take all forty of them. They're young and have a better chance to survive if they stay isolated, but she had no more beds. She got the Black Muslims and the Baptist church to truck over some old mattresses and stuff from hospital storage, and she dropped in on them every day."

"Oh hell, it was inevitable that she'd get the virus."

"I told her to be careful. She said 'we get paid for helping people'."

"How much oxygen is she receiving?"

"Twenty-three percent. I was about to raise it when the crowd broke in."

"Better do that now. It looks like she's struggling."

Mayzie reached for the knob to increase the oxygen, then stopped and picked up Big Momma's limp wrist. She froze for a long moment, then placed the still hand back on the bed and pulled the sheet up over Momma's face.

"Lost her?" Mac whispered.

"My best friend," Mayzie sobbed.

"We've all lost her." Mac nodded toward the door and the crowd outside. "What do we do?"

"Get another body-bag. A big one."

Mac called the Bed-Stuy medical center and informed them: "Big Momma is coming home."

"By ambulance or cab?" the secretary asked.

"By chariot."

Word spread quickly. A mighty wail went up from the Bed-Stuy ER, followed by people in the halls kneeling down in prayer. The wave of kneeling swept into the lobby and out into the streets. Cars stopped, and when people learned of Big Momma's passing they got out and knelt down too. A young volunteer from the Baptist church began singing: "Amazing grace, how sweet the sound..." The kneeling crowd joined in the tearful refrain.

The list of the dead in New York went over a thousand in the next twenty-four hours.

"Get me a translator!" the head of the Coney Island ER shouted. "Somebody who speaks Russian!"

"I do," called a policeman working crowd control.

"Then explain things to these guys." The doctor pointed to a group of tough-looking Russian men.

"You mean the gang members?"

"I don't care who they are. Tell them that being young and in good shape they'll survive the virus without help from us. They just have to go home and quarantine themselves. If I hospitalize them they'll get a much heavier virus-load, and possibly a stronger strain, in which case they'll die."

"Is that true?" the policeman asked.

"How the hell should I know? What I do know is

that we're out of medicine, masks and beds. They should go back home, or wherever they've been staying, and isolate themselves. Anyone over age fifty-five should see me."

"This is Mr. Abrazov," the policeman pointed. "He's their employer."

"What kind of work do they do?"

"Laborers," said Abrazov, in clear English.

"Where do they live?"

"The old Coney Island Roller Dome."

"Do they have sleeping facilities?"

"Yes, and food."

"Is there a place to take a shit?"

"Oh yes, we have toilets."

"Good. Keep your people there, and keep them quarantined. Get masks for them."

"Where?"

"Hell, I don't know. Try folding a bandanna over a coffee-filter. I haven't enough of anything for my own staff. It's important they wash their hands often and wipe everything clean. How old are you?"

"Fifty-seven."

"You stay here. I'm admitting you."

"What for?"

"Being older than the rest, and wheezing like an old buffalo. What medications do you take?"

"High blood-pressure, diabetes and heart medicine."

"You're mine! Officer, put him in stall five for evaluation."

"I protest! I know my rights! I—"

"Officer, shackle him if you have to."

Martha drove Mac to Bed-Stuy, where they found a parking space three blocks from the ER entrance. The mourning crowd still flowed out of the ER, into the parking lot and the street beyond. The two fought their way inside and grabbed the nearest nurse. "Who's in charge?" Mac asked.

"Nobody," the nurse groaned. "Big Momma went down like a rock, and it's been chaos since. We heard that she... passed."

"Yes, less than an hour ago. Martha will take over here."

The nurse loosened two bobby-pins and pinned her nurse's cap on Martha's head. "That's so they'll know you're staff and not some sleep-walker in those pajamas."

"Where are the police?" was the first thing Martha asked.

"They disappeared a couple of hours ago."

"Call the precinct and tell them to send a riot squad."

"Riot? There's no riot."

"There will be when I start throwing people out of here. After you make the call, bring the staff together and I'll talk to them."

While Martha was busy with that, Mac received a phone call from the Red Hook hospital. She immediately called Floyd. "Sorry to interrupt your honeymoon, but we've got a situation here."

"I was going to call you," said Floyd. "Kula was called back to work. Half her staff is infected. She's pulling double shifts and sleeping there."

"Same thing in Red Hook. I need you and Big

Bill to run that ER."

"I may have another problem."

"Like what?"

"Kula's father."

"What's wrong with him?"

"He's out back of the diner cooking for elderly people in lockdown."

"That's wrong?"

"He's got a dry cough, joint pains, and difficulty breathing."

"Uh-oh. Does he have a temperature?"

"He won't let me take it. When I questioned him about the Chinese family at the party, he said they'd just returned from a business trip to Wu Han. That's where the virus started."

Mac stepped back and stared at her phone as if it had bitten her. "Do you think he has a fever?"

"Oh, I do."

"Does he have pre-existing medical conditions?"

"Diabetes, gout, and low blood-pressure."

"Oh, hell. Sit Georgee down and explain to him why Wu Han is important. Call the emergency line to the Health Department and get that Chinese family's name—and if Georgee knows which airline they flew, and when. Everyone on that flight could be infected."

"Should I take Georgee to the VA hospital?"

"No! We aren't accepting Covid-19 patients. In Massachusetts they lost eighty patients overnight in a veterans' retirement home. Take him to Bushwick, and I'll meet you there. Call Kula. Tell her to come here in full protective gear. You too."

"Is it really that urgent?"

"I don't know. We lost Big Momma in three hours."

Kula made it from New York to the diner in twenty minutes. The streets were empty of cars and pedestrians. She and Floyd met outside dressed like spacemen in helmeted white suits, boots, dark gloves, and plastic face-shields. They embraced, and Floyd said: "Your father won't listen to me, and your brothers do what he says. They're making food for hundreds of people, and the food could be contaminated."

"What about my brothers? Have they got the virus?"

"If they do, it's a lot milder. They're much younger."

"Where are they?"

"In back of the diner. They're cooking cn outside burners."

"No doubt with the giant pots my grandfather used for the soup-kitchen. First get my brothers to come out here in front so I can talk to them before I speak to my father."

Kula's brothers didn't recognize her at first, all covered up with the protective suit. "I need your help," she said. "Papa has to go to the hospital. You and everyone working with you must go home and stay in quarantine for two weeks."

At first her brothers protested, but finally they agreed to help convince their father to go to the hospital. They all marched through the vacant diner and out into the backyard. There stood giant metal cauldrons steaming and bubbling over the flames of large outdoor gas burners. Some cauldrons held noodles, two large pots held chopped carrots and potatoes, and along the table lay a hundred chickens cut into eighths. The diner's staff, in improvised cloth masks, were doling out food in styrofoam bowls. A long line of older people, muffled in similar masks, trudged past the cauldrons.

At first Georgee didn't recognize his daughter in the protective gear—but then she shoved a thermometer in his mouth and kept him from pulling it out. "Don't talk, Papa," she ordered. "Just a few seconds... There." She took out the thermometer and held it up to the light. "Papa, you're going straight to the hospital."

"I'm staying right here! I'm needed—"

"Papa, you've got to go," the boys insisted. "You've got the virus. You can give it to anyone who comes near you. Everyone here has to be considered infected, and must go into quarantine for two weeks."

"Then what happens to all this food?"

"We'll serve it," the staff volunteered.

"Won't it be contaminated?" Floyd asked.

"Not if the tables and implements used to serve the food are thoroughly cleaned. Alcohol will do," said Kula. "The heat from cooking will kill the virus in the pots. I'm the dietitian, Papa. You sent me to school to learn just what's needed here. And you need to go to the hospital."

"No, no! My duty to my neighbors—"

"Papa," said Kula, pulling up her plastic mask so he could see her face, "You're going to the hospital right now. If I have to slug you, I will—but you're going." Tears trickled down her cheeks.

Georgee melted. "Oh Sweetness, don't cry…"

He reached out to touch her, but Floyd pulled his arm down. Georgee gave him a startled look.

"You're struggling to breathe," Floyd explained. "You're closer to death than you know. You can give this plague to Kula, and all of us."

"Oh!" Georgee went pale.

"You need a respirator."

"We'll go with you," the brothers promised.

"No," said Floyd. "You're contaminated, probably infected, but you're young and strong and otherwise healthy. You direct whoever comes to serve the food, until it's gone. Tell them to keep six feet apart, and put on whatever masks they've got."

"So who's going to serve?"

Floyd looked to Kula, who said: "I'll call Father Kline at Saint Barbara's. He has a group of volunteers. Meanwhile, let's check out the staff here."

Kula dialed the church rectory while Floyd took the vital signs of the diner's staff. He found one woman with advanced symptoms of the virus. She accompanied Georgee in the rear of Kula's car to Bushwick Hospital.

Mayzie met them in the parking lot, and took charge, sending everyone but Kula hither and yon.. It took age-long minutes before she returned. "Your father's going on a respirator," she reported. "The woman's being evaluated."

"What are my father's odds of recovery?"

Mayzie put her face-mask close to Kula's and whispered: "Eight to two against."

Kula collapsed in tears. Floyd rushed to her side. "I need my father!" she sobbed.

"They've taken him to intensive care," Floyd reported.

"I've got to talk to him! There's so much I have to tell him..."

"He said to tell you you're the image of your mother."

"I must speak with him."

"He won't be able to answer. They're putting a breathing tube down his throat."

"Can you stay with me?"

"For a few minutes. Bill and I are assigned to help at the Red Hook ER."

When Floyd left, Kula pulled a chair to Georgee's bedside and sat beside him, reminding her father of a picnic long ago at Jones' Beach where their little dog ran back and forth into the water until he lay exhausted on the sand. Then she spoke of her relatives making the trip from Greece to America for the wedding. Then she detailed the progress being made on remodeling the house.

The scene at Red Hook Medical Center was a replay of the Bed-Stuy melee. Floyd duplicated Martha's approach, and sent for riot police. He addressed the staff, assigned half of them to Bill, and set them to interview, examine, and send home all but those requiring intensive care.

It was Friday night, and in addition to the virus cases there were the usual number of drunks and bar-fight victims. Floyd assigned one nurse and two riot-cops to separate the groups. There was shouting, a lot of crying, and drunken brawls. The police, using their own initiative, broke out their stun-guns and zip-tie cuffs to settle the brawls quickly.

Bill and Floyd eventually restored order to the understaffed ER. Seventy percent of those examined were sent home under two-week quarantine orders.

Respirators were in short supply, and people began dying.

Alerted to the situation, the neighborhood reacted. Piggly Wiggly, the famous barbecue spot in Red Hook, sent over fifty barbecued pork sandwiches, French-fried onions and potatoes. Carvel sent twenty-four ice cream cakes. Pizza Hut sent two dozen pizzas. The food and those who donated it brought the ER staff to life. People waiting to be examined cheered, clapped, and prayed for the hospital staff. People in the tenement houses surrounding the hospital opened their windows, cheered and banged pots and pans in honor of the staff.

Joe Nolan—known in the neighborhood as Joe Skunk—now with the Metropolitan Opera, was in town visiting his mother. He stepped out onto a fire-escape and sang the Irish ballad "Mother MacCree". People stopped shouting and banging pans to listen to the refined and tearful voice of Joe Skunk. They understood that his mother had been sent home to die.

Mac returned to her office at the Ridgewood VA hospital to find Ms. Basch frantically working two phones and the computer, and looking harried. On her own desk was a list of requests from the city, state and hospital administrators. She read three notes from Jill written in heavy black marker-pen.

"Two more staff are down with the virus. I need help, masks and smocks. You had better find refrigerator trucks for us. Washington ordered us to accept veterans with the virus into our hospital. We are to make fifty beds available for non-veterans."

"The pandemic is winning. Police found fifty bodies rotting outside the Cleckly Funeral Home in Flatbush. The smell upset the neighbors, who called the police. Refrigerator trucks are difficult to find. Crematoria are backed up."

"City and private morgues are full. Unclaimed bodies are being buried in mass graves on Hart Island in the Bronx.—Jill"

Mac picked up the telephone and called the drug-dependency ward. "JJ Dougherty, please."

"Speaking."

"JJ, this hospital is about to enter a shit-storm. I need your help. I don't need another alcoholic."

"I can do my job."

"Are there any others up there who can lend a hand?"

"Two doctors and four nurses, but I'll have to leave one on the ward."

"Bring them. Who can help Ms. Basch work the

phones?"

"Is that battered wife Rosie still in the hospital?"

"You're right. She's a telephone sales manager. I'll get her. You bring the others to my office."

JJ led five scrubs-clad doctors and nurses into Mac's office, where Rosie joined them.

"No matter the depth of your medical knowledge," Mac began, "No one alive has had experience with a pandemic of these proportions. The closest comparisons we have are the Spanish Flu of a century ago, and the Bubonic Plague of the 1300s, which wiped out millions in Europe, Asia, and Africa. Because of the speed of modern transportation, this plague is spreading faster and further than those ever did. According to the Health Department, New York is losing one thousand patients a day. Those figures are questionable for political reasons, but we have to assume the worst-case scenario. Morgues are stuffed, hospitals are using refrigerator trucks, crematoria are falling behind, and the Health Department is reduced to digging mass graves. It's bad, people."

"How soon can we expect a vaccine?" one of the nurses asked.

"Six months at absolute minimum, and maybe as much as two years."Our testing results are questionable."

"And treatments?" the ward doctor added.

"Try anything that has ever worked on any kind of virus, in any reasonable combination,' said Mac. "Keep careful records, and see what works. We're scatter-gunning in the dark here."

"Why us particularly?" another nurse questioned.

"For a particular warning." Mac gave them all a grim look. "Twenty percent of my staff is down with the virus. I need your help, but if it's going to drive anyone back into the bottle or drugs, then you're not acceptable. I'm not trading your lives for others."

"I don't think that'll be a problem," murmured JJ.

"I'm not a nurse or anything like it," Rosie piped up. "What am I doing here?"

"I need you to help Ms. Basch deal with the bureaucratic nightmare that's coming," said Mac. "American veterans' hospitals throughout the world have been ordered to accept Covid-19 veterans as patients, besides providing fifty beds per hospital for non-vets. The average patient age in the VA is sixty-seven, prime targets for the virus."

"Whose bright idea was that?!" one of the nurses squawked.

"Some damned bureaucrat's," Mac sighed. "Rosie, I want you to call the families of all our patients who can be cared for at home, and ask if they can take them in."

"For how long?"

"Tell them fourteen days."

"Is that true?"

"I don't know. We'll provide medications, bandages, and whatever masks we can spare."

"What about food?"

"Possibly. We're getting local donations. Start with the orthopedic and physio wards. All amputees less than triple must leave. I need as many beds as you can free up. The charge nurses can tell you who's able to leave. Yes, you'll be paid for your time."

"Not necessary," said Rosie. "You took care of me when I needed it. I'll do the same for you."

"Oh," said Mac. She handed two business cards to Rosie. "Both these people volunteered to provide a couple of refrigerator trucks for the corpses. Tell them we'll need more."

"That reminds me," Rosie added, "I know of a company that makes ozone generators and sells them to hotels to sterilize rooms once they're empty."

"Yes, we could use those," Mac agreed. "Fellow colleagues, Jill is the ER Charge Nurse, and JJ knows his way around the ER. Go to either of them if you need help.

"Now, I have a hypothetical problem to test your understanding. Listen carefully, then decide what you'll do. Two ambulances pull up at the same time, carrying patients who are seventy year old women, both breathing only because of an oxygen mask. Their lungs are equally congested. They both require a ventilator, and you have only one. Which patient gets it?"

"Save the one who arrived first," said the ward doctor.

"They both arrived at the same time. Try again."

"The one who has the less threatening medical history," a nurse offered.

"They both have heart conditions and diabetes. Which one gets the ventilator?"

"The one closest to me?" another nurse tried.

"Wrong. JJ, tell them."

"Neither one," said JJ. "They're both sent home."

"That's crazy!" the doctor snapped. "You're asking us to decide who will live and die."

"No," said Mac, "JJ is right. Eighty percent of those who go on ventilators will die. Those age seventy and older have even less chance. Save the inhalator for a patient who can benefit from it."

"Follow me," said JJ, and he led the group to the ER to be fitted with masks, smocks, gloves and face shields. Rosie went to the outer office and pulled a chair next to Ms. Basch's desk. Mac felt her cellphone come to life, and answered it to find Congressman Waters on the line.

"I called," he said, "To see how you're coping with that order from Washington to let in the Covid-19 patients."

"We're coping by sending everybody else to their families," Mac groaned. "Still, that's nowhere near the pressure on the public and private hospitals. They have no place to put the dead."

"Tell me about it. The gravediggers' union refuses to inter the dead without proper masks. The crematoriums can't handle the work-load. Bus drivers refuse to take fares. Twenty percent of the police force are off sick. Social workers have stopped making house-calls without PPE. Liquor stores are doing a booming delivery business, and the spousal-abuse hot-line has been ringing off the hook. We had to activate cadets at the police academy to replace the absentees."

"Elijah, I got a notice—supposedly from somewhere in the mayor's office—that New York is the epicenter of the world-wide pandemic, and Brooklyn is the heart of it all, and we all have to go into lockdown for quarantine. Is that real, or is it politics?"

"It's both. I wouldn't put it past politicians to throw the whole economy into chaos, and it's all too easy to inflate the virus death-numbers. Remember what Mark Twain said about liars and figures. On the other hand, we have six hundred and eighteen nursing homes in the area. You heard about the one in Flatbush?"

"Oh yes."

"We're beginning to find out just how many of these homes have not given an account of their dead and infected. It doesn't help that there's a serious shortage of accurate tests. They're overwhelmed, and the older folks are dying like flies. Staffs are depleted from the virus or fear of catching it."

"Anything new from Washington about a vaccine or a cure?"

"Too much information, and too little verified. I swear our President does more right by mistake than he does on purpose."

"Ah, that's a democrat talking."

"I'm serious. He issued a proclamation that the lockdown should continue, and he got blasted from both sides of the aisle. Republican as well as democrat governors complained that it was a violation of their Constitutional rights to shut down their own states themselves, and Attorney General Barr ruled that the governors were correct. So Trump said, 'all right, do it yourselves'. Then the democrats happily went back to bashing Trump for not showing 'proper leadership'. So now the states have protesters rioting in the streets all over the argument, but they're blaming the governors, not Trump. Brilliant."

"Lovely," Mac groaned, pulling up another note. "One piece of good news: The garment district sent over a truckload of PPEs."

"Can you share?"

"Will do."

"Thanks. ...And you can do me and the mayor another favor."

"Name it."

"One of Pete Gotti's lieutenants has the virus. He's not a veteran, but I'd like to have him cared for in your hospital."

There was a long moment of silence from Mac's end of the line.

"Look, Doc," Waters sighed, "I don't get to choose who I play this game with, but play it I must. And there's another patient in Coney Island hospital named Taguir Abazov. Same deal."

Mac took a deep breath. "Send them," she said, "But tell them to ask for me before entering the ER. We're going to be very busy there."

"Alright. And I'll be sending over some of the most suitable volunteers, all medical professionals."

"Volunteers? Where did you find them?"

"They found us. People all over the country heard what was happening in New York, so they called in and let us know they were coming. Formed groups, collected some money, and hired buses. The first of them is arriving now."

"How many?"

"We have a telephone list of ninety thousand."

"Elijah, repeat that."

"Ninety thousand volunteers. Some just arrived. ...Mac, are you crying?"

"I'm so proud to be an American."

"Me too."

Mac accepted the Gambino lieutenant and the head of the local Russian mob into the hospital's isolation ward. Both required respirators.

CHAPTER 36:
INTO THE FIRE

RED HOOK ER

"Did you hear what I said?" Big Bill Schmersal asked Floyd. "Two more of the staff are out with fever. We may have to ask the National Guard for medics. Didn't Mac say something about volunteers coming?"

He got no response.

Bill put his hands on Floyd's shoulders and shook him. "Are you hearing me?"

Floyd looked up with unfocused eyes.

"Floyd!" Bill demanded, "What's the matter with you?"

"Kula's father died. They won't let her bury him."

"Bullshit!"

"All burial laws are in Epidemic Mode. They're afraid the bodies are contagious. The Prodromakeos family have a private mausoleum in Trinity Cemetery. Georgee wanted to be buried next to his wife."

"He will be. That man deserves respect."

"Didn't you hear? Gatherings for funerals are

against the law."

"Brooklyn laws are made to be bent." Bill put his hands under Floyd's armpits and hauled him to his feet. "Get the hell out of here. Go to your wife."

"There's no one to bury him. The gravediggers don't have PPE."

"We'll manage." Bill pushed Floyd out of the ER, watched him mount his bike and drive off, and then went to the phone and dialed the deceased Rabbi Goldman's number. When he got an answer he asked: "Is this Rabbi David Yehuda?"

"Speaking. How may I help you?"

"This is William Schmersal from the Ridgewood VA hospital Emergency Room."

"Ah, yes. You and Rabbi Goldman played chess. You were extremely helpful to our recovering his body, and the preparations for burial. Thank you."

"I have another burial to discuss." Bill explained briefly.

"*B'ha sheym sha'dai*," the rabbi muttered, taking notes. "I'll call you back."

By the time Floyd reached Bushwick Hospital, the wheels had already turned. He hurried to Georgee's room to find Kula being comforted by a bearded man dressed in black from head to toe, clearly a member of the Ridgewood Hassidic community.

Kula ran to Floyd, sobbing. "Daddy's gone! He's gone! They told me 'sorry for your loss', and I didn't understand. They meant I'd lost my father."

Floyd could do nothing but hold her and kiss her face.

She pulled back and drew a deep breath. "This is Rabbi David Yehuda. He's in charge of the Jewish Burial Society, and he made arrangements with Father Kline of Saint Barbara's to take possession of the body and see that Papa is interred with dignity in the family plot."

"When?" Floyd managed to say.

"Now," said the Rabbi, "And finish before dark."

"...Before dark?" Floyd mumbled, struggling to catch up. "Why?"

"Three reasons," said the Rabbi, holding up three fingers. "First, it's our tradition, and our way of honoring this great man. Second, to keep our dear mayor's enforcers from preventing the burial. Third, because druggies hang out and do their business in cemeteries, and with so many people unemployed it could be dangerous."

He turned to Kula. "I never met your father, and from what I hear that is my great loss. As a boy I was taught that when a person dies his soul is quizzed by an angel who asks two questions: 'what have you learned?' and 'whom have you helped?'. I know not how your father would answer the first question, but as to the second, from all I have heard of your father and his family, he helped the whole city—in imitation of God, he gave without thought to receive. A truly righteous man."

The phone buzzed in his pocket. He bowed to Kula and Floyd.

"The Greek Orthodox bishop of New York is sending an emissary to perform the rites for your father. He will be here shortly. I must leave now for another funeral. Go with God."

The rabbi's car passed the hearse carrying Georgee Prodromakeos' body, which proceeded on to the cemetery. There the four men carrying the coffin wore protective shoe-covers, gloves, plastic face-shields, and coveralls from head to toe. The young priest, with wispy beard and ornate robe and gold-encrusted head covering, came over to Floyd and Kula.

"Mrs. Kula Sorenson," he said formally, "On behalf of the archbishop of the Greek Orthodox church in New York, I bring you the warmest greetings from His Holiness. He regrets not being able to leave his post, but conditions require fulfilling his duties there. I convey to you and your brothers, in the strongest possible terms, the high regard in which your father is held by the Greek Orthodox church, here and abroad. Special services are being held for him in Athens and Cyprus."

Kula only nodded and bit her lip to keep from crying.

"Now we must proceed," said the priest. "It's getting late."

"What must we do?" Floyd asked, quietly pulling a small camera out of his pocket.

"Support your wife. The Trisagion Service is an abbreviated memorial which contains the closing hymns and prayers found in the rite of burial. It includes the hymn 'Holy God', then brief prayers which conclude with the Lord's Prayer, then hymns called the Troparia which implore God to grant eternal rest to the departed, then a litany for the departed with the faithful responding 'Lord have mercy' three times after each petition, then the final blessing in which we ask God to grant the departed rest in the bosom of Abraham, Isaac and Jacob. Finally there is the closing exclamation: 'Grant eternal rest, oh Lord, to the soul of thy departed servant and make his memory to be eternal', to which the faithful sing 'Memory Eternal'.

"You may remain with your wife and comfort her. Everyone else must keep a six-foot distance."

"There's no one else here except us and the four pallbearers."

"Ah, yes. They're from the gravediggers' union, and volunteered to inter the casket in the family mausoleum."

Kula was surprised at that. "Did they know my father?"

"Not personally, but they're good men and have heard stories about your family."

"Daddy would have been proud to meet them."

"Do you have the key to the mausoleum?"

"Yes," Kula whispered, reaching into her purse.

"Then we should get on with it." He glanced at Floyd, who was holding the camera. "I know this is heartbreaking. Your husband is filming this for your brothers and family in Greece. It's the only way for the family here and abroad to participate. The plague has changed how we live and die. Now it's time to say goodbye."

Kula stepped forward and unlocked the door to the mausoleum. The priest started to reach out and prevent her from joining the pallbearers, but stopped short of touching her. "It's best if no one else enters the mausoleum," he said.

"Too late," she replied. "I'm already infected."

"Were you tested?!" Floyd gasped.

"No, but I've been exposed and have all the symptoms, including the temperature—No, love, don't touch me. You'll have to take care of me."

He reached out anyway, but she backed away from him and followed the priest and pallbearers into the mausoleum.

The pallbearers lifted the coffin and shoved it into an open niche in the wall. The priest sang hymns and together with Kula recited the Lord's Prayer. He touched her on the right, then left, shoulders and finally on the forehead, with an ornate crucifix. "May you and your family be blessed," he said. "May the name of Georgee Prodromakeos be remembered on earth as it is in heaven." He stepped back. "This concludes our service."

"Bury me next to my father," said Kula.

"Not yet!" the priest shouted. He turned to Floyd, filming by the door. "Take care of your wife. I have to deal with another funeral before the sun goes down."

He hurried off, followed by the bewildered pallbearers. Kula locked the mausoleum door after them.

Floyd asked her, "Do you want to say anything on the Zoom to your brothers, or your relatives in Greece or Cyprus?"

"There'll be time to talk to my brothers in quarantine. To my family and friends I can only say it isn't fair. People should have time to tell their stories about my father. He gave his heart and soul to the community, to those who needed help. ...Oh, this doesn't feel real! The only good thing is that he's together with my mother again. Every evening he would kneel down by his bedside and recite: 'I pray thee, Lord, to guide my ways; and if I die before I wake, I pray thee, Lord, my soul to take—and bond me again with my Yvonne.' So he's finally with Mama. He'll be so happy to see her."

She walked to where the pallbearers were getting into their car and touched each man's elbow with hers. "You buried a good man today," she said. "He was my father. Thank you."

She broke down weeping, and Floyd led her to their car.

They returned to Georgee's house, where her brothers stood waiting. The steps and porch were covered with large and small bouquets of flowers, but only the brothers stood on the porch at the head of the floral pathway. A thinly-spread line of masked neighbors came up the stairs, one by one, to pay their respects. Kula tried to embrace her brothers, but Floyd stopped her. "You have to be tested," he reminded her.

His phone rang, and Floyd answered briefly.

"Who was it?" the elder son asked.

"Another family friend. Because of the lockdown he won't be coming, and he asked what he could do. I told him to light a candle for Georgee, and if he has a photo to put it nearby."

"Yes, that's smart," Kula murmured. "I'm so

tired."

"You're not sleeping here. Your brothers could be infected. Let's go home."

CHAPTER 37:
THE SPEED OF
BUREAUCRACY

RIDGEWOOD VA HOSPITAL

With the pandemic emergency hitting all five Brooklyn emergency rooms, Mac's plans for their future development were put on hold. She didn't need the Washington representatives warning her to allocate the grant money in time or she might lose it; she'd already assigned a lot of it to hiring more staff, buying more ambulances, more respirators, more protective gear—everything from gowns and masks to full moon-suits—and of course more tests, many more tests. She especially didn't need the Washington bureaucrats telling her that she had to give a lecture to an undetermined number of hospital administrators and their ER managers from all over the country.

"Why me?" she complained.

"Because," Congressman Waters explained gently, "New York State is the hardest hit, and Brooklyn is the epicenter. You're in charge of the five ERs on the front-line of this battle. Think of yourself as General Eisenhower in 1943.”

“I probably look like him too, by now,” Mac groaned. “Is there a specific subject?”

“What happened, what is happening, and what's going to happen.”

“Oh, thanks! The first two I can address with some degree of confidence, but as for the third, and what the future holds, nobody knows.”

“Be optimistic.”

“Thanks again. They gave me no option but to give this talk.”

“Girl, this is more than a photo-op or a stroll in the park. The Trump administration will either hang its hat on your words or hang you. Try to speak better than Fauci does.”

“Again, why me?”

“Because everybody else turned them down, and it's your turn in the barrel.”

“...The barrel?”

“Old sailor's joke. There was this shipwrecked sailor who got picked up by a passing ship, and he found that every Friday all the crew would line up in front of a barrel with a big knot-hole in the side. Each sailor in turn would come up and stick his schlong into the knothole, and whoever was inside the barrel would give him a butt or blow-job. The sailor thought this was a great tradition until one Friday he went to line up, but everyone kept pushing him to the head of the line. He asked them why, and they explained—as they picked him up— It's your turn in the barrel'.”

"How did everybody else get out of giving this talk?"

"That's another skill you have to learn. I'll pick you up for the meeting, and we'll talk on the way there."

"Aren't you worried about being close to me if I fail?"

"Fail, and I'll quietly disappear. Succeed, and I'll show you off as my protégé."

"Heads, you win: tails, I lose."

"That's the way the game is played, my dear. Survival of the quickest I'll see you Friday."

Mac visited each to the five ERs every morning, taking copious notes. Jill and JJ, and their half-dozen volunteers, kept the VA well in hand.

Mayzie hadn't gone home since the pandemic began; she ate, slept, showered and changed and worked at her hospital.

Big Momma's replacement was her longtime friend Annie Parnham, a deaconess at the Bedford Baptist church. She was a handsome woman in her fifties, with her hair tied back in a severe bun and an exotic slant to her eyes often seen in paintings on Egyptian royal tombs. Mac found Annie as bright as she was beautiful, and she had a good relationship with the staff and patients.

Big Bill ran the Red Hook ER efficiently, and difficult problems he cleared with Jill.

Martha took on the Flatbush Medical Center, but Mac thought she should return to the drug dependency ward to complete her course of treatment.

Rosie did such good work on the phones that the VA administrator hired her full-time to work Accounts Receivable.

Joyce Murphy called from Philadelphia to volunteer. "We're doing better than expected," Mac told her, "Especially with that blessed batch of volunteers. Opening the hospital ship and the Javits Center to Covid-19 patients reduced pressure on all the hospitals in the city. If there's a spike in the infections, I'll call you."

Besides that, Mac spent every free moment preparing her lecture. She had a cot brought into her office, and slept there.

The first task was to choose a virus-free venue for her lecture, so she selected the Bushwick High School auditorium. The school was in lockdown, and the National Guard sanitized the hallways, auditorium, toilets and cafeteria. Ozone generators would be left running in the auditorium all the night before. Lecture participants were limited to eighty in the three hundred and twenty seat hall. Participants would be met at the entrance with a personalized seat number to maintain spacing. Hand-sanitizer, gloves and masks would be provided. That, Mac guessed, would impress the attendees with the seriousness of the situation.

Martha solved the problem of seating priorities by placing the Washington bureaucrats on the stage to either side of the podium, where they would be readily seen. "Give them the headache of satisfying the egos of the honored guests. Let them get the questions afterward. It may be a bi-partisan working meeting, but politics is always on the agenda."

When Friday afternoon came, Mac felt she was as ready as she'd ever be—especially after the chat with Elijah Waters. They entered the auditorium from the back, Waters introduced her and quickly took himself off to a far corner of the stage. Mac strode to the podium before the polite applause died, adjusted the microphone, and plunged into her speech.

"I'd like to thank the President of the United States and Congressman Waters for this opportunity to talk about the Corona Virus pandemic. Being charged with overseeing the plan to update the emergency rooms in five Brooklyn hospitals has given me a unique perspective, since New York is currently the center of America's pandemic and Brooklyn is the epicenter. In fact, right now Brooklyn is the world epicenter of the disease. My people were, and are, at the heart of this conflict. Many of them are ill with the virus. Two have died, and several are on respirators. Thank God for the volunteers, because we need more troops.

"Now you are the controllers of the purse-strings and the opinion-makers of your communities. You need facts and accurate statistics. Yet the media appear to ignore statistics, disregard them or misread them.

"For instance, comparisons and contrasts are often made between our country and others, but the figures there are ambiguous at best, or at worst have no relationship to the facts, comparing apples to oranges. Many people assume that England is a good measuring-rod on which to predict the future of the virus. Yet all of England, Ireland, Scotland and Wales could fit into the state of Idaho with enough room left over to feed them potatoes for a year. France can fit into Texas with ten thousand square miles left over for the buffalo to roam. Most Americans believe that New York is the most populated state, but one of every nine Americans lives in California. Population density matters. Thickly populated cities spread the virus more quickly than thinly-populated countryside where people encounter non-family less than once a day. And geography matters. The Web-Foot state of Washington really can't be compared to living conditions in hot and arid Arizona.

"And taking all these factors into account, a true picture of the pandemic is still blurred. The slow and expensive serum test will show whether a person has antibodies for Covid-19, which means that the person either has the virus right now or has had it in the past and may be immune to it. The quick and inexpensive mucous test will reveal whether the patient has the virus present or is virus-free at the moment—but even that may not be true. The population of the virus present at the moment may be too low to register on the test. This virus has ways of hiding itself only to pop up later in a more virulent form. The virus may not affect the carrier enough to notice. Carriers are often unaware that they're sick—but spread it they will, and catch it you may. We need more and more accurate tests, given more often.

"The poor, uneducated, and elderly are the most vulnerable. No, I don't think that racial discrimination has anything to do with the spike of infections in the African-American community; it's just that, for well-known historical reasons, Black Americans in crowded cities are often poor and uneducated. Wherever poor and uneducated populations live in thick population densities, you have the perfect recipe for medical, social, and economic disaster. Where people are poor, they often can't take proper care of their elderly—and the elderly succumb to this disease more readily than the young and strong.

"More, even the death-numbers are misleading. The latest statistics show that more than 95% of recorded Covid-19 deaths were of patients who had potentially lethal conditions—everything from last-stage cancer to traffic injuries—which would have killed them eventually, even if the virus had not been present. We don't know how much the virus hastened their deaths, or if its presence was even relevant.

"As of right now, there are over a million and a half confirmed Covid-19 cases in America. A hundred thousand have died, at least five thousand of them from the virus alone. Three hundred and fifty thousand have recovered. How did it happen, and why? And what does this tell us about the future?

"There are two explanations for 'how'. The Chinese officials say it was a mutation of a wild virus that crossed over to humans at the Wu Han wild-animal market. This is the market that spawned the SARS epidemic eighteen years ago. The Wu Han

University's Virology Laboratory is within walking distance of the market. It's a well-known secret that Chinese labs have been experimenting with Corona virus. They admit to doing so, but deny accountability."

Mac paused to take a sip of water, and give time for anybody in the audience to make a comment. Nobody did. Clearly, nobody was about to say the words 'germ warfare', not in public. She cleared her throat and went on.

"The US government believes that a young woman technician at the Wu Han lab became infected visited her boyfriend who owns a shop in the market, and passed it on to him. He passed it on to his colleagues, customers and neighbors. His shop is next door to a vendor who sells live bats, and it spread from there.

"Since the last epidemic from that market was attributed to bats, this species of corona virus was originally thought to be another outbreak of SARS. It is not. The Covid-19 species is much more dangerous and a hundred times more contagious. One of my colleagues nicknamed it the Artful Dodger, because it hides, then reappears in a different form as a direct attack on the lungs. Ninety percent of those diagnosed early enough recover. It's too soon to estimate long-term effects.

"What is most disturbing about all this is the Chinese reaction to the outbreak. The government knew about the situation much earlier than they told anyone. As news spread, they and the World Health Organization denied the transmission from human to human. They claimed that was a figment of western imagination, invented to disable internal tourism for the profitable Chinese New Year, which occurs at the end of January. Yet the Beijing government immediately slapped a lockdown on Wu Han and imposed distancing regulations enforced by the police and the army. They forbade travel from Wu Han to the rest of China, but allowed all Chinese to travel to Europe. China also bought up national and international supplies of PPE—medical-level protective gear—in anticipation of an epidemic. Without informing other nations, China allowed its tourists travel to France, Spain, Italy and America from Wu Han. The first cases of Covid-19 in the US were diagnosed in the states of Washington, Oregon and California; those states are closest to China."

"But why is the east coast so hard hit by this disease?" someone dared to ask.

"Because," said Mac, "As soon as our president understood the situation he imposed a two-week isolation period on tourists and returning Americans from China. The governors of those three states instituted distancing laws and lockdowns."

"Why didn't New York and New Jersey do the same?" another administrator questioned.

"They were blindsided," Mac answered. "They were looking for Chinese carriers of the disease, but it was Europeans who brought the plague with them. They got it from Chinese tourists visiting Spain, Italy and France. The incubation period is two weeks, and many infected people were asymptomatic. They never knew they were sick or capable of passing on the disease in a more virulent form. New York alone receives ten million European visitors per year. They spread the virus.

"President Trump was roundly criticized for restricting Chinese travelers, and vilified for his European travel restrictions, but in fact he saved thousands—perhaps millions—of lives with his swift and decisive actions. The directions issued by the federal government have been spot on and flexibly adaptable.

"At first there weren't enough masks, gloves or smocks. Ventilators were in short supply, especially in Illinois, Michigan, New Jersey, Massachusetts and New York. The president invoked the War Powers Act and ordered factories to convert to making ventilators. This program proved so successful that the US is now sending respirators, ventilators and special equipment to Russia, England, France, Spain, Italy, and other countries—incidentally cutting into China's export market in medical supplies "

There was a faint rustling in the audience as various members turned to look at each other.

"We have learned much about this virus," Mac went on, "And more about ourselves. Mistakes have been made. We didn't know what we were dealing with. There are still aspects of this virus that are unclear. What is clear to the emergency room staffs is that everyone making a decision in response to this pandemic has honest intentions. Hindsight might prove them wrong, but I have not met anyone attempting to enrich themselves from the ravages of this disease.

"You have the right to ask 'Are we doing enough?'—and the answer is a statistical yes. By percentage, there are now more infections per capita in the general population than among first responders. ER personnel now have proper equipment and know how to utilize it. If the public will imitate the first responders, they too will reduce the transmission of infection rates dramatically. It's simple: keep your distance, wear a mask, and wash your hands often. The mask also reminds you not to touch your face if possible; the most common transmission is from breath to breath, but the second most common is from hands to face. The virus enters through the eyes, nose, and mouth. Keep your hands clean.

"We'll now take a short break for some light refreshments."

Mac stepped away from the podium and sat down on one of the stage seats. The rest of the audience got up and shuffled off toward the cafeteria. The appointed ushers moved among the seats, spraying cleanser and setting down copies of papers.

Mac was putting her notes in order when one of the Washington representatives came over. "My compliments on a well-organized and thoughtful discourse," he said. "I expected you to have more interaction with the audience."

"These are important people with powerful egos," she replied. "Each of them would want to be heard. A dialogue with them would go over my two-hour limit. I hope to present the facts so that the audience leaves with a clear and comprehensive understanding of the situation."

"You know, when you spoke of the volunteers, I expected you to mention Governor Cuomo's threat to apply New York state tax on them. He invited them."

"I considered it, but it's too political."

"Oh? How?"

"I really doubt that the governor will tax the volunteers; the political fall-out from that would be too damaging. New York State is already in arrears for eleven billion dollars, and that doesn't look good. He's pushing the president to allocate that to him, but no other governor has followed suit, no matter how much in debt their states are. The governor is trying to squeeze the president through the volunteers, and that doesn't look good either."

"I was told you were politically inexperienced. Would it be possible for you to give this same talk in the capital, say, ten days from now?"

"That would be difficult while the virus is still running rampant here in Brooklyn."

"I'll make the arrangements," the man promised, and padded off.

Elijah Waters rolled up to offer her a cup of coffee and ask quietly: "What was that about?"

"He was trying to figure out if I'm a republican or democrat."

"And what did you tell him?"

"Independent."

"Clever girl. You learn fast."

"I couldn't stop him from putting me in the Washington D.C. barrel."

"He must consider you a friend, but be careful; the DC barrel is far more dangerous."

"I've got a plan," Mac promised. She ducked her head, pulled out her phone and spoke quietly into it. Then she got up and went back to the podium.

The rest of the crowd filtered back in, and returned to their seats. Mac took up her notes and resumed speaking.

"Honored guests, I've told you what was. Now I'll tell you what is, and possibly what's to come. Some see a light at the end of the tunnel, and others see the headlight of an oncoming train. As my mother-in-law used to say, 'he's right, and you're not wrong'.

"In the papers before you, the following account is taken from the WHO's daily report on the internet. As of today, there are 5,201,549 confirmed cases of Covid-19 world-wide. Number of deaths, 337,405. In the Americas, 2,338,124 confirmed cases. In Europe, 2,004,025.

"Now these are not immutable figures; they change from moment to moment. Cases are currently reported as pending, dead, or discharged. We especially want to keep track of those discharged; their blood may contain antibodies that could be used to treat future patients."

"Like serum horses!" someone in the audience laughed.

"Exactly." Mac smiled grimly. "There are far worse fates for old horses who have been put out to pasture. Now, the death-toll may seem unchangeable, but here too we have under-reported, over-reported, and misdiagnosed cases. You can draw some meaning from these figures, but you can't trust them to be accurate.

"Our scientists and medical staff are learning how to fight the virus. At first, if a patient went on a respirator, the survival rate was twenty percent at best; if you were older, with pre-existing serious medical conditions, you were dead. This is no longer the case, not because Covid-19 became less dangerous but because we learned ways to neutralize it in most cases. Yes, we've tried other antiviral medicines, and they all show some promise: hydroxychloroquine with antibacterials and zinc, remdesivir, lopinavir and others work to some degree, but none of them is a true cure. Right now, antibodies from recovered patients seems to be the most effective treatment.

"We have no idea what the long-term consequences might be. Are the lungs permanently scarred? What about the heart? Will the kidneys and liver continue to function properly? We don't know. More, the figures on the paper before you have little relationship to European or Asian statistics. The US tested more people in less time than the rest of the world. Countries deficient in testing techniques can't give an accurate rate of infections, recoveries or causes of deaths."

"What about China?" snapped a man in the second row.

"Again, we can't trust the figures," said Mac. "A cover-up is certainly possible—and politically probable. I believe our president is correct in holding the Chinese government accountable."

"Hong Kong," a woman called, "Has the same population as New York, on less land, putting its people at greater risk. It's just across the bay from the Chinese mainland, yet they suffered only a fraction of New York's casualties. Why?"

"Experience and preparation," Mac replied. Hong Kong and South Korea fought the SARS pandemic of 2002, and they had prepared for another such outbreak. SARS is part of the corona virus family, and in many ways can be misdiagnosed as Covid-19. And yes, SARS was also traced to the Wu Han live-animal market. It affected 26 countries and caused 8000 cases in 2003. Bill Gates and others have been warning us of a possible pandemic, but in most countries little or nothing was done to prepare for it.

"So today the world is infected, and deaths are approaching the one million mark. The majority of cases will recover, but we still don't know what the long-term affects will be. We don't even know how many people have been infected and recovered without even knowing it. Are they now immune? We don't know. These are questions we're addressing."

"What about the lockdown and the economy?" called a voice that Mac could have sworn she recognized from somewhere.

"I understand the mental, social and economic toll the lockdowns are having," Mac said carefully. "But aside from the simple basics of distancing, masks and washing hands, I have to say there's no one-size-fits-all solution. This isn't my field of expertise, but our states, cities and people are so diverse that it's logical for mayors and governors to determine freedom of movement, school openings and public gatherings—not so much for the federal government. We can only slow the spread of the disease, not prevent it—but we hope to slow it enough that we can come up with vaccines and better treatments.

"You were hoping I could give you some estimate on when we'll see the end of this pandemic, and I wish I could tell you. All I can say is that it will end when everyone is immune, either by vaccination or surviving infection. I am leery of anyone who predicts spikes or reductions in this pandemic, because we're still in the learning stage. Had we known what was coming, we could have prepared better. We didn't. What happens in the future to our medical, welfare and social systems, we'll have to wait and see. Our biggest mistake was in our nursing homes; our greatest success will be protecting the elderly and infirm.

"Covid-19 will probably surpass two million infected, with deaths in the hundreds of thousands. Do we know when the pandemic will end? No. Do we have a vaccine or a cure? No. Will we get a vaccine and a cure? Yes. When? I haven't a clue. What I do know is that we are getting better at recognizing, treating and preventing the disease. Our actions are growing swifter and surer with experience. The virus is not as deadly as we first thought, and it can be beaten.

"Historians may say that we panicked and overreacted by exaggerating the threat. In retrospect that may well be true, but we tried to save lives against an invisible foe of unknown origins—and we learned. With every case, we learned. And we're continuing to learn. Given the conditions and knowledge we had to work with, I am proud to have taken part in the effort—and I'm proud to be an American.

"Thank you."

Mac received a standing ovation as she stepped away from the podium. Various audience members tried to maintain their distance while they came up to congratulate her, and that made it easier for her to back away, leaving the other officials on the stage to deal with the attendees. She slipped back until she reached Congressman Waters' chair.

"Congratulations," he said. "You did us proud. So you're going to speak in Washington?"

"Oh no," Mac confided. "I'm not getting put in that barrel."

"You can't refuse that guy; he wields a lot of power."

"He'll excuse me and probably send me a big bouquet of flowers."

"Girl, explain yourself."

"I'm about to be infected by the virus."

"How do you know?"

"I arranged it. This will put me in quarantine for two weeks or more. Ah, and here comes Martha with the thermometer; I'll have a temperature of a hundred and two, and I'm beginning to feel aches in my joints. I guess we'll be talking only by phone for the next couple weeks. Sorry 'bout that."

The congressman sat back in his wheelchair and gave Mac an appreciative grin. "Woman, you're going to go a long way," he said. "I look forward to a permanent association."

Floyd slid out of his shoes, pulled a medical packet out of his pocket, sat down on the bed beside his sleeping wife and gently kissed her awake.

"Floyd?" she murmured, looking up at him. "Did you get the test results?"

"Yes," he whispered, kissing her again. "You've got it, but it's a light virus-load. You'll recover soon, and I'm going to make sure of it." He held up the packet for her to see.

"What's that?"

"Serum. Antibodies, willingly donated by grateful patients who recovered completely. The first to volunteer were members of Rabbi Goldman's congregation."

"Oh, how kind of them."

"They also sent condolences for the loss of your father, and tales of what a great man he was."

"He was." Kula hugged Floyd and began to cry again.

Bobby Big, the chief of the Flatbush Social Club— also known as the Flatbush Bloods—, sat alone in his office above the old warehouse, frowning at the facts and figures scribbled on papers cluttering the desk before him. The takeover of his share of Bed-Stuy hadn't gone smoothly at all. There were plenty of Crown warriors still alive and fighting, his own troops were dropping like flies from The virus, the demand for crack and whores was way down, the

Mafia wasn't providing any help, and his gang was actually losing money. This just wasn't Brooklyn anymore; it felt like the end of the world. Hopefully, his expected mysterious guests could come up with some solution, any solution.

Sure enough, there came a knock on the door and then his surviving lieutenant opened it to admit the guests. One of them was a man with polished shoes and a bow tie, wearing a fine-looking business suit that didn't disguise his muscular build or the convenient space under his arms; the other was a very tall and handsome woman in a sleek black dress who looked vaguely familiar. They strolled into the office like a pair of tigers, and Bobby Big felt his hopes rise.

"I hear you've been having some business problems," the woman said. Her voice sounded measured and precise, as if she'd rehearsed her speech.

"You might say that," Bobby admitted. There was no harm in admitting what everyone knew.

"That's because," the woman smiled, showing perfect white teeth, "When the spaghetti-benders cut off the head of the snake, there was still plenty of body left thrashing around. More than a thousand Crown warriors, who don't give up easy. You can't put them down. You're gonna have to deal with them."

Bobby Big made some fast guesses. "The snake's grown a new head?"

"That would be Miss Ida here," said the man. His voice was deceptively mild. "She's Miss Lucille's sister, as proven by DNA in a court of law, and she inherited all of Miss Lucille's... resources."

"Uhuh," said Bobby, thinking of what those resources could be. "And she wants...?"

"I believe it's called a 'corporate merger'," said the man. "We negotiate the details, and we join forces."

"And what, call our new bunch the Blood Crowns?"

"Names and titles can be negotiated. So can territories and departments."

"Uhuh. And what would the Italians say about that?"

"They don't care, so long as their cut goes on like normal," said Miss Ida. "Besides, they're kind of distracted right now, what with Gotti's chief lieutenant in the hospital, dying of The Virus."

Bobby raised an eyebrow. He hadn't heard about that. The woman had good intelligence services at least. What else could she supply? "So what can the Crowns bring to the bargaining table?"

"Good friends in useful places, like the staffs in all five hospitals in Brooklyn—and other connections."

Bobby could see the usefulness of that, especially in times like these. "And what in particular do you think the Flatbush boys can offer in exchange?"

"Two things." Ida smiled again, not prettily. "First, we all support Miss Lucille's favorite charity. It's a very exclusive club that hunts down baby-fuckers, wife-beaters and woman-killers here in town, and it... makes them go away. Permanently."

"Why, yes," said Big Bobby, thinking of some

prime candidates he knew of. "I think we can surely help with that. It's a public service. What's the other thing?"

"Kill the Russians." Ida's teeth were definitely bared, and not in a smile. "Kill the whole lot of 'em. If we don't, they're gonna wind up killing all of us."

He blinked at that. It was something he'd thought about himself, but it was a tall order. "What makes you say that, Miss Ida?" he temporized.

"You know they planning to take over the whole town, and only the Mafia's holding 'em back. To get more juice, they gotta wipe out us smaller fry first—and they're racist bastards who hate us Blacks worse than the spaghetti-benders any day. That's why they started on the Crowns first. Who do you think they were gonna come after next?"

Big Bobby caught himself nodding in agreement.

"And now's the perfect time to start," Ida pushed the point home. "Their chief is in the hospital too, dying of The Virus. It'll be awhile before the Moscow bums can come up with a replacement for him. And who's going to notice a few more dead White guys in the middle of a plague? You just be careful to get 'em one by one, scattered, so nobody sees a pattern—or a war. Do it like that, and the Italians won't mind at all."

Big Bobby returned Miss Ida's smile. "Lady," he said, "Let's set up a time and place for negotiations. This just might be the start of a beautiful friendship."

THE END

AFTERWORD

By Don Silverman

Thank you.

This historical novel was originally meant to be a parable against spousal and child abuse, which I called The Widow-Makers Society; members of the ER staffs decided to take the law into their own hands to punish wife- and child-abusers. After two deaths, the characters decided not to continue because it was morally wrong. What influenced them, I asked. They were trained in a profession to save lives, not take them.

Current events became the impetus that propelled them into the fight against the Corona virus. They wanted to help. I couldn't force them to do what I wanted. The book changed to an ending I could never have anticipated.

The background of the gangs of Brooklyn fit into the story; the visible rioting was more organized by the gangs than the TV news made it appear. The passivity of the police was dictated by politicians and the plethora of weapons in the hands of gang members. If you think high-end merchandise being looted by non-gangbangers did away with the good stuff, you're mistaken. They were hijacked by the gangs and put into storage for sale on eBay and other auction sites.

TIMELINE OF EVENTS

January 31, 2020: the Wuhan Coronoavirus is officially a public health emergency in the United states, Alex Azar, Secretary of the US Department of Health and Human Services announced at a White House briefing.

January 31, 2020: the US Center for Disease Control and Prevention issued a federal quarantine for 14 days affecting the 195 American evacuees from Wuhan, China. Starting Sunday, February 2nd, US citizens, permanent residents and immediate family who have visited China's Hubei Province will undergo a mandatory 14 days' quarantine and, if they have visited other parts of China, they would be screened at airports and asked to self-quarantine for 14 days. The last time the CDC had issued a quarantine was over 50 years ago in the 1960s, for smallpox.

January 31, 2020: President Donald Trump signed an order for the US to deny entry to foreign nationals who traveled to China in the preceding two weeks, aside from the immediate families of US citizens.

On January 30, 2020: the CDC had confirmed the first case of person-to-person transmission of the virus in the US: the husband of the Chicago, Illinois case who had returned from Wuhan, China on January 13th and tested positive on January 24th. The CDC stated that "It is likely that there will be more cases of 2019-nCoV reported in the coming days and weeks, including more person-to-person spread." The virus had been confirmed in five states.

January 31, 2020: New York City health department officials vehemently denied the rumor regarding a corona-virus case in the city. On February 1st, however, the city's health commissioner did report that there was a test being performed on a person under 40 who had returned from China, developed matching symptoms, and tested negative to the seasonal flu. Most US patients had visited Wuhan. All of the first US cases were reported as mild, followed by pneumonia.

January 31, 2020: Delta, American, and United Airines announced they would temporarily suspend all their mainland China flights in response to the corona-virus outbreak. On January 28th United Airlines had announced that it would cut 24 flights between the US and China for the first week of February. On January 29th American Airlines had announced that it would suspend flights from Los Angeles to Shanghai and Beijing from February 9th through March 27th, 2020. It will maintain its 10 daily flights Dallas-Forth Worth to Shanghai and Beijing, as well as from Los Angeles and Dallas-Forth Worth to Hong Kong. Delta was the only airline with direct flights to China that had not taken action to limit flights before.

The White House considered issuing a ban on flights from the US to China on January 28th. Italy announced on January 31st that it was suspending all flights to and from China following the first two cases of Covid-19 in Italy. On January 30th the US state department issued a top-level (Level 4) Do Not Travel to China alert. Previously, on January 29th, the advisory was set at a lower level: Level 3, advising Americans not to travel to Hubei Province and to reconsider travel to the remainder of China. On January 28th the CDC had issued a Level 3 warning, recommending that travelers avoid all non-essential travel to China.

On January 17th the CDC announced that three airports in the US would begin screening incoming passengers from China: San Francisco-Oakland, JFK and Los

Angeles. Two other airports were added subsequently, and on January 28th the federal Department of Health and Human Services announced that 15 additional airports—bringing the total to 20—would begin screening incoming travelers from China.

SPOUSAL AND CHILD ABUSE:

In the US, one out of every five women, and one out of every 59 men, is raped during his/her lifetime.

9.4% of women experience sexual assault from an intimate partner during their lifetimes.

STALKING

19.3 million women and 5.1 million men in the United States have been stalked.

66.2% of female stalking victims reported being stalked by a current or former intimate partner.

(In crisis, contact: The National Domestic Violence Hotline at 1-800-799-SAFE or www.TheHotline.org

Please visit The National Coalition Against Domestic Violence website at www.ncadv.org for more information.)

CHILDREN

There is a common link between domestic violence and child abuse. Children witness violence in 22% of intimate-partner violence cases filed in state courts. 30% to 60% of perpetrators of intimate-partner violence also abuse children in the household. One study in North America found that children who were exposed to violence in the home were 15 times more likely to be physically/sexually assaulted.

AUTHOR'S NOTE

I am privileged and proud to have been born an American. On my mother's side, I am a 9th generation Brooklynite.

PS: If you believe that the riots in American cities are unplanned and spontaneous, then I failed to depict the sophistication of these gangs.

ABOUT THE AUTHOR

Dov (Robert) Silverman was the ninth generation on his mother's side born in Brooklyn, New
York. After 3 years as a US Marine in the Korean
War, he worked as a Long Island Railroad conduc-
tor, an auctioneer, and he established Autar Micro-
film Service. While working nights on the Railroad
and studying full-time days, he earned his high
school diploma and went on to graduate from Stony
Brook University, Long Island, New York, cum
laude, at the age of 39. Dov credited a spiritual
meeting with God and a *Tzaddik* (righteous man),
Jules Rubinstein, in the Brentwood (New York) Jewish Center, with setting him on the path of study,
religious involvement and settlement in Israel.

His life was filled with amazing experiences from
which he crafted novels such as the award-winning
Good Shepherds, *The Shishi* and other "factions"
(historical fictions) with an incredible amount of
amazing characters.

Brooklyn Plague was his last novel, finished just
before before he passed away in 2020.

He brought us a large amount of amazing tales –
excellent characters, daring scenarios, and triumphs

over evil and the folly of man. The world is made
poor by his departure.

Go forth bravely, Master Wordsmith.
You will be missed.

www.ingramcontent.com/pod-product-compliance
Lightning Source LLC
Chambersburg PA
CBHW070341170726
48291CB00001B/139